Ace Books by William C. Dietz

BY FORCE OF ARMS

WILLIAM C. DIETZ

ACE BOOKS, NEW YORK

BY FORCE OF ARMS

An Ace Book / published by arrangement with
the author

PRINTING HISTORY
Ace mass-market edition / June 2000

All rights reserved.
Copyright © 2000 by William C. Dietz.

This book may not be reproduced in whole or in part,
by mimeograph or any other means, without permission.
For information address: The Berkley Publishing Group,
a division of Penguin Putnam, Inc.
375 Hudson Street, New York, New York 10014.

The Penguin Putnam Inc. World Wide Web site address is
http://www.penguinputnam.com

Check out the ACE Science Fiction & Fantasy newsletter
and much more on the Internet at Club PPI!

ISBN: 0-441-00735-X

ACE®
Ace Books are published
by The Berkley Publishing Group,
a division of Penguin Putnam Inc.,
375 Hudson Street, New York, New York 10014.
ACE and the "A" design are trademarks
belonging to Penguin Putnam Inc.

PRINTED IN THE UNITED STATES OF AMERICA

10 9 8 7 6 5 4 3 2 1

For my dearest Marjorie . . . Here's to the Lizard!

ACKNOWLEDGMENTS

My thanks go to Joel Davis, co-author of Mirror Matter *for the concept of "White Holes," and how to harness them, to Dr. Sheridan Simon for his help in building this particular universe, and legionnaires past, present, and future.* Vive la Legion.

ACKNOWLEDGMENTS

> Distasteful though it may be, one stroke of the assassin's axe may have an effect greater than that produced by a large number of troops.
>
> Grand Marshal Nimu Wurla-Ka (ret.)
> Instructor, Hudathan War College
> Standard year 1957

Planet Earth, the Confederacy of Sentient Beings

The assassin moved quietly, as if her life depended on it, which it definitely did.

The house had been constructed more than five hundred years before, back when Portugal was a nation rather than an Administrative Region (AR), and the floorboards had a tendency to squeak.

The killer paused for a moment, assured herself that it was safe to move, and gestured to her companions. They wore black hoods, black bodysuits, and black slippers. They glided over the hardwood floor.

A shaft of sickly yellow moonlight came down through the transparent bubble roof to pool on the rumpled bed. Maylo Chien-Chu was awake, staring up through the plastic, listening to her lover breathe. He was asleep and had been for an hour now.

The sex had been good, *very* good, but something was missing. Was it her? Was it him? Or, and this was what she feared most, was it *them*?

Something creaked—and her thoughts continued to churn.

The hallway was long, wide and dimly lit. Huge pieces of furniture and statuary lurked in the heavily anchored gloom.

In spite of the fact that Earth's legally constituted government had been restored, and most of the mutineers had been placed in prison, where they awaited military trials, there were still plenty of renegades, outlaws, and psychopaths who would like nothing better than to assassinate Legion General William "Bill" Booly III, who, along with Admiral Angie Tyspin and a number of civilian resistance groups was credited with winning the battle for Earth. That being the case, Naa commandos, the best special ops troops the Legion had to offer, were assigned to protect him night and day.

Corporal Hardswim had served with Booly in Africa, where the officer had not only managed to restore discipline to the 13th DBLE, but had won a number of battles against the mutineers, and led the famous raid on Johannesburg. A raid the Naa had been part of—and had a medal to prove it.

The legionnaire grinned at the memory, looked down the dimly lit hall, and turned to the window. It was a likely point of entry *and* a way to break the boredom. There wasn't much to see outside, just the moon, and the lights of Sintra.

The assassins glided from one pool of shadow to the next, careful to make no sound, weapons at the ready.

Each and every Naa was gifted with a supersensitive

sense of smell. The invaders knew that and had gone to considerable lengths to counter it. Each assassin had bathed repeatedly prior to the mission, used scentless soap, donned specially prepared clothing, and been sprayed with an essence derived from the house itself. A not altogether unpleasant combination of furniture polish, fresh flowers, and a touch of mold.

Protected by their clothing and carefully honed skills, the assassins continued to advance.

Maylo turned onto her side, felt Booly stir in response, and examined his face. She couldn't really see it—the moonlight wasn't bright enough for that—but didn't need to. The short hair, steady gray eyes, and determined chin were etched in her memory.

He was intelligent, romantic, and very, very brave. When a member of the cabal had imprisoned her in Johannesburg it had been Booly who led the mission to rescue her. She would never forget the moment when light spilled into her cell, when he spoke her name, when he swept her into his arms. Just like in her childhood story books except for one very important thing: He *might* be the one, and they *might* live happily ever after, but she wasn't sure.

Hardswim looked down on the lights of Sintra, imagined the interior of his favorite bar, and cursed his luck. The general got laid, his buddies got drunk, and what did *he* get? The stinkin' shaft that's what . . .

Hardswim paused in midthought as his nose tried to tell him something. A scent that shouldn't be there? No, too much of the scent that *should* be there!

The Naa was already drawing his sidearm and turning toward the light switch when the assassins took him down. One hit the back of his knees, a second pulled his head back, and the third slit his throat. The blood looked black in the moonlight. It took less than three seconds. The body made a soft thump as it hit the floor.

Moving quickly, lest the body cool, the diminutive killers towed the Naa over to the bedroom door, raised him up, and pressed a palm against the print-sensitive lock. The mechanism made a soft but distinctive click.

Maylo heard the door lock click and frowned. Hardswim never entered the room without requesting permission first—not to mention the fact that it was the middle of the night.

Having been awake for some time, the executive's eyes were fully adjusted to the half darkness that pervaded the room. She saw the door open a crack and made up her mind. There had been a time when she would have laughed at the notion of assassins, but that was before she had spent months as a political prisoner, and been forced to shoot a man at close range. Better to look stupid than dead.

Booly felt a hand cover his mouth, came instantly awake, and felt for the handgun. It had a tendency to migrate during the night, especially when they made love, but it happened to be in the spot where he'd left it. His fingers closed around cool metal as lips brushed his ear. "Someone opened the door."

The officer nodded, nudged Maylo toward the far side of the bed, and flicked the safety to the "off" position.

Someone else might have yelled something like "Who's there? I have a gun!" but Booly didn't believe in that sort of nonsense. He figured that anyone who mistakenly entered a locked room during the middle of the night deserved to die. He rolled to the left, saw motion, and opened fire.

The first assassin staggered as two bullets ripped through her body, but the second and third made it through the door, and opened fire with handheld flechette throwers. The darts sampled the air, identified epithelial cells that matched the DNA they were programmed to seek, and steered themselves accordingly.

Booly continued to fire, saw two additional shadows fall, and felt rather than saw the missiles that accelerated past his torso. Smart darts! Targeted to Maylo!

The officer turned, threw himself out over the bed, but knew it was too late.

Having rolled off the right side of the bed, Maylo sensed the attack and raised the pillow out of reflex more than anything else. She felt the darts hit the foam rubber, fell backward in an attempt to reduce the extent to which she was visible, and saw Booly throw himself into the line of fire.

The bed creaked as the officer landed on it, three heavily armed legionnaires burst through the door, and the lights flashed on.

Maylo, surprised to learn she was still alive, lowered the pillow. Nine flechettes protruded from the opposite side. The previously white linen was yellow where some sort of liquid had started to spread. Booly yelled, "Poison!" and Maylo threw the object away.

Booly rolled off the bed, stood, and approached the bodies. He was naked, which meant that anyone who cared to look could see the mane of silvery gray fur that began at his hairline and ended at the base of his spine. Proof that he was one-quarter Naa—and a matter of pride for his bodyguard.

Sergeant Armstrong had gold fur streaked with white, a bald spot on his right biceps where a bullet had ripped through it, and carried an assault weapon in his right hand. He knelt by one of the bodies. "They murdered Hard-swim."

Booly swore, bent over, and tugged at one of the black hoods. It came off rather easily. The small almost feline head bore large light-gathering eyes, pointed ears, and horizontal slits where nostrils might have been.

Maylo peered down across her lover's shoulder. "Thraki."

"Yes," Booly agreed. "But why?"

Maylo frowned. The Thraki race was but one element in a very complicated political picture.

Humans, along with a number of alien species had founded a star-spanning government called the Confederacy of Sentient Beings. First conceived as a military alliance, the Confederacy had become much more than that, and the key to interstellar peace and prosperity. Not that all of its members could or should be trusted. The Clone Hegemony along with the Ramanthians and others had agendas of their own and had been at the very center of the effort not only to subvert Earth's duly constituted government but to destabilize the Confederacy as well.

A rather complex situation made all the more difficult by the arrival of the Thraki, who dropped out of hyperspace, formed a relationship with the conspirators, and took possession of a world called Zynig-47. Other planets had been colonized as well, most with permission from the Hegemony, but some without it.

All during a time when the Confederacy's armed forces were not only suffering from the cumulative effects of serial downsizings but were divided by the recent mutiny.

Then, as if those problems were not enough, Maylo's uncle, a businessman-politician named Sergi Chien-Chu, had learned that the Thraki were on the run from something called "the Sheen," and hoped to use the Confederacy for what amounted to cannon fodder. All of which was extremely important—but didn't begin to answer Booly's question. What did the Thrakies hope to gain? And *which* Thraki were behind the attack since their society included at least two opposing groups. The Runners and the Facers. There was no way to know.

One thing was clear, however, her uncle might be targeted too, and she needed to warn him. "I'll need a ship . . . the fastest one you can find."

Booly smiled and dropped a robe over her shoulders. "I'll put someone on it. In the meantime, you might want to consider some clothes."

2

Thou shalt have no gods before me.

Holy Bible, Exodus 20:3
First printing circa 1400

Somewhere Beyond the Rim, the Confederacy of Sentient Beings

One moment they were there, thousands upon thousands of shimmery spaceships, all seemingly motionless in space, then they were gone, absorbed by the strange dimension called "hyperspace," and launched toward a distant set of coordinates.

The Sheen fleet was comprised of approximately 1,300 separate vessels, all controlled by the computer intelligence known as the Hoon, and, with the exception of a human named Jorley Jepp, a navcomp called Henry, and a robot named Sam, was entirely crewed by nonsentient machines.

Not that Jorley Jepp and the AIs who attended him could properly be referred to as "crew," since their actual status hovered somewhere between "prisoner" and "stowaway." A situation that Jepp sought to exploit, since he viewed the fleet as the manifestation of Divine Providence and the means by which to enact God's plan. Well, not *God's* plan, since it was difficult to know what that was, but *his* idea of what God's plan should be.

All of which was fine with the Hoon so long as the human continued to support the computer's overriding purpose, which was to find the Thraki and eradicate them. *Why* was anything but clear. Not to Jepp anyway. Still, why worry about something when you can't do anything about it?

The prospector cum messiah straightened his filthy ship suit, stepped out onto the improvised stage, and raised his arms. Like the ship it was part of, the one-time storage compartment was huge and stank of ozone.

Jepp's first convert, a nonsentient robot named Alpha, sent a radio signal to more than a thousand of his peers. All of them bowed their heads. It was more dignified than the shouts of adulation that Jepp had required of them the month before. He was pleased and the sermon began.

The world called Long Jump was pleasant by human standards, having only slightly more gravity than Earth did, plus a breathable atmosphere, a nice large ocean, and plenty of raw unsettled land. Real estate, which like vacant lots everywhere, was available for a reason.

This was partly due to the fact that Long Jump was not only on the Rim, but on the *outer* edge of the rim, which meant that goods such as grain, refined ore, and manufactured products would have to be shipped to the center of the Confederacy where they would be forced to compete with similar commodities that were more expensive to produce, but had a shorter distance to travel. A competitive reality that the citizens of Long Jump had never managed to compensate for.

All of which helped to explain why Fortuna, the only city of any real size, was home to thieves, prospectors, renegades, bounty hunters, organ jackers, drug smugglers, slave traders and every other sort of villain known to the broad array of sentient races.

It was like so many frontier towns, a city of contrasts in which mansions stood shoulder to shoulder with sleaze-bag hotels, animals toiled next to jury-rigged robots and the often muddy streets wandered where commerce took them.

But Fortuna *was* civilized, and, like mostly human civilizations everywhere, was host to a complex social structure. The very top layer of this society was occupied by three different beings, all of whom liked to think that they owned the very top slot, although none of them really did.

One individual came close, however, and his name was Neptune Small. The fact that he weighed approximately 350 pounds was an irony of which he was well aware, and no one chose to joke about. No one who wanted to live.

Small's offices were located over one of the restaurants he owned, which was rather convenient, since he considered it his duty to sample the establishment's wares at least four times a day.

So that's where he was, sitting at his favorite table, when a functionary named Hos McGurk left the city's dilapidated com center, ignored the pouring-down rain, and ran the three blocks to the aptly named Rimmer's Rest. He could have called, could have asked for Small, but the businessman didn't like com calls. He preferred to deal with people face to face, where he could see their fear, and smell their sweat.

McGurk pushed the doors open, ignored the robotic hostess, and headed for the back. All sorts of junk had been nailed, wired, screwed, or in at least one case welded to the walls. There were nameplates taken off long-dismantled ships, a collection of alien hand tools, the shell from a five-hundred-pound land mollusk, a mummified hand that someone found floating in space, and a wanted poster that not only bore Small's somewhat thinner likeness, but announced the possibility of a rather sizeable reward. Some of the clientele thought it was a joke—others weren't so sure.

McGurk had started to pant by the time he arrived in front of Small's table. The entrepreneur, as he liked to refer to himself, always wore immaculate black clothing, and affected a specially made cane. The handle resembled the head of an eagle and the shaft doubled as a single-shot energy weapon. It leaned against the table only inches from it owner's well-dimpled hand. Small dabbed his fat puffy lips, raised an eyebrow, and spoke in what amounted to a hoarse whisper. "Good afternoon, Hos—what brings you out on such a miserable day?"

Thus encouraged McGurk began to babble. His eyes bulged with pent-up emotion, his hands washed each other, and the words emerged in spurts. "Ships! Hundreds of them! Maybe more! All dropping hyper."

Small frowned. Given Long Jump's location, five ships would be notable, ten would be extraordinary, and a hundred was impossible. He stabbed a piece of meat. "Have you been drinking? I thought you gave it up."

"No!" Hos said emphatically. "I ain't been drinking, and here's proof."

Small accepted the note, read the com master's barely legible scrawl, and saw that the messenger was correct. Assuming that the orbital sensors were functioning correctly, and there was no reason to think otherwise, hundreds of alien ships had dropped into the system and more were on the way.

Some, the majority from the sound of it, had adopted a long elliptical orbit around the sun, while six vessels, big honkers judging from the message, were in orbit around Long Jump.

Small removed the crisp white linen from his chest, folded the napkin along the creases, and put it aside. It was important to maintain a front, to signal how unflappable he was, in spite of the inexplicably empty feeling that claimed the bottom of his considerable gut. What was going on? A Confederate raid? Or just what the message claimed it was? Aliens out of nowhere? Neither possibility suggested an opportunity for profit.

Those thoughts were still in the process of flickering through Small's mind when something twittered. McGurk hauled a pocket com out of his coat and held the device to a badly misshapen ear. He listened, nodded, and turned to Small. "It's Hawker . . . He claims to have one of the ships on the horn—and says Jorley Jepp wants to speak with you."

The businessman felt his face flush red. He knew Jepp all right. Plenty of people did and would love to get their hands, tentacles, or graspers on him. A sometimes prospector, he owned a ship named the *Pelican*, and was eternally broke. One hundred and sixty-five thousand two-hundred and ten credits plus interest. That's how much the slimy, no-good, piece of space crap owed Small.

But Jepp had disappeared more than a year back, which meant some stupid bastard was having him on. Small was about to say as much, about to rip McGurk a new asshole, when the idiot in question offered the com set. "Here, it's Jorely Jepp."

In spite of the fact that his relationship with the Hoon was basically cordial, it was hardly collegial, which meant the computer never bothered to announce what the fleet was going to do next. A fact that bothered the human no end. That being the case, Jepp usually gathered information through his robots or via his own senses.

The human had lived on the Sheen ship for quite a while by then, and was used to the way air whispered through the ducts, the hull vibrated beneath his feet, and the push of the engines. So when the fleet dropped hyper, slowed, and dropped into orbit, Jepp sensed the change and sent his minions to investigate.

The Thraki robot was called "Sam," short for "Good Samaritan" and, though small, was able to assume a variety of configurations. Some of which came in handy from time to time. The fact that it served as a translator made the machine even more useful.

Henry, the only surviving component of the good ship *Pelican*, was a navcomp by trade and currently trapped within a body that looked like a garbage can. Though sentient and capable of speech, the host mechanism wasn't. That left the computer dependent on Sam.

The two robots, along with the ever-obedient Alpha, left Jepp's self-assigned quarters, passed an example of the religious graffiti that the prospector liked to spray paint onto the ship's bulkheads, and made for the nearest data port. Sam plugged in, sampled the flow, and found what the master was looking for. With that accomplished, it was a relatively simple matter to transmit the data to Henry, who possessed superior analytical abilities, and who if the truth be told was just plain smarter.

The navcomp scanned the data, registered the machine equivalent of surprise, and checked to ensure that it had arrived at the correct conclusion. Then, certain that the information was correct, Henry experienced a profound sense of horror. What were the odds? Millions to one? That the Hoon would randomly choose *that* particular set of coordinates?

No, much as the AI might want to believe such a hypothesis, it couldn't. Henry's memory had been plundered shortly after capture. Now, for reasons known only to it, the alien intelligence had approached Long Jump. The navcomp had witnessed similar visitations during the previous year, and none of them had been pleasant. Entire civilizations had been snuffed from existence, species left near extinction, and natural resources looted to feed the fleet. Slowly, reluctantly, Henry returned with the news.

Jepp listened to the report, asked to hear it again, and felt an almost overwhelming sense of joy. He'd been right! God had a plan. Why else would the Supreme Being direct the fleet to Long Jump? The very planet from which Henry and he had lifted so long ago?

The human literally danced around the compartment, chortled out loud, and slapped the robot's alloy back. "Here's our chance, Alpha! We'll minister to the godless and build the flock! Praise be to the lord."

"Praise be to the lord," Alpha echoed dutifully.

Henry was silent.

The Hoon transferred a portion of its consciousness from one ship to another, scanned the orb below, and considered its options. Yes, it could consume the metal on the planet below, and thereby fuel the fleet, or, and this was more intriguing, allow the soft body to interact with its peers and take the food afterwards.

Evidence had been found suggesting that the AI's quarry had traveled into that particular sector of space—and it wanted confirmation. If the soft bodies knew anything about the Thraki, they would tell the one called Jepp, and he would tell the Hoon. Or would he? Based on data gleaned from the biped's navigational entity, this was the biological's planet of origin. Perhaps he would run. No great loss, the Hoon concluded, none at all.

Jepp boarded the Sheen shuttle, followed by his robots, each one of which progressed by its own means of propulsion, which meant that Alpha walked, Henry rolled, and Sam scampered about. The human had been given grudging use of smaller ships in the past, but this felt different, as if the Hoon actually *wanted* him to go. Form has a tendency to follow function—so the control room looked like what it was. The presence of two pedestal-style chairs confirmed the fact that the ship's architects, whoever they might be, liked to sit down once in awhile.

There was a view screen, a stripped-down control panel, and a joystick. Did that mean the creators had a preference for simplicity? Or that the controls were regarded as little more than an emergency backup? Jepp favored the second theory but had no way to know if he was correct.

The ex-prospector sat down, wished the chair was more comfortable, and felt the ship lift off. It hovered for a moment, scooted out through the enormous hatch, and fell into orbit. The sight of Long Jump brought a lump to his throat. It looked like a chocolate ball dusted with powdered sugar. There were people down there, lots of them, and he hungered for the sound of their voices. Could the ship patch him through? There was only one way to find out. "Contact the surface," Jepp ordered, "and tell them I wish to speak with Neptune Small."

Three minutes passed while the robots communicated with the ship and the ship communicated with someone on Long Jump's surface.

Then, much to the human's amazement, Alpha touched a section of the control panel, waited for a small cover to whir out of the way, and removed a curvilinear tube. "Here, you can speak into this."

Jepp recognized the device as some sort of handset and heard a voice issue from a hole. "Jepp? Is that you?"

The sound of the merchant's voice was enough to trigger unpleasant memories. The prospector remembered what it had been like to wait for hours while Small sat in his office. And then, *if* he was very, very lucky, to be given five minutes in which to make his case. *Why* the existing loan should be extended, *why* he would strike it rich, *why* Small should be patient. And how, when the whole humiliating ritual was over, Small would part with a tiny fraction of the money he'd made during the last five minutes, and Jepp would slink away. But not *this* time Jepp thought to himself. "Yes," Jepp said out loud. "It certainly is. How do you like my fleet?"

Small, who had taken the precaution of draping a handkerchief over McGurk's less than sanitary com set, gave a grunt of derision. "I don't know who owns those ships . . . but it certainly isn't you."

"Oh really?" Jepp replied, eyeing the huge doughnut-shaped space hab that had appeared on the shuttle's view-screen. "How's that refueling station doing? You know, the one that charges twice the going rate, just for being out on the Rim?"

Small felt something gnaw at his gut. He made it to his feet, grabbed the cane, and walked toward the door. Maybe the folks down at the com center could tell him what the hell was going on. "Now Jorley . . . there's no reason to get all excited . . . let's talk."

A mob had formed in front of the com center but parted to let Small through. Voices babbled and questions flew, but the merchant ignored them. People scattered as Small barged into the main office and eyed the wall screen. There were ships all right, *lots* of them, more than he could count. And there, right between some red deltas was his pride and joy, the largely automated refueling station he called "*Halo.*" The computer-generated likeness of the station was gold and glistened in the sun.

Then, as if by magic, the *Halo* was gone. Small yelled "No!" but it was too late. Instructions had gone to the Hoon, weapons had been fired, and the hab ceased to exist.

Jepp tried to remember how many people lived on board but wasn't sure. He should have checked first—should have known the answer. What was wrong with him anyway? Would he go to hell? No, not so long as he furthered God's plan. His voice was filled with steel. "Prepare to receive God's servants. Make them welcome or suffer my wrath."

Small started to reply, started to ask "What servants?" but realized the connection had been severed.

All other air traffic was turned away as a procession of shimmery shuttles landed at Fortuna's much-abused space-port. Neptune Small, his flunkies, a crowd of townspeople, and spaceport staff all watched in amazement as dozens of smooth-faced robots filed out of the alien spaceships and made their way into the slums that bordered the port.

Many feared that the machines would suddenly turn violent, but there was no sign that any of them bore weapons, and none of the robots did anything to offend. What they did do, however, was take up positions on street corners, enter bars, and invade houses of prostitution. There were objections, of course, along with various attempts to eject them, but to no avail. Even after being physically accosted and thrown out into the streets, the robots simply picked themselves up and marched back in.

Eventually, after the bouncers tired of trying to stop them, the machines were allowed to stay. That's when they launched their carefully prepared sermons. Long rambling affairs that borrowed from a number of sects, denominations, and traditions, but were faithful to none.

It was only after walking around for a bit and sampling a number of presentations that Small realized the robots were speaking in unison!

Jepp, self-styled messiah that he was, had constructed the perfect cult. Each and every member thought the same thoughts, had the same beliefs, and babbled the same nonsense. Including the need to eradicate the Thraki. Whoever they might be.

People listened at first, curious as to what the silvery machines had to say, but soon grew bored and drifted away.

Three of the robots were machine-napped but set free the moment that the orbital barrage began. The buildings were chosen at random and destroyed one at a time till the Sheen were released.

Small lost two properties during the attack, and his peers lost structures as well. Finally, at their urging, the businessman was forced to go looking for Jepp. The self-styled messiah was easy to locate. Every street-corner robot seemed to know exactly where their master was.

The prefab warehouse catered to the sort of misfits that used Long Jump as a base of operations, and was subdivided into a labyrinth of heavily screened cubicles. It was difficult to see in the murky corridors, but most of the compartments seemed to crammed with semiworthless junk.

The owner, a weasel nicknamed "Pop," dogged the merchant's steps. He was as small as the other man was large and dressed in property confiscated from his nonpaying customers. A two-thousand credit spyder-silk robe flapped around his tiny body as he walked. "He's down this way Mr. Small . . . along with some of his infernal machines. They just walked in and took over."

The twosome turned a corner, passed under a dangling light wand, and located their quarry. Jepp was there all right—along with a clutch of robots. A silver globe bumped into Small's well-shod feet, transformed itself into something that resembled a spider, and attempted to scale the merchant's right leg. He bent over to peel the device off. Sam took exception. "Hey! Watch it buster! Hands off."

Startled by the robot's use of standard, the merchant took a step backward. The robot lost interest and dropped free. Jepp, who had chosen to ignore the businessman up till then, scanned the title of a holo disk and dropped it into a box. "Don't mind Sam . . . he's harmless enough. I wondered when you would show up."

Small, who felt inexplicably nervous, was shocked by the sound of his own voice. He sounded weak, and a little bit subservient, like those who worked for him. "Really? Yes, I suppose you did."

"Of course I did," Jepp said matter-of-factly. "So what did your friends say? Get rid of him? And do it fast?"

"Something like that," Small admitted lamely.

"So what will you give me?" Jepp demanded, hands on hips.

Small shrugged. "Whatever you want. So long as you leave and take the machines with you."

" 'Whatever I want,' " Jepp mused. "I like the sound of that . . . One can imagine all sorts of things. The sort of worldly garbage that a man like *you* would ask for.

"But God has no interest in such things . . . and neither do his servants. I ask only two things, one for the Hoon, and the other for myself."

Small felt a small, hard lump form in his throat. He had no idea who or what the Hoon was . . . but wasn't sure it mattered. As with all business deals, the price was what mattered. "Yes? What do you want?"

"The Sheen are looking for a race known as the Thraki. Have you heard of them?"

The merchant shook his head. Chins jiggled. "No, but we don't get much news out here. You know how it is . . . The Feddies don't care about us, and we don't care about them."

Jepp looked unimpressed. "You have contacts . . . use them. Talk to the smugglers. They know what's going on . . . they have to. I want a report by this time tomorrow."

Small nodded weakly. "It shall be as you say. And the second request?"

"Five years' worth of the best ship rations you can lay your hands on, fifty thousand gallons of purified water, a class one autodoc with plenty of supplies, ten dark blue ship suits, ten sets of underwear, two pairs of size twelve boots and ten thousand Bibles. At the spaceport by tomorrow night."

The fact that the list didn't involve large quantities of money or other valuables granted Small a tremendous sense of relief. "That sounds doable . . . Everything but the Bibles. I doubt there's more than 100 on the entire planet."

"Then print some more," Jepp replied sweetly, "or Judgment Day may arrive a little bit early."

The Hoon was both annoyed and amused by the supplies that the soft body wanted to bring aboard. Not that it made much difference since there was plenty of room.

Of greater significance was the fact that the biological

had clearly decided to stay. A thoroughly disagreeable prospect except for one thing: Prior to quitting the planet's surface, the human had acquired some valuable intelligence. It seemed that this particular world was little more than an outpost for a much larger multicultural civilization. A society still struggling to cope with the fact that the Thraki armada had dropped out of hyperspace, seized control of a planet, and taken up residence there. An extremely important development—assuming it was true.

The information had been culled from soft bodies that Jepp considered unreliable, nonfunctional, and in some cases outright hostile. In fact, based on observations the computer intelligence had carried out while monitoring its robots, some of the data had been obtained under physical duress.

Still, the claims were consistent with each other plus other data stored in Hoon's banks, and not to be ignored. The Sheen would proceed, albeit cautiously, to avoid any sort of trap.

As for the planet below, well, there were ships to feed, and even though the city would offer little more than a snack, something is better than nothing.

The shuttles landed with monotonous regularity. Larger units this time, loaded with self-propelled machines, each protected by one of the shimmery force fields that gave the Sheen their name.

Fortuna had no military as such, just criminal gangs, none of whom were willing to cooperate with each other. That being the case, the three-story crawlers were free to go about the business of consuming every bit of metal they could lay their graspers on without any interference other than the occasional shoulder-launched missile.

Neptune Small knew he should run, should head out into the bush like most of the others had, but continued to hope for some sort of miracle. The machines threatened everything that he had worked, stolen, and fought for. He was both too old and too fat to start all over again.

That's why the merchant stood out in front of the Rimmer's Rest, why he fired his cane as a crawler rounded a corner, and why Small, along with the entire facade of his building, vanished in a single flash of light.

3

Thus the highest form of generalship is to balk the
the enemy's plans; the next best is to prevent the
junction of the enemy's forces; the next in order is
to attack the enemy's army in the field; and worst
policy of all is to besiege walled cities.

Sun Tzu
The Art of War
Standard year circa 500 B.C.

Planet Arballa, the Confederacy of Sentient Beings

Originally christened as the battleship *Reliable*, the *Friendship* filled an entirely different role now, but still looked like what she was: one of the most powerful ships the Confederacy had. Her hull was five miles long and covered by a maze of heat exchangers, tractor beam projectors, com pods, and weapons blisters.

The planet Arballa hung huge behind her. The poles were white, but the rest of the world appeared as various shades of brown. Oh, there was water all right, but it was locked deep below where lake-sized aquifers had been sealed into bubbles of volcanic rock. That's where the wormlike Arballazanies took shelter from the sun's dangerous heat, spun their delicate cocoons, and built the optically switched computers for which they were justifiably famous. The *Friendship* had served the Confederacy as a traveling capital for more than fifty years now—and it was their turn to play host.

All of which was little more than a backdrop for co-conspirators, who, in an effort to escape the nonstop surveillance typical of shipboard life, boarded a Ramanthian shuttle, and used it to slip away.

The interior bore an intentional resemblance to the sort of underground cavern that Ramanthians preferred, which meant that it was not only dim but hot and extremely humid. The Hegemony's ambassador to the Confederacy, Harlan Ishimoto-Seven, sought to surreptitiously loosen his collar, and regretted the decision to come. Could the Ramanthian tell how uncomfortable he was? There was no way to be sure.

The Ramanthian resembled a large insect. He had multifaceted eyes, a parrotlike beak, tool legs in place of arms, and long narrow wings. They were folded at the moment, and nobody the clone knew had ever seen them deployed.

The clone and the Ramanthian were both members of the cabal that attempted to subvert Earth's government and thereby weaken its influence. The effort had failed, but just barely, and through no fault of their own. After all, who would have predicted an alliance between Ambassador Hiween Doma-Sa, the sole representative of the Hudathan race, and Sergi Chien-Chu, wealthy industrialist, past President of the Confederacy, and functional cyborg? Nobody, that's who.

Earth Governor Patricia Pardo had been a member of the original conspiracy but now languished in prison. Also missing was Legion Colonel Leon Harco, who had betrayed the Confederacy, the cabal, and ultimately himself. His court-martial was scheduled for later that year. Of less importance, in Ishimoto-Seven's opinion at least, was

Leshi Qwan, a corporate type who had pushed his luck too far, and allowed Maylo Chien-Chu to shoot him.

The conspirators had some *new* allies however, including Grand Admiral Hooloo Isan Andragna, the most senior officer in the Thraki fleet. He looked every bit as uncomfortable as Ishimoto-Seven felt.

Also joining the cabal was Senator Haf Noother, the duly appointed representative of the reclusive Drac Axis, who was clad from head to toe in a dull black pressure suit. His breathing apparatus, if that's what it was, made a sort of gurgling sound. Seven did his best to ignore it.

Orno noted the human's discomfort and took pleasure in how stupid the humans were. Especially this one. Little did he or the rest of the conspirators know, but the tricentennial birthing was only two and a half annums away, which meant his race would have an additional fifty billion mouths to feed. Reason enough to obtain some additional real estate. The Ramanthian made use of his tool legs to preen the areas to either side of his beak. His words were translated by the computer woven into his iridescent robes. The syntax was slightly stilted. "Thank you for taking time out of your busy schedules. Let's start by providing each of our representatives with the opportunity to report. Ambassador Ishimoto-Seven . . . let's begin with you."

The clone was ready. "Thank you. My efforts have centered on recruiting the votes necessary to admit the Thrakies to the Confederacy. In spite of the fact that my clone-brother, Senator Samuel Ishimoto-Six continues to drag his feet where our initiative is concerned, he *will* follow orders, and cast his ballot accordingly. That being the case the Hegemony is well on the way to building a pro-Thraki coalition."

"Excellent," Orno purred, "truly excellent. Once their membership has been approved, our Thraki brothers and sisters will bolster our strength. How many votes do we have?"

"Quite a few," Seven allowed cautiously, "but less than

we had hoped for. Governor Chien-Chu and Ambassador Doma-Sa have formed an alliance of their own. A strong group that seeks to block our initiative."

Admiral Andragna listened with a strange sense of detachment. His race was split into two main camps: the "runners," who believed the best way to deal with the Sheen was to run from them, and the "facers," who wanted to face the enemy and fight. The facers were in the majority—so plans had been laid for the inevitable battle. A battle in which he and his staff planned to use the Confederacy as a shield. A strategy that would be greatly enhanced if they were covered by the mutual defense pact that attended membership.

Still, in his heart of hearts, Andragna was a runner and saw the present machinations as a waste of time. He couldn't admit that, however, not to the committee or to those around him.

The Drac spoke for the first time. Maybe it was the synthesizer, or maybe it was his voice, but the result was less than melodious. "Bribery, what of?"

Seven shrugged. "We could buy Doma-Sa with freedom for his race, assuming there was a way to deliver, but what happens after that? The Hudathans were confined to their home system for a very good reason. They killed *millions* during the first and second Hudathan wars."

"And Governor Chien-Chu?"

"Hopeless," Orno concluded. "The governor is so wealthy that money holds no meaning for him. There are other possibilities however—and the Thraki are working on them. Admiral?"

The robot that rested on the Thraki's lap was part toy, part pet, and part tool. It morphed into a globe and assumed the role of translator. "Our priesthood includes a branch focused on the martial arts. A team of assassins was dispatched to Earth with instructions to kill Maylo Chien-Chu. We haven't heard from them as yet . . . but they seldom fail."

"Point is what?" the Drac inquired flatly.

"Intimidation," Ishimoto-Seven replied easily. "If Chien-Chu's niece can be killed then no one is safe. Not his wife, not his associates, and not him."

"Good it is," Noother concluded. "Next what?"

Orno glanced at the viewscreen. Special electroactive contact lenses took hundreds of separate images and combined them into one. The *Friendship* looked small and potentially vulnerable against the great blackness. "Isolated though he is, the Hudathan has proven far too effective for his own good. I plan to eliminate him . . . and do so in a very public manner. With Doma-Sa dead—the votes we require will hurry to find *us*."

"How?" the Drac demanded.

"Patience," the Ramanthian counseled. "You must have patience. Isn't that right, Horgo?"

The War Orno stepped forward into the light. Like all of his kind, the Ramanthian's vital organs were protected by an extremely hard brown-black exoskeleton. He possessed an elongated head, short antennae, a parrotlike beak, and a pair of seldom-deployed wings. He wore black body armor secured by bright metal links. A sword had been strapped across his back, and Horgo wore two hand weapons, butts forward. His rarely heard voice was deep and menacing. "Yes, lord. That is correct."

The Starlight Ballroom could handle up to one thousand guests, all protected by an immense transparent dome. The planet Arballa hung like a jewel beyond the armored plastic. Only one corner of the vast space was currently in use. About sixty beings, who represented more than a dozen different races, stood in conversational clumps where they sipped, sucked, snorted, and otherwise ingested a wide variety of mildly intoxicating substances, snacked on a variety of exotic hors d'oeuvres, and told each other lies.

All except for one lonely figure who knew he *should* mingle—but couldn't quite bring himself to do so. He stood with his back to a durasteel bulkhead, his feet planted firmly on the deck, wishing he were dead. Ambassador Hiween Doma-Sa had rendered many services to his now beleaguered race—but none involved more personal sacrifice than his presence at President Nankool's cocktail party. He not only hated such occasions but hated them with every fiber of his 350-pound body.

The food was disgusting, by *his* standards at any rate, and the conversation was highly political, which was to say full of poorly disguised flattery, outrageous gossip, and carefully calculated untruths. All of which went against the Hudathan's instincts.

Still, that was the price that had to be paid if he ever hoped to gather the support necessary to lift the blockade that currently confined his people to their home world. A chaotic place where a Trojan relationship with a Jovian binary caused the planet Hudatha to have a wildly unpredictable climate, and threatened the survival of the race. Just as *humans* threatened it, *Ramanthians* threatened it, and every other sentient race threatened it. Not because of anything they had done, but because they existed, and *might* cause harm.

All of which explained why Triads long dead had considered it necessary to attack and destroy the very races with which Doma-Sa now mingled. *Stupid* races for the most part, who, had they truly understood the nature of his race, would have killed every Hudathan they could find and sterilized the planet from which they came. But they were incapable of such pragmatism, which was good for him.

"So," a voice said, "which ones would you like to kill most, and in what order?" The joke, because the Hudathan had learned enough about humans to recognize it as such, demonstrated an almost scary understanding of the way he felt. Was he that transparent? The possibility frightened Doma-Sa as he turned to face Sergi Chien-Chu.

The industrialist's biological body had expired many

years before. That's why his brain and a length of spinal cord were housed in an otherwise synthetic body. A vehicle quite similar to the original. The face had a rounded, slightly Asian cast to it, the body was pleasantly plump, and the clothing was simple verging on plain. A look that was nearly Hudathan in its simplicity. Doma-Sa's expression changed only fractionally, but the human recognized the alien equivalent of a smile. "I would leave *you* till the last."

Chien-Chu laughed in spite of the fact that the jest contained a strong element of truth. Doma-Sa had a large humanoid head, the suggestion of a dorsal fin that ran along the top of his skull, funnel-shaped ears, and a rigid mouth. His skin was gray, but would turn white should the temperature drop, and black were it to rise.

Chien-Chu glanced to his left and right, assured himself that they were as free from surveillance as one could be on the *Friendship*, and took the opportunity to share his news. "My niece came aboard three hours ago. The Thraki tried to assassinate her."

Doma-Sa liked Maylo, as much as he liked *any* non-Hudathan, and his face grew hard. "Then they must die."

"They already have," Chien-Chu said gravely, "thanks to General Bill Booly. The larger problem remains, however. Who sent them? And why?"

"The cabal," Doma-Sa answered with certainty. "The Thraki were used."

"Yes," the cyborg agreed. "Albeit willingly—as part of their own grand scheme. Even though you exposed their intention to use the Confederacy as a shield—they continue to move the plan forward. There was a time when we could have forced them to leave, but that was prior to the mutiny, and the subsequent rebellion. They have five thousand ships, not counting what the cabal can bring to bear, which leaves Earth badly outnumbered."

The Hudathan offered a human-style shrug. "I am aware of these facts . . . why review the obvious?"

"Because," Chien-Chu said, "I have an idea. A solution nearly as dangerous as the threat itself . . . but one that . . ."

The human never got to finish his sentence. A body brushed past his, stepped forward, and sprayed what looked like red paint onto the front of the Hudathan's robe.

Chien-Chu took a step backwards, realized who the interloper was, and heard the War Orno speak. The words had a rehearsed quality. "You have not only slandered the Ramanthian race, but sullied the house of Orno, and taken liberties with our private communications. Honor has been lost . . . and honor must be restored."

Had the room fallen silent a fraction of a second *before* the challenge was issued? Chien-Chu thought that it had, which would mean that at least some of the bystanders had been warned, and were waiting for the confrontation to unfold. A quick check confirmed that Senator Orno, flanked by Ambassador Ishimoto-Seven and Grand Admiral Andragna, were watching from a hundred feet away. First Maylo, the industrialist thought to himself, now this.

Doma-Sa looked down at the stain on his chest then up into the Ramanthian's hard insectoid eyes. The entire room held its breath as the Hudathan allowed the silence to build. Finally, when some doubted his capacity to speak, the diplomat gave his response. "Challenge accepted."

There was a sucking sound as the oxygen breathers inhaled. The War Orno bowed and straightened again. "The choice of weapons is yours."

The silence built once again. What would the Hudathan choose? What would any of them choose? Energy weapons? Slug throwers? Dart guns? Each had merit.

Doma-Sa smiled but very few of them recognized the expression as such. Most saw what looked like a predatory grin. "Swords."

There were gasps of surprise, the quick buzz of commentary, and a variety of stares.

Horgo was taken aback. Though something of an expert with the sword, he had assumed that if the diplomat agreed to fight, it would be with something less personal. A weapon that would put some distance between the combatants and serve to even the odds. This was good news indeed. The duel would be short. Pleased by his good fortune, the War Orno bowed for the second time and backed away. "The surface of Arballa—two days from now."

Doma-Sa nodded. "Two days from now."

Chien-Chu sighed. The trap had been set and sprung. Would the quarry escape? Only time would tell.

It was a small compartment, just off President Nankool's living quarters, and frequently used for gatherings such as this one. Candlelight glinted from real silver, a Turr symphony could be heard in the background, and the meal was half over. President Marcott Nankool was a rather bland man who took too much pleasure in ceremonial meals, and looked a bit bloated.

The guests included Sergi Chien-Chu, Maylo Chien-Chu and Hiween Doma-Sa. The President gestured toward the Hudathan's large and rather ornate bowl. "So, Ambassador, how are you doing? Ready for another serving?"

The Hudathan eyed his second bowl of cooked grain. It was hearty stuff—full of nuts and dried fruit. Not bad for shipboard cuisine. "Thank you, Mr. President, but no. This is more than sufficient."

Nankool looked at Maylo. "And how 'bout you my dear? Some more of the fish perhaps?"

Maylo flashed back to the illicit swim that she and Senator Samuel Ishimoto-Six had shared in one of the onboard aqua-culture tanks, and wondered where he was. Why did she care? And what about Booly? The silence stretched uncomfortably long, and she hurried to fill it. "No, thank you."

"Well," Nankool continued, dabbing at his lips, "let's get to it. So, Sergi, what's on your mind?"

Chien-Chu had very little need of nourishment, and what he did require was delivered by other means. He toyed with his wineglass. The dinner was *his* doing . . . so the question made sense. He looked from one face to the next. "I would like to submit a proposal, a proposal that many of our colleagues would consider to be insane, but, given our present circumstances, may represent the only real chance we have."

Nankool finished one glass of wine and poured himself another. Light gleamed as he raised the glass. "To Sergi Chien-Chu! Author of the outrageous! Please proceed."

The most fleeting of smiles touched Chien-Chu's plasti-flesh lips. "You may feel differently in a moment. My proposal is this: Given the fact that the Sheen are hunting for the Thraki, and we lack the clout to force them to leave, the Confederacy is in need of allies. Allies with military clout."

"Yes," the President agreed. "But who? All the players have chosen sides. None remain."

"Ah, but that's where you are wrong," the industrialist insisted. "One player remains, and he's *here*, sitting at this table."

Nankool frowned, looked to Doma-Sa, and back to Chien-Chu. "I'm sorry Sergi . . . I don't understand."

"It's really quite simple," Chien-Chu replied. "After the last war ended, in an effort to prevent still another, a block-ade was established. Since that time Ambassador Doma-Sa and his people have been free to do whatever they pleased so long as they remained on the surface of the planet Hudatha."

Maylo wondered what her uncle was driving at, looked at the Hudathan, and took note of his expression. Though no expert, the businesswoman had spent a considerable amount of time with the diplomat, and thought she detected a strange sort of intensity . . . As if the alien *thought* he knew where Chien-Chu was headed . . . but was afraid to hope.

"I have no way to know," the industrialist continued earnestly, "but it's my guess that the Hudathan military has been anything but inactive during the last fifty years, and are at the very peak of readiness. All of which points to a reserve of warriors, *fierce* warriors, who have every reason to fight the Sheen and nothing to lose."

Nankool went pale. His hands started to shake. "My apologies to the Ambassador—but have you taken leave of your senses? Have you forgotten the death of your own son? The deaths of more than two million Confederate soldiers? The deaths of a billion civilians? All at the hands of the Hudathans? I'm sorry, Sergi . . . but what you propose is out of the question. Even if the Hudathans agreed, even if they fought the Sheen to a standstill, they would turn on us in the end."

Though not as responsive as his flesh and blood face had been, the highly malleable plastic did its best to reflect what the cyborg felt, and there was no mistaking the extent of his emotions. A hand slammed down onto the surface of the table, and wineglasses jumped in response. Maylo, who had never seen her uncle lose his temper in all the years she had known him, felt suddenly afraid.

"You think I haven't considered those things? Damn your impertinence! Not a day passes that I don't think of Leonid, of the fact that I sent him to Spindle, where the Hudathans killed him.

"But what of the billions for whom we are responsible? How many will the Sheen slaughter? Once dead, we have no means to bring them back. Should we defeat the Sheen, and go on to face the Hudathans, they have a chance. No offense to Ambassador Doma-Sa—but we defeated his race on two previous occasions. I believe we can do so again."

Though confused by conflicting emotions Maylo came to her uncle's assistance. "Sergi has a point . . . Perhaps the Hudathans could change, if they *wanted* to change, and integrate themselves into Confederate society. Still, even if they can't, limits can be imposed."

"Yes!" Chien-Chu added gratefully. "Limit the size of

their navy! Troops mean nothing without the means to move them around."

"Spoken like a true admiral," Nankool said dryly. "I see what you mean . . . but I still find the concept more than a little frightening."

The President turned to Doma-Sa. So, Ambassador, what do *you* think? Would you and your people fight alongside the Confederacy in exchange for limited freedoms? And to what extent could your race be trusted? Realizing that you are a bit biased of course."

Doma-Sa fought to control the unseemly feeling of joy that threatened to overwhelm the rest of his faculties. At last! Here was the opportunity he had dreamed of . . . An opening to exploit. But at what cost? The Thrakie hoped to use the entire Confederacy as a shield—and Chien-Chu wanted to employ *his* people as a spear. Oh, how he hungered for something clean and pure. The diplomat chose his words with care.

"The governor's assumption is correct. Though not permitted to leave the surface of Hudatha, my people *have* been able to maintain a high state of military readiness. A fact that in no way violates the terms of our surrender and subsequent imprisonment.

"As for our willingness to fight the Sheen, well, anyone who has carried out even the most superficial analysis of our racial psychology knows that we have a strong, some would say overdeveloped sense of survival. Given the opportunity to neutralize a threat, we will always seek to do so.

"Such decisions lie beyond the scope of my authority, but, I believe the answer would be 'yes.' *If* we were allowed some additional freedoms—and the right to settle new worlds. Hudatha grows less stable with each passing year, and time grows short."

"And then?" Nankool demanded. "If we defeat the Sheen? What could we expect then?"

The silence built as Doma-Sa considered his answer. He

could lie, or try to, but doubted his ability to carry the deception off. Not with Chien-Chu present. No, the Hudathan decided, the truth was best. "I cannot honestly say that my people will ever be able to fully merge with the Confederacy. Given too much freedom, and the opportunity to build a fleet, our instincts would take over. *If* the Confederacy allows my race to fight, *if* we are allowed some additional freedoms, it would pay to be vigilant. We are what we are."

There was another moment of silence followed by Nankool's nod of acknowledgement. "Thank you Ambassador Doma-Sa. I have come to rely on your honesty. No one could represent you race or its interests more ably. Come, let's eat, the food grows cold."

It took the better part of an hour to finish the meal, complete the usual pleasantries, and prepare to leave. Nankool saw them to the hatch. It was he who raised the topic again. "Thank you for coming . . . Terrifying though Sergi's proposal is, I promise to give it some thought.

"In the meantime I suggest that all three of you direct your energies to the upcoming vote. The attempt on Maylo's life is a sure measure of how desperate our opponents are. Once admitted, the Thraki would represent more than another vote—they would demonstrate how powerful the cabal has become. Many beings would align themselves accordingly, and a great deal would be lost, including any chance of approval for a scheme as wild as the one Sergi put forward."

Nankool turned to the Hudathan. "They intend to kill you . . . I wish you had refused."

The Hudathan shrugged. "Thank you, but such a course is impossible."

"But why swords?" the President insisted. "Have you any experience?"

"I hope to give a good account of myself," the Hudathan answered mildly. "Please notify my people should I fail to do so."

Nankool's guests left after that—but the politician was far from alone. Ghosts haunted his dreams. Many screamed in anguish.

In spite of the fact that it would have been more convenient to conduct the duel on board the ship, there were laws that prevented the combatants from doing so, which left Arballa's hot rather unpleasant surface. A fleet of high puffy clouds sailed across the land. Each threw a separate shadow. They drifted like night over broken ground.

And so the politicos arrived, their shuttles shattering the silence, landing in sloppy groups.

There wasn't much vegetation, which meant that oxygen was in short supply. Many of those who had chosen to come, and that was almost everybody, required supplemental air. They hiked in from wherever they happened to touch down with all manner of exotic breathing gear attached to their mouths, snouts, beaks, and other related organs.

All except for Doma-Sa that is, whose body could handle a wide range of atmospheric conditions, and who walked unencumbered from his shuttle. A fact that attracted no small amount of notice and fueled the speculation. Would the War Orno win? He certainly *looked* dangerous . . . Or would the Hudathan carry the day? Opinions were offered, odds were given, and bets were placed.

Doma-Sa's robe snapped in the breeze, dust exploded away from his boots, and he walked with purpose. Bystanders scattered at his approach, wondered about the bundle tucked under his arm, and some even felt sorry for him. Had anyone else been challenged seconds would have accompanied him down to the planet's surface, but the Hudathan was all alone. The onlookers followed, marveled at the size of the alien's footprints, and felt a delicious sense of anticipation.

The arena consisted of a bowl-shaped depression, scoured by the relentless globe-spanning winds, and rimmed by a circle of heavily weathered rocks. Someone, it wasn't clear who, had seen fit to stick long whip-style poles into the soil, each topped by a colorful pennant. They seemed oddly gay, given the nature of the occasion, and flapped back and forth.

The rocks offered a sort of rough and ready seating and were half occupied by the time the Ramanthian party made its way down from the hill on which they had landed and entered the crater.

The War Orno had been there before, on three different occasions, to test the surface on which he would fight. Yes, he knew each dip, each patch of gravel, and each pocket of sand. Critical knowledge, given the fact that good footing is one of the most critical components of good swordsmanship.

The Hudathan was big, *very* big, and that meant slow. Slow and potentially clumsy. There was power in those shoulders, however, the kind of power generated by an internalized skeleton, and a mistake could be fatal.

Senator Alway Orno removed his counterpart's cape, took pride in the way he looked, and stepped out of the way.

A buzz ran through the crowd. Balanced on his powerful retrograde legs, his chitin shiny with oil, the Ramanthian was very imposing. There was the rasp of high grade steel as Horgo drew his weapon, slashed the air into four equal sections, and restored the blade to its scabbard. The odds changed again. The cabal and its champion were favored to win.

Maylo made an adjustment to her nose plugs and spoke to her uncle. The words had a nasal quality. "That was impressive."

"Ceremonial displays usually are," the industrialist observed. "It's what happens when blade meets blade that matters."

The sun was hot, but Maylo shivered.

Doma-Sa looked strangely vulnerable as he entered the

arena. His robe flapped around his knees, and he carried a bundle bound with twine. He paused, turned a long slow circle, and nodded as if satisfied. Then, with the care of a surgeon preparing her instruments, he gave a tug on the string, and flicked the roll toward the east. Dust spurted up around the edges of the fabric as the quiltlike material hit the orange-red dirt. Sunlight rippled along the surface of the thousand-year-old blade

It was called *Head Taker* and had been handed down through Doma-Sa's family the way all things of value were allocated: *by force*. Like all such weapons, it had two edges, one straight, one with razor-sharp teeth.

Another buzz ran through the crowd. Did the Hudathan know how to use the weapon? Why have such an implement if he didn't? The odds turned and surged the other way.

That's when Doma-Sa dropped his robe, the audience watched his skin shift toward white, and realized how big he truly was. Leather cross-straps bulged where they sought to span his chest, muscles rippled along massive arms, and his legs looked like tree trunks. The diplomat bent to take the sword. Light danced the length of the blade and *more* bets were placed.

A robot named Harold had been designated to officiate the event. His day suit had been painted on. A hover cam appeared. Once-shiny metal had been dulled by hard use. Maylo knew who the device belonged to. Though unwilling or unable to venture out onto the surface of their planet, the Arballazanies were interested nonetheless. Somewhere, far below, they watched as Harold made his way to the center of the arena.

Harold motioned the duelists forward. His voice was amplified. "*Before* the duel begins, *before* blood is shed, the President begs both parties to reconsider. The Confederacy is built on the rule of *law*, not violence, and there are equitable ways in which to solve our differences. Will one or both parties yield to reason? No? Then let the contest begin."

There was no salute, no words of respect, since neither one of the opponents was willing to honor the other's traditions. They circled to the right. The Hudathan held his weapon in the on-guard position, his torso turned slightly inward, his rear arm touching his hip.

The Ramanthian shuffled sideways, watching the way Doma-Sa held himself, and waited for the attack. Though too young to fight in the last war, Horgo had studied it, and drawn certain conclusions. Hudathans were aggressive, impatient, and overly reliant on brute force. All of which suggested that Doma-Sa would come to him.

Doma-Sa watched the sun, waited till his shadow pointed at his opponent's feet, and launched a head cut.

The War Orno flicked his head to the right, waited for the moment of full extension, and made the forward lunge.

The Hudathan took note of the other being's speed, parried the incoming blade, and recovered his ground.

Encouraged by the small retreat, the Ramanthian brought his left foot forward, and timed the chest cut to coincide with the end of the movement. Steel flashed past his face, something tugged at his air mask, and his lungs sucked hot thin air.

A murmur of approval ran through the crowd, and Senator Orno displayed the equivalent of a frown. Ambassador Ishimoto-Seven and Senator Haf Noother stayed where they were, but others edged away.

The combatants continued their slow deliberate dance. The War Orno found that it was hard to breathe. Time was running out. He backpedaled as if afraid, waited for Doma-Sa to commit, and opened his wings. The wind rushed in, his feet left the ground, and the Ramanthian was airborne. His sword fell, found the Hudathan's shoulder, and cut to the bone. Blood flowed and Senator Orno whistled his shrill approval.

Doma-Sa cursed his own stupidity, shifted his sword

from the right hand to the left, and parried the next blow. The bug could fly! How could he miss that? Gravel slipped out from under his boots as he fell.

The Ramanthian beat his way forward—leg spurs at the ready. Shaped like claws, and razor sharp, they could rip through chitin. Still lying on his back, the Orno's wings pushing air down into his face, the Hudathan slashed with his sword. Steel sliced through the outer surface of a leg, and the Ramanthian flinched.

This was the opportunity Doma-Sa had been waiting for. The bug couldn't land—not and stand upright. That would keep him in the air . . . or so the diplomat hoped. He rocked forward, found his feet, and surged upwards.

The War Orno responded, or tried to, but discovered that his belly was exposed. *Head Taker* stabbed upwards, the Ramanthian screeched in agony, and Maylo closed her eyes.

The War Orno fell, the Hudathan jerked his weapon free, and the body hit the dirt. A cloud of bloodred dust rose, the crowd fell silent, and the duel was over. Androids rushed to dress Doma-Sa's wound and peers hurried to congratulate him.

Senator Orno felt a terrible sense of sorrow and shuffled his way forward. The War Orno and he had been hatched within seconds of each other, had courted the Egg Orno as a pair, and promised many things. Visions, dreams, things that might someday be. Now they were gone, snuffed like cave candles, forever destroyed.

Maylo actually felt sorry for the Ramanthian as he knelt on alien soil, gathered his loved one into his arms, and made his way up the hill.

Haf Noother looked at Harlan Ishimoto-Seven. The clone shrugged. The Drac walked out into the arena, located the Ramanthian's sword, and tested the heft. Then, aiming for soil still damp with the Orno's blood, drove the blade into the ground.

Later, long after the visitors had left, night came, and the stars danced on steel.

The vote came two days later. The result was never in doubt. Thraki membership was rejected, "pending further investigation," and the cabal suffered a setback.

Grand Admiral Andragna, his plans frustrated, left for Zynig-47.

Sergi Chien-Chu witnessed the vote, made his way back to his quarters, and palmed the lock. Once inside, the fold-down desk sensed his presence, dropped into position, and spoke. "You have six messages waiting—one of which carries the designations 'urgent,' and 'private.' "

"Play it," Chien-Chu said, dropping into his chair.

"Congratulations," Nankool said, as his likeness filled the holo tank. "The vote went just as we hoped it would. The cabal lost, and *you* won."

The President formed a steeple with his fingers. "All of which is good except that it won't last, won't *mean* anything, if the Sheen destroy the Confederacy as part of their effort to reach the Thrakie. "That's why I'm going to name *you* as my secret envoy, give you more power than any one being should rightfully have, and let you enter talks with the Hudathans.

"Sell them what you sold me, attach all the conditions you can, and do it quickly. Time is short—and the clock is ticking."

4

To see the future one has but to visit the past.

Naa folk saying
Circa standard year 1700

Planet Algeron, the Confederacy of Sentient Beings

It was cold. Snowflakes twisted down out of the heavens, and the Towers of Algeron were but shadows in the distance. Some of the peaks soared more than eighty thousand feet into the atmosphere, which made them taller than Olympic Mons on Mars. In fact, the mountains were *so* massive, that had they been located on Earth the Towers would have sunk down through the planet's crust.

However, thanks to the fact that Algeron completed a full rotation every two hours and forty-two minutes, centrifugal force had caused the equator to bulge outwards.

In fact, although Algeron possessed roughly the same amount of mass Earth did—its equatorial diameter was 27 percent larger. That, combined with the fact that the planet's polar diameter was 32 percent *smaller* than Terra's produced an equator nearly twice the diameter of the poles. All of which meant that the Towers of Algeron, which rode the world-spanning bulge, weighed only half what they would on Earth.

All facts that General William Booly had been aware of since childhood—the earliest part of which had been spent in a village seventy-five miles to the northeast.

The legionnaire stepped out onto the parapet, saw his breath jet outwards, and was glad of his jacket. He'd been dirtside for one standard week by then, and the sentries had become familiar with his morning walks. The habit had been born on the walls of his previous command, in Djibouti, Africa, and continued here. Precious minutes during which he could think and no one dared disturb him. He followed the top of the wall.

Fort Camerone, which had been named after what the Legion considered to be its most important battle, crouched on a dry rocky plain, and, with the exception of antenna arrays, fly-form landing pads, and missile launchers that interrupted its boxy lines, was reminiscent of Legion forts in North Africa. It was, Booly decided, the way a fortress *should* look. Hard and uncompromising.

It was strange to be there, not only in command of Fort Camerone, but of the entire Legion as well. Yes, he'd been ambitious enough to fanaticize about such an achievement, but never believed that it would happen. Not to a half-breed.

But it *had* happened—though not in the way he would have preferred. Rather than earn the position, he had inherited it from officers who, like Mortimer Kattabi, had died in battle, or like Leon Harco, who had chosen the wrong side and paid the price. Good officers, perhaps *better* officers, who, except for a moment of bad luck, or poor judgment, would have been in command. A fact that played into the feelings of inferiority that had been born right there, beyond the veil of the slowly falling snow, where he and his Naa playmates had fought their play pretend wars. Wars that he generally lost.

A sentry snapped to attention, presented his weapon, and

waited for Booly's acknowledgement. Like everyone on
the battlements, he was aware of the general's presence
and more than a little self-conscious. The officer returned
the salute and continued on his way.

Yes, it was hard to compete when your peers could
smell game from a hundred feet away, could sense heat
with the soles of their bare feet, and on a cold day, *much*
colder than this one, had the capacity to run nearly naked
through the snow, for miles on end if need be, laughing
all the way.

Booly had been smart enough, always toward the top of
his class, but had never won a footrace, wrestling match,
or other test of athletic ability until he had entered the
academy and competed with humans. The fact that he
could win, *could* excel, had been something of a revela-
tion.

The instructors taught him how to lead, and he had,
though never with the confidence of classmates like Harco.
Now that might come back to haunt him, and not just *him,*
but the thousands of men, women, and cyborgs under his
command.

The officer paused to look out over the densely packed
domes collectively known as Naa Town. As darkness fell,
he saw squares of buttery yellow light, fingers of dark gray
smoke, and the wink of the occasional torch. More than
that, his supersensitive nostrils could pick up the odor of
incense, burned to cover the smells that emanated from the
fort, and the faint scent of slowly drying dooth dung. A
valuable source of fuel.

And it was out there, beyond the edge of the slum, that
his mother and father, both of whom had served in the
Legion, had given up their lives in order to free the fort.
The plaque, which he had visited only two days before,
bore a single line:

They died that others might live.

Was it colder? A chill ran down his spine. Booly scanned the horizon, watched another two-hour-and-forty-two minute day come to an end, and turned toward a door. A private held it open. His office awaited as did his work. Plans, requests, appeals, budgets, promotions, reports, and more. All the stuff that he hated . . . but was forced to do.

Booly thought longingly of Maylo, wondered what she was doing, and stepped through the doorway. His responsibilities closed around him.

A staff meeting plus three hours of administrative work passed before Booly rewarded himself with a break. He rarely ate in the officers' mess, preferring the chow hall instead. That's where the troops were, and while they weren't about to spill their guts to a general, they didn't have to. Like most good officers, he could learn a great deal about how the legionnaires felt, what they were thinking, and their general state of readiness by simply looking at them.

Booly had named Colonel Kitty Kirby to command the fort, and she was tough but fair. She, combined with the efforts of the officers and noncoms who reported to her, had been good for morale. The results could be seen in the way that members of various units sat together, the buzz of conversation, and the occasional burst of laughter. Things had improved a great deal since the mutiny and the bloodshed that accompanied it.

The mess hall featured bright lights, artificially cheerful colors, and odors left from the previous meal. Something that Naa troopers never stopped griping about. When you *eat* lunch they reasoned, it should *smell* like lunch, and not like breakfast. Fans had been installed—but the complaints continued.

Booly joined the chow line, joked with the cooks, and headed out into the hall. A table of heavily bearded Pioneers started to rise and the officer shook his head. "At ease . . . How 'bout it, Sergeant? Is there room for one more?"

The legionnaire grinned. "Yes, sir! Watch what you say though . . . we're talking about sports. Cramer says that Earth is going to win the next powerball playoff—and Rober favors the clones. It could get violent."

Booly laughed. "I'll take my chances." The Pioneers made room—and the hour passed quickly.

Booly returned to his office to find a package waiting on his desk. His adjutant turned from a pile of printouts. Her name was Tan. She had served under Cadet Leader Voytan during the battle for Los Angeles, survived, and been posted to Algeron. She had short black hair, serious brown eyes, and quick little hands. "That came while you were away, sir. A cub gave it to one of the sentries and said it was for you."

Booly raised an eyebrow. The relationship between the Legion and the Naa was complex to say the least. Even as some of the tribes encouraged young warriors to join the organization, others continued to fight it just as they fought each other. Patrols were subject to ambush, sentries had been killed, and the occasional SLM slammed into the fort. Many of the chieftains would like nothing better than to bag a general. The box could contain anything . . . including a bomb.

Tan read his expression and shook her head. "No, sir. The package is clean. I had the demolitions folks check it out."

Booly nodded his thanks and took a moment to remove the protective wrappings. The gar wood box had been decorated with crudely cut semiprecious stones. Such containers were common among the Naa, and he had seen hundreds of them. But not like this, not with the cap badge of the 13th DBLE carved into the lid, above the motto: *"Legio patria nostra."* (The Legion is our country.)

Booly had watched his father burn the words into the wood with a laser pen. Then, long after his mother had opened the present, and remarked on how beautiful it was, he had seen it on her dressing table, next to her bed, and on her desk. For this was the box in which Connie Chrobuck kept small treasures. He remembered them well: one of *her* mother's earrings, a rock her son retrieved from a riverbed, a holo of her sister, some small, extremely sharp scissors, and, Algeron being what it was, some stray rounds of ammunition. Those and other things had lived in the box. Now, at long last, they lay before him.

The officer turned, discovered that Tan had left the room, and was grateful. Generals weren't supposed to cry—everybody knew that—but the tears continued to flow.

Booly closed the door, wiped his face with his sleeve, and sat at his desk. Was the box empty? Did it contain the odds and ends she had kept there? Or had they been looted? Or more likely lost? Treated like what most would think they were: junk.

Carefully, lest his suddenly clumsy fingers betray him, Booly opened the box. It was empty, except for his mother's scent, and a note written in her neat hand. "I knew you would return as surely as a brella must return to its roost. In spite of the fact that I wasn't born on Algeron, and lack your father's blood, his mother taught me many things . . . Among them was the importance of a peaceful heart, the beauty that dwells around us, and the way of the Wula sticks.

"They speak of a great chief, the Chief of all Chiefs, and of great sadness. A battle lies ahead, a *great* battle, the one you were born to fight. No one can be sure how it will end, not even the sticks, but look at the map. Follow it and find that which you seek.

"We love you—and always will. Watch your six . . . Your mother and father."

Booly laughed, wiped the last of the tears away, and

examined the reverse side of the note. The map was good—but the officer didn't need one. He'd been there before. He departed two hours later.

It was dark at the moment, but that made little difference to the Trooper II, who, thanks to a full array of sensors, could "see" quite well indeed. She had light-amplification equipment, infrared sensors, and the benefit of a highly accurate Global Positioning System, which, thanks to high quality maps, displayed her position to within three inches. More than enough data for a little stroll in the boonies.

The cyborg went by the name of Wilker, although her real name was something else, and was glad to clear the fort. Yeah, the rider was a pain, but what else was new? Anything beat garrison duty. She scanned the terrain ahead, spotted the heat that radiated from some recently deposited dooth droppings, and headed that way.

First Sergeant Neversmile had ridden on cyborgs before and knew better than to tighten up. The best thing to do was stick boots into the slots provided for that purpose, lean backwards, and allow the harness to take your weight. Then, with knees bent, the motion was easier to take.

Wilker followed the trail down into a gully and up the other side. Servos whined, heat radiated off her cowling, and the odor of ozone filled Neversmile's nostrils. Just one of the things he hated about box heads.

Still, they did have their advantages, not the least of which was the firepower they carried. Wilker was equipped with an arm-mounted air-cooled .50 caliber machine gun, an arm-mounted fast-recovery laser cannon, and a pair of shoulder-mounted missile launchers. Yeah, Colonel Kirby knew what she was doing. Wilker had more than enough clout to deal with a handful of bandits—or some warriors on a tear. All of which was fine, or would have been, had the mission made more sense.

It seemed that nobody was sure what the hell the general was up to. A gift had been delivered to his office. The rumor mill was clear about that, but the rest was weird. Shortly after receiving it the Legion's most senior officer had announced that he was going on a trip, would need a dooth, and would dispense with the usual escort. A dooth for god's sake! Neversmile hadn't been aboard one of the wooly beasts in more than fifteen years—and figured Booly was the only officer on Algeron that knew how to ride one.

The noncom felt a momentary sense of pride in the nature of the general's origins and remembered Kirby's orders: "Don't let the old man see you . . . and don't come back without him."

Not that the last part was necessary, since Neversmile had served under the general during the mutiny and had a lot of respect for him. Good officers were hard to come by.

A faint pink line marked the eastern horizon. Wilker followed the trail, and the Naa continued to worry. The general was crazy, the colonel was pissy, and the problem was his.

Dimwit Timewaster was standing there, pissing on a rock, when the rich pungent odor of dooth passed beneath *his* nostrils. Not *his* dooth, a mangy animal tethered to a withered bush, but a distinctly different beast. And there was something more, the tart, not altogether unpleasant smell which, along with plastic and ozone, he had learned to associate with humans. The clip clop of hooves combined with the clink of poorly secured equipment served to reinforce what the Naa already knew. A lone, presumably stupid human, was heading up into the hills. Not only that, but, judging from odors ranging from gun oil to aftershave he came bearing gifts! His mother had been right. The gods *did* smile on those in need.

The Naa shook himself off, secured his trousers, and slipped through the rocks. The bedroll looked like a long lumpy tube. Nocount Quickknife jerked as a hand covered his mouth, went for his blade, and relaxed when he smelled who it was. Dimwit nodded toward the trail. His voice was little more than a whisper. "We got company. Easy pickin's. Move your ass."

Nocount yawned. Dimwit winced at the smell of his companion's breath and started to gather his gear. There was no particular hurry, something neither of them liked to do, since every stride carried their victim further from the fort. An advantage if the idiot called for help. Not that it mattered . . . since he'd soon be dead.

Booly left the reins loose and allowed the dooth to pick its own way up the rockstrewn trail. A good decision since the animal was native to Algeron and well equipped to survive there. It had been a long time since the officer had ridden anything more challenging than a command car, and his knees were starting to hurt. His butt would come next, followed by his lower back. The legionnaire had already started to regret the journey but was too stubborn to turn back.

The dooth completed one long stretch of trail, tried to snatch a bite of greenery from a likely looking bush, and took a kick to its barrel-shaped ribs. Dooths were never ones to suffer silently and were famous for the variety of sounds they could make. This particular animal produced something that bordered between a belch and a grunt.

Booly kicked the animal again and guided it up through still another hairpin turn. The gravelly trail stretched up toward the swiftly rising sun. It was then, as the dooth started to climb, that Booly detected, or *thought* he detected, a foreign scent. The officer's hand went to his side-arm. He stood in the stirrups and took a long careful look around.

Weather-smoothed boulders littered the surrounding hillside. Many were the size of battle tanks. A full company of legionnaires could have hidden there, concealed among the rocks, and he wouldn't have been able to spot them. Especially if they were Naa—and didn't want to be seen.

Uneasy now, but not sure why, the legionnaire climbed toward the sunrise. Everything was normal . . . except for the fur that ran the length of his spine. That stood on end.

The Trooper II rounded an outcropping of rock, "saw" a patch of green smear itself across the blue grid that overlaid her surroundings, and stopped dead in her tracks. Then, weapons ready, she backed around the corner. Numbers shifted in the lower right hand corner of the cyborg's vision as the threat factor gradually decreased.

Neversmile, who had allowed himself to be lulled into a sort of half-conscious trance, came fully awake. He spoke into a wire-thin boom mike. It was jacked into a panel at the base of Wilker's duraplast neck. "What's up?"

"Naa," Wilker replied. "Two of them. Both mounted. Maybe a quarter mile ahead. Between the general and us."

Neversmile swore silently. Just his luck. The general get's a wild hair up his ass . . . and the colonel chose *him* to deal with it. "Can you nail the bastards?"

"A shoulder-launched missile would handle it, assumin' you ain't too worried about due process or how big a hole I make."

Neversmile remembered how many innocent females and cubs the Legion had accidentally slaughtered over the years and knew he wasn't willing to take that chance. Not to mention the fact that he was supposed to maintain a low profile. "No, hold your fire. Feel free to close the distance, however—but don't let the shitheads see you."

It was a stupid order—Wilker thought so anyway—but knew better than to say so. Not to a sergeant—and not to *this* Sergeant. Gravel crunched under her weight, and the cyborg continued to climb.

• • • •

Dimwit emerged from the rocks still buttoning his pants. It was the second time he had stopped to take a pee and the second time he had fallen behind. Nocount was irritated. "Hurry up! The human's slow but not *that* slow. We'll lose the furless bastard."

"It ain't my fault," Dimwit complained. "I had to pee and it hurts."

"All because you'll screw anything with a pulse," his companion replied unsympathetically. "Come on, let's go."

Dimwit mounted his dooth, kicked the animal onto the trail, and kicked it yet again. The animal groaned, sent plumes of lung-warmed air down toward the ground, and passed a prodigious amount of gas. The trek resumed.

If the mesa had a name, Booly didn't know what it was. Only that it stood straight and tall, just as it had the last time he'd been there, camping with his mother.

It was she who showed him the narrow, often dangerous, path that circled the sheer-sided cliffs, pointed out the tool marks the ancients had left on the rock, and fired his imagination. "Who were they?" she asked. "And from whom were they hiding?" For surely some great evil had been upon the land, a threat that drove them up off the slowly rising plain, to make a home in the sky.

Had they won? These hard-pressed Naa? And survived that which sought to hunt them down? Or had the group been decimated? And wiped from existence? There was no way to be sure.

And there was *another* story, a more personal tale, which came back to Booly as his dooth labored toward the top. It had to do with his grandfather, William Booly I, a one-time sergeant major who was wounded during an ambush, taken prisoner, and nursed back to health by a Naa maiden, a *beautiful* maiden, named Windsweet.

His grandfather was smitten, *very* smitten, and soon fell

in love. But the whole thing was wrong. *Wrong* according to the Legion, *wrong* according to the Naa, and *wrong* according to her father. Windsweet helped the legionnaire escape, bandits gave chase, and a patrol saved his life.

Later, after returning to his unit, the soldier tried to forget the maiden and the way he felt about her, but found that impossible to do. That's when Booly's ancestor did something which Booly himself, as an officer, could never forgive: William Booly I went over the hill.

The dooth rounded a corner, rocks clattered away from its hooves and fell toward the scree below. They rattled, started a small slide, and tumbled down the mountain.

The noise caused Nocount to jerk his animal to a halt. He turned to Dimwit. "The motherless alien is halfway to the top."

"So?" his friend inquired sarcastically. "If *he* can make it, so can we."

"I know that you idiot," Nocount responded impatiently. "But why bother?"

Dimwit frowned, processed the words, and brightened. "We could wait here!"

"Now there's an idea," Nocount replied sarcastically. "Let's try it. No point in doin' all that work if we don't have to."

Dimwit agreed, swung down from the saddle, and headed for some likely looking rocks. He needed to pee.

The trail wound through the site of an ancient rock slide, shelved upwards, passed through a rocky defile and ended on a windswept plateau. A crust of icy snow covered what remained of the ancient walls. Yes, Booly thought to himself, whatever roamed below must have been *very* unpleasant to force the old ones up here.

The officer dismounted, took the dooth by its reins, and led the animal toward a rocky spire. It was there if memory served him correctly that his mother and he had camped.

Not on the surface, at the mercy of the groaning wind, but below, in chambers created by the ancients.

He located the spiral stair without difficulty, pulled a torch out of his pack, checked to ensure that the underground common room remained habitable, and allowed the light to play over some empty ration boxes. Others had camped there since his childhood visit, but not for many years, judging from the dust on the containers.

Someone had left a mound of somewhat desiccated dooth dung, however, which meant the legionnaire could enjoy a fire and a more pleasant evening than he had counted on.

But dooths came first, as all Naa learn the moment they are allowed to ride, and Booly returned to the surface. He removed the animal's saddle, rigged a nose bag filled with grain, and hobbled its feet.

Then, confident that his mount would remain nearby, the officer carried his gear below. It took the better part of a hour to build a dooth dung fire, clear the room of trash, and prepare a simple meal. Firelight danced the walls as the story retold itself.

Having deserted the Legion, his grandfather went back for the maiden, and took her away. Knowing that her father would follow, and fearful of what might happen if the two of them came into contact, Windsweet led her lover to the high plateau.

The Hudathans attacked Algeron shortly thereafter. Booly's grandfather went off to fight them and left Windsweet by herself. And it was there, in that very room, that his grandmother threw the Wula sticks and learned that the child in her belly would be male.

Was that what his mother meant? That what he needed was here? Buried among old memories?

Something caught Booly's eye. Something white, something beyond the dance of the flames, something almost obscured by graffiti.

The legionnaire stood, circled the fire pit, and found what he was looking for: the badge of the 13th DBLE. A coincidence? Or something more? The officer discovered a lump in his throat, wondered why the room felt so warm, and took his coat off. That's when Booly knelt on his parka, felt for his combat knife, and started to dig. The well packed earth was dry and hard.

The fire, augmented by some Legion-issue fuel tabs, burned hot and bright. Nocount took a pull from his canteen, passed the container to Dimwit, and delivered a prodigious belch. "I hope the human comes down tomorrow. We're almost out of drak."

The second Naa took a drink, felt the liquor burn its way down into his stomach, and wiggled his nose. That odor . . . What was it? Not drak, not his friend's pungent body odor—it was something else. Then he had it. Dimwit's brain sent the message to his lips, told them what to say, but not in time.

First Sergeant Neversmile had stripped to the waist. His fur was black with patches of white. They seemed to glow as he stepped out into the firelight. "Greetings my brothers . . . I saw your fire and wondered if you might spare a traveler something to eat."

Both of the bandits were in the habit of *taking* things from travelers but never gave them away. They ran their eyes down the newcomer's body, saw no sign of weapons, and felt a lot more secure. Nocount decided to toy with the stranger. He pulled a Legion-issue .50 caliber recoilless out from under his jacket and waved it back and forth. "Sure, I'll give you something to eat . . . How 'bout a bullet?"

Neversmile smiled. A bad sign if there ever was one. "Sure, if you don't mind eating a few yourself."

Nocount frowned. "I have a gun, and you don't."

"True," the legionnaire said agreeably, "but I have a friend . . . and *her* gun is bigger than your gun."

Dimwit squinted into the surrounding gloom. "Friend? What friend?"

"That would be me," Wilker replied, stepping out into the light. Servos whined as weapons came to bear. "Hi, how ya doin'?"

Dimwit peed his pants. Nocount decided to gamble.

The knife point struck metal and skidded through olive-drab paint. Booly gave a small grunt of satisfaction, scooped dirt with his hands, and revealed the top of an old ammo box. Though faded, the words "Grenades 40 mm HE," could still be read. Such containers were highly prized by the Naa and used for a multiplicity of purposes. The officer dug around both ends, freed the handles, and checked for wires. There were none. Then, careful lest the box be resting on some sort of spring-loaded mine, he felt underneath. Nothing.

Confident that it was safe the legionnaire grabbed the handles and pulled the container out of its hole. It was light, *too* light for a box with grenades in it, which confirmed his initial impression. Someone had used the box for something else.

Booly carried the container over and placed it in front of the fire. Most of the dark green paint was intact, but there were patches of dark brown rust, and any number of scratches. There was no lock, just a series of latches, all of which were stiff. He pried them open, took a long deep breath, and pushed the lid up and out of the way.

The contents were sealed in clear plastic, and Booly recognized some of the items even before he sliced through the outer covering. He saw his grandmother's Wula sticks, his father's Medal of Valor, his mother's long-barreled target pistol, and much, much more. There were photos, diaries, Naa story beads, his grandfather's flick blade, and a Hudathan command stone. Not the sort of items *most* mothers would leave for their sons—but the kind that a warrior would. For each and every one of the objects told a story, was part of who he was, and a source of strength. It was her way of reminding him of where he came from, of who had gone before, and the nature of his inheritance. Not land, not money, but a legacy of honor.

Suddenly, without knowing why, the officer thought of Maylo Chien-Chu. She had doubts about their relationship. That was obvious. Could her doubts have been related to his? After all, why should she be sure of him, if he doubted himself? Or was that too easy?

Whatever the reason, he felt stronger now, confident that he was entitled to the stars that rode his shoulders and the responsibility that went with them. Because of the objects in the box? The pilgrimage to get them? The fact that his mother cared? It hardly mattered. What was, was.

Half an hour later Booly crawled into his sleeping bag, closed his eyes, and entered a dreamless sleep.

Millions upon millions of snowflakes fell from the lead gray sky, performed airborne pirouettes, and spiraled into the ground. They formed a lace curtain through which Neversmile and Wilker maintained their watch. A jumble of boulders broke the wind, provided the twosome with some cover, and screened the trail. They waited through six foreshortened "days" before stones rattled, a dooth coughed, and General William Booly made his way down off the plateau.

He paused no more than twenty feet away from them to scan his surroundings. He felt something—but wasn't sure what. Whatever it was sent a chill down his spine. The officer resisted the impulse to pull his blast rifle, kicked the dooth in the ribs, and continued on his way. He wanted to reach the fort—wanted to leave the planet. Algeron was in good hands, and there was work to do. Lots of it.

Neversmile waited until the general had established a sizeable lead, mounted the cyborg's back, and spoke into the mike. "Senses to max . . . patrol speed." Wilker obeyed.

Behind them, covered by a thin blanket of cold wet snow, lay two mounds of carefully piled rocks. Algeron continued to spin—and darkness swept in from the east.

5

Even the final decision of a war is not to be regarded as absolute. The conquered nation often sees it as only a passing evil, to be repaired in after times by political combinations.

Karl von Clausewitz
On War
Standard year 1832

Planet Hudatha (Protectorate), the Confederacy of Sentient Beings

The packet ship *Mercury* dropped into orbit, offered a burst of code, and waited for the appropriate response. Battle station *Victory*, one of four such structures constructed immediately after the last Hudathan war, hung like a dark omen over the planet below. One of the vessel's many computers checked, confirmed the newly arrived ship's identity, and gave the necessary permissions.

The *Mercury*'s control room was too small to accommodate visitors—but a viewscreen filled one of the wardroom's four bulkheads. Governor, now Envoy Sergi Chien-Chu watched with keen interest as the battle station grew to fill the smaller vessel's screen. At the conclusion of the last war, he had played a role in the seemingly endless design process that led up to the *Victory*'s construction. So, in spite of the fact that he'd never seen the finished product before, the industrialist recognized the spherical shape as well as the heavy duty weapons mounts and the other installations common to *Monitor* class warships. Because, for all her size, the battle station was capable of movement, *had* to be capable of movement, given the complex interplay of gravitational forces associated with Hudatha and her Jovian binary.

The battle station *Triumph*, now obscured by the planet itself, had nearly been destroyed during the mutiny while *Victory* and two other platforms remained loyal. A matter of no small importance lest the Hudathans escape.

Chien-Chu thought of the *Monitor* class ships as something akin to old-fashioned corks, the kind used to keep mythical genies trapped within their bottles. Now it was *he* who proposed to release them. Was he correct in wanting to do so? Or just terribly naive?

But the packet ship bore *two* passengers . . . and as the *Victory* grew larger and the landing bay opened to receive them, the second had some very different thoughts. War Commander, now Ambassador Doma-Sa looked out on what appeared to him as nothing less than a mechanical monster, a machine that could sterilize the surface of the planet below. The fact that his people had actually perpetrated such horrors on others, had reduced entire worlds to little more than radioactive slag, made no difference whatsoever. *This* was unjust, *this* was unfair, *this* must end.

The *Victory*'s cavernous landing bay swallowed the *Mercury* as if she were little more than a snack. Chien-Chu watched with considerable interest as the packet ship followed a bright orange robodrone down the center of a blast-scarred deck and toward the area reserved for transient vessels. Here was a significant portion of the Confederacy's remaining strength, resident in row after row of sleek two-seat fighters and squadrons of boxy assault vessels. None of which could be used against the Sheen lest the genie escape. Who was truly captive? The industrialist wondered. The Hudathans? Or the forces left to watch them?

There was a noticeable bump as the packet ship touched down. All manner of maintenance droids, robo hoses and other automated equipment rolled, slithered, and swung into action. The *Mercury* would be refueled, provisioned, and relaunched in less than six hours.

Doma-Sa struggled into some standard issue Hudathan space armor. Chien-Chu thanked the *Mercury*'s four person crew and hauled his duffel bag to the lock. It took three minutes to cycle through.

Self-propelled stairs stood waiting, along with a space-suited lieutenant commander and two ratings. She saluted, and her voice came over Chien-Chu's on-board multi-freq com unit. "Welcome aboard, Admiral. My name is Nidifer. We received orders to dispense with the side party. I hope that was correct."

Chien-Chu returned the salute and smiled. "Yes, thank you. Your people have enough to do . . . Let's save the ceremony for *real* admirals. Please allow me to introduce Ambassador Hiween Doma-Sa."

The naval officer bowed to the extent that the space armor would allow her to do so. "Welcome aboard, Ambassador. My name is Nidifer, Lieutenant Commander Nidifer. It's a pleasure to meet you. Please follow me."

It took the better part of fifteen minutes to cross the busy flight deck, enter the VIP lock, and cycle through. The *Victory*'s commanding officer was waiting to greet them. He was tall and thin, and looked like a skeleton brought to life. He was the real thing, meaning an officer who had graduated from the academy, and wore two stars. His hand was hard and bony. "Admiral Chien-Chu . . . Ambassador Doma-Sa . . . welcome aboard. Admiral Kagan at your service. Sorry I wasn't there to greet you . . . but one of our shuttles lost power. A tug is bringing her in. I thought we'd give you a chance to stow your gear and gather in my cabin. Sound okay to you?"

The visitors assured him that it did, and little more than thirty minutes later the visitors arrived in Kagan's cabin. The *Victory* was considered a hardship post, which meant that extra money had been spent to make the ship more livable. Wood paneling lined the bulkheads, back-lit shelving held some of the art objects the naval officer had collected during his years of service, and the furniture was worn but comfortable. The admiral gestured toward some chairs. "Please, have a seat."

Doma-Sa chose a chair backed by a bulkhead, knew it had been placed there for his comfort, and felt a little better.

Refreshments were offered, both guests refused, and Kagan looked from one to the other. He was curious and let it show. "So? What can I do for you?"

Chien-Chu gestured toward the planet that hung beyond the view port. "First we'd like a briefing, you know, surface conditions, intel reports, whatever you've got. Then we'll need some transport." He looked at Doma-Sa. "That should cover it."

Kagan felt a rising sense of anger and fought to control it. Here he was, sitting on what amounted to a time bomb, while some half-baked has-been thought up ways to waste his resources. But the bastard had pull, the kind of gees that could crush a mere two-star, and the officer forced a smile. "Yes, of course. I'll arrange for the briefing. But that's as far as I can go. The ambassador isn't cleared to receive military intelligence. As for the trip, well, Hudathan nationals can return to the surface whenever they choose, but you will have to remain in orbit. Or return with the *Merc*—the choice is up to you."

One of the things Chien-Chu liked about his status as a cyborg was the fact that when he ordered his face to remain blank it actually did so. "I'm sorry, Admiral. I forgot to present my credentials. Perhaps you would be so kind as to review them."

The cyborg withdrew a small case from his coat pocket and gave it over. The naval officer inspected the seal, applied his thumb to the print-sensitive pad, and saw the lid pop open. A disk nestled in a plastic holder. Kagan took the disk, excused himself, and entered the neighboring office. He was back three minutes later. His face was pale. The words sounded stiff and formal. "I am to place myself under your command for the duration of your stay, render all possible assistance, and keep the nature of your mission secret." He looked down into Chien-Chu's synthetic eyes. The resentment was clear to see. "What may I ask *is* the nature of your mission?"

Chien-Chu smiled in an effort to put the man at ease. "Ambassador Doma-Sa and I are here to examine the feasibility of integrating certain branches of the Hudathan military into the Confederacy's armed forces."

A look of disbelief came over Admiral Kagan's face, and he practically fell into his chair. His voice was thick with emotion. This was a joke. It *had* to be. "Surely, you jest."

"No," the cyborg assured him calmly. "Nothing could be more serious."

The snow, which had been falling throughout the night, stopped, the sun came out, and the temperature soared to eighty. All before noon. Just another day on Hudatha. Legion Captain Augustus North warned the sentries that he was coming out, palmed the hatch, and waited for it to whir up and out of the way. They still had power, something of a miracle after months on the surface, but for how much longer? A week? A month? Maybe, if the tech heads could keep the fusion generator running, and the ridge heads allowed them to live.

The officer squinted into the glare, stepped out into the slush, and returned the cyborg's salute. What remained of the battalion included four quads, plus thirty-six Trooper II's, down from twelve quads and seventy-two Trooper II's the day of the crash.

North turned, eyed the mountain of half-slagged metal, and started to climb. There were plenty of sharp edges where a wide variety of munitions had struck so it paid to be careful. Medical supplies were running low—and the doc was hard-pressed to patch people up.

The insanity had originated on the *Triumph* more than three months before. A cadre of mutineers, led by Major Pinchett, North's commanding officer, received confirmation that the mutiny was under way, and took control of the ship's bridge. Then, more than a little full of themselves, they had called on the rest of the battle stations to surrender.

The *Victory*, under the command of Admiral Kagan, along with the *Celebration* and the *Jubilant* had attacked their sister ship with a vengeance. The mutineers put up stiff resistance, and did pretty well for a while, but never stood a chance. Pinchett offered to surrender, but Kagan refused to listen, and the pounding went on.

North would never forget missile after missile slamming into the monitor's hull, the steady bleat of battle klaxons, the smell of his space armor, people running down corridors, and Hudatha hanging above.

The weird thing was that North had never been asked to join the mutiny . . . and wasn't sure how he would have reacted. Lord knew there was reason, starting with the cutbacks, the way ex-soldiers were left to beg in the streets, and what could only be described as a pathetic state of readiness. But mutiny? No, it didn't seem right. There was no way to justify what Kagan did, though, pounding the *T* to scrap, and destroying each life pod within seconds after launch. The admiral saw the capsules as bacteria, as the manifestation of a horrible disease, to which no mercy could be shown.

That's when North, with help from a loyalist naval officer, loaded the freighter with troops and tried to escape. They didn't get far.

Kagan caught the ship shortly after it left the *Triumph*'s launch bay, scored dozens of direct hits on the lightly armored vessel, and ignored their pleas for help.

Damaged, and with no possibility of escape, the freighter had fallen toward Hudatha's surface. It was a miracle that anyone had survived, but a naval officer, a woman named Borkna, knew her stuff and managed to pancake in.

The transport skidded for the better part of two miles before running into a small hill. Not just *any* hill, but a hill with what remained of a castle on top, and walls on which many lives had been spent. The kind the Hudathans had spent hundreds if not thousands of years fighting each other for.

Now, with the hull snuggled up against old stone walls, and both covered with patches of green-black mold, not to mention islands of quickly melting slush, it was hard to tell one construct from the other. Given enough time, say a year or so, and the wreck would be invisible from the air.

North was sweating by the time he made it to the top of the wreck and stood on a barely legible "C," which, along with a "T" and a six-digit number was part of the ship's official ID number. Listed as missing? As unrecoverable? There was no way to know.

Corporal Gorwin was there waiting for him. She lifted one of her energy-cannon-equipped arms by way of a greeting. "Morning, sir."

The words were cheerful enough, especially in light of the fact that the lower part of her body was missing, and, with no chance of repairs, she had volunteered to stay on the top of the ship as a semipermanent sentry.

North nodded and worked to catch his breath. He was short and stocky. His uniform was filthy but so was everyone else's. "So, Gorwin, any sign of the geeks?"

The cyborg nodded. "Yes, sir. I notified the control room by radio. Right after you left. Take a look toward the west." Her voice was dull—empty of hope.

North pulled a small pair of binoculars out of his shirt pocket and brought them up to his eyes. What he saw made him suck air into his lungs. The Hudathans had attacked before, twenty-seven times to be exact, but never like this. An army was on the march. There were *thousands* of the bastards. More than he and his handful of troops could possibly deal with.

The situation was reminiscent of the Legion's most famous battle, that day in the spring of 1863 when Legion Captain Jean Danjou and a force of sixty-four men took on more than two thousand Mexican troops and fought them to a standstill. That was the good news. The bad news was that only three legionnaires had survived. Danjou was not among them. The name of village where the fight took place was Camerone.

Gorwin, who had similar thoughts herself, read the officer's face. "Yes, sir. It looks a lot like Camerone."

In spite of the fact that Chien-Chu had been living in cybernetic bodies for many years now—he had never controlled anything like a Trooper II. Theoretically outmoded some fifty years before, T-2s continued to roll off the assembly lines because they were sturdy, effective, and, when compared with a Trooper III and its animal analogs, cheap to produce and maintain. Part of their value stemmed from the proven ability to operate in just about any environment that one could imagine, which was what awaited the industrialist below.

Doma-Sa, who had no need of technology in order to survive, watched the process with obvious amusement. The transfer took place in one of the onboard equipment bays. The cyber-techs injected some drugs into Chien-Chu's artificial circulatory system, removed his brain box from his "normal" body, and "loaded" a Trooper II.

Chien-Chu endured the brief moment of sensory deprivation, felt the new body react to his presence, and experienced something akin to a drug-induced rush as system after system came on-line.

Though theoretically analogous to what he had experienced before, there was no real comparison. The war machine was faster, more powerful, and loaded with systems civilians had no need for.

The industrialist's left arm was an air-cooled .50 caliber machine gun, his right arm was a fast-recovery laser cannon, and he could run at speeds up to fifty miles per hour. He spoke, realized how loud the PA system was, and turned it down. "I'm ready for anything—even Hudatha."

Doma-Sa looked him over. "That may be true, my friend—but the switch did nothing for your appearance."

"Look who's talking," Chien-Chu replied. "Come on, let's see if I can walk."

The thousands of Hudathan troopers marched as if on parade, which essentially they were, crossing the Plain of Skulls toward the castle Glid, where the great Kasa-Ka had ruled during feudal times, and the aliens now lived. An insult that must be expunged . . . but not till Ikor Ifana-Ka was finished with them. Training was important, and, if properly husbanded, the humans could be stretched for another couple of weeks. *Real* combat, with *real* aliens, was hard to come by. That's why they had been allowed to live for such a long time.

Besides, the Hudathan liked the look of his troopers, the banners that flew above their heads, the gleam of their weapons, the sound of the drums, the way the whistles shrilled the air, and the wind in his face. This was the way things had been, should be, *would* be if his people were free.

Ifana-Ka sat on what amounted to a half-enclosed sedan chair, winced as pain stabbed his fully extended leg, and listened to his aide. The youngster had little difficulty keeping pace. The words were clear—but the message wasn't. "Doma-Sa? Landing with a high-ranking human? Impossible! Shoot the translator."

Mylo Norba-Ba was used to such excess. His words were both patient and respectful. "There was no translation. War Commander Doma-Sa spoke directly with me. He said the matter is urgent and of the highest importance. Their shuttle has entered the atmosphere."

Ifana-Ka adjusted his leg. "All right then, if we must, we must. Pass the word . . . the troops will stand down. We may as well feed them. Not for long mind you . . . We march two hours from now."

A sudden gust of high altitude wind hit the shuttle's hull. It rocked from side to side. The cargo compartment was empty except for the Trooper II that stood at the center of it, the Hudathan who overflowed a fold-down seat, and the orange exoskeleton secured toward the stern. Admiral Kagan had elected to ride up front with his pilots.

Chien-Chu felt his body tug against the cargo straps and questioned his own sanity. Was the trip to Hudatha's surface truly necessary? So he could negotiate face to face? Or driven by curiosity? The desire to see the place that had given birth to such an implacable foe? He looked at Doma-Sa. "So, how would you rate our chances? Who sits on the Triad? And how will they react?"

The shuttle shuddered as the hull hit the bottom of an air pocket and continued to fall. Doma-Sa had known that the question would arise—and spent a considerable amount of time formulating a reply. A response calculated to conceal the infighting that years of planetary confinement had caused, the sense of hopelessness that commanded his people, and the fact that one member of the ruling body was more than a little eccentric. "I can't speak for the rest of the Triad, but I favor your proposal, depending on what your race refers to as 'the fine print.' "

Chien-Chu wondered if he had misunderstood. "*You*? You belong to the Triad?"

"Of course," Doma-Sa replied easily. "What could be more important than our freedom? Besides, we have no diplomatic corps. Outside of myself that is."

Chien-Chu wondered how he could have missed what now appeared to be obvious. The Hudathans favored a highly vertical almost dictatorial political system. They had never negotiated for anything, not until now, a fact that should have tipped him off. No one *except* one of the rulers could have been entrusted with something so critical. So, while many of those on board the *Friendship* treated Doma-Sa like a low level functionary, they had actually been dealing with a head of state.

Chien-Chu struggled to remember everything he had said or done. Doma-Sa, who had come to know the human pretty well by then, gave the Hudathan equivalent of a chuckle. It sounded a lot like a rock crusher in low gear. "No, you never said anything to offend me, not that it would make much difference, since the *Victory* could sterilize the surface of my planet. "Ikor Ifana-Ka is another matter, however. He's a lot more emotional than I am. It would pay to be careful in his presence."

Chien-Chu frowned, or tried to, but discovered that the Trooper II wasn't equipped for that sort of communication. "Grand Marshall Ifana-Ka? The officer that our intelligence people referred to as 'the Annihilator?' "

Doma-Sa looked as surprised as he was capable of looking. "You have a remarkable memory. Yes, Ifana-Ka carried out his duties with what you would refer to as 'ruthless efficiency.' "

"Meaning that he murdered hundreds of thousands of sentient beings," Chien-Chu said coldly.

"Why, yes," the Hudathan replied calmly. "And isn't that why you came here? To recruit some killers?"

Chien-Chu sought some sort of comeback and was unable to think of one. Silence filled the cargo compartment.

• • •

Clouds rolled in to cover the sun, rain fell in sheets, and Captain North struggled to penetrate the gloom. He'd gone below to grab a ration bar, and now he was back. The Hudathans should have arrived by then . . . and he wondered where they were. His troops, what were left of them, were dug in and waiting.

Gorwin was quick to provide an unsolicited opinion. "The infrared is clear enough, sir. It looks like the ridge heads broke for some R&R."

North lowered the glasses. Rain peppered his face, ran down the back of his neck, and sent damp fingers into his clothing. "Okay, but why? They could take us anytime they want."

"Maybe it has something to do with the shuttle," the cyborg replied mysteriously.

North was annoyed. Gorwin was playing some kind of game with him—and the only thing that saved her from a good ass chewing was the fact that the enemy had already blown it off. "Shuttle? What frigging shuttle?"

Gorwin, who knew when to quit, underwent a sudden change of attitude. "The assault boat that passed over our position a few minutes ago, circled the Hudathans, and landed over there somewhere." The cyborg used her arm-mounted energy cannon to point toward the northwest.

North felt his heart try to beat its way out of his chest. "A *human* assault boat? You're sure?"

Gorwin nodded. "Sir, yes sir. Some of the other borgs saw it too. We told the loot. She said you were on the way."

North peered into the rain, made his decision, and gave the necessary orders. "Wait ten, and tell the loot I went for a stroll. If I don't return by 1800 hours she's in command."

"She ain't gonna like that," Gorwin replied sincerely, "and neither do I."

"Sorry," North replied, "but rank hath its privileges. See you later."

The officer disappeared over the side. The corporal tried to stand and cursed her missing legs.

The wind picked up, the rain came in sideways, driven by forty mile per hour gusts of wind. The clouds were so thick that it seemed night had fallen. Rocks that had been too hot to sit on steamed as the moisture hit them. Some, stressed by years of abuse, cracked in two. The sound resembled rifle shots—and came from all around.

The assault boat crouched like some sort of gray-black monster, water streaming off its heavily armored back, beacons strobing the murk.

A hatch whirred open, Admiral Kagan directed the exoskeleton out through the opening, and was glad he had agreed to use it. This was the first time he had set foot on the planet, and he felt vulnerable, *very* vulnerable, in spite of the steel cage that protected his rain-soaked body.

Still, if Chien-Chu could do it, then he could do it, never mind the fact that the industrialist was all snuggy inside a T-2. The ramp bounced under his weight, a gust of wind attempted to push him over, and the officer was forced to focus the majority of his attention on the normally simple task of walking. Once on the ground, the officer confronted six heavily armed Hudathans. They stood and stared. Kagan stared back.

Chien-Chu stepped into the hatch, scanned his surroundings, and walked down the ramp. The admiral's servo-assisted exoskeleton was equipped with amber shoulder beacons. They flashed through the downpour.

Doma-Sa was the last to deass the shuttle, and Kagan saw a distinct change where the reception party was concerned. They came to rigid attention as the Hudathan diplomat cleared the ramp and stomped through the rain. Water ran over his shoulders, down his chest, and spurted away from his boots. A series of short sentences were exchanged, and the ambassador turned to explain. "We landed in the middle of a field exercise. Ikor Ifana-Ka has agreed to receive us . . . but hopes to resume training in an hour or so."

Having said his piece, Doma-Sa set off for a pole-supported shelter that had been erected a few hundred yards to the east. It was gray, like the world around it, and shivered in the wind. The Hudathan savored the warm damp air, the way the rain pelted his chest, and the feel of gravel under his boots. It was good to be home.

Chien-Chu drew abreast of the admiral, took note of how pale the officer looked, and spoke via a heavily encrypted com channel. It took less than a minute to brief Kagan regarding Doma-Sa's actual rank—and urge him to use caution. The meeting would be critical.

Kagan took the information in, realized what it meant, and felt a deep sense of betrayal. After all the Hudathans had done, after all the murders they had committed, Chien-Chu, along with a bunch of suck-ass politicians were going to sell the Confederacy out. All to defend against a bunch of machines that might not exist. The whole thing made him sick.

That's when Kagan came to an important realization: *He* could end the insanity, *he* could save the Confederacy, *he* could go down in history. *If* he got the opportunity—*if* he had the guts.

North jogged through the rain, availed himself of what cover there was, but knew it was just a matter of time before somebody intercepted him. Would they shoot him? Before he could reach the people in the shuttle? That was his second greatest fear.

His *greatest* fear was that he had unintentionally betrayed the Legion, his battalion, and himself. Danjou had had many opportunities to surrender but had refused to do so. Here was an opportunity for glorious death, the kind the Legion respected, but rather than embrace it, as so many others had, he was trying to cheat his fate. Why? For the sake of his troops? Or out of cowardice? The possibility gnawed at his belly.

The legionnaire angled toward some rocks. Water splashed his ankles and wandered into his boots. He swore, allowed himself to slow, and pushed in among the boulders. One of them had cracked right down the middle during some previous storm leaving a V for him to peer through. It looked like an old-fashioned rifle sight. The enemy could be seen just beyond, preparing a meal.

The legionnaire shoved both his assault weapon and his sidearm under a rock, used stones to wall them in, and returned to the viewpoint. North swallowed the lump in his throat, stepped out through the V-shaped crack, and raised his hands in the air. Nothing happened at first, and the officer was about to move, when a shout was heard. The words were in Hudathan, but there was no doubt as to what they meant. The officer stood fast.

The rain seemed to part like a curtain. The troopers were huge. They gathered around. One grabbed the officer from behind. Another punched him in the stomach. The blows came hard and fast. North felt himself fold.

If there were negative things about Hudathan culture, such as their tendency toward genocide, there were some positive characteristics as well. One was a distaste for the trappings of power that so many humans lusted after. It could be seen in Doma-Sa's matter-of-fact no-nonsense manner, in the plain rather utilitarian shelter erected for Ifana-Ka's benefit, and the way that he waved them over. Much to Chien-Chu's surprise, there had been no attempt to disarm Kagan or neutralize the Trooper II's weaponry. A sign of respect? A sign of contempt? There was no sure way to know.

The exoskeleton and the Trooper II were big . . . but so was the tent. They whirred, whined, and crunched their way across the rain-soaked gravel. The fact that the shelter had no floor other than what the planet saw fit to provide was consistent with the lack of pomp. Ifana-Ka spoke Hudathan, but Chien-Chu's onboard computer took care of the translation.

"Welcome. Please excuse me if I don't get up. A Ramanthian war drone shot me more than fifty years ago. The butchers wanted to take the leg off but I wouldn't let them. Now I'm too old for regeneration therapy, too set in my ways for a bionic replacement, and too mean to die. Isn't that right, War Commander Doma-Sa?"

"I don't know about the first two," the Hudathan replied, "but there's no doubt about the third."

Chien-Chu took note of the military title and assumed the grunting noise equated to laughter. "So," Ifana-Ka asked, "who are you? And what do you want?"

The question was addressed to Admiral Kagan, since he was the only being who looked even slightly human. Doma-Sa, who was smooth by Hudathan standards, entered the gap. "Grand Marshall Ifana-Ka, this is Admiral Kagan. He commands the Confederate forces in our sector."

The contempt on Ifana-Ka's face was clear for even a human to see . . . and Doma-Sa hurried to forestall whatever gaffe was in the making. "And this," the Hudathan said, gesturing toward the hulking T-2, "is none other than Sergi Chien-Chu, past President of the Confederacy, reserve admiral, Governor of Earth, and special envoy to the Hudathan people."

Chien-Chu essayed a bow. "I apologize for my appearance. The body I normally wear was less than suitable for a visit to your planet."

Ifana-Ka pushed himself up out of his chair and staggered forward. Norba-Ba rushed to support him. "Chien-Chu? The same miserable piece of excrement who fought Poseen-Ka off the planet Algeron?"

Chien-Chu tried to swallow but didn't have anything left to do it with. "Yes, I'm afraid so."

"It's an honor to meet you," Ifana-Ka said. "I served under the bastard, and he was tough. *Very* tough. So they sent a soldier to make their case? Smart, damned smart. Maybe there's hope for humans after all."

Disappointed by the warmth of Chien-Chu's reception, and disgusted by the politician's conciliatory tone, Kagan stood a little straighter. Others could bend . . . *he* would refuse.

Chien-Chu experienced a profound sense of relief, and was about to offer some sort of reply, when a disturbance was heard. All five of them turned toward the source of the noise. Captain North was a mess. His hair was matted from the rain, blood smeared his face, and his uniform was covered with mud. He had lost consciousness at some point during the beating and come to on a stretcher. That's when he rolled off, dodged a slow moving trooper, and ran toward the tent. Maybe there would be someone in authority . . . someone who could . . .

A sentry yelled. North dashed for the tent, and waited for the inevitable bullet. It didn't come. Not with two members of the Triad just beyond. He burst through the entryway and looked left and right. "My name is North! *Captain* North. Who's in charge here? I want a word with them."

That's when the legionnaire saw Kagan, their eyes locked, and hatred jumped the gap. "Butcher!"

"Mutineer!"

Kagan went for his sidearm just as a 250-pound Hudathan sentry flew through the entrance and hit North from the side. The two of them skidded across the gravel.

Undeterred, the naval officer raised his weapon, and was about to fire, when an ominous whine was heard. Chien-Chu looked through the sighting grid and knew the .50 caliber machine gun was ready to fire. "Hold it right there, Admiral . . . this man has something to say. I'd like to hear what it is."

Slowly, reluctantly, Kagan allowed the pistol to fall.

Ifana-Ka was amused. "I thank the Giver that humans spend most of their time at each other's throats. Guard, help that officer up, and report for punishment. Twenty lashes should put you right. If the human were an assassin, I'd be dead by now."

The sentry, who showed no reaction whatsoever, came to attention, did a smart about-face, and marched into the rain.

North, who had the wind knocked out of him, spoke in short painful gasps. He described the battle, the attempt to escape, and what Kagan had done. The legionnaire had no hope of mercy from the admiral, assumed the cyborg was some sort of escort, and addressed himself to Ifana-Ka. "So, that's it, sir. My people are ready to fight. Your forces will win, I know that, but we will kill a lot of them. And for what? Nothing will be gained."

Ifana-Ka looked at Chien-Chu. "He is yours—do with him what you will."

Kagan heard a roar in his head, felt heat suffuse his body, and understood his duty. Here was an opportunity to not only stop Chien-Chu but put the mutineer down. He would shoot the Hudathans, North, and himself in that order. The cyborg would survive—there was no way to prevent that—but not for long. Ifana-Ka's troopers would see to that. He raised the slug thrower, turned toward Ifana-Ka, and felt the exoskeleton stagger as .50 caliber slugs tore his body apart. The vehicle shuddered, toppled to one side, and crashed into the ground.

Guards stormed into the tent, and Doma-Sa barked an order. Slowly, reluctantly, the troopers lowered their weapons. The soldier-diplomat turned toward Chien-Chu. A wisp of smoke drifted away from the arm-mounted machine gun. "You see my friend? We aren't as different as you thought."

The cyborg, who found the thought depressing, was forced to agree.

• • • •

The ensuing negotiations lasted for six local days. Long, seemingly endless affairs punctuated by hail, sun, rain, wind, snow, and combinations Chien-Chu had never experienced before.

North, along with his sort-of mutineers, were evacuated to await court-martial. Chien-Chu, relying on his on-again off-again status as an admiral gave his word that they would be treated fairly. That was relatively easy. The mutual defense pact cum treaty was a good deal more difficult.

First came the question of who could and should conduct the negotiations. Chien-Chu made it clear that while he could help draft a proposal, the senate would have to review it, and the President would need to approve it.

Due to the fact that the third member of the Triad had been killed during an inter-clan feud and that a replacement had yet to successfully assert himself, Ifana-Ka and Doma-Sa would speak for the Hudathan race.

They opened the negotiations by demanding full unqualified freedom for their people. Understandable—but completely out of the question.

Literally dozens of models were discussed and eventually discarded. Chien-Chu discovered that the Hudathans were dogged negotiators . . . never giving ground till the battle had been fully fought and lost.

Still, when the process was over, the final draft was very close to what Chien-Chu had proposed to begin with. It was bound to be, given that his race held most of the cards, and *any* degree of freedom would be an improvement over what the Hudathans had prior to signing.

The key to the agreement's appeal, if there was any, would be in the treaty's clarity and simplicity. The essence of the document was that the Hudathans would resume their status as a sovereign state, would be entitled to a representative in the senate, would be free to engage in nonmilitary commerce with other members of the Confederacy, would pay their fair share of taxes, and, with one significant exception, would be subject to the mutual defense pact. The qualifier, the all important restriction, stated that the Hudathans would not be allowed to build, maintain, or operate a space-going navy.

The responsibility for transporting Hudathan troops to and from their home planet or colonies, should they be permitted to retain some of the worlds previously under their control, would fall to other space-faring races such as the humans and Ramanthians. Because without a navy, and the independence that went with it, there would be very little chance that the Hudathans would try their hands at conquest.

This was a bitter pill to swallow, one that not only hurt the Hudathan's pride, and made them dependent on other races. Something their inborn sense of survival argued against.

But facts were facts, and Doma-Sa, who had spent a great deal of time observing the senate, knew that this was the best deal he and his people were likely to get for the next hundred years or so, and it certainly beat the alternative, sitting on Hudatha until their own combative culture turned inward and destroyed them, or the planet was torn apart. Besides, even the most superficial study of human history revealed what extremely short memories they had, a fact that augured well for the future.

And so it was that an agreement was reached, that Chien-Chu and Doma-Sa returned to space, and that Admiral Dero Delany Kagan II remained behind.

The marker, which stood alone on the rocky, often windswept plain, was cut from hull metal, and bore the best inscription that Chien-Chu could come up with. A poet named Carl Sandberg provided the words:

Pile the bodies high at Austerlitz and Waterloo,
    Shovel them under and let me work—
    I am the grass; I cover all.

6

Power never takes a back step—only in the face of more power.

Malcom X
Malcom X Speaks
Standard year 1965

Somewhere beyond the Rim, the Confederacy of Sentient Beings

Far out in space, beyond the largely imaginary border that the Confederacy referred to as the Rim, the very fabric of space and time was momentarily altered. Hundreds of ships appeared, glittered like minnows, and swam through the surrounding darkness.

The Hoon's scout ships detected the other fleet the moment it dropped hyper, issued an electronic challenge, and were answered in kind. Recognition codes were received, analyzed, and validated. Signals were sent, courses were altered, formations were merged, and for the first time in more than two hundred years the fleet was whole.

Whole, but divided, since the *original* Hoon, which had divided itself into two identical halves in order to cover more space and increase the odds of finding the Thraki, had yet to reintegrate itself. A process of high-speed bilateral updating, which if successful, would result in an artificial intelligence that incorporated all the knowledge and experience each entity had gained during the years of separation. A substantial gain that could lead to a high chance of success.

However, the same minds that had granted the computer the capacity to split itself in two had enacted certain safeguards as well. One such safeguard included a complicated matrix of truth tables intended to ensure that neither of the two halves had been corrupted during their years apart.

Neither entity felt any qualms regarding the test, not at first anyway, viewing the process as entirely natural.

Hoon number one, defined as the receiving intelligence, sampled the inflow at intervals frequent enough to ensure that its counterpart had been operating within the specified parameters.

Everything was fine at first. The incoming data was not only acceptable, but judging from equally spaced nibbles, made an excellent meal. It seemed that Hoon number two had journeyed far, fed off many civilizations, but failed to turn up anything more than some Thraki splinter groups. But it was then, while number two reported on one such encounter, that number one spotted the potential problem.

Careful to conceal its activities, lest the other AI realize that an investigation was under way, number one diverted part of the data feed to a parallel processor where it could be dissected without interrupting the main flow.

The essence of the discrepancy had to do with the outcome of that particular contact report. Having located a breakaway colony, Hoon number two had allowed itself to be drawn into a two-way conversation, and even worse, had been convinced to spare that particular group. Something that should have been impossible.

Worried lest it be contaminated by some sort of virus— Hoon number one ran an in-depth review of the facts: Having identified a Thraki debris trail consisting of a wrecked ship, a hastily mined asteroid, and a spent fuel core, his opposite number had given chase. So far so good.

Fleet number two followed the soft bodies, discovered that approximately three hundred Thraki had established themselves on a class two planet, and prepared to destroy them. That's when a command override was received. Somehow, someway, one or more of the Thraki had come up with a way to spoof the Hoon.

It appeared that a very sophisticated virus had been planted in the Thraki wreck, a scout had been infected with the corrupted programming as it ingested the ship's AI, and passed the disease along to its superior as part of an intelligence report. Not only that, but whoever built the virus was so clever that they had imbued it with the means to fool Hoon number two's virus hunters, and take up residence in the AI's central processor.

Once in place, the false input took on the appearance of original programming, programming that confirmed the existence of a special breed of Thraki, a group that could and should be allowed to live. An assertion that Hoon number one knew to be false.

That being the case, the AI routed the data to a sacrificial memory module, ran a high priority scrub on its primary, secondary, and tertiary backup banks, and did the only thing that it could: lay plans to murder its twin.

The cabin was dark, intentionally dark, in keeping with the way Jepp felt. Empty ration boxes littered the normally spotless floor, clothes lay heaped where they'd been thrown, and the would-be messiah lay huddled beneath a none too clean blanket.

The ex-prospector had been in a foul mood for weeks now, ever since the visit to Fortuna, and the manner in which God's message had been ignored.

Yes, the sentients who lived there were the dregs of the Confederacy and committed to their evil ways. Still, he had assumed one or two of them would respond and form the core of what would eventually be a galaxy-spanning religion.

But he'd been wrong, *very* wrong, and was depressed as a result. Nothing, not even Sam's most entertaining antics had been sufficient to rouse the human from his emotional stupor.

In the meantime, the fleet continued to travel through space, the Sheen continued to hunt Thraki, and his followers continued to attend the daily prayer meetings. Humans, bored by the repetitive nature of the gatherings might have stayed away, but not the machines, who listened to Alpha's rantings with limitless patience, and always came back for more.

In fact, had Jepp been in a better mood, he might have taken heart from the fact that more than two thousand machines routinely attended services held in the vast nano-draped launch bay where hundreds of vessels sat, waiting for their next assignment.

It was at the conclusion of one such session, as the congregation walked, rolled, and crawled to their various tasks, that a pair of recycling droids, the closest thing the Hoon had to police, took Alpha into custody.

The robot complained, but his various utterances and transmissions were to no avail. The recycling machines were not only larger than it was, but stronger and equipped with the ability to override the acolyte's motor functions.

That being the case, Alpha could do little more than pepper some of his escorts with some of Jepp's favorite admonitions while they conveyed him through the main lock and into a labyrinth of passageways. " 'He who lives by the sword shall die by the sword.' 'As you sow so shall your reap.' 'What goes around comes around,' " and half a dozen more.

But the recycling droids remained unmoved and continued to chivvy their charge through the brightly lit passageways. It took less than ten minutes to reach the cabin Jepp had assigned to himself.

Then, with the signal lack of courtesy typical of mechanical devices everywhere, the robots pushed their way in. The human took exception. "Alpha? Is that you? I don't want to be disturbed. Please go away."

In spite of the fact that the answer came via Alpha's speech synthesizer, it sounded entirely different. It was harder, stronger, and much more insistent. "The ship belongs to *me*. I will do as I please. I am the Hoon."

Jepp felt the bottom drop out of his stomach. The Hoon! Coming to him! Nothing of that sort had ever happened before. What did it mean? He swung his feet off the bunk and placed them on the hard cold deck. "Yes, of course. I apologize. Please excuse the mess."

The Hoon processed the message, concluded that an answer would constitute a waste of time, and moved to the matter at hand: While its counterpart, Hoon number two, possessed all the same defenses that it had, the other entity shared the same vulnerabilities as well. That's where the soft body came in. The trick was to use the biological without allowing the human to know it had been used. It might balk otherwise, or even worse, obtain more data than it was entitled to have. "There is a task that you will perform."

Jepp noted the apparent lack of courtesy but knew there was no reason for an alien artifact to observe social niceties appropriate to human culture. Besides, the Hoon saw everything that existed within the structure of the fleet as falling within its domain, and the human was forced to agree. If the AI wanted him to do something, Jepp could either comply or face the not too pleasant consequences. He cleared his throat. "Yes, well, if I can help . . ."

The Hoon seemed oblivious to the human's words. "The unit through which I am communicating will escort you aboard vessel 17-9621 where you will be asked to perform a simple maintenance procedure. Once the task is complete, you will be allowed to return here."

"You can count on me," Jepp replied, determined to

sound positive. "I have one question however . . . If the maintenance procedure is so simple—why can't one of your robots take care of it?"

"*You* will perform a maintenance procedure," the computer reiterated sternly. "*You* are leaving now."

"Okay," Jepp said, getting to his feet. "No need to get your processor in a knot . . . Allow me to get dressed, grab some tools, and we're out of here."

The one-time prospector hurried to pull some fairly clean overalls on, selected some of the tools salvaged from the *Pelican*, and stuffed them into a pack. "All right your supreme Hoonship . . . lead the way."

But the AI had more important things to do than stand around and wait while the somewhat sluggish biological wrapped itself in fabric. That being the case, it was Alpha who replied to the human's comment. "The supreme intelligence will meet us later."

"*God* is the supreme intelligence," Jepp growled. "The Hoon is a pain in the ass. Well, come on, let's get it over with."

Sam, the Thraki robot, cartwheeled across the cabin, transformed itself into something that looked a lot like a spider. Then, climbing quickly, the device took its place on Jepp's shoulder. The three of them left together—but it was Alpha who led the way.

Vessel 17-9621 glowed with the same shimmery force field that gave the Sheen their name.

Like Hoon number one, Hoon number two could project itself to any ship in the fleet, but if its intelligence could be said to reside anywhere, it was aboard that particular ship. For it was there, within a carefully secured compartment, that its various components were located.

Having been alerted to expect a biological and asked to render an opinion as to its usefulness, a very small portion of the AI's total consciousness tracked the incoming shuttle, noted its arrival, and monitored the creatures that disembarked.

There was an all-purpose unit similar to thousands on board the ship, an alien construct of no obvious value, and the biological that Hoon number one had warned of. An inquisitive creature who seemed headed for the very compartment in which number two was centered. That observation was sufficient to generate a low-level threat warning and to focus more of the computer's attention on the visitors and their activities.

As with all Sheen vessels, 17-9621 was equipped with a multiplicity of surveillance devices. Some took the form of tiny silicon imaging chips that had been "painted" onto the bulkheads. The computer preferred infrared to video, however, which meant that what it "saw" looked like a bipedal green blob. It seemed intent on approaching number two's sanctuary. Why?

Hoon number two sent a message to number one, ran into an electronic wall, and became immediately suspicious. Pathways were verified, systems were checked, and a second attempt failed just as the first had. The AI jumped to the logical conclusion: The other half of itself had severed their relationship and declared the electronic equivalent of war!

A biological might have waffled, might have questioned its own judgement, or been hesitant to take action. Not number two. The second Hoon went to the highest state of alert, directed fifty robots to intercept the intruders, and locked itself in. Monsters roamed the corridors . . . and the computer was scared.

Servos whined as Alpha moved down the passageway. Jepp's shoes squeaked when they came into contact with the deck, and Sam nattered in the ex-prospector's ear. Insofar as Jepp could tell, this vessel was the twin of the one in which he had spent most of his captivity. That being the case, he was familiar with the basic layout and could have navigated on his own, right up till the moment when Alpha approached a heavily armored hatch. The human was familiar with the door, or its analog, but had never been able to open it.

One of Alpha's armlike extensions whirred as it telescoped outwards, made a clicking sound as it mated with some sort of receptacle, and was immediately withdrawn.

Air hissed as the barrier disappeared overhead, a whiff of ozone found its way into the human's nostrils, and they were in. "I didn't know you could do that," the human said, as he followed Alpha down the brightly lit hall.

"It *can't*," Hoon number one replied, "but *I* can. Now listen carefully because there are limits to how far I can go. Robots will be sent against us, I will neutralize most if not all of them, while you proceed to the goal."

Jepp felt a rising sense of panic. Whatever he had landed in the middle of was more than a routine maintenance chore. That much was clear. Questions begged to be asked. "Robots? Goal? *What* goal?"

Hatches opened up ahead, a swarm of silvery robots flooded the corridor, and the Hoon hurried to answer. "After you pass through the last door you will find yourself in a circular space. Go to the bright blue module located at the very center of the compartment, take hold of the red handle, and give it one full turn to the right.

"Once that's accomplished, you must pull the handle, and the component to which the handle is attached, clear of the console. Then, assuming that you survive, you can return to my ship. Questions?"

Questions? Jepp had dozens, but the robots attacked right about then, and the conversation came to an abrupt end. Metal clanged as the oncoming wave smashed into Alpha. None of the units had weapons or were programmed for grasper-to-hand combat. That being the case, they fought like Sumo wrestlers, pushing, shoving, and bumping with their torsos. Alpha staggered under the onslaught, Sam danced the width of Jepp's shoulders, and the human was forced to retreat.

There were lots of attackers, but the width of the passageway acted to concentrate them, thereby limiting the number that could make contact at any given moment. Still, the phalanx had force, and the intruders gave ground.

The whole thing was strange . . . If the Hoon had taken over Alpha's body, and the robots worked for the Hoon, why would they attack?

Jepp was still pondering that question, still trying to figure it out, when the Hoon/Alpha extended an arm. Bright blue electricity arced between it and one of the oncoming Sheen. A black spot appeared between the robot's sensors, a wisp of smoke drifted away, and the construct collapsed on the deck.

Another machine took the first robot's place, another spark jumped the gap, and another unit fell.

Jepp backpedaled, ducked a clumsy roundhouse right, and backpedaled again. That's when something unexpected took place. Sam morphed into a configuration the prospector had never seen before, threw itself at one of the oncoming robots, and drilled a hole through the top of its shiny metal skull. The bit screamed, bright metal shavings curled toward the deck, and sparks jetted upwards. The machine jerked spasmodically, its joints locked, and it toppled forwards.

Sam rode the robot down, popped loose, and rolled away. The next victim didn't even know it had even been selected until the diminutive machine swarmed up one of its legs, scampered onto its head, and started the drill.

Emboldened by the inroads achieved by his electromechanical allies, Jepp uttered a primal war cry, charged the machine in front of him, and pushed it over. Metal screeched on metal as the defender hit the deck. The human stepped on the robot's abdomen and tackled the next unit in line.

The battle raged hot and heavy for the next few minutes,

started to wane as the causalities increased, and came to a sudden halt. The drill bit screamed as Sam left its most recent victim twitching on the deck.

Eyes wild, adrenaline pumping, Jepp turned and charged for the opposite end of the corridor. Never mind the fact that he didn't know who he was fighting, or why, the human wanted to win. "Come on! This is our chance!"

Sam scrambled onto the prospector's shoulder as Alpha charged forward and hit a force field of some sort. The robot staggered and started to convulse. The Hoon spoke but the words arrived one at a time. "The-force-fields-were-designed-for-robots. Continue-to-the-objective."

Of course! Jepp thought to himself. *That's why the tricky pile of nuts and bolts recruited me—the security systems are designed to stop machines! Sheen machines since Sam remains unaffected.*

That's when the thinking ended, lost in the rasp of his own breathing and the pounding of his pulse. The hatch! At the far end of the corridor—how would he get the damned thing open? That's when Jepp remembered the pack, still pounding the lower part of his back, and the tools it contained. Maybe . . . just maybe . . .

Hoon number two monitored the biological's approach with a growing sense of dread. Hoon number one had not only conceived the assault but had actually participated in it. Why? A software problem? No, not unless number two wanted to consider the possibility that *it* was vulnerable as well. The Thraki then . . . a virus of some sort . . . or . . .

The greenish blob knelt in front of the hatch, removed a colder object from its pack, and triggered a green-white flame. A torch! The soft body planned to burn its way in! Hoon number two gathered the most critical aspects of itself into one digitized file, sent it down a fiber optic pathway, and hit some sort of blockage. The escape route had been severed!

There were others, backups, and backups for the backups. The computer intelligence tried each and every one of them. None were open. The trap had closed.

Metal glowed cherry red, turned liquid, and trickled toward the deck. The heat, reflected off the hatch, warmed Jepp's skin and drew sweat from his pores. Now, with a little time in which to think, ice cold fear trickled into the pit of his stomach. What lay in wait on the other side of the hatch?

The question went unanswered as metal surrendered to heat and a locking rod was severed. The door sagged, Jepp hit the "Off" switch, and the torch made a popping sound. He placed the tool on the deck. The recesses had been engineered for use by hands smaller than his but still managed to accommodate his fingers. Jepp lifted and felt the hatch roll reluctantly upwards. Success!

The human retriggered the torch, held it like a handgun, and crept forward. Woe be to the machine that got in *his* way!

The interior looked the way the Hoon said it would look. The compartment was circular. A blue console stood at its center. The ex-prospector pulled a 360 to ensure he was alone, released the trigger, and heard the torch *pop*.

The handle was red all right . . . and easy to spot. Jepp placed the torch on the deck, felt Sam leap off his shoulder, and wiped the palms of his hands. Here it was, what he'd been sent for, ready for the taking. The voice made him jump. It spoke highly stilted standard and came from all around. "Why are you doing this?" It sounded like the Hoon—only different somehow.

"Because *you* told me to," Jepp said defensively.

"*I* told you nothing of the kind," the voice answered evenly. "The orders you received came from Hoon number one."

"Hoon number one?" the human asked hesitantly, scanning the bulkheads for some sign of the intelligence he was talking to. "So who are *you*? Hoon number two?"

"Precisely," the AI replied. "Now, leave this compartment, and return to wherever you came from."

Metal scraped on metal. Jepp turned to find that Alpha had entered the compartment. The robot walked with a limp but its voice was clear. "Resist the devil, and he will flee from you. James 4:7."

Who had spoken? Alpha? Or Hoon number one? Jepp decided it didn't make any difference. God had would have his way. He took the handle, gave it one turn to the right, and pulled it free.

There was only one sensor built into Hoon number two's main processor module, but that was sufficient to monitor the carefully computed launch, the fall toward the sun, and one last moment of existence. *What is a devil?* the AI wondered. *And what would such a being look like?* An image etched itself onto the computer's consciousness and it looked a lot like Jorely Jepp.

7

Just as the process of natural selection will determine which species shall ultimately prevail, a logical tendency toward self-interest applies similar pressure to the covenants, treaties and other agreements that govern affairs of state.

Mowa Sith Horbothna
Turr academic
Standard year 2227

Planet Arballa, the Confederacy of Sentient Beings

Conscious of the fact that his movements were monitored, Senator Samuel Ishimoto-Six palmed the panel, waited for the hatch to open, and nodded to the embassy guards. Both had been cloned from a much celebrated soldier named Jonathan Alan Seebo whose badly mangled body, and the DNA stored there, had given birth to entire armies.

Each trooper had experienced different things, leading to different personalities, but remained very similar. They had strong bodies, the intelligence necessary to operate sophisticated weapons systems, and a near fanatical devotion to duty. The guards came to attention, but there was nothing respectful about the look in their eyes, or the expressions on their identical faces. The soldiers had been briefed by either his clone brother, Harlan Ishimoto-Seven, or his assistant, Svetlana Gorgin-Three, both of whom were aligned with Alpha Clone Magnus Mosby-One and his brother Pietro. They, along with a significant number of the advisors who served them, had been seduced by the Ramanthian-led cabal. Something that Six, along with *his* sponsor, the reclusive Alpha known as Antonio, both opposed. That being the case, the sentries would make a note of his departure and enter it into a log.

The politician nodded an acknowledgement and stepped out into the nonstop foot traffic. The corridors, busy during the most lax of times, positively hummed as the senators and their staffs prepared for the half-session hiatus. A rather important opportunity to return home, rub elbows, tentacles, and pseudopods with constituents, and enjoy some R&R.

Six allowed himself to be absorbed into the crowd but was far too experienced to think that it would shield him from surveillance. No, not on board a vessel that crawled with every sort of bug known to more than a dozen races. Information was power—that made it valuable—and everyone sought to obtain as much as they could.

Private meetings *were* possible, however, provided that the participants took elaborate precautions and left nothing to chance. That being the case, the clone adopted a quick decisive pace, stepped onto a fully packed lift at the precise moment when the doors started to close and rode it down. Then, following the crowd into a labyrinth of corridors, he took a shortcut through one of the passageways reserved for robots, paused in a public restroom, donned a privacy mask, changed into some electronically laundered clothes, and left via the back door.

The mask smelled of plastic, and made the area around his eyes itch, but did offer a modicum of anonymity. The fact that about ten percent of the crowd wore similar disguises hinted at the number of last-minute schemes, deals, and agreements being hammered out as the hiatus began.

Finally, after the senator had done everything he could to shake surveillance, he entered a one-person lift tube, dropped to the less-trafficked boat deck, and took a careful look around. Nothing. Nothing he could see anyway.

Then, with the quick, positive movements of someone who knows his way about, the politician followed the gently curving hull to a multilingual sign that read: "Lifeboat-46, Oxygen Breathers Only."

Then, after another backward glance, the clone removed a card from his pocket and inserted the rectangle into a slot. The lock mechanism read what it thought was one of 749 acceptable DNA-based codes and released the hatch. It hissed open and closed.

The lifeboat was equipped with a tiny lock, but it was located toward the stern—and away from the main hatch. Seconds would count should an actual emergency occur, and the entry had been designed to accommodate a large number of beings in a short period of time. The air was cold, and the lights were on. The interior smelled like the inside of a brand-new ground car. Six removed the mask. "Maylo? Are you here?"

There was a whisper of fabric, followed by the slightest whiff of perfume. Six turned, and there she was. An overhead spot threw light across her face. She wore a plain high-collared sheath-style dress. It clung to her body the same way *he* wanted to and was slit up both legs. Wonderful legs, which on one memorable occasion, had been used to pull him in. But that was months in the past, a moment he'd never been able to replicate, much as he desired to do so. His voice was husky. "You are very, very, beautiful."

Maylo smiled. The truth was that she liked Samuel Ishimoto-Six, liked him more than she should have, or even wanted to, given her relationship with Booly. Whatever *that* was. The clone was about six feet tall, had a slightly Japanese cast to his features, and looked *very* handsome. "Thanks. You look pretty good yourself."

Both were silent for a moment—taking each other in. The clone spoke first. "I didn't know about the cabal—not till your uncle and Ambassador Doma-Sa forced the whole thing out into the open."

Maylo nodded. "Yes, I thought as much. I'm sorry they threw you into the brig with Ishimoto-Seven."

The politician shrugged. "It was for the best. Otherwise, the conspirators would have assumed the worst and arranged for some sort of accident. The cabal will stop at nothing. The so-called duel proved that."

"So?" Maylo asked gently, "why the meeting?"

Six grinned. "Because I want to seduce you."

"I believe you have already accomplished that," Maylo observed dryly.

"Which is why I know it's worth the effort," Six replied.

"That's it then?" the executive inquired mischievously. "You put your life on the line in order to get in my pants?"

The politician laughed. "No, I have an ulterior motive as well."

"Ah," Maylo replied. "I thought as much . . . My career as a sex goddess comes to an end. Come on, let's find a place to sit."

The lifeboat's interior was somewhat spartan. An emergency services droid stood motionless at the rear of the compartment. A forehead-mounted "Ready" light blinked on and off. There were overhead bins packed with supplies, pressure suits racked along the bulkheads, and rows of adjustable seats. Maylo sat on one, heard a whirring noise, and felt it conform to the shape of her body. Six took the chair opposite hers. "So," the executive continued, tell me more . . . What's on your mind?"

The clone forced his thoughts away from the way she looked and focused his mind on business. The business of *politics*. "I know that *you* know there's been a schism within our government. It would be hard to miss. What you *don't* know, or I *hope* you don't know, is how deep it went."

"I couldn't help but notice the use of the past tense," Maylo observed. "Has the schism been healed?"

The senator shrugged. "No, not yet. I think such a thing is possible, however, remembering that I'm something of an optimist. The essence of the situation is this: Alpha Clones Magnus and his brother Pietro allowed themselves to be drawn into an alliance with the Thraki in hopes that the aliens would serve as a counter to the cabal's steadily growing influence. A situation the Hegemony could have avoided by steering clear of the conspiracy in the first place. *My* sponsor, the Alpha known as Antonio opposed the plan—but lost the vote.

"During the period immediately after Magnus and Pietro authorized the alliance with the Thraki, the aliens took possession of Zynig-47 and were allowed to establish military bases on a number of our sparsely settled planets.

"The strategy, as conceived by my brother Ishimoto-Seven, was that anyone who attacked the Hegemony would be in the position of attacking the Thraki as well, and, given the size of their armada, would have second thoughts."

"A strategy your leaders have since come to regret," Maylo finished for him. "Especially in light of the fact that the Sheen are headed this way—and seem bent on destroying the very armada that you spoke of."

"Exactly," the politician agreed. "Which equates to a one-of-a-kind opportunity. This is the time to speak, to offer countervailing counsel, and turn them around."

Maylo nodded. "What you say makes sense . . . But why tell me?"

His eyes locked with hers. "If, and I repeat *if*, we are able to convince Magnus and Pietro of the truth, we'll need Nankool's support. The Thraki value their bases and will strive to keep them."

"And you believe that I can secure Nankool's support?"

The clone nodded. "Yes, but more than that, I want you to accompany me home. Your experience, your views, and your connections will add weight to my arguments . . . We must convince the Alpha Clones that *if* they change, if they break with the cabal, the Confederacy will take us in." His eyes pleaded with her. "So, will you come?"

Maylo felt a rising sense of excitement. If the Sheen *were* on their way, and should they turn out to be even half as powerful as the Thraki claimed that they were, the Confederacy would need every bit of strength that it could muster. The Hegemony, along with its highly developed military, could make an important difference. Her uncle would want her to go.

There was another reason however—one that had more to do with *him* than politics. Maylo smiled. "Yes, I'll come."

The two of them left after that, but the emergency services robot stayed where it was, waiting to repeat what it had seen and heard.

Exhausted by the long hours he'd been keeping, and still grieving over the War Orno's untimely death, the Ramanthian senator retired to his warm, somewhat humid quarters.

The politician noticed the ultraviolet message light, decided to remove his computer-assisted contact lenses, and saw the light replicate itself dozens of times. He had grown used to the transition but it still made him dizzy.

Orno listened to the message, listened again, and wondered how two seemingly intelligent beings could be so stupid. Meeting in a lifeboat, discussing how they had mated with each other, then switching to politics. It made him feel unclean. Well, there was a solution for that, one of the few pleasures the Ramanthian allowed himself.

The politician made his way back to his private quarters, took pleasure in the low murky light, and released his robes. The garment was left for a drone to deal with while he shuffled toward the sand bath. Though smaller than the ones typical of dwellings on his native planet, the transparent duraplast box was functional nonetheless. The Ramanthian entered, descended a set of stairs, and mounted the equivalent of a stool. The switch was located next to his left pincer. The Orno triggered the prewarmed sand, and felt it rise around him, and experienced something verging on bliss.

Then, when the finely grained stuff lapped around his neck, it stopped. That's when the entire mass started to vibrate, each grain acting like a tiny scrub brush, removing dirt while it polished his chitin. The senator allowed his mind to drift and knew that it was here, within the warm embrace of the sand, that some of his most inspired schemes had been hatched. And, painful though the knowledge was, the Orno realized that some of his *worst* plans had been concocted there as well, as measured by the extent to which they had been successful.

Now, as he prepared to return home and report to the hive mother, it was necessary to evaluate the situation as dispassionately as *she* would.

The plan to destabilize the Earth government, and thereby lessen the extent to which the humans controlled the Confederacy, had been successful initially, and might have achieved the desired end had it not been for the sudden reemergence of the damnable Chien-Chu, and for the meddling by Hiween Doma-Sa. A dangerous pair who had suddenly dropped from sight. Why? Where were they? And what were they up to? There was no way to be sure.

What the Ramanthian *did* know was that the newly stabilized Earth government, plus the arrival of the Thraki, plus the threat posed by the Sheen had altered the political landscape. Yes, it would take idiots like Ishimoto-Seven and his ilk awhile to notice, but the nature of the game had changed.

Certain elements within the Hegemony were in the process of reconsidering their options. The conversation between Ishimoto-Six and Maylo Chien-Chu was proof of that, and the possibility of war lurked just beyond the horizon. War between the clones and the Thraki, war between the Thraki and the Sheen, and war between the Sheen and the Confederacy.

Should the Ramanthians choose sides? No, the politician decided, not with so many variables clouding the outcome. His race had been scavengers once and could so profit again. The most intelligent strategy was to pull back, allow the cabal to wither, and wait to see who or what reigned victorious. Then, their strength undiminished by war, his people would emerge to claim the worlds they so desperately needed.

Orno settled into the sand and allowed the substance to take most of his weight. Warmth sought his center. Yes, the Ramanthian decided, there are times to act and times to wait. The trick was knowing the difference. Sleep pulled him down.

Clone world Alpha-001 was extremely Earthlike in keeping with the nearly endless edicts laid down by the Hegemony's founder Dr. Carolyn Anne Hosokowa. Though beautiful when viewed from orbit, the surface of the planet was less attractive from thirty-five thousand feet, and even less so as the courier ship came in for a landing. Not because of some failure on nature's part but due to what human beings had done to it.

Maylo watched with a growing sense of dread as the carefully laid out farms gave way to low-slung factories and rank after rank of identical high-rise buildings. They looked like what they were meant to be: cold, cost-effective boxes in which workers were "stored" during nonproductive "rest and regeneration periods."

The business executive glanced sideways, saw the look of eager anticipation on Ishimoto-Six's countenance, and was reminded of how adaptable human beings were. First, they had colonized every conceivable corner of their native

world, and later, other planets as well. Even those that
swirled with methane, were almost entirely clad in ice, or
subjected them to 1.5 gees. More than that, they frequently
came to love them, like ducks that imprint on the first
animate object they see, and claim it as their own. And
here, where an effort had been made to establish the "perfect" society, one could expect to see even more of that.
"Beautiful isn't it?" Six inquired as the ship flared in for
a landing.

"Yes," Maylo lied, remembering similar questions from
Booly. *He* enjoyed looking at rank after rank of carefully
arranged legionnaires . . . and couldn't understand her lack
of interest. Men. They were the *true* aliens.

There was a noticeable thump as the ship settled in. The
senator's assistant, Gorgin-Three, appeared at the center of
the aisle and announced the obvious: "We're on the surface
now—I will check on the ground transportation."

Ishimoto-Six wanted to stand and choke her into sub-
mission. The bitch had boarded the ship at the last possible
moment, and by her miserable presence, had prevented
him from enjoying some time with Maylo. Some zero gee
sex, a pleasure he had enjoyed only once before, would
have been a wonderful way to pass the time.

Now, determined to dog him, and report everything he
said or did, she was like a cloud hanging over the clone's
head. Solely because she was a fanatic? Or because she
had a crush on him? It hardly mattered. The senator
growled a reply, gathered his belongings, and prepared to
disembark. Maylo did likewise.

The tarmac shimmered in the afternoon heat, drives roared
as an in-system freighter fought its way up through the
atmosphere, and the courier settled onto the blast-scarred
pad.

The kill ball had been waiting for the better part of a
local day. But machines are patient, especially those designed to assassinate people, so the delay was unimportant.

Some environments are difficult to operate in, especially those where a spherical self-propelled droid has a tendency to stand out, but there was no such problem here. The kill ball had simply lowered itself onto a pylon-mounted sensor pod where it looked very much at home. So much so that any number of birds landed on the machine, crapped on the brushed aluminum housing, and made it appear that much more natural.

Now, as the courier's lock cycled open, the mechanical assassin activated its weapons and rose into the air. The moment had arrived. There was a task to perform. What it was made no difference. A variety of droids converged on the spaceship. The kill ball joined the throng.

Gorgin-Three stepped out onto the roll-up stairway, nodded to the Jonathan Alan Seebo who'd been sent to greet them, and scanned her surroundings. The assassins were waiting, of that she was sure, but where were they? In among the hangers that lined the tarmac in front of her? The thought that cold-blooded killers might be staring at her through high-powered telescopic sights sent a chill down the staffer's spine.

However, while Ishimoto-Seven had told Three *what* to expect, he hadn't told her who, or even how. Perhaps death would find Maylo Chien-Chu, while having a drink or taking a shower. It made little difference. The slut needed to die, *deserved* to die, for any number of reasons: for her opposition to the Hegemony's legitimate interests, for the exploitation of workers, and for having sex with Ishimoto-Six.

Gorgin-Three heard movement behind her, turned, and allowed Six to pass. He looked so handsome that feelings bubbled up from deep within her. *What did it feel like?* she wondered. To let a man . . . But no, such things were forbidden. She pushed the thought away.

Maylo nodded to the staffer and descended the stairs. They bounced slightly. The sun warmed her face.

Gorgin-Three caught movement from the corner of her eye, turned, and saw the sphere closing in. Some sort of guide drone? On its way somewhere else? No, those were orange. Then it struck her . . . Something was wrong! The droid paused, hovered, and fired a targeting laser. The dot wobbled across the top of Ishimoto's head.

Gorgin-Three screamed, "No!" at the top of her lungs, launched herself off the stairs, and hit Six with both her outstretched hands. He fell facedown. The high velocity slug tore through the staffer's body, and the shot echoed across the spaceport.

Jonathan Alan Seebo-11,212 saw what took place and fired a quick series of shots. Later, after the investigation had been completed, official documents would show that twelve of the fourteen shots fired hit the target and four caused serious damage.

The kill ball took note of the fact that it had failed to hit the assigned target, knew it was damaged, and tried to self-destruct. The mechanism failed, the device lost altitude, and crashed into the tarmac. All in a matter of five seconds.

Six did a push-up, made it to his feet, and turned toward the ship. Gorgin-Three lay in a pool of her own blood. The politician rushed to her side. The clone was very near to death. She knew it, and so did he. There was something in her eyes, a tenderness the clone had never seen before, and suddenly wished that he had. "Samuel?"

"Yes, I'm here."

"I would have done it, if you had asked me to."

Ishimoto-Six looked surprised. "Done it? Done what?"

Blood rose to fill Three's mouth. She worked to swallow it. "You know . . . what you did with her."

Maylo was there—pressing a makeshift compress against the entry wound. The politician's eyes flicked to her and back. He shook his head. "I'm sorry, Svetlana. I wish I had known."

But her face was slack, the light had faded from her eyes, and Gorgin-Three was gone.

The villa, which had been constructed to meet the exacting standards set forth by Antonio-Seven, crowned a verdant hill. The roof was covered with locally manufactured tile, the walls were painted pristine white, and bright-red fire trees guarded the grounds. A series of gracefully proportioned arches admitted large volumes of air into the dwelling along with semicircles of warm orange-yellow sunlight.

Simply put, the villa flew in the face of the sort of institutional architecture the founder favored, and it was indirectly responsible for the rounded, more organic shapes that were starting to appear out away from the cities.

There was nothing especially luxurious about the house, however. The furniture was of good quality but far from ornate. Nor was there much of it, which meant that Alpha Clones Magnus Mosby-One and the flamboyant Pietro-Seven could either take the seats that were offered, or sit on the floor.

Magnus, who had been born of a union between the Alpha Clone Marcus-Six and Marianne Mosby, one of the Legion's most storied officers, had his father's black hair, his mother's tendency to put on weight, and a deep booming voice. He wore a plain white toga held in place by his favorite double-helix pin. A pair of plain but sturdy sandals completed the outfit.

Pietro, who had exactly the same features as his host, wore a gauzy lime-green pullover top, matching pantaloon-style trousers, and a pair of leather slippers. A single earring dangled from his left lobe.

It was an embellishment Antonio considered to be excessive, like a dish with too many ingredients or a contrived work of art. He preferred a spartan black tunic, matching pants, and bare feet. They padded across the floor and stopped in front of his favorite chair. It was made of cane and creaked under his weight. His voice was slightly higher than that possessed by Magnus but a good deal more melodious. He looked from Magnus to Pietro. "Much has changed."

"Yes," Magnus agreed thoughtfully. "It has. Much as it pains me to say so . . . it appears that you were correct."

Pietro looked surprised. "He was? About what?"

"Almost everything," Magnus replied somberly. "Starting with his opposition to the cabal—and extending to his suspicions regarding the Thraki. The first strategy failed to achieve its purpose, and, should the Sheen arrive, the second could actually destroy us. Especially if the alien military bases come under attack."

Pietro, who was a much better administrator than a strategist looked alarmed and defensive. "That's not what our experts say . . . they say . . ."

"*They* are fools," Antonio finished for him. "Many of them are sincere but misled. Much of the counsel they received originated with *this* man."

The Alpha Clone touched a button and a holographic likeness of Ambassador Ishimoto-Seven blossomed at the center of the conversation area. The footage had been obtained surreptitiously. It stabilized and started to rotate. The diplomat was talking to someone.

"Nonsense," Pietro replied. "Ishimoto-Seven is not only genetically appropriate to his task, he has years of relevant experience, and has been rated ready for promotion."

"The very thing he seeks most," Magnus observed. "*Before* all else."

"Surely you are mistaken," Pietro insisted, looking from one face to the other. "Where is your proof? Something objective?"

"Right here," Antonio replied calmly. "Watch this."

The holo of Ishimoto-Seven dissolved into a shot of a spaceport. Judging from the way it was framed and the duration of the subsequent zoom, the camera had been a long way off. All three of the men watched as the kill ball closed on a courier ship, lined up on Senator Ishimoto-Six, and fired a single shot. The clones remained silent as Gorgin-Three died—and was carried away. Antonio was the first to speak. "My agents were caught by surprise and have some explaining to do . . . The kill ball was dispatched by Ishimoto-Seven. He knew Six was on the way to see us . . . and hoped to intervene."

"So you *say*," Pietro replied stubbornly. "Prove it."

"All three of the Alpha Clones were equipped with implants. Antonio cocked his head as the message came in. "The accused has arrived," Antonio replied. "Make no mention of what you've seen, wait for the rest of our guests to arrive, and watch Seven's face. His personal communications devices were spoofed hours ago . . . He will convict himself."

Pietro considered the matter for a moment, gave a jerk of his head, and wondered if the rumors were true. Had his brother's DNA been obtained from one of their predecessor's backup copies rather than stored material? And if so, could that account for the differences between them? There was no way to know.

A chime sounded. Three officials were shown into the room and left to choose from the few remaining chairs. There was Catherine Chambers-Nine, the secretary of state, Morley Hyde-Thirteen, deputy secretary of state, and Harlan Ishimoto-Seven, the Hegemony's ambassador to the Confederacy.

Magnus, who had long wished that he were someone else, watched them in a way that he never had before. How, the clone wondered, had he failed to see the cruel almost predatory curve of the secretary's lips? Her deputy's sleek, overfed assurance? And the diplomat's oily self-satisfied smirk? They were like fingers on a hand. Their joint perfidy seemed so obvious now, so amazingly clear, that he could barely believe his own lack of clarity. His mother would have seen it, his father would have seen it, but *he* was blind. Damn them anyway! For giving him a life that he neither wanted nor was qualified to have.

There was small talk, the awkward, somewhat stilted kind of conversation that occurs when human beings attempt to communicate across a social chasm, followed by the same chime heard earlier.

Chambers and her subordinates turned toward the main hallway. They were curious—but far from alarmed. *More* officials they supposed or—and this seemed more likely—senior military officers who, in spite of their lack of expertise, never tired of dabbling in statecraft.

None of them noticed that the Alpha Clones remained as they were, watching, and waiting.

Harlan Ishimoto-Seven felt a sudden sense of alarm as Maylo Chien-Chu entered the room, wondered how she had managed to find her way alone, and what the development would mean. That's when the diplomat spotted his clone brother, knew the assassination attempt had failed, and heard Chambers gasp. It was the moment Antonio had been waiting for. He turned to Pietro. "So, my brother, look at their faces. What do you see?"

"Surprise," the Alpha Clone replied sadly. "All of them are surprised."

"Yes," Antonio agreed. "Not proof of guilt . . . but that will come. A citizen is dead and the investigation has begun. One of them will rat on the rest. Guards! Take them away."

Ishimoto-Six was confused, then angry, as the meaning became clear. He lunged forward, stopped when a guard seized his arms, and confronted his brother. "Svetlana is dead. *Why?*"

Seven saw the hatred in his brother's eyes, felt Antonio's contempt, and couldn't believe it was happening. "Wait! Stop! You don't understand!"

Oh, but we do," Magnus replied. "We understand all too well. Take this trash away."

•   •   •

The subsequent meeting lasted the better part of two local days. Though not empowered to act on behalf of the Confederacy, Maylo was knowledgable regarding the political climate, and well worth listening to. The Clones did so.

It was clear from the beginning that the Alpha Clones had already decided to form a closer relationship with the Confederacy—the question was how and within what time frame. Finally, when the session was over, Ishimoto-Six was empowered to open certain areas for negotiation, and the two of them left.

They had the courier ship all to themselves this time. Maylo, who had never tried zero gee sex before, decided that she liked it. The only problem was that the act left her feeling sad somehow—as if something had gone missing. She wrestled with her dreams and felt tired when she awoke.

8

In war I would deal with the Devil and his grandmother.

Joseph Stalin
Army Staff College Papers
Standard year circa 1909

Planet Arballa, the Confederacy of Sentient Beings

Sergi Chien-Chu awoke where he usually did—standing
in one corner of his small, and rather sparsely furnished
stateroom. It had been a long time since he had made use
of a bed. He'd been back for about three standard days by
that time but was still in the process of reintegrating with
his own body and the *Friendship*'s daily routines.

He thought the word "vision" and scanned the interior
of his cabin. It was dark, so he switched to infrared. The
com console glowed green, as did the battery-powered ho-
los of his family, and the overhead heat duct.

The cyborg wondered what time it was, saw 0633 appear in the lower righthand quadrant of his vision, and
knew he should get to work. *Hard* work—since the task
the industrialist had set for himself would be anything but
easy.

The Hudathans had agreed to fight . . . but would the senate allow them to do so? Millions of deaths argued against it. Even *he* wondered about the wisdom of the idea.

Slowly, reluctantly, the industrialist unlocked his joints, brought all of his systems on line, and departed his quarters. The first meeting would be held over breakfast. A meal he had once enjoyed. Life was anything but fair.

The *Molly B* popped out of hyperspace like a cork out of a bottle, fired her in-system drive, and immediately started to tumble.

Willy Williams swore a long string of colorful oaths, took the Navcomp off line, and assumed manual control of the ship. Located deep within the durasteel hull, the computer depended on external sensors for input, and roughly half of them were out of action.

Both the ship and its owner, a man of somewhat elastic morals, had been on Long Jump, minding their own business, catching a little R&R when the Sheen dropped in for a visit. Machines that preached on street corners . . . What was next? Talking dogs?

Willy *wanted* to leave, wanted to boost ass as fast as possible, but needed his cargo. A nice load of custom-designed bacteria, all destined for a dirtball called Clevis, where the colonists were hanging by their fingernails while they waited for microscopic reinforcements. The kind that eat rock, burp oxygen, and shit fertilizer.

They weren't gonna get 'em, though, not anytime soon, not since the machines slagged Fortuna, Willy hauled butt, and a Sheen fighter put the hurts to *Molly*.

But that was then, and this was *now*. The ship rolled, the smuggler fired a jet, and she stabilized. He was about to check his position, find out where the hell he was, when something hit the hull. The *Molly* shook, and some buzzers went off.

Willy tapped some buttons, discovered that the delta-shaped fighter was *still* on his ass, and wondered how.

None of the civilizations *he* was familiar with had the technology to lock on to another ship and follow it through hyperspace. But this sucker *did* . . . and was determined to kill him.

The *Molly B* shuddered as a missile exploded in the vicinity of her hull—and shuddered once again when Willy took evasive action. His eyes were bloodshot, veins traced his nose, and stubble covered his cheeks. The words went out over freq four. "You want some of me? You wanta dance? Well, come on you pile of metallic shit, let's get it on!"

The Sheen fighter took note of the transmission, had no idea what it meant, and filed the message away. Such matters were handled by the Hoon—and the Hoon was a long way off.

President Marcott Nankool nodded to Chief Warrant Officer Aba, the senate's master at arms, climbed the short flight of stairs and made his way to the podium. Ironically enough it was Senator Orno who was tasked with the introduction by right of seniority. He rose from the specially constructed chair located to the right of the speaker's position. His voice, translated by the computer woven into his iridescent robe, filled the chambers. The chatter died away. "Please allow me to welcome each and every one of you back to this; the sixty-ninth gathering of this august body, and the second half of this year's session.

"Here to open the proceedings is the Right Honorable Marcott Nankool—the Confederacy's President and Chief Executive Officer. President Nankool?"

There was sustained applause followed by the usual rustle of fabric, creak of chairs, and whir of servos. Nankool smiled. Most of the senators knew what the expression meant. The rest ignored it. "Thank you. It is a great pleasure to be here. You have an ambitious slate of legislation to consider—and I have no wish to delay your deliberations. With that reality in mind, I will keep my comments short and to the point.

"We have reason to believe that a force known as the Sheen is headed our way. The purpose of this fleet is to destroy the Thraki plus any race that gets in the way or offers them support."

Many of the senators had heard rumors and offered gestures of agreement while some looked confused. They turned to neighbors, and words were exchanged.

Nankool scanned his audience, prepared the next volley of words, and delivered them with care. "Even as we meet, efforts are under way to marshal what forces we have and prepare a defense. However, a series of budget cuts, combined with troubles on Earth, have left our forces at little more than half strength. That being the case, it is my hope, no, my *prayer*, that you will understand me when I say that desperate times call for desperate measures."

Nankool looked out into the chamber, located the eyes he was looking for, and continued his speech. "You may be interested to know that Governor Chien-Chu, acting at my request, accompanied Ambassador Hiween Doma-Sa to the planet Hudatha, where they met with senior officials.

"The result of those discussions, pending your approval, was the outline of what could become a mutual defense pact. An agreement that would allow the Hudathans some measure of additional freedom in exchange for their assistance against the Sheen."

It was as far as Nankool got. Shouts were heard, and someone threw a glass. It shattered against the podium. Aba moved to protect the chief executive, and democracy turned to chaos. Every being present had lost someone to Hudathan aggression—and was opposed to any sort of rapprochement.

Chien-Chu looked at Doma-Sa. The Hudathan shrugged. There was nothing else he could do.

•   •   •

The *Molly B* shuddered, rolled, and corkscrewed away. The fighter followed. Willy had been in his share of scrapes during more than forty years of working, stealing, and smuggling, but couldn't remember one worse than this. He needed to beat the machine and do it soon. Coherent light blipped past the view screen and raced past the ship. The human scanned the instrument panel, was frightened by how many red and amber lights he saw, and took a firm grip on the control yoke. He pulled back. The *Molly B* broke out of the corkscrew and started to climb. Not really, since "up" was relative, but that's the way it felt. The smuggler's mind started to race.

The machine was a machine. That constituted both its strength *and* its weakness. It would do what it supposed to do, which, if its programming followed the dictates of logic, meant achieving its objective in the shortest possible period of time, while expending the minimum amount of energy required to get the job done.

He, however, was human, which meant he could do anything he frigging wanted to do, no matter how stupid that might seem.

Williams turned the yoke to the left, fought the gee forces that threatened to distort his movements, and checked the heads-up display (HUD). The enemy fighter appeared as a three-dimensional red outline. Suddenly, the ships were headed at each other at a high rate of combined speed. The smuggler steered into the center of the sighting grid, gave a whoop of joy, and sent another transmission. "You got balls? *Steel* balls? Let's find out."

The fighter's processor made note of the change, ran the numbers, and received negative results. Since it was bow-on, the target vessel would be extremely hard to hit. Not only that, but there was the very real possibility of a head-on collision, which while it would almost certainly destroy the enemy, would have similar implications for the fighter. Something the Hoon was almost sure to disapprove of.

Added to that was the fact that the tactics employed by

the opposition didn't make much sense, suggesting that the enemy intelligence was inferior, defective, or—and this seemed unlikely—possessed of a plan so sophisticated that only one such as the Hoon would be capable of understanding it.

The oncoming vessel was closer now, a lot closer, and showed no sign of turning away. A subprocessor signaled alarm. The Sheen fired two missiles, turned to the left, and ran into a beam of coherent light. It was powerful, much more powerful than a ship of that displacement would logically have, and therefore unexpected. The force field that protected the fighter, and was the origin of the name "Sheen," flared and went down. Steel turned to liquid, a drive went critical, and the machine exploded.

Willy *saw* the fireball, *heard* the tone, and *felt* the impact all at the same time. One of the enemy missiles had missed—but the other struck its target. The *Molly* took the blow, seemed to hesitate, and took a jog to starboard.

Most of the remaining green lights morphed to red, a klaxon began to bleat, and the control yoke went dead. Willy swore, attempted to kill power, and discovered that he couldn't. The ship was hauling butt, heading out past the sun, bound for nowhere. The planet Arballa, to which the smuggler had been headed, was off to port. *Way* off to port.

Williams bit his lip, checked to see if the auxiliary steering jets were on line, and discovered most of them were. He fired two in combination, the vessel jerked to port, and the smuggler dared to hope. Maybe, just maybe, he could bring her in.

It took the better part of ten minutes, plus a dozen minute adjustments, but he brought the *Molly* around. Finally, convinced that the ship was on course, Willy sent a message: "Confederate vessel CVL-9769 to any Confederate warship—over."

There was a pause while the signal made the necessary journey, but the reply was as prompt as the laws of physics would allow. The voice belonged to a com tech named Howsky—and she was bored. Nothing interesting had happened for weeks. "This is the vessel *Friendship* . . . we read you loud and clear. Over."

"Glad to hear it, *Friendship*, cause I'm declaring an emergency and comin' in hot. Over."

Howsky sat up straight, signaled her chief, and eyed an overhead holo. CVL-9769 appeared as a blue delta. It was coming in fast. "Declare your emergency, 69 . . . What kind of problem do you have? Maybe we can help. Over."

"Thanks for the offer," Willy replied, "but I went head-to-head with a Sheen fighter. I nailed the bastard . . . but took some damage. Navcomp's down, controls are shot, and the drives won't answer. They're maxed, repeat maxed, and my board reads red. Other than that—things couldn't be better."

"Got it," Howsky replied. "Hold one . . . will advise. Over."

The chief called the division commander, who called the executive officer, who confirmed the remote possibility of collision, and notified Captain Boone. He hit the crash alarm and hell broke loose. Klaxons sounded, signs flashed, and traffic was diverted away from the ship. The *Friendship*'s crew raced to their damage control stations, hatches dropped into place, and the ship's PA system came to sudden life. Translations followed.

"This is the captain. Nonessential personnel will take seats, strap themselves in, and remain in place till further notice. There is a *remote*, I repeat remote chance that an incoming vessel will collide with the *Friendship*, but there is no need for concern. Based on current calculations the ship should miss ours by more than a thousand miles. If that were to change, we have plenty of ways to deal with it. I will provide more news the moment it becomes available. Thank you."

Down in the senate, where pandemonium reigned only moments before, silence claimed the chamber. Marcott

Nankool felt a sudden sense of relief. Suddenly, as if by magic, the arguments had stopped. Not forever, but for the moment, which would act as a damper. The emergency was an opportunity in disguise.

There was a rustling of fabric and the occasional clink of metal as the senators strapped themselves in. The President had just secured his harness when Captain Boone spoke via the implant in his skull. Very few people had either the authority or the means to do so. That being the case, there was no need for an introduction.

"Sorry to bother you, sir, but the owner of the incoming vessel, one Willy Williams, desires to speak with you. He says it's urgent, and, given his present situation, he may be correct. There's a very real chance that he will hit Arballa at two or three thousand miles per hour."

Nankool frowned and subvocalized his reply. "I'm kind of busy . . . did he mention a subject?"

"Sir, yes sir. Williams claims that the Sheen attacked a planet called Long Jump, destroyed the city of Fortuna, and are headed this way. One of them followed him through hyperspace A freak accident most likely—but the effect is the same."

The tone was clear: Boone didn't believe much if any of what Williams had to say. But Nankool, politician that he was, felt his heart beat a little faster. The truth didn't matter . . . not right then. What mattered was perceptions . . . An idea flashed through his mind. If the strategy worked, it could save day. If it failed he would look like an idiot.

Ah well, Nankool thought to himself, *it's all on the line in any case. My reputation won't matter if I'm dead.* He cleared his throat. "Tell Williams that I will take his call . . . Monitor the chamber, and the moment I give the word, pipe him through the PA. I'll take a holo if you have one available."

Boone thought the President was out of his mind but was far too professional to let it show. "Sir, yes sir."

Nankool released his harness and stepped to the podium. "May I have your attention please? Thank you."

Most of those present assumed the President had information pertaining to the emergency and were quick to quiet down.

Like most high-ranking politicians Nankool was a consummate actor. He had even gone so far as to study some of what he considered to be the more important alien cultures, not striving for a fluency that would take a lifetime to achieve, but settling for a basic understanding of what constituted a gaffe, or an out-and-out insult. Now, as the President looked out over his audience, he applied all that he had learned.

"Most honorable gentle beings . . . please watch and listen as the pilot of the incoming ship describes what happened to him. Captain, if you please . . ."

The holo blossomed, and the senate found itself staring into Willy Williams' grizzled countenance. Though conscious of the fact that he was on camera, the smuggler's eyes flicked from side to side as he checked the wildly fluctuating readouts. "Sorry to bother you Mr. President, but I reckon you need to know. I was on Long Jump, mindin' my own business, when a fleet dropped hyper. There were lots of ships, hundreds, maybe thousands of 'em, all wrapped in some sort of shiny force field.

"No bio bods, though, not unless you want to count Jorley Jepp, and most people think he's crazy. That's cause he's been loadin' the machines with some sort religious gobbledygook. Sent 'em down to preach on the street corners. Not sure what happened after that. The Sheen attacked Fortuna and reduced the place to rubble. A few of us managed to lift. I came here to warn you. Guess that's it 'cept for the pickle I'm in. Sorry 'bout the inconvenience . . . but the *Molly* took a whole lot of damage."

Nankool cleared his throat. "Thank you, Citizen Williams. What you did required a great deal of courage. I'm sure that Captain Boone and his crew will do everything in their power to assist you. Once this matter is resolved, please ask to see me. The Confederacy owes you a debt of gratitude.

"Now," Nankool continued, turning his attention to the senators arrayed before him, "you see what I've been talking about. This is no phantom menace . . . The Sheen are real, we must ready ourselves to meet them, and they are knocking on the door. Fortuna lies in ruins . . . It could have been one of *your* cities. *Will be* should you fail to take action.

"Your reservations regarding the possibility of an alliance with the Hudathans are understandable—and deserve reasoned discussion. A discussion that must be held in light of what we *know*: The Sheen are coming."

Most of the senators were moved by Willy's story and convinced he was telling the truth. That, plus the fact that they were strapped in place, fueled some rational discussion.

Doma-Sa sat toward the rear of the chamber next to Chien-Chu. "Your President fires words like bullets. They hit the mark."

Chien-Chu nodded. "Yes, he's very skilled. *If,* and I stress *if* he pulls this off, Nankool will be President of *our* Confederacy. Yours *and* mine."

Doma-Sa felt the reality of that sink in. The Hudathans? Led by an alien? Unthinkable! Yet what of the alternative? The annihilation of his people. Equally unthinkable. There was no way out. The debate droned on.

The *Friendship*'s control room was huge—as befitted a ship of her importance—and self-consciously quiet. The multispecies crew took pride in their professionalism and always sought to meet emergencies with exactly the right amount of effort. Captain Boone scanned the screen for a second time and gave a sigh of relief. There would be no need to break the former battleship out of her parking orbit. The *Molly B* would clear his vessel by more than a thousand miles. There was so much clearance in fact that he would have lifted the shipwide lockdown had it not been for Nankool's insistence that the restrictions remain in place. A nonsensical request the naval officer thought absurd.

Still, the situation did allow him to turn his attention from the spacegoing capital to the *Molly B* and her somewhat disreputable owner. It seemed that Williams, aka Kline, Peters, and Howe, the last being the name he'd been born with, was a wanted man. A fact that might or might not get in the way of the reward promised by Nankool.

None of which mattered to Boone, who knew his duty, and was determined to save the smuggler if such a thing was possible. He opened a com link. "Captain Williams? This is Captain Boone. What kind of emergency gear have you got on board? A lifeboat? Escape pod?"

Willy gritted his teeth as the drive cut in and out. The ship was doomed and so it seemed was he. "My lifeboat needs some repairs . . . and the pod was damaged during the fight."

Boone bit his lip. The very idea of lifting with a lifeboat in need of repairs went against every bone in his naval body. Such things were common among civilians, however—just one of the reasons why they required supervision. "Yes, well that's a bit unfortunate. How about space armor? You have some I trust?"

Willy looked up at the camera. "Of course I do! What do you take me for? An idiot?"

Boone decided it would be best to let the question pass unanswered. "Excellent. That being the case you'll be able to abandon ship. I suggest you step out of the lock in two hours and twenty-seven minutes. One of our search and rescue sleds will pick you up."

"What about the *Molly*?"

The naval officer glanced off screen then back. "Our calculations suggest that your ship will impact the surface of Arballa at approximately three thousand miles per hour.

The Araballazanies have given their permission for you to land or, more accurately, to crash. I doubt your ship will be worth much after that."

Willy squinted into the camera. His mother plus all three of his former wives knew the expression well. "No."

Boone raised an eyebrow. " '*No?*' What does that mean?"

"It means I ain't gonna do it," Willy replied stolidly. "The *Molly*'s been hurt worse than this . . . I can repair her. All you gotta do is stop her."

The bridge crew, all of whom were surreptitiously monitoring the conversation, snickered. "And how," Boone said patiently, "would we do that?"

"Simple," Williams replied. "You got tractor beams don'tcha? Well, use 'em."

The naval officer frowned. "Yes, we do. But snatching a fast-moving object like your ship takes a great deal of effort and skill. You claim your ship can be repaired. I doubt it. Why should I go to the effort?"

Willy leaned forward until his heavily veined nose looked like an overripe tomato. "Because if you don't help me, I'll end up spread across twenty square miles of Arballa's surface, and *you'll* have to explain why."

Boone felt a rising sense of anger but knew the civilian was correct. He *would* have to launch an investigation, convene a board of inquiry, and sit through days of boring testimony. "I'll think about it."

Willy grinned. "You do that, Captain. I'll be waiting."

Ishimoto-Six had to bully traffic control before getting permission to land in the *Friendship*'s cavernous launch bay—and was surprised to see how quiet the facility was.

It wasn't until Maylo and he had cleared the lock and entered the ship that they heard about the emergency. Given a choice between sitting in their staterooms or joining the senate, they chose the latter. Sergi Chien-Chu and Hiween Doma-Sa waved them over. Some whispered conversation was sufficient to bring the newcomers up to speed. Ishimoto-Six was amazed at how audacious the plan was, saw how it could serve the Hegemony's interests, and wondered if the Alpha Clones would support him.

The debate was well advanced. Senator Hygo Pulu Darwa, who represented the Dwellers, had come forward to oppose the proposal. The senate listened as he spoke.

"So," Darwa concluded, "while I can see the benefit to be realized from an alliance with the Hudathans, the dangers are much too great. What happened to the legion could happen again. While it's true that the lack of a deep-space navy might serve to brake their expansionist tendencies, a revolt by one or more of the Hudathan military units could wreak havoc on our defensive efforts, and threaten the Confederacy as a whole. I'm sorry—but that's how I see it. Thank you."

Nankool, who had expected the Dwellers to support rather than oppose his initiative, struggled to conceal his disappointment. A rare moment of somewhat awkward silence fell over the chamber. Those who sought to block the proposal relished their moment of victory—while those who favored it stared defeat in the face. Chien-Chu wished he had the right to speak—and Doma-Sa struggled to hide his rage.

Ishimoto-Six felt himself stand was surprised to find that he had. "The Clone Hegemony seeks to be recognized."

Senator Orno looked for Ishimoto-Seven and wondered where he was. Not that it made much difference. Ishimoto-Six had every right to speak. The Ramanthian ran his tool legs back along the sides of his beak. "The chair recognizes Senator Ishimoto-Six."

Six saw his image appear at the front of the chamber. Most of his peers settled for that—but a few turned to look. He established eye contact with those that did. "I suggest that in addition to the proposed restrictions on the Hudathan navy, that their ground forces be integrated into the Legion, so that there will be little to no possibility that an entire unit could or would revolt. Thank you."

Slowly, inexorably, every ocular organ in the room turned, swiveled, and in one case slithered toward Ambassador Hiween Doma-Sa. Every single being in the room knew how xenophobic the Hudathans were. Would the race submit? Agree to take orders from those they had long sought to annihilate?

Doma-Sa felt the scrutiny and knew what they were thinking. In spite of the fact that the thought was new to them, *he* had already considered the possibility and hoped it would never come up. But now it had, which forced him to confront a terrible choice: Accept the clone proposal, thereby ceding control of the Hudathan military to the Confederacy, or—and this was equally unthinkable—open his people to an attack by the Sheen. He ignored Orno and spoke without benefit of a mike. The words were bitter— like poison. "My people stand ready to accept the clone proposal *if* we receive a full membership in the Confederacy, *if* all trade restrictions are lifted, and *if* the Hegemony agrees to a joint command structure."

There was a hiss of in drawn breath as everyone turned to stare at Ishimoto-Six. Here was a brilliant counterstroke. A piece of political legerdemain that would be discussed for months if not years to come. Though a member of the Confederacy, the Hegemony had always been very independent. A unified command structure would limit that . . . How would the clone respond?

Ishimoto-Six wondered the same thing. How would his government *want* him to respond? But more importantly how *should* he respond? Because this was one of those moments, the kind he had once dreamed of, when a single person could make a difference. *If* he had the courage. Whatever he said, whatever he did, would be hard if not impossible for the Hegemony to retract.

The politician looked at Maylo, saw the question in her eyes, and got to his feet. Like Doma-Sa, he decided to ignore Senator Orno. The almost perfect silence was permission to speak. "The Sheen are on the way . . . It will take every bit of our strength to stop them. The Hegemony will place its forces under a unified command for the duration of the crises. What happens after that will be subject to negotiation."

Stroke and counterstroke! Every single one of them understood the qualification. It gave Six a way out, an escape hatch, should his superiors take issue with the decision. Not immediately—but down the line. It was a smart, gutsy move.

President Nankool released his harness, stood, and started to applaud. The rest of the senate did likewise, or, in the case of those who lacked hands, made an assortment of celebratory noises.

Chien-Chu felt a sudden surge of hope. He looked from Doma-Sa to Ishimoto-Six. Both were close enough to hear. "Thank you—thank you both. We have a chance now, a slim one, but a chance nonetheless."

The Hudathan offered a human-style nod. "My people have a saying . . . 'hope lights the way.' "

Arballa had grown from little more than a pinprick of light to a luminous brown ball. The elation that had accompanied Willy's victory over Captain Boone had faded to be replaced by a growing sense of concern. What had he been thinking anyway? Shooting his mouth off that way . . . Yes, he needed *Molly*, but only if he was alive, not spread all over the surface of some godforsaken dirtball.

Pride prevented the smuggler from saying anything, however—which accounted for his silence. Perhaps Boone was playing a game with him, waiting to see if he'd crack, or, and this seemed more likely, the miserable swabbie was off on a coffee break, sipping java and trading scuttlebutt while he . . . The voice sounded bored. "Stand by CVL-9769. We intend to seize control of your vessel with two, repeat two, tractor beams. You may feel a bump."

Willy ran his tongue over dry lips. "And if I don't?"

There was a momentary pause. The woman was amused. "Then either we did one helluva good job or we missed."

"And if you miss?"

"Say hello to the Arballazanies for me. I love the computers they make."

Willie could almost hear the swabbies laughing, forced himself to smile, and leaned back in his seat. He'd hold that position all the way to the surface if necessary, to the point when the *Molly B* drilled her way into the planet's crust, and the worms came to . . .

The bump was more of a violent jerk, and Willy's head flew forward then back. The drive screamed, edged into the red, and shut itself down. "Congratulations," the voice said cheerfully. "You're going to live. The first round is on you."

9

The commander must try, above all, to establish personal and comradely contact with his men, but without giving away an inch of his authority.

Field Marshal Erwin Rommel
The Rommel Papers
Standard year 1953

Planet Drang, the Confederacy of Sentient Beings

General William Booly climbed the same metal stairs that he had climbed more than twenty years before, opened the naval-style hatch, noticed the fact that the hinges had been heavily greased, and knew why.

The indigs, more commonly referred to as the frogs, owned the lake in which Firebase Victor had been constructed, and loved to take potshots at anyone unfortunate enough to "pull the O," which was slang for walking endless circles around the metal observation deck. The locals had excellent hearing, which meant that the sound of a squeaky hinge could attract a bullet from a preregistered sniper's rifle, about head-high straight through the hatch. How had that lesson been learned? The hard way—from someone who had been dead for a long time.

The legionnaire stepped out onto the metal grating, nod-ded to a heavily armored private, and knew she was an old hand. Newbies, also known as "frog food," had a ten-dency to salute officers and thereby pick them out for the snipers. She smiled and a network of creases exploded away from her bright blue eyes. "Welcome back, sir. The name's Harris. I hear you've been here before."

Booly nodded. "They sent me here right out of the Academy. Said I'd learn a thing or two."

"And did you?"

"Hell, no. I was a second lieutenant . . . and you can't teach them anything."

Harris laughed. "Well, you survived, sir, and that's more than some can say."

"Yes," Booly replied soberly, "it sure is."

The legionnaire continued her rounds as the officer scanned his surroundings. The water had a dark, oily look, mist hovered like ectoplasm, and some unseen thing sent ripples radiating in all directions.

The firebase sat at the exact center of the lake, which seemed like a stupid place to put it unless you were fa-miliar with Drang and its relentless jungles. The water kept the vegetation back and provided a natural fire-free zone.

That didn't stop the indigs from swimming in close, though . . . They liked to take potshots at the sentries, am-bush Trooper II's as they returned from patrol, and place charges against the tower's supports. *If* they got that close—which was a rarity. The firebase was protected by sensor arrays, robotic weapons emplacements, and some pretty sophisticated booby traps.

Something clanged off the metal behind him, and Booly heard the report of a distant gunshot. Harris materialized at his elbow. "It doesn't pay to stand still, sir. A gunrunner managed to land about two months ago. Sold the frogs some fairly decent hunting rifles. Scopes, infrared, the whole shebang. That shot came from the jungle. The swimmers get in close. Nailed Oki last week. Miserable bastard."

There was no way to know if the "miserable bastard" was Oki or the sniper who shot him. Booly thanked the trooper and started to walk. His boots clanged on metal. Dark gray clouds merged to produce a spattering of rain. Each drop hit the surface of the lake and gave birth to concentric rings. A lot like recent events. Who would have envisioned a time when Hudathans, Hegemony, and Confederate forces all came under a single command? *His*.

Not because Booly was best qualified, not in his judgement anyway, but because better men and women had been killed, or, as was the case with officers like Colonel Leon Harco, were rotting in prison.

All of which left the officer with little choice but to muddle through. The challenge was enormous. He had what? Weeks? Months at most to deal with the Thraki military bases, fold three vastly different military cultures into one, and mount a credible defense. In the meantime, the Sheen could do as they pleased. Including roll over the Confederacy in less than a month, should they decide to move more aggressively.

That's why Booly had selected the best officers he could find and tasked them with building the command, communications, and logistics systems necessary to unify such a diverse force. And they were hard at work, doing the sort of things he could have done, would have *preferred* to do, rather than risk his life on Drang.

But that's where he was because leadership starts at the top and is built on trust, plus a set of common standards, beliefs, and values. The task, *his* task, was to select officers from each of the disparate military traditions, assess their strengths, understand their weaknesses, and forge a single blade. A weapon so strong, so sharp, that it would cut the Sheen to pieces. Was he up to the task? Were they up to the task? There was no way to know. All he could do was try.

The officer paused and allowed the rain to hit his face. The rail felt cold beneath his fingers. Something screamed in the jungle . . . and night swallowed the sky.

The rain stopped just before dawn, and the sun came out of hiding. It rose through a clear blue sky, claimed its place in the heavens, and bathed everything in gold. A layer of mist floated over the surface of the lake, jerked in response to the ebb and flow of the early morning breeze, and parted for the flat-bottomed boat.

The scow was constructed of aluminum, was twenty-two feet long, and heavily loaded. General William Booly sat toward the bow, War Commander Wenlo Morla-Ka occupied the next seat back, General Jonathan Alan Seebo-346 shared a seat with Battle Leader Pasar Hebo. Staff Sergeant Mordicai Mondulo commanded the stern. He steered the boat and kept his eyes fixed on the shoreline.

The small electric motor whirred, water rippled away from the bow, and the jungle waited. The trees were taller now, hosts to a tangled mass of intertwined vegetation that was involved in a nonstop slow-motion working out of complex symbiotic, commensualistic, and predatory relationships. Here was an enemy even more implacable than the frogs—a biomass eager for nourishment. Booly had survived the forest once before, but just barely, and felt something cold trickle into the bottom of his gut.

Mondulo had black skin, wore tattoos on both brawny forearms, and possessed a deep resonant voice. It carried all the way to the bow. "The water looks real nice, don't it? Well, it ain't. There's all kinda critters in there . . . some of which have mighty sharp teeth. That bein' the case, don't stick nothin' in there you wanta keep."

None of the officers said anything, and Booly wondered what they were thinking. That he was crazy? That the whole exercise was a joke? Maybe. One thing was for sure however, even if *he* didn't manage to get their attention, Drang sure as hell would.

Mondulo killed the motor, allowed the boat to coast, and felt it slide onto the mud bank. None of the occupants noticed the sleek head that surfaced behind them, the yellow eyes, or the ripple left when the creature submerged.

Booly stood, scanned the area ahead, and noticed boot prints in the muck. He eyed the tree line, saw something move, and flicked the safety off his assault rifle. "We have movement in the trees, Sergeant . . . you make the call."

"Not bad for an officer," the noncom said grudgingly. "There's an entire squad concealed in the undergrowth along with three T-2's. They secured the area just before daylight. This is the last time we'll have that kind of support."

Mondulo nodded towards Booly's subordinates. "Safe your weapons and deass the boat . . . The general gets a word with you, then it's my turn."

Booly felt mud suck at the bottom of his boots as he stepped out of the boat and climbed the gently rising bank. He hadn't carried a full combat load in a long time—*too* long, judging by how heavy it felt.

The training exercise, if that's what the evolution could properly be called, was scheduled to last three days. Shorter than he would have liked but all the time that could be spared. No one knew when the Sheen would make their next appearance, and he wanted to be there when they did.

Like the others, Booly carried a waterproof com set capable of reaching the firebase from any location on Drang, an extensive first aid kit, six days worth of rations, two canteens, a hammock made of superstrong netting, a dozen hand grenades, an assault rifle with a built-in grenade launcher, twenty magazines, each containing thirty rounds, twenty shotgun-style 40 mm rounds, his favorite sidearm, two extra clips, a combat knife that hung hilt down from his harness, and numerous odds and ends. No big deal when he was twenty-three—but a pain in the ass now.

Morla-Ka looked as if he were underloaded, Seebo wore

a self-confident smile, and Hebo, who carried his gear in something that bore a resemblance to a pair of saddlebags, appeared unaffected. The Ramanthian was something of an enigma. What was the insectoid sentient thinking? There was no way to know.

The officer met each set of eyes in turn. "One of my people's greatest military thinkers, a man by the name of Sun Tzu, wrote a book called the *Art of War*. It begins: 'The Art of War is of vital importance to the state. It is a matter of life and death, a road either to safety or ruin. Hence under no circumstance can it be neglected.' "

"Another great warrior, this one Hudathan, wrote, 'The survival of the Hudathan race cannot be left to chance. Anything that could threaten our people must be destroyed. Such is the warrior's task.' A little more preemptive than humans would prefer—but to the point."

A look of newfound respect had appeared in Morla-Ka's eyes. The words had a sibilant quality. "Those words were written by Mylo Nurlon-Da in standard year 1703."

Booly nodded. "Yes. *The Life of a Warrior* should be mandatory reading for anyone who takes up the profession of arms. And that's what *this* is all about.

"We represent different races, come from different military traditions, and share a common enemy. In order to fight that enemy and defend those who depend on us, we must operate from a set of common values. The concepts I'm about to put forth may be consistent with your native culture, or they may not. I don't care. They are the precepts by which you will lead our troops. Fail to do so at your peril.

"So here they are . . . First: Strategy and tactics will be formulated and implemented for the *greater good*. That means what's good for the Confederacy as a whole. *Not* Earth, *not* Alpha-001, *not* Hudatha and *not* Hive.

"Second: We will lead by example and never order our troops to do something we would refuse to do ourselves, and treat them respect. *Regardless* of what species or group they represent.

"Third: We will think first—and fight second. The Sheen will be as smart as someone was able to make them. We must be smarter.

"And fourth," Booly continued, "is the need to conserve lives, options, and supplies. Our resources are limited. Use them wisely. Any questions? No? Then it's time to hear from the sergeant. He has orders to treat us the same way he would treat raw recruits, so the next few days will be a bit rough, but it will teach us to work as a team. Listen to what he says—it could save your life. Sergeant? We're all yours."

Mondulo nodded. "Sir! Yes, sir." He took three paces forward, performed a crisp right-face, and stood at parade rest. The voice was the same one perfected on parade grounds at a dozen forts. "You pukes want know what my claim to fraxing fame is? Well, I'll tell you what my claim to fraxing fame is . . . I've been on this pus ball for two years, and I'm still alive. That's *my* claim to fame, and there ain't a fraxing one of you who can say the same thing. That makes me numero uno, the big dog, and the main enchilada."

Booly watched his officers out of the corners of his eyes and fought to restrain a smile. With the possible exception of Seebo; none of them had ever run into a noncom like Mondulo before.

"Now," the sergeant said, gesturing to the verdant foliage. "That's the jungle . . . *My* fraxing jungle, and it's full of nasty-assed shit. Take a look around. See those trees? Tall suckers ain't they? Tall enough and thick enough to block out the sun. That means a low light level down on the ground, damned little undergrowth, and relatively easy walking. The frogs aren't very comfortable on land so you're relatively safe from them.

"You gotta watch for reptiles, though, includin' the dappled Drang adder, the vine viper, and a nasty piece 'o work called the stick snake, cause that's what the bastard looks like, till you grab his ass and he kills you."

Mondulo looked from one face to the next. "You got any questions? No? Okay, then. Once we leave the jungle, we're gonna travel through some suck-ass swamps. The fraxing frogs *love* the swamps so they'll be waitin' for us."

Mondulo glared at them from under a craggy brow. "That ain't the only problem—not by a long shot. I don't how many of you have dicks, you bein' XTs an all, but take my word for it, don't pee when you're wadin' through the water. Not unless you want a tiny wormlike critter to swim up your uretha and lay eggs in your bladder. The medics tell me that the young 'uns *eat* their way out."

The noncom shrugged. "Course we got water snakes, blood suckin' plants, and some nasty-assed parasites all waitin' to take a bite out of your ignorant butts as well . . . That's why you're gonna do what I say, do it fast, and do it right. You got any questions? No? Then saddle up. Booly, you take the point. Morla-Ka, Hebo, and I will follow. Seebo has drag. Practice those hand signals— you're gonna need 'em."

Booly experienced a strange sense of déjà vu as he eyed the jungle, spotted a break in the foliage, and headed that way. A heavily camouflaged human peered out of the undergrowth, offered a thumbs up, and faded from view.

Then, some fifteen or twenty steps later, the friendly forces were behind them, the lake was little more than a memory, and the jungle wrapped the interlopers in its warm-wet embrace.

Booly—worried lest he miss something and lead the team into a disaster—focused on the environment around him. Memories came flooding back. Memories and knowledge. The kind gained the hard way. The trail had been used many times before. That made for some easy walking. But Booly, mindful of similar patrols twenty years earlier, knew that easy things were dangerous. Once the enemy knew where you were likely to go, it was easy to lay traps, set mines, or establish ambushes. None of which would be good for their health.

That being the case, the officer checked the patrol's position on his wrist term, glanced at the waterproof map strapped to his left forearm, and stepped off the trail. It would have been different if he'd been looking for the enemy, rather than trying to avoid them, but such was not the case.

Staff Sergeant Mondulo observed Booly's decision and gave the officer some mental points. At least one of his charges knew a thing or two . . . which increased the odds of survival. Theirs—and *his*.

Hebo had removed the special contact lenses that converted hundreds of images into one and felt very much at home. The jungle reminded him of Hive, his youth, and good times past. He relished the warmth, the slight odor of decay, and the well-filtered light. The Ramanthian held his weapon at the ready, watched to ensure there was sufficient space between his body and the black-skinned human, and felt a steadily growing sense of superiority. This was *his* world, or should be, by right of adaptation. No matter what happened to the others *he* would survive.

Morla-Ka fought to control a rising sense of panic. Not in regard to the jungle, which he felt competent to deal with, but from prolonged contact with non-Hudathans. Contact—bad enough in and of itself—was made worse by forced interdependency. To rely on aliens, to place his life in their hands, went against his most basic instincts. Yet that was his duty to the Hudathan race, since without the alliance, and the strength it would provide, his kind would almost certainly perish. The knowledge brought small comfort. The fact that a heavily armed human was following along behind added to the officer's discomfort.

Seebo watched the Hudathan's back, thought about how easy it would be to put a few rounds into it, and made a silent vow: If anything went wrong, if it looked like he was about to die, the geek was going first. The thought brought a smile to his lips.

Conscious of his role, the clone turned, and walked backwards for awhile. How long had it been since he had taken part in an honest-to-god patrol, rather than the endless staff meetings, review cycles, and readiness reports that claimed most of his time? Too long that was for sure . . . Truth was that it felt good. Seebo turned, hurried to close the gap, and was glad to be alive.

Eyes watched, vanished behind nictitating membranes, and reappeared. Their owner hissed softly, slithered upwards, and sampled the air. Breakfast was waiting.

The morning passed without incident. Each individual rotated through point and drag. Hand signals were perfected. Their surroundings became more familiar. Nobody blew a foot off. Not bad for a bunch of greenies.

Mondulo called for a break, ordered Hebo and Seebo to stand guard, and allowed the others to eat. The human rations included built-in heat tabs, but the noncom liked his cold. He peeled the top off something that claimed to be beef stroganoff, stirred the mess with the tip of his combat knife, and used the same implement as a pointer. "We'll spend the better part of the afternoon hiking thata way, haul our butts up into the trees, and wait for daylight."

" 'Haul our butts up into some trees?' " Morla-Ka inquired warily, "What for?"

"So nothin' can eat 'em," Mondulo replied matter-of-factly. "Let's say one of you generals gets killed . . . You got any idea how many forms I'd have to fill out? Too *many*—so you're goin' up into them trees."

The Hudathan weighed more than three hundred pounds and didn't fancy climbing anything as insubstantial as a tree, but he didn't want to say so. He nodded, finished his rations, and sealed the empty into a bag. Both went into his pack.

Morla-Ka relieved Seebo, who came in to eat. The clone jerked a thumb back over his shoulder. "I think the big guy is all pissed off. What's his problem anyway?"

Booly looked up from the log where he was sitting. "It's hard to know for sure—but it's my guess he doesn't like to climb trees."

Seebo frowned and gave a noncommittal shrug. "Is that all?"

"That's all," Mondulo answered. "I'll relieve Hebo."

Seebo watched the noncom go. It seemed strange to serve with beings who looked so different from the way he did. Strange and a little scary, since he knew how his clone brothers would react in an emergency. Simply put, they would react the way *he* did—which was the genius behind the founder's plan.

Still, Mondulo was sharp, anyone could see that, which made him feel better. When Booly spoke, it was as if the free-breeder could read his mind. "It's going to be different, isn't it?"

"Yes," Seebo replied thoughtfully, "it certainly is."

"Do you think it will work?"

Seebo activated the heat tab and felt the container start to warm. "Yes, sir. Where the humans are concerned. We're different but the same. As for the geeks, well, the jury's out on that one."

Booly raised an eyebrow. "We need to walk the talk . . . so please avoid using terms like 'geek.' Personally, I think it will work."

The clone tore the cover off his food. Steam thickened the air. "Sir, yes sir. But that's what you *have* to think. Isn't it?"

"Yes," Booly replied. "I guess it is."

The Pool of Fecundity had been created by digging a canal from the river into a natural depression. A second ditch carried the water back to the river for a real as well as symbolic union. Only one individual was allowed to use the pond, and she floated about ten feet from shore.

The Clan Mother was *very*, very pregnant. So much so that her swollen abdomen made it next to impossible to walk. Because of that her attendants marched into the pool, positioned the specially constructed litter under her grotesquely swollen body, and carried her ashore.

The path from the pond to the village had been paved with a thick layer of crushed white shell. It made an attractive surface and provided excellent traction. A small detail but a critical one, since the Clan Mother was the only female permitted to reproduce. One slip, one accident, and hundreds of eggs could be damaged or destroyed, an important matter for a race in which normal infant mortality ran to sixty percent.

The village, which was know as the "Place Where the Water Breaks White over Old Stones before Turning South toward the Great Swamp," consisted of some thirty beehive-shaped mud huts clustered around a larger mound that served as warehouse and provided the Clan Mother with a residence commensurate with her considerable status.

She had a tendency to become irritable during the final stages of pregnancy and was quick to make her annoyance known. The snakelike head rose and rotated from left to right. Speech came from deep in the back of her throat and emerged as a series of variegated croaks, burps, and coughs. "What's taking so long? *We* are hungry."

The "we" was a not so subtle reminder that she spoke for not only herself but for a generation unborn. Cowed, but careful lest they drop her, the litter bearers hurried up the path.

The warriors, their mottled green-black bodies still damp from the trip downstream bowed respectfully as the conveyance passed. Many of them, all of those in their prime, had mated with the Clan Mother, and might have fertilized her eggs. That being the case, they would fight to the death to protect not only her but her progeny.

The litter passed out of broken sunlight and into the mound's cool, dark interior. Once the stretcher came to a stop, the Clan Mother used her long willowy arms to support her grossly distended belly, lurched to her feet, and shuffled toward the carefully constructed throne. It was made from tightly woven reeds fitted onto a frame made of steam-bent wood and decorated with colorful flyer feathers, clan charms, and beads provided by gunrunners. It creaked under her considerable weight. "Well?" she demanded. "Where is our food?"

A platter appeared. It was laden with dried water skimmers, spiced flit fish, and recently harvested grot roots. A fine feast indeed. The Clan Mother dug in. The eggs were hungry. Words emerged between bites of food. Some of it landed on her stomach, tumbled off, and fell to the floor. Minute scavengers moved in to harvest the crumbs. "Who lurks in the darkness? What do you want?"

Drik, who had been waiting patiently toward the back wall, took three steps forward. He had fertilized the Clan Mother for the first time that year and felt certain it was his strong sperm that had so efficiently quickened her eggs. "I come bearing news."

"So?" the Clan Mother said imperiously, "out with it!"

But Drik, who had long fantasized about such a moment, refused to be hurried. He chose his words with care. "Five of the off-world intruders left their metal island, crossed the food lake, and entered the jungle."

The Clan Mother paused in midbite. Food dribbled down onto her well-rounded belly. "How many of them were hiding in machines?"

"None," Drik replied, "although two looked strange, like weed dreams come to life."

The Clan Mother chewed thoughtfully. There was very little point in attacking the machines, or off-worlders protected by the machines, due to the heavy casualties that her warriors were certain to sustain. But this was something different. This was an opportunity to capture weapons *and* punish the sky people at the same time. "Wait for them in the swamp. Kill them there."

Drik bowed. "Yes, Clan Mother . . . It shall be as you say."

It rained like hell about two in the afternoon, a downpour that drenched the treetops and sent water cascading from leaf to leaf, to soak those down below. Hebo seemed even happier, Morla-Ka barely noticed, and the humans were miserable. The water found its way under their collars, seeped over their shoulders, and entered their boots.

The ground turned soft, sucked at their boots, and drained their energy. The branches that brushed their shoulders, the vines they slashed in two, and the knee-high foliage all conspired to deliver even more water to their moisture-laden clothing. And, as though that weren't bad enough, many of the local life forms seemed energized by the afternoon soaking. The hopped, slithered, and swung from branch to branch.

Hebo knew the point position was dangerous, knew he was showing off, but couldn't help himself. Drang was so pleasant, so much like Hive, that he felt at home. Maybe that's why he missed the vine viper, mistook the reptile for one of the green runners that dangled from the canopy, and whacked at it with his machete. Not edge on, which might have killed the creature, but with the flat of the blade, which served to make it angry.

The snake, which hung head down, released its grip on a branch twenty feet over the Ramanthian's head, allowed the full weight of its long sinuous body to fall on the officer's torso, and struck for the alien's neck.

The tactic would have worked on a frog, or on a human, but not on a jungle-evolved Ramanthian. Fangs grated on dark brown chitin, tool arms grabbed a section of the viper's body, and a razor-sharp beak slashed through skin and muscle.

The reptile reacted with understandable violence. It

whipped coils of rock-hard flesh around the Ramanthian's thorax and started to squeeze.

Seebo, true to the DNA for which his ancestor had been chosen, took immediate action. Not because he had developed a sudden fondness for geeks, but because he was who he was, and couldn't stand idly by.

The human's assault weapon was useless, not unless he wanted to kill Hebo as well, so the clone drew his combat knife, threw himself into the fray, and grabbed a thigh-thick section of the viper's muscular body. The blade had two edges, one straight, the other equipped with sawlike teeth. It was the second that proved most effective as Seebo sawed through the red-tinged white meat.

Hebo made a note of the human's attack, felt the snake shudder in response, and knew it was distracted. That being the case, the Ramanthian felt for the short sword that projected up over his right shoulder, pressed a button on the hilt, and felt the weapon come to life.

The force blade made a sizzling sound as it burned through the reptile's flesh. The viper's head bounced off the jungle floor, the body gave one last convulsion and finally lay still.

Mondulo stepped over a section of the long serpentine body and said, "Good thing it was only half grown," and took the point.

Seebo started to laugh, Hebo made strange popping sounds, and Booly shook his head in wonder. It wasn't the kind of bonding he had envisioned—but something was better than nothing.

Dinner looked a lot like lunch, hell, it was *exactly* like lunch, which suited Mondulo just fine. The jungle offered enough variety, and it was nice to deal with something you could count on. The noncom stirred the stroganoff with the tip of his combat knife and watched his charges prepare for the night.

The Ramanthian turned out to be one heck of a tree

climber, which came as something of a surprise and made
the noncom just a little uneasy. The bugs were allies today—but how 'bout tomorrow? Fighting an army of He-
bos in a triple-canopy jungle would be a nasty business.
Still, a rough and ready sort of teamwork had emerged,
which was the point of the exercise.

Morla-Ka whacked trees down with five or six blows of
his machete, Seebo cut the resulting poles into sections,
and Hebo carried them aloft. That's where Booly took the
raw materials, made some modifications, and added them
to the steadily growing platform. He used a timber hitch
to get started, followed by square lashings to secure the
basic framework.

Then, when that task was complete, he tied a series of
forty manharness hitches into a doubled piece of rope,
passed sturdy sticks through the matching loops, and
pulled them tight. The result was a crude but serviceable
ladder. Not a necessity where he, Seebo, and Mondulo
were concerned, and useless for a body like Hebo's, but a
courtesy for the Hudathan. It creaked when Morla-Ka
made his way upward, but it held and was easy to hoist
up onto the platform.

Once everyone was in place and the humans had
smeared their bodies with Drang-specific insect repellent,
it was time to eat. Mondulo stood guard as the officers
grumbled over their rations, the day creatures went into
hiding, and the night hunters started to emerge.

The first hint of their presence was heard rather than
seen. There were the clicks, pops, and buzzing noises associated with the local insect population, quickly followed
by the grunts, howls, and occasional screeches made by
higher life-forms. All of which made Booly glad that they
were up off the jungle floor. He finished his meal, used
some water from a canteen to speed the last lump on its
way, and let his weight rest on a tree trunk. The moon was
up, and that, combined with a hole in the canopy, provided
some light to see by.

Seebo and Hebo were reliving their battle with the snake, while Mondulo sat with eyes closed, and Morla-Ka cleaned his assault weapon. It was strange how the trip into the jungle had served to transform these officers into regular troops. Nowhere was that more visible than in the way they talked. The conversation was about the day's adventures, about the food, and presumably, when he stepped out of earshot, about what an asshole he was. Because if there's anything grunts like to do, it's bitch about the command structure, which in their case came down to one single individual.

Booly felt an insect land on his cheek, swatted, and knew it had escaped. A tree dweller screeched and was answered from a long way off. Seebo said something to the Ramanthian, who made the popping noises that equated to laughter.

So, Booly asked himself, which one of them should I designate as second in command? Which one can the Confederacy count on? Seebo? Because he's human? Morla-Ka because he isn't? Hebo as a compromise? No, those were political considerations. The one I choose should be the best leader available—and to hell with the way they're packaged.

The thought served to remind him of his own mixed ancestry, of the fact that some people would regard his command structure as something of a freak show, a thought that struck him as funny. Booly laughed.

Seebo looked at Hebo, Morla-Ka looked up from his weapon, and Mondulo opened a single eye. The old man was a nutcase . . . but what else was new? Officers were weird, and sergeants, who served as the Legion's backbone, would never be able to understand them.

Something made a gibbering sound. A cloud cloaked the moon. The noncom smiled and drifted off to sleep.

•   •   •

Drik floated just beneath the surface of the dark, murky water. It was thick with algae, sediment, and hundreds of tiny life-forms all vying for their share of the swamp-born soup. Air bladders located beneath his armpits allowed the warrior to control the extent of his buoyancy. That being the case, he could hang suspended in the water for hours or even days should that become necessary.

But it *wouldn't* be necessary—not unless his senses had suddenly decided to betray him. A flock of flyers had fluttered into the air moments before. A school of swamp darters had propelled themselves toward deeper water, and he could *feel* an alien presence. None of the clan members had ever asked him about such impressions, since they had them too, but a xenoanthropologist would have been interested in the fact that while some portion of the data required to generate them flowed from "normal" sensory input, the rest stemmed from something else, which if not telepathy, was somehow related.

In any case, Drik "felt" the aliens approach, could distinguish between different personas, and, had he been allowed to observe them for a longer period of time, might have been able to describe their various emotions.

His emotions were clear. The off-worlders had murdered members of his clan, poisoned the planet's water, and interfered with the Great Mother's plan. The crimes were clear—and so was the punishment: death.

Booly smelled the swamp long before he actually saw it. The damp, slightly malodorous scent of decayed plant life, combined with the stink of stagnant water, sent invisible tendrils into the jungle as if to warn of the terrain ahead.

That being the case, the legionnaire was far from surprised when his machete slashed through the final screen of vegetation to reveal a broadly shelving mud bank and an expanse of coppery brown water backed by a stand of what Booly remembered as sponge trees, tall woody tubes that contained membranes through which swamp water was continually filtered. Nutrients were removed, waste products were added, and what remained oozed into the estuary.

Booly scanned the area for danger, failed to identify any, and moved to one side. Morla-Ka stepped forward, followed by Mondulo, Seebo, and Hebo. The latter shuffled backward, his world divided into hundreds of images.

The noncom squinted into the brighter light, directed a stream of spit into the toffee-colored water, and removed a grenade from one of his cargo pockets. The pin had been pulled, and the object was high in the air before Booly managed to spit the words out. "Sergeant, what the hell are you . . . ?"

An explosion, followed by a geyser of momentarily white water, served to punctuate the sentence. "Just some reconnaissance by fire, sir. Stir things up, see what's what, if ya know what I mean."

Booly swallowed his anger. "So much for keeping our presence secret."

Mondulo looked surprised. "*Secret?* Beggin' the general's pardon, but we ain't got no fraxin' secrets. The frogs know where we are and what we've been doin'. Well, not *what* we're doin', since that wouldn't make any sense to a frog, but what *they* think we're doin', which is stompin' all over the Great Mother's sacred body and pissin' on her face. The slimy bastards are out there all right—the only question is where."

Booly swallowed his pride, nodded, and said, "Carry on."

Mondulo did—and more grenades flew through the air. The geysers formed a tidy row.

Though moderated by the density of the surrounding water, the explosions wounded a warrior named Gril and delivered what felt like a series of blows to Drik's abdomen. He felt the air rush out of his lungs, stuck his nose up through the surface, and drew some much-needed air. If the aliens saw, they gave no sign of it, and the warrior was gone before the water started to settle.

Other warriors, too far from the bang thing to be affected by it, towed the half-conscious Gril away. The first blow had been struck—but far from the last.

The Hudathan's machete made a solid thunking sound as it bit into the side of the T-T tree, produced another wedge of flying wood, and squeaked free. The blade, harnessed to three hundred pounds of bone and muscle, had already made short work of fourteen carefully matched eight-inch trunks. The trees, which bore only four branches apiece, were strong but buoyant, important qualities for a raft.

Seebo had lobbied for a lunch break but been forced to give way under Mondulo's insistence that the team construct their vessel prior to eating. Now, with hunger driving them on, the officers were hard at work. The first task was to assemble the materials in the proper manner. The noncom was a strict taskmaster. "This is called a 'gripper bar raft' 'cause of the way we place two lengths of wood on the ground and place logs on top of them. "Now, if you would be so kind as to lay the logs at right angles to the crosspieces, we'll be damned close to done."

Booly assisted Seebo, and the majority of the logs had been rolled, dragged, and kicked into place by the time Morla-Ka arrived with his latest arboreal victim.

Then, with the tree trunks lying side by side, the last two crosspieces were lowered into position and secured to the first pair, "gripping" the logs between them.

Once that was accomplished, it was a relatively simple matter to construct an A-frame-style support structure, secure it in place with guylines, and add the pole-mounted paddle-style rudder. Once the last knot had been tied, the entire team took a moment to admire their work. The finished raft was about twenty feet long and nine wide. Though flat, and not especially pretty, Seebo figured it would float. "I christen thee *Pancake*," the clone said, sprinkling some canteen water on the craft's bow. "Long may you sail."

Other and in some case more colorful names were submitted for consideration, but *Pancake* stuck, and they broke for lunch. No one had given much thought to Hebo's rations up till that point, but when he opened a container of grubs, squirted some sort of stimulant into the mix and brought the creatures to squirming life, *that* got their attention.

The entire group watched in horrified fascination as the Ramanthian speared one of the creatures, shoved it under his parrotlike beak, and bit down. A mixture of blood and intestinal contents sprayed outwards. Seebo shook his head in amazement. "Jeez, Hebo . . . that was gross."

The statement would have been a breach in etiquette within diplomatic circles but was well within the realm of what one legionnaire would say to another. Which way would the Ramanthian react? Booly waited to see.

There was a pause while the insectlike alien considered the human's comment. When he spoke, the words had the hard, flat sound of his computer-driven translator. "Screw you, Seebo, *and* the test tube you were born in."

It was *exactly* how the typical legionnaire would respond. The rest of the group laughed, and Booly smiled. The team was coming together. The officer closed his eyes, thought of Maylo Chien-Chu, and wondered what she was doing.

The *Pancake* was launched with more swearing than ceremony. By constructing the raft up on the mud bank, the team had kept their feet dry. Now, in order to launch their vessel, the officers had to lift it. Morla-Ka made his part look easy, while the rest of the group strained, stumbled, and swore as they struggled to break the logs free from the mud, hoisted the *Pancake* into the air, and carried her down into the water. She landed with a splash. Everyone got wet, and waves rolled toward the opposite side of the estuary.

"All right," Mondulo said, squinting into the sky. "We got ten miles of swamp to cross before nightfall. Time to get our asses in gear."

Drik, along with fifteen of the clan's most fearsome warriors floated just below the surface of the water and watched the aliens board their clumsy-looking craft. They knew the little bay was little more than a fingerlike extension of the great northern swamp. There was one way in and one way out. All they had to do was sit at the entry point and wait. The ambush was ready. Drik felt a rising sense of excitement, allowed more water to enter his auxiliary bladders, and sank further below the surface. His war party did likewise.

Mondulo stood with the long half-peeled steering oar clamped under one arm while he read the coordinates supplied by his Legion-issue wrist term and examined a map. Seebo, and his Ramanthian counterpart stood back to back, scanning for trouble. Morla-Ka and Booly used poles to push the *Pancake* out and away from the shore.

The scenery seemed to glide past as if mounted on rollers. A weed-draped snag appeared off to the left, bobbed as a bird launched itself into the air, and fell behind. That's when Booly noticed how quiet their environment had become, as if the entire swamp was holding its breath, waiting for something to happen. The legionnaire felt the fur rise along his spine, started to say something, but never got it out.

Four warriors rose as one. Each held a well-sharpened blade, each cut through the bindings that held the gripper bars in place, and each flutter kicked out of the way. It took a moment for the raft to come apart. Seebo was the first to notice. "The raft! Something's wrong!"

But there was no time to respond, no time to make repairs, no time to mount a response. One after another they fell into the water. It was blood warm. Booly assumed the raft had come apart of its own accord, and realized how wrong he was when a two-foot long harpoon bounced off his chest armor. Mondulo gave the alarm: "Frogs!"

Bubbles exploded around Booly's face as he went under, thought about the assault rifle, and remembered that it was slung across his back. The officer groped for the combat knife, thumbed the release, and saw a narrow snakelike head emerge from the surrounding murk.

Something gleamed, and the legionaire managed to catch the warrior's arm as a blade flashed for his throat. He brought his own knife around in a long loop, felt the steel hesitate as it sliced through flesh, and saw the face convulse. The body fell away. Something jumped him from behind. An arm slithered around his neck and began to tighten. He needed air! The frog pulled him down.

Hebo had a secret. Like most members of his race he could swim when forced to do so but hated the water. Land was what his body had evolved to deal with—and where his psyche was at ease. Fear rose like a wall as the logs drifted apart. Frogs! He saw them floating below the surface! The Ramanthian squeezed the triggerlike firing sleeve that activated his weapon. The water acted to slow most of the bullets but an individual named Ralk had the misfortune to be only inches beneath the surface when the alien fired. The hard ball ammo cut him nearly in two, flooded the already murky water with his blood, and cut the opposition by one. The logs parted, Hebo floundered, and thrashed toward shore.

Mondulo felt the harpoon slide up under his arm, where the armor couldn't protect him, and enter his chest cavity. There was time, not much, but time to press the 9 mm handgun against the phib's gut, feel the recoil, and harvest the look of surprise.

Then, before the pain could make itself felt, there was another increment of time in which to wonder why it was *he*, the fraxing expert, who was going to frigging die, while Booly and his team of XT weirdoes would probably emerge unscathed. But that's how it was with officers . . . they . . . A knife sliced through Mondulo's throat, and the thinking was over.

Morla-Ka felt the logs part beneath his massive boots, heard Hebo open fire, and drew the machete, Had Drik and his companions known to look and been trained to interpret the Hudathan's expression, they would have been frightened. Morla-Ka smiled as he launched himself over the side, landed on something solid, and carried it down. Drik felt the crushing weight, managed to flip himself face-up, and wished that he hadn't. The alien looked monstrous, like something from a nightmare, like the last thing he would ever see.

Seebo fired into the water, wished he could see what he was shooting at, and felt something grab his ankle. The clone looked, saw the long sinewy arm, and corrected his aim. The 5.56 mm rounds chewed the limb off at the elbow, the logs rolled under his boots, and he hit the water sideways.

Booly back-elbowed his assailant, felt the arm loosen, and ducked through the loop. He wanted to surface, wanted to breathe, but knew he shouldn't. The frog would follow, nail him from below, and that would be the end of it.

The human turned, saw the warrior raise some sort of spear gun, and felt the shaft race past the side of his face. A single shot weapon? The officer hoped so as he lunged forward, grabbed the launcher with his left hand, and pulled it toward him.

The frog could have let go, *should* have let go, but was reluctant to part with his most prized possession. He paid with his life.

Booly rammed the knife up into the warrior's unprotected abdomen, felt the gun come free, and kicked for the surface. His gear plus the weapon across his back weighed him down. His body urged him to breathe anything, water if that's what was available, but his mind refused to do so.

The legionnaire pulled with his arms, kicked with his feet, and willed himself upwards. The murk seemed to clear after a bit, his head broke the surface, and he opened his mouth. Air entered his lungs, a log bumped his shoulder, and he managed to capture it with an arm. Nothing had ever felt so solid and reassuring.

Hebo flailed right and left, felt one of his pincers encounter something soft, and a frog fell away. A ribbon of blood trailed behind. The bottom! Where was the bottom? The Ramanthian aimed himself toward shore and started to paddle. Then, just when it seemed as if he would swim forever, the alien felt mud under his feet. He paused, tested to see if the bottom would take his weight, and discovered that it would. That's when the War Hebo uttered a long chittering challenge, turned his back to the jungle, and invited attack.

Morla-Ka broke the surface like a breaching whale. He spouted a mouthful of foul-tasting water and turned his attention to the warriors who hung from various parts of his mighty frame.

Drik, who had the signal misfortune to be clutched to the alien's chest, felt the hug start to tighten. What seemed to last for an eternity took less than three seconds. The warrior felt his spine snap, lost contact with his extremities, and wondered where the pain was. Darkness came instead.

In spite of the fact that the Hudathan had successfully dealt with one attacker, three remained. Hebo saw that and knew he should go to the other officer's assistance but was reluctant to leave the security of solid ground.

Morla-Ka bellowed his anger as a knife entered his shoulder, threw one of his assailants into the air, and struggled with the others.

Hebo saw the splash, cursed his luck, and threw himself forward. The Ramanthian hadn't traveled more than three feet when warriors rose to either side of him, threw a fishnet high into the air, and used ropes to pull it down over his head. Pincers trapped, legs thrashing, Hebo waited to die.

Seebo kicked a frog in the stomach, felt the top of his head hit the underside of a log, and swallowed a mouthful of water. It went down the wrong way. The soldier kicked, broke the surface, and fought to clear his airway. He did so just in time to see Morla-Ka break the surface, covered with frogs. A phib went flying. A knife flashed downward. The Hudathan bellowed in pain. There was no room for error, not given the tolerances involved, but Seebo knew the extent of his skill. Where it started, how far to trust it, and when to stop. By some miracle, the assault weapon was still there—clutched in the clone's hands. He brought the rifle up, fired a burst of three shots, and saw a frog take the bullets. It screeched, fell back into the swamp, and quickly disappeared.

Steel flashed. Morla-Ka roared with rage, broke the grip that encircled his neck, took hold of an arm, and jerked the warrior up over his shoulder. The long sinuous neck was an obvious point of vulnerability. The Hudathan got a grip on it, twisted, and heard something pop. The body went limp. He let the warrior go.

Though filled with the rage of battle, his body pumping chemicals into his blood, Morla-Ka's mind had stayed in control. He *saw* the net fall over Hebo's torso and considered his options. He could let the bug die, a rather reasonable course of action given the manner in which the Ramanthian government hoped to annex Hudathan-controlled worlds, or—and this possibility went against all of the officer's instincts—Morla-Ka could wade out, pull his sidearm, and shoot the frogs in the head.

The sound of his own gunfire served to alert the War Commander that thought had been translated to action. The bodies fell away, splashed into the water, and floated with arms extended. Silence descended over the lagoon. Those frogs that were still alive had escaped.

Booly saw some mottled fabric, swam over, grabbed

Mondulo's battle harness, and towed the body to shore. The others salvaged what gear they could, recovered most of the logs, and pulled them up onto the mud. Once that was accomplished, Booly took control. "We'll bury the sergeant, make camp, and spend the night up in the trees. Seebo, Morla-Ka needs some first aid. See what you can do. The raft can wait till morning."

"We will use wire to lash the binders on next time," Hebo said reflectively. "That should stop them."

"Yes," Booly replied wearily, "I think it will."

Dinner was a somber affair, the night passed slowly, and dawn brought rain. Not a downpour, but a steady drumbeat, that peppered the surface of the lagoon.

Each member of the team paused by the mound of newly turned earth and said good-bye in their own special way. But it was Seebo who quoted a long-dead poet—a legionnaire named Alan Seeger:

> When Spring comes back with rustling shade,
> And apple blossoms fill the air,
> I have a rendezvous with Death,
> When Spring brings back blue days and fair.

Booly nodded solemnly and followed the rest of the team down to the muddy beach. The work went quickly, and the heavily reinforced raft was ready less than three hours later. No one bothered to name this one, no one questioned the grenades that blew holes in the water, and no one looked back.

The Clan Mother awoke to an overwhelming sense of loss. The eggs? No, they were safely contained within her abdomen.

Then it came, the sudden realization that the thin tenuous thread that connected her to the leader of the war party had been severed. Drik was dead.

The Clan Mother cried out in sorrow, attendants rushed to her side, and the entire village began to mourn. For the warriors, yes; but for themselves as well, since each death weakened the social organism. For there were crops to be harvested, fish to catch, and repairs to be made. And ultimately, should the village be unable to defend itself, another clan would force the group to surrender its identity and accept outside rule.

Clouds hid the sun, darkness settled into her heart, and the Clan Mother started to cry.

The pick-up zone consisted of a flat scrub-covered island. The clearing, which had been enlarged with machetes, was barely large enough to accommodate the fly-form already on its way.

Outside of their weapons, which looked as clean as the morning they had left, the team was dirty, ragged, and tired. Still, they lay in a circle, facing outwards, ready for anything, a disposition that was indicative of the mutual dependency, respect, and trust developed during the last few days.

Booly considered saying as much, heard the approaching aircraft, and decided to let it go. Words have their place . . . but blood binds all. The officer turned his face upwards, gloried in the way the raindrops struck it, and was grateful to be alive.

10

The key to opening new markets is to establish
two-way communication. Failing to do so will often
lead to disaster.

Prithian Handbook for Merchant Apprentices
Standard year 2842

Somewhere Along the Rim, the
Confederacy of Sentient Beings

The Prithian freighter bore a vague resemblance to the beings who had designed it, in that the ship possessed wings
for use within planetary atmospheres, which were folded
while traveling through space, a strategy that allowed the
birdlike beings not only to indulge their love of atmospheric flight but to avoid the delays so often associated
with orbital parking slots. It was all part of doing what the
Prithians did well, which was to carry small, highly valuable cargoes over relatively short distances leaving the
high-volume long-haul business to the big conglomerates.

It was a niche market, which was perfect for a numer-
ically small race having a low birthrate and rather insular
ways. So insular—and some said self-serving—that the
Prithians had ignored repeated invitations to join the Confederacy, while continuing to profit from the markets the

organization had created and the stability it fostered. A policy that saved the merchant race a significant amount of money.

All of which explained why the *Dawn Song* was jumping from one system to the next, delivering freight to a series of undistinguished planets, when it surfaced in the wrong place at the wrong time.

Having arranged for the soft body to delete its other self, the Hoon had lingered for a bit, taking the time necessary to review the fleet's operating system and root out those instructions authored by its recently deceased twin. A tedious process, but one that would ensure that the Hoon's orders would be followed by every unit in the fleet, regardless of which entity had controlled it during the recent past.

That's why its forces were waiting there, with very little to do, when the *Dawn Song* dropped hyper, appeared on the detector screens as a spark of light, and attempted to run.

The Hoon noted the event, dispatched two fighters to deal with it, and returned to what it had been doing: Reviewing each and every line of code that comprised the operating system for the fleet's maintenance units. After all, the artificial intelligence thought to itself, *I'm* clever, which means my twin was clever, which means traps could have been laid. And where better than deep within some aspect of my own body? Which was how the computer regarded the thousands upon thousands of machines that comprised the reconstituted fleet. Time passed, the AI searched, and the *Dawn Song* ran for her life.

Whereas the control rooms on Hudathan ships resembled those on human vessels, and vice versa, the Prithians took an entirely different approach. There was no single place from which to pilot the *Dawn Song* anymore than there was a special place to sleep or eat. After all the birdlike beings reasoned, why limit oneself when there was no reason to do so?

The entire concept of a human-style control room stemmed from the days of sailing ships, steam locomotives, and early ground vehicles—times when the need to see where one was going, plus analog-style controls, forced the helmsman, engineer, or driver to stay in one place. But now, more than a thousand years later, there was no need for such limitations beyond that required for their own psychological comfort.

All of which explained why Prithians like Per Pok preferred to con their vessels via audio interface and simply "sang" their instructions to the ship's central computer.

Pok, who had a yellow beak, blue eyes, white head feathers, and the crimson shoulder plumage that marked his membership in the scarlet flock, cocked his head to one side and listened as the ship warbled its report. A report so strange, so essentially nonsensical, that merchant demanded to hear it again.

Then, convinced that he really had dropped into the midst of an enormous fleet, Pok "called" for his daughter. Her name took the form of a short three-syllable song.

Veera, who was a good deal smaller than her father but bore the same cape of reddish feathers, looked up from the component-strewn workbench. As with any vessel of her size and complexity, the *Dawn Song* required a good deal of maintenance—something Veera and a half dozen robots had responsibility for. There were twelve ways to sing her name each having a different meaning. This one meant, "come to me—and do so immediately." It was one of the first communications a youngster learned, and Veera warbled the appropriate response.

The teenager placed the tuning wand on the tray-shaped work surface and entered the tunnelway that led to the portion of the *Dawn Song* where her father spent most of his time, a circular space that functioned as office, roost, and galley.

As with any space-going creature, Veera was very at-
tuned to the feel of the ship. She noted the slight increase
in vibration, one or two degrees of additional heat, and a
change in the neverending "ship song," a sort of humming
sound that provided the crew with feedback and was as
unique to *Dawn Song* as Veera's variegated back plumage
was to her. The vessel spoke of how difficult it was to
make more speed while simultaneously charging the accumulators—a process that preceded a hyperspace jump
and normally took most of a day. They were in trouble
then—and running from something. The youngster increased her pace and emerged into the all-purpose living
area. "Father? What's wrong?"

Pok finished his latest instruction to the ship, forced his
feathers to fall into something resembling "peaceful rest,"
and turned toward his daughter. The extent to which the
teenager resembled her mother never ceased to amaze him.
The same expressive eyes, slender body, and gorgeous
plumage. How long had Malla been dead now? Only two
years? It seemed longer. But all things end—separations
included. "Some sort of fleet, my dear, though nothing
we've seen before. It's *huge* . . . and clearly hostile. At
least two ships are closing with us as I speak. I tried to
make contact but no response. I want you to enter the
lifeboat and strap yourself in. *If*, and I emphasize *if*, they
attack, we'll try to escape."

Veera knew her father better than anyone else in the
universe. The lie was as obvious as the brittle manner in
which the song was sung, the high conflict-ready way in
which Pok held his head, and the neck plumage that refused to lie flat. "No! I won't go. Not till *you* do."

Per Pok was far from surprised. His daughter was not
only willful, but less deferential than was appropriate, the
direct result of living with her father in such confined quarters. He fluttered the feathers along the outside surface of
what had once been wings. The gesture meant "I love you"
and served to distract Veera just long enough for her father

to produce the spray tube, aim it in her direction, and press the trigger.

The inhalant, which was found in every Prithian's on-board medical kit, functioned as a powerful anesthetic. Veera barely had time to register the nonverbal communication and realize what the tube was before darkness pulled her down.

The merchant managed to catch the teenager before she hit the deck and swept her into his arms. She was light, *very* light, and easy to carry. Careful not to breathe, lest he inhale some of the still-lingering gas, the Prithian hurried away.

The ship song had changed by then, had grown more intense, and warned of approaching vessels. Pok scurried down a passageway into the ship's belly. A hatch opened in response to the Prithian's command, and indicator lights began to flash. The very act of entering the bay had activated the lifeboat's various on-board systems. Any one of the four seats would do. The merchant placed his daughter in the one nearest to the hatch and strapped the youngster in place.

Then, knowing he would never see Veera again, Pok backed out through the lock. He sang "I love you," and the hatch cycled closed. The *Dawn Song* shuddered as a missile exploded against her protective force field and started to cry. It was a keening sound like an animal in pain. The Prithian had one more thing to accomplish . . . something that might make all the difference. He turned and hurried away.

The fighters launched their weapons against the Prithian ship with no more emotion than a pair of maintenance bots might demonstrate while scrubbing a deck. They locked onto the target, activated their launchers, and waited for the range to close.

Then, just as the fugitive vessel came within reach of their long-range missiles, it seemed to vanish as a container fell free, exploded, and scattered preheated chaff in every direction. It was an old trick—and one the Sheen were well-prepared to deal with. It did buy some time, however, because as the fighters waited for their sensors to clear the *Dawn Song* continued to flee.

Bio bods might have missed the lifeboat as it tumbled end over end through the chaff, dismissed it as unimportant, or, in a moment of pity, allowed the fugitive to escape. But not the Sheen. They identified the seemingly inert lump of matter as having an 82.1% match to the identification parameters typical of a Type 4 auxiliary spacecraft, which, based on a reading of its core temperature was equipped with a hyperdrive. This information was transmitted to a nearly insignificant aspect of the Hoon, which routed it to a salvage ship, which was already under way.

In the meantime the chaff had cleared, the machines took note of the fact that the quarry had turned on them, and fired their weapons.

Knowing that the *Dawn Song*'s relatively puny arsenal would have very little impact on his pursuers, and knowing he was about to die, Per Pok chose to target all the offensive weaponry he had on only one of the incoming fighters. Then, eyes closed, he thought of home and his fervent desire to go there.

Unit AV-7621769 registered the machine equivalent of surprise as the incoming missiles hit his shield and hammered their way through. Most destroyed themselves in the process but one managed to penetrate the hull.

Thousands of miles away the Hoon "felt" what amounted to a tiny pinprick, a unit of machine pain so small as to barely register on its consciousness, yet annoying nonetheless. The AI accessed the back feed from the surviving fighter just in time to witness the explosions. There were three of them, each more powerful than the last, as the Prithian vessel ceased to exist.

Satisfied, and eager to return to what it had been doing, the machine intelligence severed the connection.

Veera felt pain at the back of her head, struggled to penetrate the thick gray fog, and remembered the tube. Had her actually father aimed the device at her? Or was that a dream? The teenager forced her eyes to focus, saw where she was, and knew the truth. She remembered the fleet, the argument with her father, and the hiss of anesthetic. The youngster threw herself forward, felt the harness cut into her shoulders, and called out loud, "Father? Where are you?"

But there was no answer. He was gone. Just like her mother. The weight of Veera's sorrow threatened to crush her chest. But there was no time to mourn, to sing the death song, or to enter the traditional fast.

Something grabbed the lifeboat, jerked it back and forth, and drew it in. Something *huge*. Veera touched controls located in the arm of her chair and a 3-D vid screen popped into life. What she saw was a ship, a *strange* ship that shimmered as if lit from within, and a steadily growing rectangle of light. A hatch! The aliens planned to take her in! Veera felt her heart race and wondered what to do. The Sheen swallowed the lifeboat whole.

Though successful, from the Hoon's viewpoint at least, the assassination, and Jepp's role in it, left the human feeling depressed. He had been manipulated, used, and subsequently ignored, none of which was consistent with his status as God's prophet, *or* his position as head of the New Church, an organization that would be of critical importance to all sentients once they realized how wonderful it was.

Still, even the creation of a glorious new position for himself had not been sufficient to lift the human's spirits. The truth was that he was both bored and lonely. Yes, members of his mechanical flock attended to his needs round the clock and, with the occasional exception of Henry, agreed with everything he said. But that wasn't half as pleasant as he had assumed it would be . . . not without genuine feedback.

All of which accounted for why the one-time prospector had resumed his once habitual explorations of the ship and the fleet it was part of. Except that now, aided by both Alpha and Sam, the human had a good deal more access to things than he had had before. Things like the fleet's electronic nervous system. That's how Jepp heard about the fugitive ship, the lifeboat, and the fact that it had been salvaged.

The process of being there when the salvage ship landed, of entering the bay only moments after it was pressurized, reminded the ex-prospector of his childhood. There had been two or three birthdays when he received presents . . . and the emotions were very similar. The way the excitement started to build, the rising sense of anticipation, and the delightful delay. Then, when he could stand it no longer, the pleasure of opening the packages, except *this* present was wrapped in metal.

The lock opened, the human stepped out, and eyed the bay. Silvery strings of nano hung from the overhead, slithered along the deck, and caressed the waiting ships. There were thousands, no *millions* of the tiny repair and maintenance machines, all linked together to create mechanical organisms. Organisms that could take ships apart *and* put them back together. Mindful of the fact that the "snake" nano had a tendency to slap unauthorized intruders, Jepp was careful to watch his step.

The Prithian lifeboat was coaxed out of the salvage vessel's hold by two tractor-sized robots. It might contain anything, or *anybody*, since the very existence of such a craft hinted at a survivor, or at least the possibility of one. Something Jepp wanted—or thought he did.

Finally, when the pod-shaped lifeboat had been removed and placed on the deck, a hatch started to open. The prospector, who prided himself on his knowledge of ships, was stumped. The vessel wasn't human, Turr, Dweller, or . . .

Veera, terrified of who or what she might encounter, peeked out through the newly created opening. She wore a translator, an Araballazanie device common to Prithian merchant vessels, and her song sounded strange indeed. It was randomly transformed in Ramanthian, standard, and a half dozen other languages on the chance that one of them would be understood. "Is anyone there?"

Jepp heard a snatch of standard, cleared his throat, and yelled to ensure that she would hear him. "Yes, you can come out. The Sheen won't hurt you. They have very little interest in biologicals."

Veera heard the words as a series of chirps and twitters. A human! What was *he* doing here? Could she trust him? Not that she had much choice.

Slowly at first, head swiveling back and forth, the Prithian emerged from the lifeboat. The nano-draped compartment was strange, very strange, and took some getting used to. The human was flanked by two robots, one to each side, with a third perched on his shoulder. He approached slowly, as if worried he might scare the teenager away. "Hello, my name is Jepp."

Veera, more from habit than anything else, offered the curtsy due anyone older than she was. "My name is Veera Pok."

The Thraki robot transformed itself into the "jump" mode, leaped onto her shoulder, and sang the original sentence back to her. "My name is Veera Pok."

Prithians don't smile—but they do ruffle their neck feathers. Hers fluttered accordingly. "You speak Prithian."

"You speak Prithian," Sam chirruped. "My name is Veera Pok."

Jepp smiled and waved at their surroundings. "Welcome to the family Veera—Come on, let's salvage whatever rations you have before the nano disassemble your boat."

The suggestion made sense. Like it or not—Veera was home.

Life's picture is constantly undergoing change. The spirit beholds a new world every moment.

Rumi
Persian Sufi poet
Standard year circa 1250

Planet Zynig-47, the Confederacy of Sentient Beings

Having found it impossible to sleep, Admiral Hooloo Isan Andragna slipped out of bed, shivered in response to the breeze that found its way through a still unrepaired crack, and cursed the technicians who were supposed to have sealed it. While it was true that each and every one of them had spent their entire lives in space and knew next to nothing about the restoration of glass buildings, they *did* know something about airtight structures, or were *supposed* to, which made the transgression all the more annoying.

Careful lest he disturb his mate, Andragna dressed in the dark and slipped out into the courtyard. His pet robot jumped off a chair and scuttled along behind.

Used as he was to life aboard spaceships, the courtyard struck the military officer as unnecessarily large, although he did admire the fused glass tiles and the manner in which they went together to make complex geometric patterns. Some glowed as if lit from within—and served to illuminate a ghostly path. It led toward the remains of a gate. The Hudathans had attacked the planet many years before, murdered most of the inhabitants, and lost the ensuing war. Most of the surviving structures, his house included, had been left to the vagaries of the weather. The robot beeped softly and scrambled up a leg. It settled onto a shoulder and warmed his left ear.

Sentries, placed there to protect his wife and him against the possibility of assassins, stood a little straighter. They *looked* dangerous, what with their assault rifles and all, but could they really protect him against the increasingly disaffected Runners, elements of the Priesthood, and the odd psychopath?

No, it didn't seem likely. What protection he had stemmed more from tradition, from the rule of law, than the obstacle posed by his guards. The military officer gestured for the sentries to stay where they were and ventured out into the center of the ancient courtyard.

Two moons hung against the velvety blackness of space. One of them was natural, the result of cosmic chance, or the work of the great god Rathna, depending on who you cared to listen to: the scientists or the priesthood. The other satellite was one of the arks his ancestors had built and used to propel their progeny out among the stars. Both glowed with reflected light.

Something about the thin, pale light brought the ruins to life. Andragna imagined the clutch of structures the way they must have been, humming to some forgotten purpose, unaware of the horror ahead. The Ramanthians said that the indigenous sentients, a race of wormlike creatures, had been slaughtered by the Hudathans and driven to the edge of extinction—the same fate that he and the rest of the Thraki people could expect should the Sheen gain the upper hand. Could they? *Would* they?

The Runners, for whom Andragna felt a considerable amount of sympathy, had deep misgivings about Zynig-47 and the future of the race.

The Facers, who were in control of the Committee, had never been happier. Never mind the fact that Zynig-47 was little more than an enormous dirt ball orbiting a so-so sun, they reveled in running about the surface, squabbling over how much land each individual was entitled to, rummaging through the multicolored ruins and collecting bits of shattered glass. They called the bits and pieces "art," and he called them "rubble." The whole thing would have been laughable if it hadn't been so dangerous.

Well, that was *his* job, to make them see and understand. And today, when the Sectors met, he would make one last attempt.

The sun started to rise in the east, pushed the darkness off to the west, and took control of the sky. It was red, pink, and blue all at the same time. Like the glass in the courtyard walls. Andragna turned and returned to bed. Sleep brought peace.

Commensurate with its owner's wishes the prefab shelter had been deposited at the summit of a gently rounded hill not far from the still rising community officially known as "Base NH-426," but increasingly called "Starfall" by those with more romantic sensibilities.

As the sun rose and kissed the hilltops with soft pink light, a door whirred open, and a tiny female emerged. In spite of the fact that her body was small, *very* small, the spirit that dwelt there was large and fierce. Energy crackled around her like electricity, her movements were quick and precise, and fire filled her eyes. This was what she had fought for! To fill her lungs with pure unrecycled air! To feel the sun's slowly growing warmth on her face—and call a planet home.

And here it was, all around her, just as she had imagined that it would be. *If* she could hold the coalition together, *if* she could counter doubters like Admiral Andragna, *if* she could coax two or three more years from her steadily aging body.

Reenergized, Nool Nortalla, also known to her people as "Sector 4," whistled for her pet robot, waited for the device to climb up onto her shoulder, and took walking stick in hand. It would take the better part of an hour to walk down into the city of glass. A journey she would relish.

The Chamber of Reason was lined with *real* stone, said to have been quarried on the Thraki home world, though no one was sure, since there were very few records that pre-dated the fleet.

Originally maintained aboard one of the moon-sized arks that functioned as both habitats and battleships, the Chamber had been painstakingly disassembled, transported to the surface, and installed in a dome of rose-colored glass. The sun flooded the interior with blood-warm light as Andragna nodded to the sentries, entered through a tubelike door, and emerged into a formal reception area.

Like the rest of his species, the military officer had a natural tendency to respond to certain colors in certain ways. The soft pink light made him feel good, a fact which though innocent enough, might be of concern. Could such a phenomena impact the quality of the Committee's decisions? And was the placement part of a plot conceived by Nool Nortalla and her home-crazed Facers? Or, and this seemed more likely, had he become so immersed in his job that politics colored *all* his perceptions? There was no way to be sure—but Andragna feared that it was true.

The admiral's boots made a clacking sound as they hit dark heat-fused glass. A group of Sectors, alerted by the sound, turned to greet him. There was Sector 12, a short somewhat pudgy female known for her bombastic ways, Sector 27, who was tall and something of a wit, Sector 9, a rather conservative Runner, and a half-dozen more.

Handcrafted "forms," or robots, scampered about their feet, peered out of carrying cases, or lay cradled in their arms. Andragna greeted each of them by name, exchanged the usual pleasantries, and continued on his way. His form made little noises and scooted from one shoulder to the other while exchanging data with its peers.

It was the admiral's right to enter the Chamber first . . . and to make the long somewhat humiliating crawl from the perimeter of the stone table to its center without the embarrassment of anyone looking on.

Eager to conclude the process, Andragna dropped to his knees, crawled toward the splash of rose-colored light, and surfaced in front of his chair. Doing so brought with it the usual sense of pride, awe, and, yes, fear. Fear that he might fail.

The Thraki took his chair and eyed the recently completed enclosure. The roof of the Chamber was shaped like a dome, which, as the result of luck or divine providence echoed the native structure above. It was pierced by thirty-seven slit-shaped windows, each arranged to admit a single shaft of light, which thanks to the use of servo-operated reflectors, was quite steady. *Artificial light* up in orbit . . . *sunlight* here on the surface. *All* the beams of light converged on the table's granite surface, just as the Sectors were supposed to meet and guide their race.

Having allowed the admiral an adequate amount of time to take his place, the Committee filed into the room and set their pets loose to roam the top of the table. Andragna's form was quick to join them. The machines tumbled, rolled, and jumped, all vying for attention. Nothing was said, but each machine was awarded points for appearance, flexibility, and charm. Functionality, or a base level thereof, was assumed. Nortalla entered, still smiling as a result of her walk, followed by Sector 19 who liked to be last and usually was.

Once all of them were seated, the chamberlain called the meeting to order by administering a single blow to a large metal disk. It was known as the Shield of Waha. The sound echoed between the stone walls as it had so many times before. That's when the forms were recalled, deactivated, and removed from the tabletop.

Under normal circumstances, Andragna would have waited for one of the Sectors to speak rather than open the session himself, but the situation was anything but normal. He took the initiative. "Assuming that no one objects, I would like to open today's session by discussing our strategic position."

Andragna paused, scanned the faces around him, and saw that he had their attention. "Thank you. The first thing to talk about is the political situation within the Confederacy. Based on intelligence provided by the Ramanthians, it appears that certain factions have used the threat posed by the Sheen to not only pull the organization together but make it stronger. The reality of this can be seen in the way that the once hospitable Clone Hegemony has begun to distance itself from us, and the fact that the Hudathans, once confined to their home system, are now referred to as 'allies.' "

"So, what's your point?" Sector 12 demanded querulously. "The stronger the Confederacy is the more damage they will inflict on the Sheen."

"Possibly," Andragna replied carefully, "assuming they behave as the Ramanthians predict that they will. But how likely is that, given that our Ramanthian friends told us the Confederacy was about to crumble?"

"An excellent point," Sector 9 put in. "I believe it was our friend Nool Nortalla who suggested that we use the locals as a screen, allow them to bear the brunt of the Sheen attack, and deal with the survivors at our leisure. A silly plan with a predicable outcome. Enough time has been wasted. It's time to run."

There it was, the very idea Andragna wanted the Committee to consider. Now it was out in the open. And, given that the meeting was available to the entire armada, the idea would circulate. But not without opposition.

Nortalla came to her feet. Her eyes probed the room like laser beams, her body was rigid with the intensity of her emotions, and her voice was hard as hull metal. "Run you say? For what? So we can keep running? So our cubs can be born in the blackness of space, live their lives in fear, and run till they die? Is *that* what you want? Is *that* worth the price? Is *that* who we are?"

Nortalla let the question hang there, not just in the Chamber of Reason, but throughout the fleet. Then, with a perfect sense of timing, she broke the silence. Her voice was low now—little more than a whisper. "The answer is 'no.' Many of us will die fighting the Sheen, but there are worse things than death, such as a life spent running away from it. I say we face the machines, fight them to a standstill, and claim what's ours. *This* sun! *This* planet! *This* home!"

There was a moment of silence followed by the thump of a single foot, and another, and another until the individual sounds were lost in one massive beat. The female known as Sector 4 sought the admiral's eyes. He tried to conceal how he felt, tried to erase all expression from his face, but the oldster knew the truth. A battle had been fought and won. How many more would it take? Nortalla felt tired and sank into her chair. The foot-stomping died away.

The sun, which was high in the sky, beat down on the officer's back as he followed the slightly concave worm path upward. Although Andragna took pride in his body and worked hard to keep in shape, he had discovered that a lifetime of shipboard living had left him weak and out of breath. Something he was reluctant to admit to himself, much less to the fit, young bodyguards who trailed along behind.

The errand—or was it a mission?—was something of a chore. Andragna had encountered a number of alien cultures during his lifetime. Many featured religions and were in some cases governed by religions. All of them had one thing in common, and that was a propensity to build monuments or other structures that were so large, so visible, that the population would hold them in awe. Sadly, from the naval officer's perspective, the Thraki priesthood were possessed of the same unfortunate instincts.

The steadily growing city of Starfall offered plenty of choice building sites, many of which were on level ground, but had one of those been chosen? No, not when there was a hill to build on. A hill that would make any edifice built placed there even more visible. Broken glass crunched under the admiral's boots as he arrived on a level area and paused to take a breather. His bodyguards paused as well, but didn't need to, which he tried to ignore. Yes, he could have ordered up an air car, but that would smack of self-importance, and admirals, *Thraki* admirals, were politicians first and officers second.

The view was quite pleasant. Starfall occupied the foreground. Sun glittered off glass, worm orchards circled beyond, and hills shimmered in the distance. Pretty now, but what about later? After the Sheen came?

Andragna turned his back to the scene and resumed the climb. Refreshed, or at least partially so, the officer focused on the trail. The worm ruts had been filled with a mixture of gravel and bits of broken glass. They glittered like lost jewels as the admiral made his way to the top or, if not the top, a flat area where the remains of a once prominent building stood. Three of the four violet walls remained and, thanks to the work of a dozen robots, stood free of debris. In fact, so beautiful was the U-shaped enclosure that a stranger might have taken it for a piece of architectural art, and mistakenly assumed that it was supposed to look that way.

Now, as Andragna entered what felt like open arms he saw the mouth of a tunnel, one of many the indigenous population had left behind, and a magnet for the Thraki priesthood. The early histories had been lost, but much had been said and written during the last couple of hundred years regarding the possibility that the Thraki race was descended from subterranean ground dwellers. The theory was certainly tempting, accounting as it did for the race's excellent night vision, the complex nearly warrenlike manner in which their space ships were laid out, and the average adult's diminutive stature. Which, when combined with the prominence of the hill, would explain why the site had been selected.

An acolyte stood at the entrance of the tunnel, back straight, spear grounded at her side. It was a rare individual who wasn't acquainted with Andragna's face. Both the challenge and the response were a matter of form. "Who comes?"

"A seeker of truth."

"Enter then . . . for all who seek truth are welcome here."

Andragna stepped into the mouth of the tunnel, but his bodyguards were forced to remain outside. Weapons were not allowed on holy ground, unless they belonged to the priests themselves or their highly trained assassins. A fact that spoke volumes about the amount of power vested in the priesthood, the extent to which they influenced the government, and the reason for the officer's visit.

A second acolyte, this one male, came forward to greet him. A triangle had been shaved into the fur on his forehead, a second-year kilt was buckled around his waist, and his demeanor was respectful. "The high priestess is expecting you, Admiral . . . please follow me."

The passageway, which had been blocked at various points, was clear now, but work continued. Construction robots, many of which had only recently been retrieved from deep storage, would handle most of the work, with acolytes pitching in to help.

What light there was emanated from a spray-on fungus that Thraki scientists had harvested from a planet visited more than a hundred anums before and stored in the Armada's extensive "life" banks.

Some of the Facers opposed the wholesale use of off-planet "bio-tools," fearing the manner in which native species might be impacted, but the Runners, who still harbored hopes that the stop on Zynig-47 was little more than a pause, had no such concerns. In spite of the fact that the priesthood was a theoretical mix of Facers and Runners, the leadership had a pronounced pro-Runner bias. A fact which had everything to do with Andragna's visit.

While the priests didn't swing enough votes to stop the Facers, and feared the backlash that might result from any attempt to leverage the secular political process, they could be counted on to support conservative initiatives. Or, so he hoped.

Suddenly, the passageway opened to an enormous cavern. Light poured down through a partially restored dome to paint the lake below. The water was smooth as glass. "Beautiful, isn't it?" the acolyte said softly, and the admiral, who took the stars themselves as *his* standard of beauty, was forced to agree. "Yes, it certainly is."

The trail, which had formerly resembled a gently turning trough, followed the cavern's wall and wound down toward the lake. Once they arrived at the bottom Andragna discovered a large relatively flat area only partially visible from above. It was there, where numerous tunnels met, that the priesthood was in the process of establishing its headquarters. The temple was only half built but had already started to resemble those seen in the ancient texts. A swarm of robots, priests, and acolytes were hard at work, their tools screeching and clattering. It seemed that, Runner sympathies not withstanding, the church was building a home. Not a good omen from Andragna's point of view.

A tall, rather regal-looking female spotted the visitor, handed her power wrench to a priest, and made her way over. Her name was Bree Bricana, and beyond the almost palpable magnetism that surrounded her, there was nothing to distinguish the high priestess from her subordinates. Certainly not the rough work clothes, tool belt, or heavily abraded boots. Both were leaders and knew each other well. The tu, or nonsexual embrace appropriate to male-female friends felt both natural and unforced. Each took a step back. "You look well, admiral."

"As do you," Andragna replied truthfully. "Work clothes become you."

Bricana laughed. "I understand that you chose to walk . . . Who would have thought that legs could be so useful?"

"Yes," Andragna agreed soberly. "But for how long? The Sheen are on the way."

Fur rippled down both sides of Bricana's face. "I share your concern. Come . . . we'll find a place to sit."

Andragna followed the high priestess through a maze of neatly stacked construction materials and into a fungus-lit tunnel. It wasn't until he was within the corridor itself that he realized that he felt more comfortable there. Why? Because it resembled one of the passageways in a spaceship, that's why. If he had his way, if the race continued its journey, how long would it be until Thraki were no longer comfortable beyond the hulls of their spaceships? A thousand anums? *Ten thousand?* And was that good or bad?

The question went unanswered as the tunnel opened into a cavern. Alcoves had been carved into the sides of the chamber, creating rooms of various sizes. Bricana chose the largest of these, dropped her tool belt, and gestured toward some upended boxes. "Which would the admiral prefer? Rations or wall fasteners?"

"Rations," Andragna replied solemnly, "in case I get hungry."

The priestess laughed and took the other seat. "So, my friend, tell me the worst."

Andragna's facial fur rippled in different directions. He chose his words with care. "In spite of the fact that this

planet meets many of our needs—the Confederacy becomes stronger with each passing day."

"Yes," Bricana agreed, "I listened to the audio portion
of this morning's meeting. You were quite articulate. I
think it's safe to say that there's no possibility whatsoever
that the aliens will allow themselves to be manipulated in
the manner first described by Sector 4."

Andragna felt a sense of relief. "I'm glad we agree."

"However," the priestess continued soberly, "we foresee
the possibility of an even greater danger."

The admiral's ears stood straight up. An even *greater*
danger? One that had already been discussed? Here was
something he didn't know about but should have. He ordered his ears to relax and adopted a matter-of-fact tone.
"Yes, our people face many threats . . . To which do you
refer?"

But Bricana had seen the officer's involuntary reaction
and knew the truth. The possibility, no, the *reality* of what
the Confederacy would do, hadn't occurred to him yet. She
kept her voice neutral. "We think the aliens will attack and,
depending on how the conflict goes, might join forces with
the Sheen."

Andragna felt the fur bristle along the back of his neck.
Of course! How could he have missed such an obvious
possibility? Because he'd been trained to focus on the
Sheen . . . and the tactics of flight. A threat such as the one
posed by the Confederacy lay outside the framework of
his training and experience. And his subordinates, who had
the same background, were no better equipped. He felt a
crushing sense of shame.

It must have shown. Bricana was gentle. "You musn't
feel that way . . . We are what we have been. It could happen to any of us."

Andragna looked up. "It *didn't* happen to you."

"Ah," Bricana replied, "but it *did*. The only reason we
have discussed the matter is the fact that something very

close to this situation is mentioned in the *Book of Tomorrows*."

As with many members of his monotheistic culture Andragna had a pretty good understanding of the gods, their attributes and powers, but didn't really know very much beyond that. The truth was that like his military peers, the officer had more faith in the laws of physics than the somewhat wordy *Tomes of Truth*, one of which was called the *Book of Tomorrows*. The fact that it covered something that might have practical value came as a pleasant surprise. "Really? What does it say?"

Bricana seemed to look through him to something else. Her voice, which had been conversational up till then, seemed to deepen. The words, written hundreds of years before, had an archaic quality. ". . . And our people will settle a new world. Some will call it 'home,' and wish to stay there, while others will point to the stars, and the menace that follows. Beware of those who call themselves 'friends,' for they may attack, or align themselves with the menace. Run if you can, but failing that, call on the twins."

Andragna allowed the fur to bunch over his eyes. "The twins? *What* twins?"

The high priestess stood. "Follow me. I'll show you."

Bricana rose, led him across the open chamber, and entered a side tunnel. It was guarded by acolytes armed with blast rifles rather than ceremonial spears. Andragna registered surprise but kept the emotion to himself. What did the priesthood have that required such heavily armed sentries? It was difficult to imagine.

The tunnel turned left, ran for twenty units, turned right, ran for twenty units and turned left again. Each right-angle turn represented a potential point of defense, each was monitored by a clutch of sensors, and each had been executed with machinelike precision. These walls appeared raw, as if only recently excavated, and still wore marks left by the tools used to make them. The odor of ozone mixed with some sort of sealant hung heavy on the air.

Bricana stopped before a blast-proof hatch. Andragna noticed that it still bore the number of the ship from which it had been salvaged, still another sign of the power that the priesthood continued to wield. She placed her forehead on a reader, lasers scanned her retinas, and a blue light appeared. Servos whined, the door swiveled open, and the visitors stepped through. A priest was waiting. He was armed and wore the black robes favored by the Brother-Sisterhood of Assassins. Andragna couldn't see them—but felt sure that others lurked nearby. The priest bowed. "Welcome. How can I be of assistance?"

Bricana bowed in return. "Thank you. The admiral and I would like to visit the twins."

If the assassin was surprised by the request, he gave no sign of it. He bowed a second time. "Of course . . . Please follow me."

Thus began a second journey that was much like the first, a series of carefully planned right-angle turns that led to a second blastproof hatch. Andragna was more than intrigued . . . he was angry and fearful. What terrible secret had the priesthood been keeping? And if they had one, did they have others as well?

The second door opened. Bricana went first, followed by the males. There was nothing especially attractive about the cavern that lay beyond. No worm glass, no special lighting, no effort to smooth the recently machined walls. It was perhaps fifty units across and twenty units high. A pair of what appeared to be golden cradles, each heavily decorated with scroll work, sat on a raised dais. The twins, if that's what they were, consisted of bright metal tubes. They were approximately ten units in length. It appeared that each construct was protected by a force field, which, if not identical to those used by the Sheen, then were very, very similar. There was no need to tell Andragna what they were . . . He knew. The twins were weapons.

The priestess waited for her military colleague to reach the obvious conclusion. He asked the same question she had asked so many years in the past. "How do they work?"

Bricana offered the Thraki equivalent of a shrug. "Given the nature of your responsibilities, I'm sure you are familiar with black holes."

Andragna was. He knew that when gigantic stars explode, or go supernova, something remains. A "hole," or an object so dense that nothing could escape its gravitational field, not even light itself. Anything that ventured sufficiently close, including starships, asteroids, or planets risked being sucked in. What happened after that was unknown since there was no way for information to come back out. "Of course. It's part of my job to avoid them."

Bricana offered what amounted to a smile. "Yes, and we appreciate your efforts!" Her expression grew more serious. "Ask yourself this . . . what happens to all the matter captured by a black hole? It's reduced to amorphous energy. Ships, asteroids, planets, whatever. All transformed into radiation. Maybe it stays there, trapped in time and space, or maybe it exits somewhere else. Were it to emerge, the exit point could be referred to as a 'white hole.' Imagine how much energy we're talking about—imagine how destructive it could be."

Andragna took a moment to do so. The results would be awesome. His eyes met hers. "So that's what these are? White holes?"

"*Artificial* white holes," the high priestess corrected him, "created and suspended within an antimatter container, and housed in a normal matter shell."

Andragna eyed the twins. Here was something any military officer would appreciate. Power on an unparalleled scale. "How? How do they work?"

"I'm no expert on such matters," Bricana said evenly, "but it's my understanding that each tube can be launched like a missile. Once the weapon enters the target area a signal is sent, the magnetoelectric locks are released, and an atom-sized white hole pops into existence. It would last for no more than a millisecond, but the result would be devastating. If used against us, the entire armada would cease to exist."

Andragna wasn't sure which was more amazing, the fact that such weapons existed, or how they came to be. So long ago that they were mentioned in the *Book of Tomorrows*. "So the old ones foresaw our situation? *Knew* what would face us? How could that be?"

Bricana looked uncertain. "I honestly couldn't say. They were given into our possession when the great journey began. That's as much as we know."

"Why *two*? Why not one, three, or fifty?"

"There is no mention of what the old ones were thinking."

"But why keep such weapons secret?" Andragna demanded. "How can the church justify such a thing?"

Bricana's eyes met his. "There has been no need—not until now."

It was the answer he might have expected from the priesthood, more than a little arrogant, and completely unapologetic.

Both were silent for a moment. The naval officer was first to speak. "This changes everything."

"Yes," the high priestess replied, "I think it does."

12

In forming the plan of a campaign, it is requisite to foresee everything the enemy may do, and be prepared with the necessary means to counteract it.

Napoleon I
Maxims of War
Standard year 1831

Planet Arballa, the Confederacy of Sentient Beings

The *Friendship*'s sick bay smelled of disinfectants, plastic, and the faint odor of coffee that emanated from the much abused pot that crouched on a counter. General William Booly sat in Treatment Room 4. He was stripped to the waist. The medic, who happened to be female, grabbed a handle and directed the overhead light onto his torso. She couldn't help but notice the breadth of his shoulders, the muscular arms, the ridge of fur that ran the length of his spine. There were scars, too, some old, and some newly healed. The latter came courtesy of a planet named Drang. Most were what they appeared to be, but the blister looked suspicious. The medic pointed toward the carefully draped Mayo stand. "Place your arm on that, General."

Booly did as he was told. "I have a meeting in ten minutes or so."

The tech passed a scanner over his forearm, nodded in response to the reading, and returned the device to its holster. "Well, it's your call, sir, but it appears as though a foot-long parasitic worm has taken up residence in your right arm. The good news is that she wants to come out and lay her eggs. We can help her—or you can attend that meeting. Which will it be?"

The medic was something of a smart-ass, but Booly knew she was right. He growled, "Go ahead," and watched her prep his arm. He had lifted from Drang a good four weeks earlier but been so busy stitching the Confederacy's command structure together that he barely found time to sleep, much less worry about a rash. But that was before the rash turned into a blister, which not only hurt but itched like crazy.

"I could squirt some local in there," the medic said cheerfully, "but the pain will be equivalent to a small incision. What's your preference? Local or no local?"

"Skip the local," Booly replied grimly. "Just get on with it."

"Yes, sir," the rating answered evenly. "Here goes . . ."

She squinted her eyes, brought the blade down onto the surface of his skin, and cut a cross into the blister. Yellowish fluid jetted out followed by a small white head. It had tiny jet black eyes. The worm looked from left to right.

The tech had been waiting for that moment and was quick to seize the parasite with some forceps. "Gotcha! Now, this is the difficult part," she cautioned, "some people pull too hard. That's when the head comes off . . . Makes for a nasty infection plus minor surgery. The trick is to wind the little bastard around a probe and reel his ass in."

Booly watched in queasy fascination as the young woman pulled inch after nauseating inch of worm out of his arm. Finally, after what seemed like an eternity, she was finished. Then, with the parasite twisting and turning at the bottom of a kidney basin, it was time to disinfect the wound, close the incision, and apply a self-sealing dressing. "There you are, sir, good to go."

Booly thanked the tech, donned his shirt, and took one last look at the worm. It squirmed every which way. Kind of like the politicians he was about to deal with. His smile lasted all the way out into the corridor.

Senator Orno was angry, *very* angry, as he entered the conference room, saw that he was first to arrive, and located the Ramanthian-style chair. A quick check revealed that the back adjustment was broken. It sometimes seemed as if everything he touched was cursed. The plan to destabilize Earth, and thereby weaken the Confederacy, had very nearly succeeded, *would have* succeeded, had his co-conspirators been more competent. Subsequent efforts, such as the plot to kill Doma-Sa, had proved equally disastrous. Still, he who tunnels must move some dirt, so that's what he would do.

Orno took his seat, preened the areas to either side of his beak, and allowed his mind to wander. It was spring in Hive's northern hemisphere—and the politician wished he could see it.

Doma-Sa stepped out of his cabin, checked to ensure that the hatch was locked, and strode down the corridor. Beings who had previously gone to considerable lengths to ignore the Hudathan nodded, smiled, or waved. All because their perceptions had changed. Now, after weeks of surprisingly positive media coverage, the Hudathans had miraculously been transformed from villains to heroes. Never mind the fact that they hadn't changed in the least and viewed their new allies with the same level of paranoia reserved for the oncoming Sheen. The stupidity of their psychology astounded him. The entire lot of them were beneath contempt. Yet, there he was, nodding in return, giving the scum what they craved. The illusion of solidarity. Why? Because they had him by the testicles that's why. Imagine! Hudathans fighting for a human general . . . The great Hiween Poseen-Ka never would have believed it.

Ah well, the War Commander thought to himself, *nothing lasts forever. Not even our shame.* The thought brought comfort and put a bounce into his step.

Senator Ishimoto-Six stabbed a button with his index finger, waited for the platform to arrive, and stepped aboard. It carried him upwards. Any number of things rode on the upcoming meeting: the safety of his people, his position as a senator, and the way in which Maylo perceived him— something he still wasn't sure of. Which would be worse, the politician wondered. Failing my government? Or losing Maylo? Not that I have her. The platform coasted to a halt. Six nodded to a staffer and stepped out onto the deck. The corridor led him away. A younger version of the same man had fantasized about being at the center of things, about making a difference, and his dreams had come true. But what was the saying? Be careful what you wish for? You might just get it? Suddenly it made sense.

The watch had changed, breakfast was over, and the *Friendship*'s corridors were relatively empty. A senator rushed past, nodded, and kept on going. Maylo Chien-Chu forced a smile. Her heels clacked on the deck. General William Booly had boarded the ship some twelve hours before and would chair the meeting. Ishimoto-Six would attend as well. The knowledge left a hollow place at the bottom of her stomach. It was silly, she knew that, but true nonetheless. Would Booly detect the nature of her relationship with Samuel? And why did she care? The officer was yesterday's news . . . Or was he? Some very expensive lab-grown roses had arrived just a few days before. Right smack on the six-month anniversary of what amounted to their first date. Damn it! She was too old for this sort of crap. The executive cursed her own stupidity, increased her pace, and passed a maintenance bot. It scrubbed the deck.

The conference room was packed by the time Booly arrived. There were familiar faces, like those that belonged to Admiral Angie Tyspin, the naval officer who had risked her life and career to help the 13th DBLE during the mutiny, Major, no *Colonel* Nancy Winters, his newly named chief of staff, Major Andre Kara, his interservice liaison officer, and CO of the 1st Foreign Regiment, Colonel Kitty Kirby, CO of the 13th DBLE, War Commander Wenlo Morla-Ka, CO of the newly integrated 3rd Foreign Infantry Regiment, his superior, Ambassador Doma-Sa, Battle Leader Pasar Hebo, CO of the 4th Foreign Infantry Regiment, Senator Alway Orno, representing the Ramanthian government, General Jonathan Alan Seebo-346, CO of the 2nd Foreign Parachute Regiment, plus a lot of beings he hadn't met, and last, but certainly not least, Maylo Chien-Chu.

She sat toward the front of the room, next to Ambassador Doma-Sa, and smiled when his eyes made contact with hers. A spark jumped the gap, and the legionnaire remembered how those same eyes had stared up at him from the misery of a prison cell. And later, over a dinner table on a beach in Rio, and eventually in the warmth of his bed. What had gone wrong anyway? And how could he fix it?

Winters cleared her throat, and Booly realized that he should have spoken by then. He forced a smile. "Good morning—if that's what this is. Thank you for coming. We have a lot to accomplish, so let's get started."

Booly paused and allowed his eyes to drift across the room. "This is a truly historic occasion. The creation of new alliances, the structures required to make them viable, and the problems that naturally follow.

"As I look out on your faces, I see both soldiers *and* civilians. There are a number of different cultures represented here, so the mix may or may not seem natural to you. Please suspend whatever doubts you may have, and give the process a chance. We have very little time. Civilian support is critical. Without it, we cannot possibly win. It's my belief that everyone must come to agreement on the overall strategy, and once that's accomplished, the military will do its best to carry the plan forward. Does anyone have questions regarding that approach?"

There *were* questions, niggling matters for the most part, as various beings sought to establish their importance, impress their counterparts, or simply exercise their mouth parts. Ishimoto-Six, who sat to Maylo's right, tuned them out. He was much more interested in watching *her* out of the corner of his eye. And what the senator saw disturbed him. Her relationship with General Booly was over—everyone said so—but what of her eyes? They suggested something different.

The clone looked at Booly. The soldier answered a question. The Sheen were coming—that was the point of the meeting—so what would happen then? Booly was brave—everyone agreed on that—which meant he would participate in the fighting. Perhaps the machines would kill him. It was a small thought, a *horrible* thought, but one he couldn't shake.

"So," Booly said, "did I answer your questions? Good. Let's move to the next step. The presentation materials have been downloaded to your personal comps so there's no need to take a lot of notes. I would remind you that this material is secret and not for disclosure to anyone who hasn't been cleared."

Orno listened to the translation, wondered if the last comment was directed at him, and decided it didn't matter. The Thraki were the only party that might be interested, and they were losers. Or would be, assuming Booly made the logical moves. "Here's the situation," Booly began, and turned to watch a holo bloom at his side. The star map, prepared with the aid of clones themselves, showed most of the Hegemony. "Reduced to the simplest possible terms, the Sheen have been chasing the Thraki for hundreds if not thousands of years, and plan to eradicate their race. Why? They aren't sure, and neither are we.

"Thraki politics revolve around two groups, the Runners, who favor continued flight, and the Facers, who want to turn and fight. About the time that the Thraki armada entered Hegemony-controlled space—the Facers took control of the government."

Conscious of the clones in the room—the officer chose his next words with care. "The Hegemony greeted the newcomers in what can only be described as a peaceful fashion, allowed them to establish some bases, and settled into what they assumed would be a peaceful coexistence."

All as part of a cynical attempt to use the Thraki against the Confederacy, Maylo thought to herself . . . Not that she blamed Booly for leaving that out—since his job was to strengthen the alliance not destroy it.

"Unfortunately," Booly continued, "the Hegemony had no way to know that the Thraki hoped to use them as a sacrificial pawn."

There was a pause while someone explained the game of chess to a Dweller at the back of the room. "More than that," Booly went on, "it now appears that the Thraki hierarchy hoped to use the rest of the Confederacy in much the same manner. A plan that could still succeed if we allow them to remain where they are.

"We don't know a whole lot about the Sheen, only what the Thraki have chosen to share, and the report citizen Williams brought in. However, assuming that those reports are accurate, the machines are absolutely ruthless and will lay waste to any planet found to harbor the Thraki."

"So let's go to Zynig-47 and root the bastards out," the senator from Turr growled. "It would serve the unnamable interlopers right."

Booly had been expecting a comment of that sort and nodded his head in agreement. "Yes, it would. But there's a problem. Even now, after the consolidation of our forces, the Thraki have more ships than we do. A *lot* more. Admiral Tyspin?"

Tyspin rose and made her way to the front of the room. She wore a blue flight suit, the star that denoted her rank, but none of the many decorations to which she was entitled. Though not especially pretty, there was strength in her face, and her eyes gleamed with intelligence. They were green and swept the compartment like lasers. "What General Booly told you was correct . . . The Thraki fleet, or armada as they prefer to call it, consists of more than five thousand ships, plus auxiliary craft equivalent to shuttles, tugs, tankers and so on."

Tyspin pointed toward the holo that appeared next to her. A series of computer-rendered ships appeared. "The main body of the armada consists of supply ships, which might more accurately be referred to as 'factory ships,' since they carry raw materials plus the robotic machinery required to manufacture every item the fleet requires.

"The factory vessels are protected by three types of warships roughly analogous to what we refer to as battleships, destroyers, and fighters, though of differing displacements. It should be noted that all of their vessels are equipped with standardized weapons and propulsion systems, something that gives them a logistical advantage and represents an area that we haven't even started to address."

It was a telling point and one that some of the civilians hadn't considered as yet. There were thousands of differences between the ships built on Hive, Earth, and Alpha-001, a factor that would add a great deal of complexity to any effort aimed at using them in a concerted fashion. Some, dismayed by what they heard, felt their hearts begin to sink.

Tyspin scanned their faces. "Sorry, but that's not the worst of it. Thanks to countless years of unremitting warfare the Thraki have evolved into a race of warriors, which, with the possible exception of the Hudathans, is something none of us can claim to be. That culture—that toughness—is a weapon in and of itself. Questions?"

There was silence for a moment, followed by a voice from the back of the room. The figure who rose wore a black pressure suit, which made him instantly recognizable. The senator from the Drac Axis seemed to grind the words out. "Ships, many have we?"

Tyspin was barely able to recognize the syntax as a question. She didn't trust the Drac, knew they were among the least dependable members of the Confederacy, but had very little choice. To conceal such information, or *seem* to conceal the information, could weaken the already flimsy alliance. She could feel Booly, Maylo, and others staring at her, wondering how she would respond.

"We are still in the process of assessing the extent of our assets—but current estimates run to about thirty-five hundred ships of various classes and sizes."

"Plenty should be," the Drac gurgled. "Ships too many get in each other's way."

"There's some truth to what you say," the naval officer conceded. "Large fleets require advanced command and control infrastructures and generate all manner of logistical problems. There is one additional factor, however . . . Besides the ships mentioned earlier, the Thraki possess a number of moon-sized arks—all of which are heavily armed. We on the other hand have nothing that even begins to compare with that sort of throw weight."

The answer seemed to satisfy the Drac, or at least silence him, because he took his seat. Booly stood. "Thank you, Admiral. Now, with that information in mind, let's examine the alternatives."

The holo swirled and morphed into text. It dissolved from one language to another. "We have a number of choices," Booly continued. "We could take no action whatsoever, hoping that the Sheen will ignore us, we can attempt an alliance with the Thraki, remembering their plans to use us, or we can pursue unilateral action. My staff and I recommend option three."

Booly paused and, not hearing any objections, took the next important step. "So, assuming we opt for unilateral action—some additional choices open up. We could wait to see what the Sheen do and react accordingly . . ."

Senator Orno stood and gave himself permission to speak. "A reactive strategy is best—we fully endorse it."

Ishimoto-Six was well aware of the fact that his clone brother had been a member of the Ramanthian-sponsored cabal and felt the blood rush to his face. He came to his feet. "You'd like that wouldn't you? You'd like to see the machines attack Thraki colonies—some of which are on Hegemony worlds!"

"Established with permission from *your* government," the Ramanthian observed mildly. "Or had you forgotten?"

"That's enough," Booly said firmly. "We're here to establish a strategy . . . not debate the past. Senator Ishimoto-Six is correct about one thing, however, the penalty for adopting a reaction-based strategy is that the Sheen may decide to attack some of our assets, leading to heavy casualties."

Maylo, who paid close attention to the debate, felt sorry for Six. It wasn't his fault that the Hegemony had made itself vulnerable.

Oblivious to what Maylo was thinking, the military officer continued. "All of which suggests a second alternative: Root the Thraki out of their bases so the Sheen have no reason to attack, realizing there are no guarantees—and that they may decide to come after us regardless of where the Thraki happen to be."

Doma-Sa had been silent up till then—but couldn't remain so any longer. He lurched to his feet. "With all due respect, General—why be so subtle? The Thraki took Zynig-47 and are in the process of colonizing it. Let's attack, take the planet back, and send them on their way. The chances are good that the Sheen will follow."

Booly, who was well aware of the Hudathan's military background, gave a slight bow. "The *Intaka*, or 'blow of death,' mentioned by Grand Marshal Hisep Rula-Ka in his book *Analysis of the Legion*, is a proven strategy. And, if it weren't for the arks that orbit Zynig-47, I'd be tempted.

"However, I believe it was none other than the esteemed

warrior Mylo Nurlon-Da who said, 'Lives are as arrows—fire no more than you can afford.' "

Doma-Sa found himself not only neutralized, but honored, and possessed of new respect. Here was a human, one of the few, who deserved Hudathan troops. He cleared his throat. "Thank you, General. You have more than answered my question."

"So," Booly concluded. "Here is the strategy that my staff and I recommend. With *your* permission and support, we intend to attack the Thraki colonies and allow most of the inhabitants to escape."

"Escape, allow them to?" the senator from Drac growled. "Mind, have you lost?"

"No," Booly answered patiently. "Why kill more of them than necessary? Or more of *our* troops for that matter? Once dislodged, the colonists will run for Zynig-47."

"Providing the Sheen with a single target," Ishimoto-Six said gratefully, "and sparing our planets."

Booly shrugged. "That's the plan . . . but plans can and do go awry. For example, we assume that the machines operate in a logical manner, and are primarily interested in the Thraki. We could be wrong."

The meeting broke up shortly after that. Booly made eye contact with Maylo but was mobbed by back-patting, hand-shaking politicians. The businesswoman waited for a moment, realized it would take a long time for the room to clear, and made her way into the corridor. Ishimoto-Six was waiting. They walked toward the lift. "So, what do you think?"

"About what?"

"About General Booly's plan."

Maylo shrugged. "I think it will be difficult, but if anyone can pull it off, *he* can."

Six glanced sideways. Was the statement what it seemed? A straightforward endorsement of a competent general? Or something more? He decided to take the chance. "Maylo . . ."

"Yes?"

"There's a dance tonight, in honor of the President's birthday, and I wondered if you would come?"

Maylo noted the hesitancy in the clone's voice and considered her response. The truth was that she would have been there anyway—everybody who was somebody would be—but this was something different. A date or something very similar. If she said "yes," he would take her answer as permission to proceed, to take the relationship to the next level, and if she said "no," he would be hurt and wouldn't ask again.

So, what *did* she want? To open the door or close it? And what of Booly? Why couldn't he pursue her with the same ardor that Six did? Because he was so desperately busy? Or just didn't care? The words formed themselves. "That sounds like fun Samuel—thanks for asking."

Ishimoto-Six followed Maylo into the lift, knew the platform was falling, but felt his spirits soar.

In spite of the fact that only the humans, dwellers and a few other races liked to dance, or even had a name for it, nearly everyone wanted to participate in President Nankool's birthday celebration—some because they truly liked the chief executive, some because it pays to suck up, and some because there was nothing else to do.

That being the case, the corridors were overflowing with revelers, would-be revelers, or reveler watchers all heading for the Starlight Ballroom. They were dressed to the nines, or whatever the nines were in their particular cultures, which made for a nearly overwhelming assault on the senses.

Booly stepped out of his sixth meeting of the day, felt the crowd pull him along, and was stunned by the bright shimmering reds, blues, and greens. Capes, gowns, and robes rustled, swished, and in once case chimed. The smell of perfume, incense and things the officer wasn't quite sure of filled the air. Add the drone of multilingual conversation to the mix, and it made for a stunning combination.

It was the sort of thing that the officer in Booly dismissed as a complete waste of time. Still, odds were that Maylo was somewhere about, raising the distinct possibility that he could talk to her, or better yet, convince her to leave early.

Booly was considered a player by then, a being to be reckoned with, which meant that he was forced to shake all manner of limbs, answer nonsensical questions, and dodge various types of supplicants, the worst of whom were arms dealers, eager to sell him everything from pocket knives to nukes.

Finally, after what felt like a swim upstream, the officer heard music, managed to break through a screen of onlookers, and made it to the dance floor. It took less than a second to spot Maylo and recognize the man she was with, Senator Samuel Ishimoto-Six.

They were dancing to something slow and stately. Maylo wore a bright red dress and positively glowed. Her teeth flashed when she laughed. They looked happy, as if made for each other, and the spectators thought so too. Comments came from all around. "Aren't they wonderful together?" "Look at that dress!" "He's so handsome!" "What a beautiful couple."

Booly looked down, realized how plain his class-two khaki's were, and felt suddenly out of place. Maybe it stemmed from his upbringing on Algeron, maybe it was the result of too many years on the rim, but the entire atmosphere made him uncomfortable. This was Maylo's world and one in which he would never be able to compete. Slowly, reluctantly, the soldier turned and forced his way back through the crowd.

Meanwhile, out on the dance floor, Maylo caught a glimpse of khaki. Her eyes followed, she saw his face, and then he was gone. Something, she wasn't sure what, seemed to squeeze her heart. The music played, her feet moved, but the dance was over.

13

Any and all available resources can and should be used while searching for the Thraki.

The Hoon
General Directive 00003.0
Standard year 2502

Inside the Rim, the Confederacy of Sentient Beings

The Sheen fleet swept through the Istar Seven system with the slow sureness of an organism that knows where it's headed but is in no particular hurry to get there. And with good reason. In spite of the fact that the Hoon had completed its inventory and destroyed all remaining vestiges of its other self, the computer intelligence had something new to concern itself with.

Scouts had come across signs that the Thraki armada had not only come that way—but done so within the relatively recent past. There were other portents as well . . . Ships that flashed into existence at the far end of detector range, the presence of computer controlled drones that exploded if tampered with, and hundreds of free-floating relay devices that "squirted" data to each other as the fleet drew near.

The occurrences were interesting for any number of reasons, beginning with the fact, that, old though the Hoon was, the computer had never observed such phenomena before. They suggested coordinated activity of some sort and presented a 92.3 percent match with instructions the AI had never been called upon to use before.

How had the creators been able to provide instructions regarding events that would transpire hundreds of years in the future? The machine neither knew nor cared.

The essence of the newly revealed directions were actually quite simple: Although the Sheen had pursued the Thraki armada for centuries now, the day would almost certainly come when the hunted would turn and make a stand. And, as part of that effort, they might attempt to lure the Hoon into some sort of trap. The AI would know that day had arrived "when signs start to thicken, when ships harry the fleet, and when mysteries appear."

The first pair of parameters made sense, but the last didn't. "Mysteries?" What did that mean? Ah well, what the computer didn't or couldn't understand it had been programmed to ignore.

So, cautious as to the possibility of a trap, the Hoon doubled the number of units assigned to reconnaissance, ordered the rest of the fleet to the highest possible state of readiness, and slowed the overall rate of advance.

That's how the Sheen discovered that a Thraki convoy had taken refuge on the eleventh planet out from a rather undistinguished sun and turned to investigate.

Veera was playing with Sam, something she did at least once a day, and Jepp was watching. Their cabins were too small for such activities . . . so they had moved out into the long, sterile corridor. Well, *mostly* sterile, since the human's quasi-religious graffiti added what he considered to be a much-needed touch of color.

The game, which Jepp watched from the comfort of a chair that Henry had fashioned from metal tubing, was as old as man's relationship with dogs. Veera, her iridescent underfeathers occasionally catching the light, would throw the crudely made ball down the passageway, and Sam, pleased to be the center of attention, would chase it. Not only *chase* it, but perform tricks while doing so, each calculated to outdo the last. Jepp watched the device scoot along the ceiling, drop from above, and swallow the ball.

The robot's reward for this activity, if "reward" was the right word, were trills of approval from Veera. Trills that Sam answered in kind and made Jepp jealous. He couldn't "sing" her language, hadn't even tried, and felt left out.

Still, some company was better than none, and he had vaguely paternal feelings toward the little alien. Though competent in many respects, and almost impossibly bright, she was vulnerable, too. Both her mother and father were dead, she was passing through a stage analogous to human adolescence, and was trapped aboard an alien ship.

Dealing with Veera, which also meant dealing with her moods, had altered Jepp's life. When *she* felt good then *he* felt good—and when *she* felt bad then *he* felt bad. The back and forth of which nearly drove the human crazy but beat loneliness. Something he had experienced all to often over the last six months.

Sam did a series of cartwheels, disgorged the ball at Veera's feet, and dashed away. The Prithian uttered a series of chirps, threw the sphere down-corridor, and seemed to stiffen. Her crimson shoulder plumage rose slightly and stuck straight out. Though unable to converse with the alien without the assistance of a translator, Jepp understood some of her nonverbal communications. He sat up straight. "Veera? What's wrong?"

The Prithian cocked her head to one side. "The ship changed direction—and picked up speed."

The human hadn't felt a thing but believed her nonetheless. The teenager had mentioned such changes shortly after coming aboard, and Jepp, having doubts regarding the veracity of her claims, ordered Alpha to check them out. The results were amazing. The Prithian was right at least 95 percent of the time. Her senses were more acute than his. So, given the fact that the ship had maintained the same course and speed for the last week or so, why change now? He frowned. "Tap into the Hoon and find out why."

What could have been phrased as a request was expressed as an order. Veera felt mixed emotions. Her father ordered the youngster around all the time. And, as someone who was older than she was, and presumably wiser, Jepp was entitled to the same level of respect due Prithian elders.

Or was he? Veera's father was dead, her companion was eccentric by *human* standards, and she was alone. It was tempting to say "no," on principle. To take a stand and maintain some personal space. The problem was her own highly developed sense of curiosity. What *was* behind the change in course? Where was the Hoon taking them? The teenager wanted to know.

Veera trilled an order, Sam cartwheeled in her direction, and followed the Prithian down the corridor. Data ports were located at regular intervals along the bulkheads. The Hoon's mechanical minions used them whenever they had a need to access certain types of information.

The Thraki device scuttled up the wall, created the necessary adapter, and plugged itself into the ship's electronic nervous system.

The way in which Veera communicated with machines was different from the manner in which Jepp accomplished the same thing. Her songs were comprised of individual notes, each one of which could easily be translated into binary code, and manipulated by any device having the intelligence to do so. The resulting transfer was that much more efficient. Just the sort of thing that the average machine is likely to appreciate.

More than that was the fact that most soft bodies required a machine interface to communicate with other ma-

chines, which marked them as clearly inferior. All except
for Veera, that is, who, from a machine point of view,
spoke something very close to unadulterated code. An ac-
complishment that marked her as superior to the biped with
whom she chose to associate herself. That's why the Hoon
had a tendency to indulge her. A tiny, nearly insignificant
part of the AI's consciousness listened as the interrogatory
arrived. "The ship [I am on] changed course. Why?"

The computer intelligence spent a fraction of a fraction
of a second considering the question and formulating a
response. "Thraki have been detected. The fleet must respond."

Jepp had arrived by then, and Veera relayed what she
had learned. The human felt a variety of emotions: a sense
of excitement born of boredom, feelings of guilt that
stemmed from his last encounter with the Thraki, and a
sort of spiritual lust. Because if there was anything the
human hungered after it was live, honest to goodness converts.

Yes, it was true that the last group of Thraki had gone
so far as to deny the existence of a single all-powerful, all-
knowing god, and having done so, had paid with their
lives, but they were outcasts, and *these* Thraki might be
more amenable to reason. It was worth a try. "Tell the
Hoon that I wish to speak with the Thraki in the hope that
we might convert them to the cause."

Though relatively young, Veera was possessed of an
excellent mind and knew the human wanted to convert the
Thraki to *his* cause, rather than the Hoon's. But she was
also smart enough to know that escape, if such a thing
were possible, was more likely to result from her relationship with Jepp than from any connection to the Hoon. She
decided to comply.

The request stuttered through the ship's fiber optic nervous system and made the jump to Vessel 17–9621 where
the Hoon was currently in residence. Not just *any* resi-

dence but the one time electromechanical home of the ill-fated Hoon Number Two.

Having received the request, the machine intelligence spent a quarter of a second thinking about it. The idea had obviously originated with the "human" soft body, and while it seemed like a waste of time, there were reasons to approve it. True to its nature, the Hoon listed them in descending order of importance: The being called Jepp had not only been useful where the elimination of Hoon Number Two was concerned, but had proven his willingness to slaughter the Thraki, and never stopped advocating the necessity for other others to do likewise. Add that to the new soft body's ability to communicate via code—and the Hoon was ready to indulge the strange twosome. Veera cocked her head, listened, and made the translation. "The Hoon says 'yes.' A shuttle awaits."

Jepp gave a whoop of joy, jumped into the air, and landed with a thump. "Come on! Let's get ready!"

Veera uttered the Prithian equivalent of a sigh, waited for Sam to scramble up onto her shoulder, and followed the alien toward his quarters. Once again, her father was proven correct: humans *were* a pain in the posterior.

The control area was neat, but homey, as if those assigned to it lived there, which they basically did. There were monitors, gently curving control panels, and holes into which the pilots and other crew members could insert their hands. Once positioned within a laser beam matrix, the ship's Navcomp "read" the complicated hand-finger signals that controlled not only the vessel itself, but the various subsystems of which it was comprised.

Convoy Commander Pol Bay Seph struggled to maintain her composure as alarms sounded, hatches hissed closed, and her crew went to battle stations. She *should* have been focused on the situation, on the fact that her forlorn group of stragglers had been overtaken by what appeared to be the entire Sheen fleet, but was filled with self-pity instead. Why now? After so many years had been left behind? After the fire that once burned in her eyes had dimmed? Why had the gods waited till now to fling the challenge in her face? Not that it mattered, since even a younger version of herself would have been helpless in the face of such an enemy.

Subcommander Ith Tor Homa shook her shoulder. It was a serious breach of etiquette and a sure sign of how desperate he was. "Commander! Every captain in the convoy requests orders . . . what shall I tell them?"

Seph glanced at a display. Once the Sheen were detected, she had ordered the convoy to land in the hope that they could avoid detection. The ships were arrayed around her. There were no signs of life on the airless planet, and the enemy was closing in. She felt like telling her captains to pray, since there was nothing else they *could* do, but she knew the unyielding younger version of herself would almost certainly disapprove.

Seph was about to offer some sort of meaningless platitude when a holo popped into existence in the upper right hand quadrant of her command space. The technical looked worried. "Commander, I have an incoming message . . . A Sheen envoy is on the way."

Seph was surprised. *Very* surprised. Not by the arrogance involved—that was expected—but by the act itself. Why send an envoy when there's nothing to negotiate? The Sheen *never* took prisoners, *never* made deals, and *never* showed mercy. The convoy was doomed. What were the machines up to? There was no way to know.

An envoy implied time, however, time the officer never expected to have, and she was determined to make good use of it. Years seemed to drop away. She felt younger and filled with energy. "Homa, you wanted some orders? Well, here they are: I want every youngster under the age of sixteen to suit up, grab what they can, and head for the hills. *Any* hills. Got it? Good.

"The minute that effort is under way have the technicals

alter all of the crew manifests, supply inventories, and
other lists to reflect the reduced muster.

"While the technicals work on that have someone clean
out their cabins and destroy anything they can't take with
them. And Homa . . ."

"Yes?"

"Prep some class two beacons. I want them to activate
thirty cycles from now. Maybe, just maybe, one of our
ships will happen along."

Homa considered the possibilities . . . Death at the hands
of the Sheen—or by slow starvation. Which was worse?
The decision was made, so it didn't matter. He saluted,
said "Yes, ma'am," and turned away." His daughter was
on one of those ships . . . and there was no time to lose.

Like the Sheen shuttles Jepp had used in the past, this one
was equipped with a small almost perfunctory control
space consisting of little more than a view screen, minimal
controls, and a pair of uncomfortable seats.

Unlike previous outings, however, was the fact that
Veera had agreed to accompany him and, after a quick
survey of the lifeless control panel, had warbled a series
of seemingly random notes. The human watched in annoyance as four additional displays appeared. One showed
the relative positions of the shuttle, the planet they were
about to land on, and the Thraki ships. The second consisted of colored bars that fluctuated in length. There was
no way to be certain, short of asking Veera that is, but
Jepp figured each bar was associated with one of the shuttle's major systems.

The third display shimmered with color but remained
blank, as if not in use, and the fourth, which the human
found to be especially interesting, scrolled through line after line of alien hieroglyphics. Jepp had seen similar symbols before, printed on bulkheads, hatches, and other
surfaces, but never obtained a large enough sample to attempt some sort of analysis.

He was about to signal Sam and order the robot to record the alien text, when the surface rose to meet them. The planet was barren and seemingly lifeless. A mountain range stretched from north to south. It rose sharp and jagged—like the teeth of a saw blade. And, judging from the nav display, twelve Thraki ships waited up ahead, grounded at the bottom of a monster crater. In order to hide? Probably, though the attempt had been futile.

Jepp remembered the text, turned toward the holo, and discovered it was dark. Then, before he could give the matter further thought, the shuttle flared in for a landing. The human sought his space suit. There were heathens to convert—and God was waiting.

There were sixty-seven youngsters in a line that wound away from the *Spirit of Gatha* and out toward the perimeter of the crater. They were clad in spacesuits, bulky affairs with which they were well acquainted and decorated to their liking. Some bore markings, some sported text, and others had been painted in fanciful ways.

Lis was one of the oldest and, along with some other sixteen-year-olds, nominally in charge. It was her job to bring up the rear, urge laggards to greater speed, and keep an eye on the robot assigned to erase their tracks.

A little one, no more than five, tripped on something. He went head over heels, hit the dry, powdery soil, and sent a wail over Channel Two. Were the machines listening? It was best to assume that they were.

Lis hurried to pick the youngster up, rapped on his faceplate, and gestured for silence. Wonderfully, amazingly, he obeyed. She put the cub down and looked back over her shoulder. The sweeper, oblivious as to the reason behind its current assignment, continued to run backwards, as it erased its tracks.

Satisfied that the machine was operating properly, Lis turned and hurried to catch up. A male named Rak had set the pace—and the little ones had a hard time trying to keep up. Legs pumped, arms windmilled, and dust marked their passage. Would it settle before the machines arrived? And did she really care? Subcommander Homa was her father—and would die with all the rest. No, they hadn't told her that, but didn't need to. It, like most of the really important events in her life, needed no explanation.

Another youngster went down. A pair of ten-year olds pulled her back up, and the column wound in among some ancient rocks. Many were quite large. The ground sloped upward now, reaching toward the crater's rim, leaving the flat behind. Lis slipped, managed to regain her footing, and looked back over her shoulder.

The robot had stalled. Its drive wheels threw plumes of dirt up into the airless atmosphere as it struggled to find purchase. Lis said a word she wasn't supposed to say, directed the youngster to proceed without her, and waited to make sure. He waddled up the slope. An eight-year-old saw and took his hand.

Conscious of how the seconds were ticking away, Lis dashed down the slope, eyed the robot, and knew the situation was hopeless. The maintenance unit had been designed to operate within the confines of a spaceship and couldn't handle the uneven terrain.

Something flashed off to the east. The sun reflecting off a rock face? Or the hull of an incoming shuttle? Lis threw herself forward, hit the robot with her shoulder, and pushed to machine over. It hit the dirt and struggled to right itself. She slapped the kill switch. The robot went inert, the youngster showered the machine with dirt, and fell facedown as a shadow slipped past.

The shuttle, which shimmered with light, dropped toward the ground. Had the machines been able to spot her? Lis didn't think so—but hurried anyway. The ground rose in front of her, the incoming air rumbled in her ears, and sorrow filled her heart.

•   •   •

Convoy Commander Pol Bay Seph met her visitors at the main lock. They were different from what she had expected: two biologicals and a robot of Thraki origins. Where were the fire-breathing shiny-assed machines? It really didn't matter, not if the aliens had the power to negotiate for the machines, which apparently they did. Both removed their helmets. The larger of the two spoke. His robot handled the translation. "Hello, my name is Jepp, Jorely Jepp, and this is Veera. The Hoon asked that we speak with you."

Though a bit misleading, the human felt the lie was justified. He realized that the Thraki was female, guessed she was older rather than younger, and saw the intelligence in her eyes. She offered some sort of gesture. "You are welcome . . . especially if your presence will help to avoid bloodshed."

"It may," Jepp answered agreeably, "God willing."

"One never knows what games the gods may play," Seph said politely. "Come . . . let's find a more comfortable place to talk."

The Thraki led their guests down a passageway, and Veera, who had no role in the negotiations, took everything in. She noticed that in spite of the fact that the ship was in good repair the fittings bore the patina of hard use.

Another item that attracted the Prithian's attention was the considerable number of robots deployed throughout the ship and their degree of sophistication. Based on travels with her father, Veera knew that most spacefaring sentients had such machines, but couldn't remember another race that was quite so dependent on them or had taken the science of robotics so far.

It seemed that most members of the crew had what amounted to pet robots, which scurried, pranced, rolled, and jumped wherever they chose. The result of all this activity was a sort of benign chaos that Veera found annoying but the Thraki seemed completely unaware of. Not Sam, however, who uttered a squeak of delight, jumped off Jepp's shoulder, and joined a round of wall tag. Veera had the distinct feeling that these observations all added up to something, but she couldn't figure out what it was.

Commander Seph took a turn and led the visitors into a relatively large space. It looked and felt like a communal living room. She gestured toward some amorphous looking chairs. "You are welcome to sit . . . although I'm not sure how comfortable you'll be."

Jepp eyed the furniture, decided it was too small to support him, and did his best to sound friendly. "I'm afraid you are correct. Besides, our pressure suits would get in the way, and we don't have enough time to remove them. May I be frank?"

"Of course," Seph answered smoothly, wondering how the youngsters were doing. "Say whatever's on your mind."

"Thank you," Jepp replied. "Here's the situation . . . The Sheen are governed by a machine intelligence called the Hoon. It has orders to destroy the Thraki race."

Seph felt a crevasse open at the pit of her stomach. Contrary to the dictates of both logic and common sense, she had allowed herself to hope—that the stories were wrong, that the machines had changed, that something good would happen. Fur rippled away from her eyes. "Then why did you come? To tell us our fate?"

The words had a hard almost metallic edge to them. The human didn't blame her. "No, that was not our purpose. I came to ask that you embrace the one and only all-knowing, all-seeing, all-powerful God."

Like 99 percent of her race Seph believed in a pantheon of gods and considered the god the alien described to be patently impossible. After all, how could one god, no matter how capable, possibly handle the running of the universe? The idea was laughable. Still, there were the children to consider, and if the alien proved sufficiently gullible, the rest of the convoy as well. "*One* god? What an interesting notion. Tell me more."

Veera, whose father had trained her to look for lies, watched in silent amazement as the ex-prospector turned amateur messiah not only fell for the Thraki's attempt at deception, but proceeded to spew the same line of nonsense he had tried on her.

It took the human the better part of twenty minutes to rattle off all the stuff about how the machines were a gift from God, the mission to which he alone had been called, and the opportunity that stretched before them. "I can save your souls," Jepp said importantly, "and deliver them to the Lord."

"We accept," Seph answered earnestly. "What should we do?"

This was a much different response from the one given by the earlier group that Jepp had encountered. He was surprised. *Very* surprised. "Really? You mean it?"

"Yes," Seph lied fervently, "I do. Save our souls from the Sheen, and give them to the one all-knowing God."

The words summoned up images of a triumphant Jepp presenting a gift to God. This was it! The moment he'd been waiting for! "God bless you, Commander—and all your people. My assistant and I will return to the shuttle where we can petition the Hoon. A warning, however— the machine is stubborn. It may be necessary to tell a few untruths."

Seph struggled to control her expression, realized it wouldn't mean anything to the creature in front of her, and let the matter go. The alien was an idiot, and she couldn't imagine why the Sheen continued to put up with him. "Really? What sort of untruths?"

Jepp appeared hesitant. "That you and your companions are not only renegades—but willing to aid the Sheen."

"Of course," Seph replied calmly. "Do as you must."

Jepp, victory almost in his grasp, was eager to leave. Real live converts! Doubters? Yes, almost certainly, but that would change. He knew that it would.

Seph saw the aliens to the hatch and waited for it to

close. She turned to Subcommander Homa. "The little ones? Where are they?"

Homa, acutely aware of the fact that one of the young-sters was his, discovered the lump in his throat. He strug-gled to swallow it. "They made it to the edge of the crater—and hid among the rocks."

Seph looked her subordinate in the eyes. She had never produced any offspring of her own—but could imagine how the other officer felt. "The alien is a fool. The Hoon will refuse. The Sheen will attack."

Homa met her gaze. "If you are correct, and they attack from space, the little ones will be killed."

"Exactly," Seph agreed. "*Unless* we run."

"Which would force them to chase us," Homa said thoughtfully. "Saving the cubs but negating any possibility that the machines will accept your lies."

"So," Seph said gently, "what should we do?"

Homa felt a great upwelling of sorrow, for the daughter he would never see again, for himself, and for the entire Thraki race. Why? Why did the machines continually hunt them? The priests offered platitudes but no one really knew. All of it was so stupid and unnecessary. The words were little more than a croak. "We must run."

Seph, who felt strangely detached, bowed her head. "I'm sorry old friend—but I'm forced to agree."

As the Hoon listened to the human's rantings with a min-ute part of its consciousness, it also monitored streams of data from even the most distant parts of its far-flung body. That's how the AI knew when the Thraki convoy started to power up. It seemed that the biological's plan had failed, a rather predictable outcome that confirmed the Hoon's preexisting bias: Though mostly harmless, and occasion-ally useful, Jepp was an idiot. That being the case, the computer intelligence ordered the human's shuttle to lift, severed the incoming communication, and ordered his forces to attack. They confirmed the nature of his instruction, and insofar as the Hoon was concerned, the incident was over.

Jepp staggered and nearly lost his footing as the shuttle pushed the planet away. Veera, who had been serving as interpreter, quit in midsentence and was quick to strap herself in. The human looked left and right. "What's happening? I demand to know! Veera . . . Sam . . . tell the Hoon."

The teenager warbled to the robot. It answered in kind. Jepp collapsed into the ill-fitting seat. "Switch to standard, damn you! And hurry up."

"The Hoon broke the connection," Veera said simply. "That's *his* way of ending a conversation."

"But the Thraki!" Jepp objected, "They are under my protection!"

Veera could have said something regarding how much his protection was worth but chose to remain silent instead. Though not of his species, and not capable of tears, she knew how he felt. When the Thraki died, his dreams died with them.

Lis and the other youngsters watched from the rocks as repellors stabbed the hard oxide-rich soil. The ships hovered head high until the in-system drives were engaged. Then, with the precision born of long practice, the spaceships accelerated away. With them went fathers, mothers, brothers, sisters, uncles, aunts, friends, and more, never to be seen again. The battle, if that's what the massacre could properly be called, would take place on the far side of the planet where the thin, nearly nonexistent atmosphere gave way to vacuum. A small mercy—but a meaningful one.

The cubs, especially the younger ones, made little noises toward the backs of their throats. Lis thought about saying something, warning them to be quiet, but decided to let it go. There was only a limited chance that the machines would pick up on such a low-powered transmission.

One of the males said, "Look!" and pointed toward the center of the crater.

Lis looked, and there, exactly where her father's ship had been, sat a cargo lighter. Like an egg in a nest. The vessel was small, *very* small, but capable of a hyperspace jump. It was gray, about the same temp as the surrounding rocks, and completely innocuous. Had a course been entered into the ship's navcomp? Yes, she knew that it had.

They waited for three long days before concluding that the battle was over and the Sheen had left. Slowly, almost reverently, the youngsters filed down out of the rocks and made their way toward the ship. It was only when they stopped to look up that Lis saw the name spray-painted across the bow. It was hers.

14

I always say that, next to a battle lost, the greatest misery is a battle gained.

Attributed to the Duke of Wellington
Standard year circa 1815

Clone World BETA-018, the Clone Hegemony

Vice Admiral Haru Ista Rawan, who, as the senior officer on the ground, had the dubious honor of commanding all Thraki forces stationed on Clone World BETA-018, secured the fasteners on his standard-issue parka, waited for the form to climb onto his shoulder, and left the relative comfort of his office. Metal clanged under his boots as he crossed the catwalk that bisected the cavern and eyed the fighters arrayed below. They were Owana III Interceptors and, like the admiral himself, had seen long, hard service.

The aerospace fighters were parked in two opposing rows. Wraithlike wisps of vapor leaked from the umbilicals that connected the ships to the ground-support systems. Some twenty transports, easily identified by their larger hulls, lurked deep within the shadows.

The interceptors would be busy soon, Rawan reflected as he returned a technical's salute, stepped onto a freight platform, and stabbed the "Down" button. His breath fogged the air as a motor whined, the lift jerked in protest, and sank toward the flight deck below. Ships had dropped in system, *Confederate* ships, with not a word of protest from the normally contentious Hegemony.

The same clones who had welcomed his people with open arms only months before, had turned decidedly less hospitable of late, even going so far as to cut off communications. It didn't require diplomatic credentials to understand why. The Hegemony feared that if the Sheen attacked their guests *they* would suffer as well.

The officer could have felt bitter, could have felt betrayed, but didn't. It seemed as if his people were destined to go friendless, to roam the stars forever, bereft of peace. The clones were nothing more than the latest manifestation of a hostile universe.

The platform clanged to a stop, Rawan stepped off, and turned toward the cold gray light. It flooded through the cavern's entrance and glazed the deck in front of him. Walking into the alien glow, then peering out over the semifrozen landscape, was part of his daily routine. Officers saluted from a distance, technicals went about their chores, and the robots ignored him. The admiral's breath came in gasps as his lungs struggled to extract oxygen from the cold thin air. The medical officer claimed they would get used to it after a while, but Rawan had his doubts.

A wrench clattered as the officer neared the opening. A cold, clammy wind caressed Rawan's face and sent his hands into his pockets. The gloves he had intended to bring remained on his desk.

Warning lights chased each other around the opening, deck icons warned of danger, and snowflakes swirled beyond. The sun struggled to push its pale yellow light through a corona of white mist and failed. Rawan stepped over the knee-high safety chain and paused to eye the twin energy cannons positioned to either side of the passageway. Stripped from a decommissioned cruiser and protected by localized energy shields, they could defend against both aircraft and a ground assault. Even the Sheen would be forced to take such weapons seriously. It was a comforting thought. The admiral leaned into the wind and forced himself onto the outer platform. Moisture formed at the corners of his eyes and he blinked it away.

Though technically classified as "Earth normal," the Hegemony planet designated as BETA-018 was actually quite marginal, which had everything to do with why the clones allowed the Thraki to establish a colony there.

The entrance, and the base to which it led, were located at the head of a U-shaped canyon, and, more than that, were roughly one hundred units off the ground. That meant that any pilot so foolish as to attack would have to fly between the computer-operated weapons positions that lined both walls of the valley and into the combined fire of the energy cannons that flanked the entrance. Not a pleasant prospect.

The same thing would apply to ground forces, since Rawan and his staff had gone to considerable lengths to ensure that all of the defensive weaponry could depress their barrels and launch tubes far enough to reach the canyon floor.

In addition to those precautions, Rawan had laid a minefield across the canyon's mouth, ordered his robots to construct a variety of obstacles, and even gone so far as to prepare trenches for the six hundred ground troops assigned to protect his air squadron.

The wind renewed its assault on the officer's face and only the fact that the Thraki had short, bristly fur prevented him from getting frostbite. He stared down into the valley below but was unable to see his marines. Because their camouflage was so good? Or because *he* was getting old?

Whatever the reason Rawan feared that the ground forces represented the chink in his armor. The navy was strong, very strong, thanks to hundreds of years spent fighting duels with the Sheen, but the ground arm was weak and relatively inexperienced. Just one of the things that explained his Runner sympathies.

A klaxon sounded somewhere behind him. Fighters probably—back from a sortie. He could clear the deck or risk being blown off the ledge. Rawan took one last look at the valley and turned away. The cavern yawned and he stepped inside.

The holo, shot during a rare break in BETA-018's cloud cover and augmented by footage supplied by recon drones, ran its course and faded to black. The *Gladiator*'s hangar deck had been pressurized and, with the addition of folding chairs, transformed into a serviceable auditorium. The lights came up as Booly stood and made his way to the portable podium. The ship's motto, "For glory and honor," faced the audience. He looked out at the crowd. It was the most unlikely gathering the officer could have imagined.

The Jonathan Alan Seebos claimed the first couple of rows and, if it hadn't been for differences in age, would have been as identical as the hard-eyed stares fastened on his face. Immediately behind the clones sat the men, women, and Naa warriors still at the Legion's core. Further to the rear, like mountains rising from a human plain, the Hudathans loomed. Their skins were gray, their backs uncomfortably exposed, and their expressions were grim.

And behind *them*, like a race unto itself, the cyborgs stood. Some human, some Hudathan, they were *big*, but dwarfed by the aerospace fighters beyond and by the scale of the *Gladiator* herself.

Here, Booly thought to himself, are the *real* aliens, beings who no longer resemble the species from which they came, and no longer perceive life in the same way.

None of the Ramanthian ground forces had been assigned to the assault on 18, both because of their lack of experience in fighting on ice worlds and their participation in other initiatives. *These* were the minds that would take

Booly's ideas, translate strategy to tactics, and lead their troops into battle—not in segregated units, as certain politicians had suggested, but in integrated groups in which Hudathans, Naa, and humans would fight side by side. It was a risk, a *big* risk, but so was the alternative.

Assuming the Confederacy managed to win most of the upcoming battles, assuming that it managed to survive the Sheen onslaught, the heat of the conflict would bake the military into its final form—a form that would be difficult to break without causing considerable damage. The kind of damage that might lead to another rebellion or civil war.

Still, it was with a sense of deep-seated concern that the officer started to speak. His words were translated as necessary. "You've read the reports, heard the analysis, and seen the footage. So you know what we're up against. Given the threat posed by the Sheen, the *Gladiator* is the only ship the Confederacy could put against BETA-018. One ship—one planet. Why use more?"

Booly waited for the laughter to die away. "The Thraki are extremely experienced warriors. They have their backs to the wall and are well dug in, not only dug in, but dug into an *allied* planet, with civilians in residence. The settlement called 'Frost' lies only six miles away from the Thraki base. An orbital attack would destroy both.

"To root the Thraki out, Admiral Tyspin's fighters are going to have to penetrate the valley and put weapons on hardened targets . . . the most important of which is the base itself." Booly paused to scan their faces. Pilots stared up at him. "In order for the jet jockeys to hit their targets, the ground pounders will need to silence at least some of the batteries that line both sides of the canyon."

A major yelled, "Camerone!" and a substantial portion of the audience roared the appropriate response. "CAMERONE!"

Booly noticed that many of the Jonathan Alan Seebos remained silent, as did a substantial number of the Hudathans, but some joined in. *That* was progress. He grinned.

"Thank you. I'm glad to see that someone's awake out there."

Laughter rippled through the audience. Booly picked up where he had left off. "You and your troops come from different worlds, pack different DNA, and have different cultures. Those differences could manifest themselves as a weakness, a *fatal* weakness, or, and tremendous progress has been made in this direction, they could become the source of our strength, and the reason we emerge victorious. Not just *here*, but elsewhere, when the Sheen drop hyper.

"Long hard days have been spent establishing a chain of command, integrating our varied systems, and selecting best practices. Every single one of you deserves credit for making that happen. Now comes the test, the moment when steel meets steel, when courage owns the day."

A human legionnaire rose at the back of the audience and shouted the ancient Hudathan battle cry: "BLOOD!"

The audience roared the response: "BLOOD!"

A Hudathan stood, raised his fist, and shouted "CA-MERONE!"

Booly smiled, waited for the noise level to drop, and brought the meeting to a close. "You know what to do—so go and do it. Insertion teams Blue, Red, Yellow, and Green will drop about six hours from now. Kick some butt for me."

The flight of six daggers shuddered as they forced their way down into the planet's hard, thin atmosphere. Lieutenant Commander Rawlings bit her lower lip. She'd seen combat before, back during the mutiny, but not like this. She had been a watch officer then, standing shoulder to shoulder with the bridge crew, staring into a three-dimensional holo tank as brightly lit sparks fought duels in the dark.

This was different. There was the loneliness of her one person cockpit *plus* the knowledge that five pilots were

counting on her for guidance and leadership. One Hudathan, two Seebos, and a couple of "greenies" right out of
the navy's Advanced Combat School. Rawlings didn't
know which scared her most, *their* lack of experience or
hers. A group of red deltas wiped themselves onto her
HUD and Lieutenant Hawa Morlo-Ba, who never tired of
being first, made the call. "Blue Five to Blue One . . . bandits at six o'clock!"

Rawlings listened to herself say, "Roger that, Five," and
took pride in the flat laconic sound of the words. "Tally
ho!"

Clone intelligence claimed that Thraki interceptors were
protected by cloaking technology obtained from a race
called "The Simm," and it appeared that they were correct.
The enemy interceptors were a good deal closer than she
would have preferred. The naval officer "thought" her aircraft to starboard, felt it side slip into a dive, and brought
the ship's weapons systems on-line.

The others watched her go, followed the officer down,
and scanned their readouts. Power was critical, weapons
were critical, *everything* was critical or would be soon.

Flight Warrior Hissa Hol Beko watched the Confederate
aircraft descend, checked her wing mates, and confirmed
their positions. The pilot's weapons, like the rest of her
ship, were controlled by the special gauntlets she wore.
Each movement had meaning. Index to finger to thumb:
"Safeties off—accumulators on." First two fingers in parallel: "Ship-to-ship missiles—safeties off—guidance on—
warheads active." The pilot's displays flickered with each
carefully articulated movement. Then, as the enemy fighters came into range, a circuit closed, and her fingers began
to tingle. Beko fired and the air war began.

Rawlings heard tone, fired chaff, and rolled. The enemy
missile sped past and exploded. The fighter that had fired

it pulled a high-gee turn and attempted to flee. The rest of the Thraki interceptors did likewise.

Both of the Seebos responded with a nearly identical cheer, applied full military power, and gave chase.

Rawlings wanted to stop them, wanted to call the pilots back, but wasn't sure why. Good fighter pilots were aggressive, competitive, and little bit obnoxious. But this was *too* easy, *too* tempting, *too* . . .

Beko checked her screens and grinned as the enemy ships took the bait. The Hegemony had been most accommodating during the early stages of the Clone-Thraki relationship and shared some of their knowledge regarding Confederate technology. That was how Beko knew the range at which her adversaries would be able to detect her fighters and was able to put that knowledge to work. By leaving two heavily cloaked interceptors behind, and leading the enemy towards them, she and her wing mates had closed the trap.

The Seebos saw deltas appear as if by magic, tried to react, but ran out of time. Rawlings winced as the orange-red flowers blossomed, gritted her teeth, and took the challenge.

The Thraki had reversed direction by then . . . which meant that she and her three surviving pilots were about to go head to head with six enemy aircraft. That's when the naval officer noticed how precisely the enemy was grouped. Because they had a taste for discipline? Or because the pilots were trained to fight tightly controlled machines? Computer controlled machines that behaved in predictable ways? Words followed thought: "Break! Break! Break! Take 'um one on one, over."

Beko frowned, and the fur crawled away from her eyes as the oncoming formation seemed to explode. Confederate vessels went every which way as she struggled to understand. But there wasn't enough time, not at combined speeds of more than a thousand units per hour, and the sky went mad.

The Confederate ships rolled, turned, dove, and climbed. Missiles left their racks, coherent light stuttered toward their targets, and 30 mm cannon shells tunneled through the air.

Beko yowled in frustration as the formation disintegrated around her, fired at one of the oncoming ships, and knew she had missed. And then, before she could recover, the interceptor took a hit. Alarms went off, systems failed, and a computer made a decision. The cockpit blew itself free of the ship, a cluster of chutes popped open, and the planet swayed below. Beko saw no less than three of her pilots die or bail out during the next two minutes. Shame filled her heart, and the weight of it pulled the warrior down.

The Command and Control Center, or CCC, was almost eerily quiet. Near disasters, disasters, and total disasters were announced in the same emotionless drone used to describe the most important of victories. It was a large compartment by shipboard standards, buried deep within the *Gladiator*'s armor-clad hull, and the place from which Booly, his staff, and a group of highly skilled technicians ran the assault on BETA-018.

Screens lined the bulkheads, video flashed, rolled, and stuttered; indicator lights signaled from the darkness, and "Big Momma," the ship's primary C&C computer murmured in the background. Booly cocked his head as the latest summaries came in over the speakers. "Preliminary totals indicate casualties more than 16 percent in excess of plan. Estimate that 86.2 percent of enemy force engaged. Approximately 72.1 percent of enemy aircraft destroyed."

Something moved through the officer's peripheral vision, and a coffee cup landed at his elbow. Admiral Tyspin lowered herself onto a chair. She looked tired. He smiled. "Thanks for the coffee."

She lifted her cup by way of an acknowledgement. "De nada."

"So how're we doing?"

Tyspin eyed him through the steam, took a sip, and lowered the mug. "You heard Big Momma . . . We took causalities . . . *too* many . . . but the sky belongs to us."

Booly nodded. "And the insertion teams?"

"Ready to drop."

"Give 'em my best."

Tyspin smiled. "I already did."

Once Dagger Commander, now *Lieutenant* Drik Seeba-Ka felt the landing craft fall free, checked the seal on his anus, and was relieved to find that it was intact. He hadn't been so lucky the first time out—and spent the day wallowing in his own shit. No one had noticed though, not in the stink of the training swamp, and disgrace was avoided.

But what of today? the Hudathan asked himself, as he stared down the aisle. What of the twenty-five Hudathans, twenty-five legionnaires, four Naa and six cyborgs placed under his command? How would *they* regard him when the sun finally set? Assuming some survived? Would they honor his name? The officer was determined that they would. But what did barbarians know of honor? And could he trust them? War Commander Doma-Sa said "yes," but who could be sure?

Seeba-Ka touched the Legion-issue wrist term and watched video blossom on the inside surface of his visor. He saw the ridge, two of the weapons emplacements that topped it, and the initial objective: a cluster of Thraki airshafts. The mission was simplicity itself. Neutralize the defenders, drop through the airshafts, and destroy everything in sight. *If* they made the LZ, *if* they could penetrate the complex, *if* the enemy gave way. The purpose of the assault was to take some pressure off the forces detailed to drive the length of the valley floor. The landing craft shuddered as the hull hit the upper part of the atmosphere, but the Hudathan didn't even notice. He ran the sequence again.

About four feet away, thumbs hooked into his battle harness, First Sergeant Antonio "Top" Santana eyed his commanding officer through half-closed lids. What was the hatchet head thinking anyway? Jeez, the sonovabitch was ugly. He seemed to know his shit, though, which was good, because Santana was ready if he didn't. Two slugs in the back of the head, and the matter would be settled. Not a pleasant thought but better than letting a geek waste his team. The noncom smiled.

A little further down the aisle, over on the starboard side, Quickfoot Hillrun started to snore. Oneshot Surekill took exception and kicked the other scout's foot. The sound stopped for a moment but quickly resumed.

Lower in the hull, below Surekill's feet, cyborgs hung within cylindrical drop tubes. The team consisted of four humans and two Hudathans. The tech types had gone to considerable lengths to ensure their com equipment was compatible. That being the case, and borgs being borgs, the "machine augmented" troopers chatted on a low-power utility band. Corporal Lars Lastow, one of the 1,021 cyborgs that then Colonel Bill Booly had rescued from Fort Portal back during the mutiny, was interrogating one of his Hudathan colleagues. "So, Sergeant Horla-Ka, how's your sex life?"

"The same as yours," the noncom answered stolidly. "Nonexistent."

"That's not what I hear," the human continued. "I hear they wired you guys to come every time you kill someone."

"Come?" Horla-Ka responded, "I don't understand."

"You know," Lastow went on, "shoot your load, blow your rocks, have an orgasm."

"Oh that," Horla-Ka answered evenly. "Yes, it's true."

"Damn," the human responded. "You are one lucky bastard."

The Hudathan eyed his readouts, saw the seconds ticking away, and knew the enemy was waiting. And not just waiting, but locked, loaded, and ready to fire. "Yes," he replied dryly. "I am one lucky bastard."

One level up, and all the way forward, Navy Lieutenant Mog Howsky "thought" the nose up, wished she had something to do with her hands, and kept her eyes on the HUD. The "backdoor" as she and her copilot called it consisted of a broad U-shaped valley that lay behind the Thraki stronghold and ran parallel to it.

The plan was to approach from the south and then, when the enemy base was due west, make a hard turn to port. Conditions permitting, Howsky would make two separate passes. The cyborgs would drop during the first, engage the weapons emplacements, and secure the LZ. With that accomplished, the assault boat would return, off-load the soft bodies, and haul ass. Assuming I have one to haul, Howsky thought to herself.

Mountains rose on both sides, sparks floated up to greet them, and the hard part began. "All right," Horla-Ka growled, using his external speakers in spite of the fact that there was no need to, "we are two from dirt. Remove safeties—prepare to drop."

Conscious of what awaited them and the importance of their role, the cyborgs were silent. They could "feel" the side-to-side motion as the ship jinked back and forth. Thanks to the fact that they could "see" via the landing craft's external sensors, the team knew what to expect.

A missile raced over her head and a green tracer whipped past the cockpit as Howsky completed the run. Commands that originated in her brain burped through the computer-assisted interface to make things happen. Flaps fell, jets fired, and the ship started to stall. Repellors stabbed the darkness, the belly gun fired, and slugs hosed the ridgeline. There it was, just as the simulators said it would be, a flat area, a series of duracrete weapons emplacements, and the stacks beyond.

There was a cracking sound as a high velocity slug punched a hole in the canopy and took Second Lieutenant

Gorky's head off. Howsky felt her friend drop out of the control matrix, swore as blood splattered the side of her helmet, and forced herself to concentrate. The tubes opened on command, the borgs dropped free, and she turned to port. If anything happened, if the boat took a hit, the hard bodies would be safe. Well, not *safe*, but safer. She lined up the targeting reticule on the pillbox and thumbed the pickle. Slugs marched their way up to a pillbox and forced their way inside. Something exploded, and flames belched out through the side-mounted cooling vents.

Lastow "heard" the buzzer, "felt" the clamps release, and nothing happened. He *should* have been falling, *should* have cleared the ship, but hadn't dropped more than an inch or two.

Okay, okay, the cyborg said to himself, it's a jam. How many simulated jams have you cleared? A hundred? Yeah, easily. Test the circuits, look for shorts, reroute the signal. Electricity did as it was told, a relay closed, and the clamps opened.

It was only then, as the Trooper II body dropped clear of the ship, that the legionnaire remembered to check the target, discovered that the boat had cleared the ridge, and realized he was still in the process of falling. Not ten feet as he had planned, but a *hundred* feet, onto the rocks below. Those who monitored his scream, and that included Horla-Ka, would never forget the sound.

But there was no time for sympathy, for grief, or any of the other emotions that tried to push their way in. Thraki shells exploded all around. The Hudathan gave his orders. "Form a line abreast! Missiles first! Engage the weapons emplacements!"

Dor Duplo, with Lastow's scream still echoing through his mind, launched two missiles at once. They sensed heat, accelerated away, and hit the closest pillbox. Light flashed, thunder cracked, and the bunker came apart.

"Passable," Horla-Ka commented calmly as the cyborgs

advanced along the ridge, "though wasteful. One missile would have been sufficient."

Duplo started to object, started to tell the hatchet head he was crazy, and realized it was a waste of time. *All* of them were crazy.

Someone, Horla-Ka thought it was Himley, yelled "Hit the deck!"

The noncom obliged, "felt" something warm pass over his head, and "heard" the assault boat crash. Metal screeched, a turbine roared, and something exploded. Santana staggered, tried to pull the shard of hull metal out of his chest, and collapsed. Horla-Ka got to his feet. "The airshafts! Follow me!"

Bak Borlo-Ka, the second Hudathan on the team questioned the order, but followed it. What of those on the landing craft? Some were clansmen.

But there was no time to think, only to act. Thraki troops boiled up out of the ground and opened fire. That was a mistake. With no cyborgs of their own, the defenders were outgunned. Arm-mounted Gatling guns roared, energy cannons burped, and the soft bodies ceased to exist. Horla-Ka felt orgasm after orgasm ripple through a body he no longer possessed—and found the split-second necessary to hate the scientists for what they had done to him. To take the pleasure associated with the creation of life and use it as a reward for destroying it . . . What could be more twisted?

But there was no time to think, to do more than run, as the airshafts rose, and the resistance started to fade. The first objective had been secured—but what of the second? The borgs were too big to fit inside the airshafts and too clumsy to lower themselves to the bottom. The mission was at risk.

Lieutenant Seeba-Ka felt the SLM hit the ship, heard the explosion, and knew they were in trouble. He yelled, "Hang on!" took his own advice, and saw the deck tilt.

The pilot was fighting for control, the infantry officer could tell that, and struggled to suppress his fear. Fear he wasn't supposed to feel, fear that signaled his weakness, fear that . . .

The ship side-slipped into the ground. Howsky died instantly as did a third of the troops seated with their backs to the port bulkhead. Toba, Ibens, Ngugen, Al Saiid, Ista-Sa, Porlo-Ba, Boro-Da, and Norno-Ka—all dead.

Seeba-Ka, who was seated just aft of the impact zone, released his harness and lurched to his feet. Though conceived in Hudathan the words were not all that different from what a human might have said. "What the hell are you waiting for? A full-blown holo presentation? Hit the dirt!"

Hudathan, human, and Naa alike released their harnesses, struggled to make their way the length of the steeply slanted deck, and headed towards the bright green lights. Due to the fact that the ship had fallen onto the port side that door was blocked. Thanks to the manner in which the hull had rotated, the opposite hatch was high, and very difficult to reach. A legionnaire boosted another legionnaire up, but he lost his balance. Both tumbled to the deck.

Private Lars Lasker solved the problem by triggering the belly-mounted escape hatch and jumping up and down on the door. It gave, and he fell through the hole. Sergeant Quickfoot Hillrun pointed and yelled. "Move! Move! Move!"

Legionnaires poured out onto the ground, took defensive positions around the wreckage, and waited for orders. Wounded were dragged outside, carried beyond the reach of the potential blast zone, and given first aid. Seeba-Ka called for an air evac and was assured that it was en route.

Once that was accomplished, it was a relatively simple matter to check with Horla-Ka, confirm that the air shafts were secure, and send the report. Like so many of its kind the communication said nothing of the sacrifice required to make it possible. "Red Team is on the ground . . . The first objective is ours."

The cabin had been designed for use by admirals and more than met Booly's needs. He sat in an easy chair guarded by two stacks of printouts. One that he had read and one that he hadn't. In spite of 18's importance, the Confederacy covered a lot of space, and Booly, as Military Chief of Staff, had responsibility for the whole thing. That's why he was busy scanning an intelligence summary on Zynig-47 when the message came in. Tyspin chose to bring it herself. She entered without knocking, dropped into a chair, and offered the slip of paper. "Here, add this to your reading."

Booly read the words, nodded, and handed the slip back. "Casualties?"

Tyspin shook her head. "No data as yet . . . but Red One requested a medevac."

"And Objective Two?"

"They're tackling it now."

Booly paused, imagined what it would be like to rappel down one of those airshafts, and grimaced. "And Blue One? How's she doing?"

Tyspin grinned. He noticed her eyes were rimmed with red. She hadn't slept in days. "McGowan? Are you kidding? She was born ready."

Booly nodded. "Turn her loose."

"Yes, sir."

"And Angie?"

"Sir?"

"Take a nap."

The assault team was located on a plain just beyond the canyon's mouth. A thin layer of snow covered the rocks, low lying vegetation, and the ground itself.

Four widely spaced piles of burned wreckage marked

sorties by low flying Thraki aircraft. The balance of Blue Team was hunkered down, weapons scanning the sky, waiting for the next assault. The fur balls knew where they were, and, if it hadn't been for the swabbies patrolling the airspace above, would have greased the entire force by then.

Captain Bethany "Butch" McGowan had been dirtside for more than eight hours by then. She cursed the cold, blew on her hands, and prayed for a green light. Every hour that passed meant that her troops were a little more tired . . . and a little more likely to make mistakes. Her force consisted of six quads, sixteen Trooper II's, twelve Hudathan "heavies," and a mixed force of infantry under the questionable command of Lieutenant Jonathan Allan Seebo-872. The ground-pounders included more Jonathan Alan Seebos plus a platoon of legionnaires under Gunnery Sergeant Rolly True Bear.

Blue Team was supposed to negotiate a minefield, find its way through the tank traps, and, should Red Team fail, make their way up the length of the valley through a withering crossfire. Not a stroll in the park.

McGowan's com tech, a woman named Bagano, stuck her head up through a hatch. She wore a com helmet, a non-reg nosering, and a shit-eating grin. "The big dog is on line one . . . We're good to go."

McGowan sighed. Bagano had a problem where military courtesy was concerned, had been disciplined any number of times, and didn't seem to give a shit. The officer could have brought the soldier up on charges, and probably would have, except for one little problem: Bagano, or "Bags" as her buddies referred to her, was the best damned com tech on that side of galaxy. McGowan had seen the woman take three mangled PR3s, fieldstrip them, and build a new unit in less than three minutes. When it came to a trade-off between formality and competency, McGowan would take competency every single time. Her voice was intentionally loud. "All right! That's the kind of news we've been waiting for! How's Red?"

"Red is down," the com tech confirmed. "Objective One is secure—and they're working on Two."

McGowan considered what that meant. The cyborgs would hold the stacks while the balance of the team dropped through the shafts, located the enemy command and control center, and blew the computer. That should silence the remotely operated weapons emplacements that lined the canyon walls. Weapons emplacements that the jet jockeys had been unable to overcome. Not that the swabbies hadn't tried. The remains of one dagger was scattered about halfway up—pointing at the ultimate goal—while a second was smeared across the face of a cliff.

Then, assuming that some of the Red Team managed to make it through—the poor bastards were supposed to throw themselves at the heavily shielded energy cannons mounted to either side of the main entrance—and attempt to shut them down.

Meanwhile, assuming McGowan made it past the many obstacles that lay in her path, she could expect to come into contact with some nasty-assed tanks the Thrakies had stashed at the base of the cliff. "Ah well, it was like they said: 'Don't join if you can't take a joke.' "

McGowan triggered the command push. A wire-thin boom mike captured her words. "Blue One here . . . we are green to go. Repeat green to go. Return to your vehicles, saddle up, and strap in. The last sonofabitch to reach the wall buys the beer!"

There were cheers, some of which were muffled, as steel clanged on steel.

McGowan grinned, circled a quad named Yen, and switched to another frequency. The ramp bounced under her boots. "I'm in—seal the hatch." Servos whined as the armor-plated ramp rose to mate with the cyborg's durasteel hull.

About a hundred feet away, sealed into the belly of a Hudathan heavy, Lieutenant Jonathan Alan Seebo-872 eyed his clone brothers. They sat in double rows facing each other. In spite of the fact that each one wore battle armor and carried a full complement of weapons plus ammo for the crew-served machine guns and rocket launchers, they were still dwarfed by the Hudathan-sized seats.

That, plus the fact that he and his brothers were actually sealed *inside* an alien cyborg, added to the somewhat surreal atmosphere. In spite of the fact that the Legion had used cyborgs for a considerable length of time, even going so far as to station them on Hegemony-held worlds, the Alpha Clones had never seen fit to commission intelligent constructs of their own.

Now, trapped within the belly of such a being, 872 had reason to question their wisdom. Of even more concern, however, was the fact that his superiors had not only acquiesced to the Confederacy's decision to place a free-breeder in overall command of the allied forces, they failed to intervene when the same officer placed McGowan in charge of Blue Team. A serious error, given not only her gender but the likelihood that she would sacrifice his brothers and him rather than risk her precious legionnaires.

All the infantry came under him, however—which would make it more difficult for McGowan to implement her plan. The officer grinned but knew it looked more like a snarl. *If* he died, *if* he wound up in hell, the legionnaires would arrive there first.

Power went to the axles, tracks started to churn, and the cyborg moved forward. Blue Team was on the way.

The sun had broken through. Sergeant Quickfoot stood in the hard black shadow cast by a spire of rock. He along with twelve legionnaires were gathered around one of the Thraki-constructed air shafts. Each was approximately ten-feet wide and lined with metal. The protective covers had been cut free and removed. The Naa peered down, but outside of the blue-green glow of the flare, there was nothing much to see.

The mechanism that pushed stale air up toward the surface remained operational, however, and there were plenty
of odors. The noncom's nose, which was at least ten times
more sensitive than the nearly useless protuberance humans were equipped with, sent information to his brain.
There was the harsh odor of the demo charge they had
lobbed in first, followed by the tang that was characteristic
of Legion-issue flares, and yes, the faint odor of cooking.

Satisfied that he knew everything about the shaft that
his senses could tell him, the noncom looked up. His team-
mates included Sureseek Fareye, Rockclimb Warmfeel,
Oneshot Surekill, and Quickhand Knifemake. The words
were in Naa: "The enemy will reach the bottom of the
shaft soon. I think we should be there to greet them."

Teeth gleamed in the half-lit murk. All of the Naa were
equipped with rock-climbing gear, including sit harnesses,
carabiners, descenders, and other equipment required for
rappelling, but carried none of the hardware associated
with climbing. The reason was simple: Once down, they
would fight their way out through the complex itself.

Coils of half-inch kernmantle fell into the void, un-
wound, and pulled themselves straight. Hillrun grabbed a
rope, stuck a loop through the hole in the figure-eight de-
scender, and used a locking D-carabiner to secure it to his
harness. Now, with his heels on the lip of the shaft, the
noncom was ready to go.

That's when he looked up to find that Lieutenant Drik
Seba-Ka's eyes were fixed on his. And that's when Hillrun
saw something he'd never expected to see. Though still
close to expressionless, it seemed as if there was a little
bit of warmth in the Hudathan's expression and, more remarkable yet, a measure of respect. The officer's voice
sounded like a rock crusher in low gear. "Watch your step,
Sergeant . . . I'm short of noncoms."

Hillrun grinned, said "Yes, sir!" and stepped backward
into the void.

•   •   •

The office, modest to begin with, seemed even smaller now. No less than three Thraki officers waited to report. None were happy. Flight Leader Pak Harpu was upset about the fact that the aliens had been allowed to seize the orbital highground without so much as a shot fired. Base Commander Mot Bara wanted to know what she should do about the invasion of her air shafts. And Armored Commander Stik Colep wanted permission for a counterattack, all of which was quite logical given who and what they were.

But Vice Admiral Ista Rawan had to consider the larger picture, focusing on that which was best for the race, that which was good for those under his command, and that which could actually be carried out.

And there was the difficulty. Yes, they could hold for a while, could make the invaders pay, but to what end? BETA-018 was a long way from Zynig-47 and of limited strategic value.

Yes, he could request assistance, but even if Andragna decided to send some, what would the relief force find? A Confederate ambush? And the smoking ruins of a devastated base?

No, it didn't make sense. Unfortunately, and the thought pained him, it was time to retreat—to take what he could, run while he could, and head for home. The word surprised him. Like it or not, for better or worse, his people had a home. A place from which they would refuse to run. Something worth defending.

There was silence in the room, and, judging from the expressions of his subordinates, Rawan knew it had been that way for quite some time. He looked from face to face. "Here's what I want each of you to do: Base Commander Bara will use part of her security troops to delay the invaders and the rest to prepare for evacuation. Flight Leader Harpu will ensure that the transports are loaded and ready to lift. Commander Colep will engage the enemy in an attempt to delay them for the maximum amount of time."

Rawan eyed his subordinates. Their pain was clear to

see. They wanted to fight. *All* of them. Even the Runners like Bara. "Timing will be critical. All three of you will share the responsibility of making sure that the maximum number of people escape."

Rawan's eyes shifted to the Armored officer. "And that includes you . . . I expect you and your troops will engage the enemy, fall back, and run as if the gods themselves were nipping at your heels. Understood?"

Colep stood gunbarrel-straight. The orders ran contrary to everything he believed in, everything he was, everything he had ever wanted to be. Here, served from on high, was eternal dishonor. Be that as it may there was only one answer that Rawan would accept. "Sir! Yes, sir!"

"Good," Rawan finished. "You have your orders. Carry them out."

Gunnery Sergeant Rolly True Bear put a chunk of granite between himself and the enemy, brought his binoculars up to his eyes, and scanned the terrain ahead. The bottom of the canyon was relatively flat, increasingly narrow, and dotted with sizeable boulders. The walls were too steep for a quad to climb and were covered by loose scree. Everything wore a coat of crusty white snow, thinner where the seldom-seen sun occasionally struck, but thick where shadows fell thick and black. Data scrolled down the right side of the screen. It included the range of whatever fell under the crosshairs, the prevailing wind direction, the surface temperature and more. Lots of information, but not what the noncom needed most.

Blue Force was stalled. Crab mines, which roam from place to place, would disturb the snow, but there was no sign of that. So, assuming the mines existed, *where* were they? It was a job for robots . . . but none had been issued. The voice arrived over the company push, which meant that everybody could hear it. "Blue Two to Blue Four . . . over."

True Bear grimaced. He didn't care for Lieutenant Jonathan Alan Seebo-872 and knew the feeling was mutual. Maybe that's why he and his troops were out looking for mines while the clones napped in a heavy. "This is Blue Four . . . go. Over."

"What's taking so long? We haven't got all day. Over."

True Bear wrestled with his temper and managed to win. "Roger that, Two. We'll know in a moment. Hold on, over."

The noncom broke the link and turned to the legionnaire crouched to his right. "You heard the loot . . . we're in a hurry. Knock on the door."

Dietrich grinned, raised his drum-fed grenade launcher, and fired a six-round burst. A mixture of snow and soil fountained into the air as the grenades detonated. A loud boom followed the third explosion and echoed off the valley walls. Sand and gravel geysered upwards.

Dietrich shouted "Bingo!" and grinned from ear to ear. The response was nearly instantaneous.

"Blue Two to Blue Four! Who authorized you to fire? Over."

True Bear, no longer able to conceal his feelings, said what he felt. "Common fucking sense, *sir*. Over."

Laughter was heard. Lieutenant Seebo sputtered and was about to reply, when McGowan activated the command push. "That will be enough of that, gentlemen . . . You can compare the size of your dicks later on. Let's clear those mines and put this team into high gear."

Both men scowled, a specially equipped Hudathan cyborg rolled forward, and the clearing began.

Sheet metal boomed as Quickfoot Hillrun dropped five feet and his boots hit the side of the air shaft. There were similar sounds as the other scouts did likewise.

Then, while halfway through the next drop, Hillrun heard the sounds he'd been dreading: A shout followed by six shots. He suspected that they had been fired by an officer, who, having been alerted to the invasion, had opened an inspection hatch, thrust his or her torso inside, and turned to look upwards. Then, having spotted the enemy, it was natural for the Thraki to pull a sidearm and open fire. Natural but stupid, since the muzzle flashes provided Oneshot Surekill with a clear aiming point. *His* weapon, a highly modified service pistol made a soft popping sound, and reentered its holster.

The Thraki went limp and, in doing so, blocked access to the shaft. Security troops struggled to pull him free, swore when his pistol belt caught the edge of the hatch, and stumbled backward as the corpse came loose. That gave the Naa the seconds they needed to land on the steel mesh that protected the slow-moving fan, release their ropes, and prepare to fight.

The Thraki were still recovering, still struggling to stand, when a grenade landed amongst them. One saw the object, started to reach, and ceased to exist. The explosion tore bodies asunder and painted the bulkheads with blood.

The scouts wasted little time signaling for the group to come down and pushed their way out through the hatch. That's when Hillrun realized that someone was missing. He looked upwards and saw the dangling body. Quickhand Knifemake—dead at twenty-five.

Someone yelled "Stand clear!" and cut the rope. Metal clanged as Knifemake's body hit the mesh. A replacement rope tumbled the length of the shaft and swayed as a Hudathan started down.

Hillrun stooped to unclip the handmade combat knife from the scout's harness, made a promise to return the weapon to the warrior's family, and ducked out through the hatch. The carnage was sickening, even for a veteran like Hillrun, and he averted his eyes. He felt sorry for the Thraki and knew the same thing could happen to him. *Would* happen if he wasn't careful. The first thing to do was to establish some sort of defense perimeter. The Thrakies would send reinforcements soon, and the majority of Red Team was still on the surface. The NCO eyed his surroundings. "Fareye, Warmfeel, take that end of the corridor. Block the point where it turns. Surekill . . . come with me. We'll take the other end."

Lieutenant Seeba-Ka followed the Naa down, was glad when his boots hit the mesh, and swore when he saw the hatch. Though sufficiently large for a Naa, or the average human, there was no way in hell *he* was going to fit *his* bulk through that hole. He got on the radio. Red One to Red Team . . . I want humans first . . . Hudathans last. We need a laser torch down here . . . and I mean *now*!"

Private Lars Lasker was among the first humans sent down. He landed on the mesh, freed himself from the rope, and turned toward the hatch. One glance at the Hudathan officer and the Thraki-sized rectangle of light told him everything he needed to know. The legionnaire laughed, gave thanks for the protective visor, and ducked through the hatch.

There were boot prints in the blood, and the legionnaire followed a set down the corridor to the point where the passageway took a sharp right-hand turn. Fareye and Warmfeel were waiting. They gestured. Lasker had no more than skidded to a stop when a bolt of energy hit the bulkhead to his left, made a black blotch, and left the odor of ozone floating on the air.

"Shit!" Fareye exclaimed, not wanting to stick his head around the corner. "What the hell was that? Some sort of crew-served energy cannon?"

"No such luck," Lasker replied grimly. "Feel the deck."

The scouts followed the human's suggestion, felt the floor vibrate, and looked at each other in alarm. "It's a robot," Warmfeel exclaimed, "or robots plural."

"Damn the fur balls anyway," Lasker said darkly. "I heard they were into robots."

"*Fur balls?*" Fareye growled. "You got a problem with *fur*?"

"Hell, no," the human replied hurriedly. "You ever seen my back? I got more fur than *you* do."

"Let's try to stay focused," Warmfeel put in. "Are either one of you idiots packing a rollerball?"

"That's affirmative," Lasker replied. "I'm toting a satchel of six."

"Well?" Fareye inquired sarcastically. "You gonna use them? Or send 'em to your momma?"

"Sorry," the human replied contritely, "here you go."

Another energy bolt hit the wall, heat washed over the legionnaires, and air thumped their eardrums. "Damn," Fareye complained, dipping into the haversack. "This bastard is starting to piss me off! Let's see how the sonofabitch likes these babies . . ."

Just as the name would suggest the rollerballs were spherical in shape. The Naa felt for the thumb-sized depression, pressed three times in quick succession, and tossed the weapon around the corner. It bounced off the opposite wall and caromed down the hallway. Three more followed. The explosions shook the walls.

The legionnaires waited for a full thirty seconds before risking a peek. The rollerballs had accomplished their purpose. The attack robot was down. That's when the newly liberated Seeba-Ka arrived, eyed the mass of twisted metal, and frowned. "So what the hell are you waiting for? A thank you note from General Booly? Let's move out."

Ice crackled, snow crunched, treads clattered, engines roared, and explosions pushed fountains of soil high into the air as a pair of Hudathan cyborgs advanced toward the end of the canyon. They operated side by side, tracks pushing them forward, while arm-mounted rollers applied pressure to the half-frozen ground. Mines blew in response, a path was cleared, and the rest of Blue Team followed behind.

Captain McGowan stood atop the second quad back, braced herself against the side-to-side motion, and checked her wrist term. Blue Team was still on schedule, but just barely, and the hard part lay ahead.

Staff Sergeant Kreshnekov materialized at her side. He was a little man, no more than five-foot-five, but nobody thought about him that way. His face, sorrowful even during the best of times, looked positively funereal now. "No offense ma'am, but if you park your butt up here, the Thraki will blow it off."

McGowan laughed. "What are you trying to say, Sergeant? That the target's so big they couldn't miss?"

Kreshnekov shook his head. His expression remained the same. "No, ma'am. I'm saying that we're coming up on those automated weapons positions, and the moment *you* die Lieutenant Seebo will assume command."

The comment, which bordered on disrespectful, would have been cause for rebuke had it originated from another NCO. But McGowan had known Kreshnekov for a long time, and that made a difference. Neither put much trust in Seebo. She grimaced. "Point taken, Sergeant. Button it up."

Weapons Emplacement 14 took its orders from the Command and Control computer located deep within the Thraki complex, but had its own localized intelligence as well, to lighten Central's load and provide tactical redundancy. Sensors registered heat and movement. Scanners checked the atmosphere and detected no signs of incoming aircraft. Convinced that it was safe to engage surface targets, the computer brought 14's weapons on line, and ordered the target lasers, energy cannon, and launch racks to tilt downward. The computer confirmed a lock, checked with Central, and opened fire. Emplacements 12, 13, and 15 did likewise.

Energy beams stuttered toward the ground, missiles raced to their targets, and the valley seemed to explode. Sheltered as his brain tissue was by layers of steel armor, the heavy known as Bak Borlo-Ba took note of the incoming ordinance but was more annoyed than frightened. *That* kind of fear, the type associated with the possibility of physical harm, had been left with his biological body. The

sense of invulnerability was deceptive—he knew that—
and had been warned to be on the lookout for it, but felt
it anyway. Columns of snow-tinged dirt soared into the
air. A quad exploded, killing all of those within. Steel fell
like rain.

Borlo-Ba thought death toward those who sought to
harm him. Servos whined as a pair of tubes rose and spun
to the right. The Hudathan's energy cannon burped coherent light, pulverized rock squirted away from the canyon
wall, and pebbles clattered across the top of the hull.

The attack, which had been coordinated by Central, met
with a well-orchestrated response. By using hardware and
software developed for that very purpose, the borgs were
able to construct a temporary or "flying" parallel processor
that divided the overall problem into subtasks and worked
them simultaneously.

Return fire was prioritized, coordinated, and adjusted.
Emplacement 12 was the first to go off-line, quickly followed by 14, which took two missiles in quick succession.
It opened like an orange-yellow flower. The sound of the
explosion was still bouncing back and forth between the
canyon walls when the surviving cyborgs entered the maze
of obstacles.

Corporal Norly Snyder found the first tank trap the hard
way by guiding her enormous body out onto what looked
like solid ground, only to have it give way beneath her.
The pit, which had been dug based on intelligence obtained
from the Hegemony during the early days of the clone-
Thraki alliance, was a perfect fit. Though only ten feet
deep, it was sufficient to prevent Snyder from climbing out
without assistance.

The mine, which exploded the moment she landed on
it, settled the matter. Her armor held, protecting the troops
riding in her belly, but the cyborg's right rear leg was
damaged beyond repair.

McGowan, who along with Staff Sergeant Kreshnekov,
was among those riding in Snyder's cargo compartment,

felt the bottom fall out of her stomach, swore when the barrel of her assault rifle tagged her chin, and knew something was wrong. The explosion, which she experienced as a dull thump, served to confirm that impression. She activated the intercom. "Snyder? What the hell happened?"

"Sorry, ma'am," the cyborg replied sheepishly, "but I fell into some sort of pit. A mine blew one of my legs off."

"Any tissue damage?"

"No, ma'am. I feel stupid that's all."

"Could happen to anyone," the officer replied. "How 'bout the Gatling gun? Is it still operational?"

"Green to go," Snyder replied eagerly. "It will clear the edge of the pit if I push it all the way up."

"Then do so," McGowan instructed. "Watch for friendlies, mark your field of fire, and stand by. The traps are there for a reason. We can expect a counterattack any moment now."

"Roger that," the quad acknowledged grimly. "I'll be ready."

McGowan replied with two clicks of the switch and nodded to Kreshnekov. "Is everyone okay? Let's bail out."

The rear hatch whined open, boots thundered down the ramp, and a familiar cry was heard. "Camerone!"

McGowan joined the response. "CAMERONE!"

Section Leader Hak Brunara prepared himself to meet the gods. Like all the Thraki under his command, the marine had never fought an actual engagement before and knew that most, if not all, of the enemy troops had.

Now, with half of their cybernetic vehicles trapped in the maze, and the rest backed up behind them, battle-tested infantry were boiling up out of the pits, trenches, and channels that cut the snow-crusted ground.

Even as Brunara stood, even as he signaled the advance, the section leader knew the transports were being loaded. Many would escape, would live to see their loved ones, but not him. Everything seemed so bright, so very, very clear as the marine yelled "Advance!" and led his troops into battle. Snowflakes caressed his face, bullets ripped through his chest, and light flooded his mind. The gods . . .

Lieutenant Jonathan Alan Seebo-872 was pissed. Consistent with his worst suspicions, the Hudathan heavy had wandered into a labyrinth of concrete barriers where it had been ambushed by a Thraki antiarmor team. They were dead—but the problem lived on. How to take the objective with minimum casualties to his clone brothers? The answer presented itself in the form of Gunnery Sergeant Rolly True Bear's leathery face. "The heavy is dead, sir—that's the way it seems anyway—and we're taking fire."

Armor rang as bullets bounced off the Hudathan hull. "Thanks for the intelligence summary," Seebo said sarcastically. "*Genius*, pure genius. Now that you have proved your worth as a strategist—it's time to earn your spurs as a tactician. Take your people out there and secure our perimeter."

True Bear looked the officer up and down. Seebo appeared small in the Hudathan-sized seat. The legionnaire's voice dripped with contempt. "Sir! Yes, sir. Let us know when you boys are ready to come out. We'll be waiting."

True Bear turned and nodded to Dietrich. The grenadier hit a saucer-sized button. Servos whined, double doors opened outwards, and the noncom waved to his troops. "Vive le Legion!"

Dietrich hung back as the rest of his platoon double-timed out through the hatch, waited for the doors to swing inward, and nodded to the clones. "See ya later assholes . . . sweet dreams."

Lieutenant Seebo saw the legionnaire's mouth move, saw something fly between the steadily closing doors, and heard the grenade clatter across the metal deck.

At least six of the clone brothers realized what had occurred and wore identical expressions of horror. They threw themselves forward, but harnesses held them in place.

Lieutenant Seebo screamed, but the sound of the explosion filled his ears.

Dietrich watched the doors seal, heard a muffled thud, and watch the borg's body rock from side to side as some demo charges cooked off. Some people hated the Legion, and couldn't wait to get out, but he wasn't one of them. No, the Legion was family, the only family he had. And family comes first.

The heavy shuddered as metal sheared and a locker full of ammo exploded. A hatch cover sailed into the sky. Flames shot out of the cooling stacks. Heat blasted the legionnaire's face. A voice crackled through his earplug. "Dietrich? Where the hell are you? Get up here and do your job."

The grenadier backed away. "Sorry, Gunny. I had to take a pee . . . I'm on the way."

Vice Admiral Haru Ista Rawan stood high on the catwalk, hands clasped behind his back, contemplating the scene below. The interceptors were hot and ready to launch. They crouched in flights of three, sitting on their skids, waiting to lift. The transports, all of which were fully loaded, sat ready to follow. Assuming the fighters could punch a hole through the Confederate air cover and assuming the larger vessels could escape the orbiting warship, the majority of his people would make it to Zynig-47.

As for the rest, well, they had done their duty. First against the troops who had dropped through the air shafts—and then on the canyon floor. Even now, he could hear the dull thump, thump, thump of cannon fire interspersed with the crackle of assault weapons. His marines were dying. The officer's thoughts were interrupted by the voice in his ear. "The transports are ready, Admiral . . . and the launch parameters are optimum."

Rawan worked his jaw for a moment. The order would

hurt . . . but his duty was clear. "Tell them to launch . . . and may the gods protect them."

The words were barely out of the admiral's mouth when repellors flared. The first flight of fighters rose into the air and fired their main engines. They were gone within seconds. Flight after flight took off, until the cavern was as empty as Rawan's heart.

Finally, after the last ship had departed, the Thraki made his way down to the flight deck and faced the wind. The light was hard and cold. He had time for one last walk.

Tyspin listened to the reports, eyed the forward-mounted screens, and confirmed what she'd been told. The Thrakies were pulling out. Well, some were, while others continued to fight. The naval officer could have delivered the news via the ship's intercom system but chose to do it personally instead. She eased her way out of the command chair, made eye contact with the ship's XO, and said, "You have the con."

He nodded. "Aye, aye, ma'am. I have the con."

With little to do beyond the need to recover the ship's fighters, the atmosphere aboard the *Gladiator* was relatively serene. Tyspin's shoes made a clacking sound as she marched the length of the corridor. A somewhat bored voice announced that the mid-watch chow call was about to begin. A rating nodded as she passed, and a robot hurried to get out of the way.

Booly was where Tyspin had expected him to be—hard at work in his makeshift office. Message torps continued to arrive every few hours or so bringing an unending flow of intelligence, status reports, and a mind-boggling array of administrative work, which, if left undone, would soon bring the Confederacy's armed forces to their knees.

A conference room table served as a desk. It was covered with printouts, half-consumed cups of coffee, the remains of a breakfast, and a computer-designed model of both the canyon and the Thraki complex. The legionnaire heard the knock, said "enter," and looked up from his comp screen. "Thank god! A rescue mission!"

Tyspin grinned, spent a second wishing the other officer had never met Maylo Chien-Chu, and took a seat. "You were right, Bill. The Thrakies pulled up stakes. Do you still want to let them go?"

Booly nodded. "Yes, I do. Let 'em run all the way to Zynig-47. A constant stream of refugees will sap morale. Besides, there's been enough dying. How's the Blue Team? Did the Thrakies disengage?"

Tyspin shook her head. "No, the battle rages on."

Booly rubbed his temples. "Why? It's pointless! We can leave a detachment and starve them out. Get McGowan on the horn . . . tell her to break contact. And pass the message to Seeba-Ka."

Tyspin stood. "Aye, aye, sir. Anything else?"

Booly looked around him. "Yeah, tell the OOD to watch for the next in-bound message torp, and blow it up."

Lieutenant Seeba-Ka turned his back to the heavily armored hatch, heard Lasker yell, "Fire in the hole!" and felt the air nudge him as the charge went off. The officer turned back, saw that the door hung askew, and waved what remained of his team forward. The Thraki had put up one helluva fight and forced the invaders to pay dearly for every foot of corridor, every intersection, and every hatch. Roughly half his force remained on their feet. The rest had been killed or wounded. The result was that the team was behind schedule, had failed to neutralize the enemy's command and control computer, and hadn't even *seen* the energy cannons much less attacked them. The Hudathan had failed, and the knowledge ate at the lining of his stomach.

There was the cloth-ripping sound of an assault rifle, a cry of "Blood!" and the team charged ahead. Seeba-Ka was third or fourth through the entry, wasted a fraction of a second thinking about the extent to which the Hudathans,

humans, and Naa had learned to work together, and heard
a tone through his earplugs. "High Horse to Red One . . .
Over."

Seeba-Ka, who was still struggling to assimilate Confederate com procedures, saw something move, fired a
three-round burst, and managed a reply. "This is Red
One . . . Go. Over."

The voice was hard and metallic. "Break it off, One.
Objective achieved. You can pull back."

Seeba-Ka thought about the bodies left behind, the team
he had come to be so proud of, and anger filled his chest.
The swear words were part of his recently acquired vo-
cabulary. "No frigging way, High Horse! We'll break
when the furry little bastards are dead! Over."

A Thraki noncom popped out of a maintenance bay, shot
Jamal in the back, and staggered as Lasker put half a mag-
azine into the Marine's chest.

Seeba-Ka roared his approval and charged the next set
of doors. They were open, and he saw rock walls beyond.
It was the chamber! His objective! Finally within reach.

What remained of the team charged, limped, and in one
case was carried out into the gallery. The rail had been
designed by Thraki for Thraki. It hit the Hudathan at mid-
thigh. The voice was louder this time and more insistent.
"High Horse to Red One . . . That is negative . . . Repeat
negative. Break contact immediately."

Seeba-Ka took a long hard look around. The flight deck
was empty—but the battle continued down on the canyon
floor. He could hear the dull thump, thump, thump of
outgoing cannon fire interspersed with the rattle of auto-
matic weapons and a loud "boom" as a missile struck its
target. Blue Team was taking a beating—that much was
clear. *If* he could make his way down onto the floor below,
if he could neutralize even one of the energy cannons, lives
would be saved. Hudathan lives, Naa lives, and yes, ap-
palling as the notion was, *human* lives.

The Hudathan waved his troops forward and opened the

com link. "Red One to High Horse . . . Roger your last . . . contact broken."

Booly was standing toward the rear of the makeshift Ops Center, talking to a naval intelligence officer, when the chief petty officer approached. She looked clean and almost unnaturally crisp. "Excuse me, sir, sorry to interrupt, but the lieutenant has something he wants you to see."

Booly nodded, assured the intelligence officer that he would read the latest report ASAP, and followed the CPO to a bulkhead covered with flat panel displays. Some naval vessels had been designed to support ground actions, but the *Gladiator* wasn't one of them. The wardroom had been converted to an Ops Center, and everything had a temporary makeshift feel.

The lieutenant was young and earnest. He had dark hair, a nose that was slightly too large for his face, and a wire-thin body. "Red One agreed to break contact . . . but look at this."

Booly looked at screen, realized it was a trooper's-eye view of the Thraki military complex, and that his host was running. Not just running, but running *toward* a brightly lit entryway, flanked by a pair of alien energy cannons. Both batteries were depressed, to command the valley below, and both burped cold blue light. The name at the bottom of the frame read: "Corporal Sureseek Fareye."

The naval officer saw the glance and pointed to an enormous body that lumbered along the right side of the frame. "That's Red One, sir. Lieutenant Seeba-Ka. We don't have compatible cameras for the Hudathans yet . . . but that's him all right . . . What should we do?"

It was a good question. Seeba-Ka had chosen to disobey a direct order—but one that Booly now realized was wrong. "Is Blue One on-line? Show me her video."

The lieutenant nodded and pointed. "Yes, sir. She's right there."

McGowan looked up into the slowly twirling snowflakes, saw the energy cannons burp, and watched geysers of mud-sullied snow march her way. "Put some more SLMs on those guns! Take the bastards out!"

Missiles, all of which had been fired prior to her order, hit only fractions of a second apart. The Thraki energy screens flared, shimmered like silver, and faded as the force of the explosions dissipated.

A quad exploded, an entire squad was cut down, and McGowan yelled through the link. "I want some air support damn it—and I want it now! Where's the Red Team? We're dying out here."

Booly gripped the back of the chair with both hands and knew it was too late. Blue One was so far up the canyon, so close to the target, that an air strike would hit her, too.

"What about Lieutenant Seeba-Ka?" the naval officer persisted. "What should I do about him?"

"Pray the insubordinate sonofabitch makes it," Booly grated, because he's the only hope we have."

Vice Admiral Haru Ista Rawan stepped away from energy cannon number two, raised the assault weapon, and thumbed the safety into the "off" position. The four remaining members of the security team did likewise.

The Thraki officer could *see* the oncoming soldiers, could feel the wind at his back, could *smell* the ozone that swirled around him. The force field caused his fur to stand on end, and his bladder felt unnaturally full. This was it, the last moment of his life, and the end of the journey. At least, the officer thought to himself, I will die with my face to the enemy. His weapon chattered, others did likewise, and the world ceased to be.

"Blow those emplacements!" Seeba-Ka ordered, waving his team forward. "There's no point in saving ordinance— pack every charge you have around those hatches."

The protective shields, which were effective against anything packing sufficient mass and velocity to damage the energy cannons, were useless when it came to a low-tech infantry assault. The legionnaires moved forward, felt a tingling sensation as they entered the force field's footprint, and set about their tasks. The cannons continued fire, and the Blue Team continued to suffer as the explosives were put in place.

Then, having moved everyone back, the Hudathan gave the order. "Lasker, you know what to do, pull the plug." The human nodded, flipped the safety cover off a remote, and pressed the big red button.

McGowan, looking up from below, saw two flashes of light, heard two overlapping explosions and fell as the shock wave knocked her off her feet. The first thing she noticed was how peaceful it was, lying on her back, watching chunks of debris somersault through the cold, frosty air. They would land—she knew that—but couldn't quite muster the energy to deal with it. Most fell short of Blue Team, however—for which she was thankful. That's when a strange sort of silence fell on the valley, when McGowan wondered if her eardrums were damaged, or if everyone else was dead.

Then came the first reedy cheer, soon joined by others, until the officer heard her own voice join the rest.

The Blue Team rose like ghosts from so many graves, marveled at the fact that they were still alive, and knew the ultimate truth: *This day was theirs*. Not through good fortune—but by force of arms.

15

Beware of false prophets which come to you in sheep's clothing, but inwardly they are ravening wolves.

Matthew 7:15
First printing circa Standard Year 1400

Transit Point NS-690-193, the Confederacy of Sentient Beings

The combined fleets, now numbering more than six thousand ships, emerged from hyperspace in groups of one hundred, formed clusters around the transit point, and waited for instructions.

If the Hoon had been something other than a machine and if the Hoon had been possessed of emotions, it might have been excited. For here, after a journey that spanned half a galaxy, the quarry was finally at hand.

But there were variables, factors the computer had never encountered before, and these argued for a certain degree of caution. Early reports, along with those that continued to trickle in, suggested the same thing: The Thraki were not only present in that particular sector of space, but present in large numbers, and showed no sign of trying to escape. This was unprecedented . . . and therefore of concern.

Adding to that concern was the fact that non-Thraki probes, *hundreds* of them, had already arrived on the scene, with more popping out of hyperspace all the time. Who were the interlopers? How strong were they? And what if any relationship had been established with the Thraki? Such questions deserved answers, and the Hoon was reluctant to proceed without them.

If the computer was cautious, however—Jepp was ecstatic. The news sent the human dashing back and forth, powerless to affect what took place, but desperate to do so. Hopeless though it had seemed at times, his faith had finally paid off! There was a plan, *God's* plan, and it was *his* job to see it through.

Though no longer invested in a ship of its own, the Navcomp named Henry still took a passionate interest in things navigational and had taken advantage of Jepp's momentary credibility to monitor the fleet's progress.

The realization that the Sheen had entered Confederate-controlled space in a system known as NS-680-193 came as a shock, since the human-designed intelligence had given up any hope of scanning familiar constellations a long time before. It hurried to notify its human master and, if not capable of joy, processed a sense of satisfaction.

But now, with Jepp literally jumping up and down, and running around like a madman, the computer wasn't so sure. The Sheen brought nothing but pain and misery to the systems they had visited in the past, and there was no reason to think this stop would be any different. There could be an increased possibility of escape, however—which the computer was quick to bring to the human's attention.

"What?" Jepp responded, his face filled with consternation. "Are you out of your silicon-packed mind? This is the moment we've been waiting for! The fleet is God's instrument—*his* way of bringing the sinners around. Judgment Day is upon us."

Henry had heard such pronouncements before, most recently in connection with some very dead Thraki, but knew better than to comment. Jepp was Jepp, and whatever would be, would be.

The cabin was dark, air whispered through ducts, and Tyspin was asleep. More than that she *knew* she was asleep and relished the knowledge. The officer heard the intercom bong, resolved to ignore it, and swore when it sounded again. She regretted the words the moment they were spoken. "Yes? What the hell do you want?"

"Sorry, Admiral," the OOD said apologetically, "but a probe was waiting at Transit Point WHOT-8965-3452. It appears that the Sheen have arrived."

Tyspin sat up, rubbed her eyes, and swung her feet off the bunk. "Where?"

"In system NS-680-193 . . . about halfway between the Ramanthians and the Arballazanies."

"Notify the general—I'm on the way."

The OOD *had* notified the general—but didn't see any need to say so. "Ma'am, yes, ma'am." The intercom popped and went dead. The officer scanned the bridge, spotted one of the less essential ratings, and made eye contact. "The admiral is on her way—how 'bout getting her a cup of coffee?"

The tech said, "Yes, sir," and disappeared.

Tyspin liked, no *needed* coffee, and everyone knew it. The bridge crew looked at each other and chuckled as the OOD considered what he knew. If the intel was correct, and there was no reason to doubt it, the machines had six thousand ships. Booly was one hell of an officer, and so was Tyspin, but that was twice the number of vessels the Confederacy could bring to bear . . . Not to mention the fact that the Thraki armada consisted of more than four thousand ships.

The OOD's father had opposed his son's choice of careers urging the youngster to pursue the law instead. Now, knowing what he knew, it appeared that dad was correct.

Planet Zynig-47, the Confederacy of Sentient Beings

Sun poured down through rose-colored glass to bathe the Chamber of Reason with soft pink light. Much of it was trapped there, blocked by the carefully laid stone, but some found its way to the beings below.

Grand Admiral Hooloo Isan Andragna had been listening to negative reports for the better part of three days now, and he was tired of it. The initial news had come as a shock. He had expected more time. A lot more time. The fact that the Sheen had arrived—were only weeks away— frightened him.

But now, having accepted the situation, the naval officer was ready to fight and more than that to win. All he needed to do was put the resources in place, execute his carefully considered plan, and do something about morale. Regardless of where he went, the gloom was palpable.

Most of the negativity was centered on the Sheen—but the constant stream of refugees from planets like BETA-018 certainly didn't help. Each convoy, each ship, was like a harbinger of doom. There was something strange about that, something suspicious, but there hadn't been time to focus on it. Not with thousands upon thousands of killer machines to cope with. But that was for later—this was now.

Sector 19 was late as usual, murmured her apologies, and slipped into her assigned chair.

The chamberlain struck the Shield of Waha, and a single note reverberated between the walls. That was the signal for the rest of the Sectors to retrieve their forms. Signals went out, and the miniature robots crawled, walked, and tumbled back to their owners, where they were deactivated and restored to cases, bags, or laps. Though normally the subject of considerable discussion, not to mention competition, there was little interest in the forms on that particular day.

So serious was the situation that High Priestess Bree Bricana had been invited to participate and, as the table was cleared, rose to give the traditional benediction. The final words, which Andragna had always found to be moving, were even more so now: ". . . And may the gods guide us through the labyrinth of stars to the peace that lies beyond. For it is there, in the promised place, where our spirits may rest."

In most cases, Andragna preferred to let one of the Sectors set the agenda and open the meeting, but this was different. Focus was important. The Admiral cleared his throat and scanned the faces before him. Thousands watched via live feeds. The expression on his face and the tonality of his words were as important if not *more* important than what he said. "The moment we have both dreaded and anticipated is upon us. The Sheen have entered Confederate space, know where we are, and will attack soon."

"I think we know *that*," Sector 12 said sarcastically. "We need a leader . . . not a clerk."

Sector 12 was a Runner and, in spite of Andragna's Runner sympathies, never tired of needling him. Many of the committee members thought her comments were amusing—but not today. Sector 27 rapped the surface of the table. He was a high-ranking member of the priesthood, a xenoanthropologist, and a levelheaded pragmatist. "Enough! There is no time for the game of politics. The admiral has a plan . . . and I want to hear it."

Sector 12 actually looked contrite for once—and the admiral enjoyed her discomfort. He leaned forward as if to add weight to his words. "We had hoped to join the Confederacy of Sentient Beings and bind some allies to our cause. That particular path has been blocked," Andragna continued earnestly, "but the strategy continues to be valid."

Sector 18 looked at Sector 4 to see if the Facer understood what the admiral was driving at, but she was as mystified as he was. Nortalla signaled as much with the set of her ears.

"The Sheen have sent probes and scouts to find us," Andragna added, "and six have been detected within the boundaries of this very solar system."

Though known to senior military officers and the top level of the priesthood, this was news to the majority of the population. Andragna paused for a moment to let the information sink in. Then, knowing how worried they were, he took them off the hook.

"We could have destroyed every single one of the intruders—but allowed them to survive. Why you may ask? So that when the vast majority of our fleet enters hyperspace, as it will soon, the Sheen will follow."

Some of the Sectors looked confused—but the rest started to brighten. Did he mean?

"Yes," Andragna confirmed, "I plan to drop our fleet into the system dominated by the race known as the Arballazanies . . . Because *that's* where the Confederate government is momentarily convened, *that's* where a significant number of their ships will be gathered, and *that's* where the battle will be joined."

It was a masterful plan, one that would force the Confederacy to side with the Thraki, or, failing that, enable Andragna to use them as a highly disposable shield. It was a good plan, a *brilliant* plan, and feet started to stomp, not just within the Chamber of Reason, but elsewhere on the planet, on the arks that orbited above, and out in the blackness of space.

Andragna heard the noise and felt it through the recently reconditioned floor. The timing would be critical—but hope had been restored.

•   •   •

One moment the *Ninja* was in the nowhere land of hyperspace, and the next moment it was bathed in light from NS-680-193, a rather benign sun in the prime of its life.

Tyspin forced herself to remain impassive, or at least *look* impassive, as every detector, sensor, and warning system the ship had started to buzz, bleat, and speak in technical tongues.

The *Ninja*'s command and control computer, better known as Big Momma, delivered the news with the same inflection used to announce the lunch menu: "More than three thousand targets have been acquired, indexed according to standard threat protocols, and tagged with firing priorities. This vessel will be destroyed approximately twenty-two seconds after the engagement begins—but may be able to inflict at least some damage on .001 percent of the enemy fleet. This intelligence recommends a preemptive strike."

Tyspin glanced at the ship's commanding officer. Captain John Hashimoto had been with her during the Battle for Earth. He was one of the most trustworthy officers she knew. Hashimoto was short, muscular, and eternally cheerful. The computer assessment made him grin. The *Ninja* had not been dispatched to attack the Sheen all by herself but it was nice to know that Momma was game.

"Stand by," Tyspin said grimly. "One wrong move, and we make the jump."

Hashimoto nodded. The calcs were complete and loaded. The Navcomp, affectionately known as Old Screw Head, was on standby. All it would take was a single word to fling the ship into the void. Would they make it before the Sheen blew the ship to bits? It seemed doubtful, but the possibility made everyone feel better.

Seconds ticked away. The bridge crew stood like statues, hesitant to breathe lest the action somehow trigger an attack, yet determined to appear fearless.

Tyspin felt fear gnaw at her belly and struggled to ignore it. Five, maybe ten seconds had passed, and her heart continued to beat. That was good wasn't it? Careful lest her voice betray how she actually felt, she raised an eyebrow and glanced at Hashimoto. "Well? What are we waiting for? You know the drill . . . Tell the servo heads that we'd like to parley."

The words, plus the knowledge that they were still alive, acted to free the bridge crew from their momentary paralysis. The admiral was pulling the old man's chain! Situation normal. Hashimoto, who was fully aware of the role he'd been given, looked appropriately stern. "Ma'am, yes, ma'am. You heard the admiral . . . send it out."

The message was sent in Thraki and standard: "Greetings on behalf of the Confederacy of Sentient Beings. This sector of space is controlled by out-member states. Please state your intentions."

President Nankool and his advisors had invested a considerable amount of time and energy in constructing the text. The phraseology was cool but short of hostile. That was the intent anyway, and how *they* would interpret such a message, but what about the machines? *Could* they? Would they read between the lines? Tyspin regarded the possibility as unlikely—but what did she know? At least two AIs had been part of the process, and if *they* believed the text would work, then maybe it would.

The reply was not only expeditious but unexpected. A com tech watched a holo bloom, listened to the audio that accompanied it, and raised his hand. "Over here, ma'am . . . the machines replied . . . or at least I *think* they did."

Tyspin stepped over to the com tech's console and eyed the video. No wonder the rating was confused. In place of a machine, or some sort of graphical interface, a human being had appeared. He was in obvious need of a haircut, his face looked slightly cadaverous, and his eyes were unnaturally bright. They seemed to bore through Tyspin's head. Judging from what the man said he had more than a passing familiarity with naval insignia. The tone was arrogant. "I see they sent an admiral to greet us . . . kind

of an insult wouldn't you say? President Nankool would
have been more appropriate."

A memory tickled the back of Tyspin's mind. Something the loquacious Willy Williams had discussed during
the intelligence debriefings. Something about a human who
had been present during the attack on Long Jump, and of
even more importance, had directed at least some of the
ensuing violence. Was this the same man? A renegade with
blood on his hands? Yes, Tyspin had a feeling that it was,
which meant she was eyeball to eyeball with a psychopath,
war criminal, or both. Knowing that, or being reasonably
sure of it, raised a very important question: How should
she deal with him? The most obvious strategy was to ap-
pease him, assuming such a thing was possible, in hopes
of gaining his favor.

But something cautioned the officer against that approach, something she couldn't quite articulate, but which
stemmed from his motivations. What were they? Perhaps
that was the key, what Jasper, no, Jepp *really* wanted was
a sense of legitimacy, of respect for what he saw as his
accomplishments.

The thoughts flickered through her mind at lightning
speed, and while it wasn't much to go on, Tyspin decided
to gamble. She could, the officer reasoned, back off,
should that become necessary. "President Nankool is rather
busy," Tyspin said coldly. "Give me a message, and I'll
pass it along."

The ex-prospector found himself torn between his desire
to impress the Hoon with how tough he was and the somewhat unexpected need to win Admiral Tyspin's respect.
He tried another tack.

"Look, I'm sorry if I seem a bit over the top, but we're
on the same side. My name is Jorley Jepp. You've heard
about the attack on Long Jump by now . . . so you know
what the Sheen can do. Their main objective is to find a
race known as the Thraki. If the Thrakies are around, and
the Sheen say they are, then you're in contact with them

by now. The best thing the Confederacy can do is to provide the Sheen with information, plus some fuel for their ships, and get out of the way."

"And then?" Tyspin inquired skeptically, glad that the entire interchange was being recorded, "what happens after that?"

"That depends," Jepp said evasively, "on any number of things. The Sheen trust me . . . and I may be able to influence them. I know the President is busy—but I would appreciate his advice."

Tyspin didn't believe that the last part of the comment was sincere . . . but took note of the less truculent tone. Could the earnest-looking man in the soiled jumpsuit influence what the Sheen did next? The initial answer seemed to be "yes," given the events on Long Jump, the fact that he was still alive, and was allowed to speak. But how far did that influence extend? And what would Jepp want in return? Those questions and dozens more begged to be answered. The key was to buy time—time Booly could use to prepare, time Nankool could use to perform maintenance on the alliance, and time she could use to learn more about Jepp. The naval officer forced a smile. "Of course . . . Let's see what I can arrange. Would you or your, er *companions*, have any objections to my dispatching a message torp?"

Jepp looked offscreen, seemed to converse with someone, and turned back. "No, so long as you and your ship remain."

Tyspin nodded. A battle of sorts had been won. The message torp would carry a copy of the interchange, a request for instructions, and more important than that, data regarding the Sheen fleet. *Valuable* data that could help Booly win.

The Hoon monitored the exchange, assigned a probe to follow the message torp through hyperspace, and processed something akin to a feeling of satisfaction. The soft bodies were gratifyingly stupid, data would be gathered, and the mission furthered. Life, or what passed for it, was good.

Planet Arballa, the Confederacy of Sentient Beings

A clutch of nervous-looking advisors stood and waited while President Marcott Nankool read the message for a second time. It was warm with so many bodies packed into the chief executive's office, and the ship struggled to cope. Cold air blasted out of an overhead vent, and Chien-Chu felt his cybernetic body adjust accordingly. Doma-Sa shuffled his feet, and servos whined as an exoskeleton-clad Dweller shifted his weight from one foot to the other.

Nankool placed the printout on the surface of his highly polished wood desk, arranged it just so, and met their eyes. "So? Your presence speaks more eloquently than words. You know what Admiral Tyspin sent me—what would you suggest?"

Doma-Sa waited to see if anyone would speak, realized they weren't sure of what to say, and broke the silence. "BETA-018 has been secured, but the Thraki occupy other worlds as well. The more time we buy, the more General Booly has to work with."

Nankool scanned their faces. "How 'bout the rest of you? Do you agree?"

Chien-Chu nodded and glanced around. There was no dissention for once . . . a rare and memorable moment.

A message torp was dispatched an hour later. A Sheen probe was allowed to follow it. They hit the outward-bound transit point within minutes of each other and seemed to wink out of existence. A reply was on the way.

Transit Point NS-690-193, the Confederacy of Sentient Beings

The launch bay was no different from the last time Jorely Jepp had been there. Ships sat in what appeared to be random fashion but was actually a mathematically precise arrangement that allowed the Sheen to use the available space in the most efficient possible manner. Ropes of silvery nano hung, crawled, and in one case squirmed across the bay. The tang of ozone flavored the air.

Only one thing was different and that was the way the human felt: happy, excited, and nearly giddy with joy. The message torp had returned. An agreement had been reached. He, Jorely Jepp, ex-prospector, debtor, and all around loser was on his way to visit with President Marcott Nankool!

No, he told himself, not *visit*, but *negotiate* on behalf of God and the heathen waiting to be saved. An account would be written one day, a tome on a par with the Holy Bible or the Koran. A book that would tell the tale of the savior who emerged from the cosmic wasteland accompanied by a silvery host. The very thought of it filled the human's heart to the breaking point. He seized Veera's clawlike hand. "Come on! This is *our* moment!"

Veera knew the human was trying to be generous—but suffered no illusions. *Her* moment would come when she was back among her own kind. In the meantime, with no other possibilities in sight, the lunatic at her side offered the best opportunity of escape. They boarded the shuttle. Henry, along with Alpha, followed behind.

Given how unstable her guest appeared to be, and given the extent of the power he might be able to call upon, Tyspin planned to be at the lock to greet him. That's why she was down in the ready room—watching a bank of monitors.

The shuttle slowed as it approached the ship, followed a brightly lit drone into the bay, and settled onto its skids. The vessel was sufficiently streamlined so that it could operate within a planetary atmosphere. It shimmered as if lit from within. Here, at least, was something of an intelligence coup since an entire battery of sensors had been specially rigged to gather information on the enemy ship. Even if the contact with Jepp proved futile, anything they could learn about Sheen technology could prove very valuable indeed.

The shuttle landed, a hatch opened, and a ramp hit hull metal. The *Ninja*'s deck master wore bright orange space armor. He approached the ramp and waited for the visitor to disembark. Jepp, or a figure that Tyspin assumed was Jepp, was a sight to see. In spite of the fact that he had an entire fleet to back him, the ex-prospector wore the same suit of dilapidated, much-patched space armor in which he had been captured. And what was that perched on his shoulder? Some sort of machine? That's what it looked like.

There was more, however—including an entourage which caught Tyspin by surprise. The second individual to emerge from the shuttle wore a type of space armor she didn't recognize until her intel officer turned in her direction. His name was Dorba-Ka, and he spoke standard with a slight hiss. "Where did the Prithian come from? What's going on here?"

What indeed? Tyspin wondered as the odd couple made their way across the repulsor-blackened deck toward the entry lock. That's when the robots appeared. Form follows function, and the first pair looked similar to the navy-issue general-purpose androids assigned to her ship. The units that followed were considerably different. There were four altogether, as similar as ball bearings, and protected by force fields. Arms ended in what appeared to be energy projectors, heads swiveled from left to right, and they moved in unison.

"They look dangerous," the intel officer said conversationally. "Can the marines handle them?"

It was a good question, but Tyspin had other things to worry about as well. Should she treat Jepp like a head of state? Someone entitled to armed guards, even within the hull of a Confederate warship? Or refuse to admit them? And risk a confrontation? A confrontation with catastrophic results? It was a nasty decision and one she would have preferred to avoid.

But Jepp had arrived in front of the lock, and time had run out. The entire side party, which consisted of the intel officer, a chief petty officer, and a squad of smart-looking marines all turned to look at her. The decision, which she would live to regret, emerged as a croak. "Let them in." The hatch cycled open, the visitors spent the requisite time in the lock, and were admitted to the ship.

Jepp, who, with the exception of his brief stay on Long Jump, had been cut off from humankind, stopped to take it in. The faces, the sounds, the faint odor of cooking all rushed to fill his senses. The admiral said something but the ex-prospector failed to process the words. He felt a little bit dizzy but managed to keep his feet. Those around him seemed unaware of his discomfort and led him down a long, sterile corridor.

The robots followed behind. Alpha discerned little of interest, Henry was on the lookout for some way to escape, and the Hoon, who occupied all four of the security units, was beaming data back to the shuttle. Useful data that would come in handy when the battle started.

The AI was struck not by the technology that surrounded it, which was average at best, but by the diversity of the life forms that crewed the ship. At least three or four different species, if appearances were any guide. They seemed to be cooperating—to be working together—the way machines would. Something the Hoon had never witnessed before.

Veera, her heart beating faster, wondered what to do. The Hoon had accompanied them, she was fairly certain of that, but doubted that Jepp even cared. The truth was that the human had accepted the computer's primacy—and even come to depend on it.

As for the other humans, those who ran the ship, they had no idea what they were dealing with. The Prithian glanced over her shoulder. Alpha and Henry followed along behind, backed by the ominous security units, and a squad of soldiers. What would the Hoon do if she tried to escape? Shoot her? Or ignore the whole thing? There was no way to know. It seemed prudent to wait and see what developed.

As with most warships, the *Ninja* had no quarters for guests, but Jepp was thrilled with XO's cabin, and never gave a moment's thought to where the unfortunate officer had disappeared to. Though actually smaller than his compartment aboard the Sheen battleship, this space had been designed for the convenience of humans and seemed luxurious by comparison. There was a small but serviceable shower, hot water that shut itself off after three minutes had elapsed, and a stack of brand new clothing. There was crisp white underwear, three dark blue ship-suits, plus a cap with the *Ninja*'s star emblem on the front of it. Life was good.

When Jepp entered the cabin, and left the robots to wait in the passageway, Henry was far from surprised. Even though the human *knew* the Navcomp was sentient, he had always treated the AI like a machine, and assumed it would remain loyal. And, up till that very moment, Henry had been. Partly because of the programming he'd been equipped with, and partly because he chose to be.

Now, with freedom all around, the Navcomp had decided to put its own interests first for a change.

Veera was shown to a cabin farther down the passageway and entered without protest.

That's when the Sheen security units assigned themselves to stand guard over both cabins—two per hatch—while heavily armed marines were posted to both ends of the corridor. Tyspin's way of keeping the machines in check.

Henry eyed the Hoon-controlled robots and wondered if the AI was even aware of him. There was one way to find out. The Navcomp looked from one group of humans to the other, decided they were roughly equidistant, and turned to the right. Henry hadn't moved more than a few feet when the Hoon made itself known. The message came via low powered intercom. "The unit will remain where it is."

The command, which should have frozen the previously hijacked body right where it was, had no discernable effect. Henry addressed himself to the marines. They stared straight ahead. "My name is Henry . . . I am an artificial intelligence held captive by the Sheen. As such, I place myself under your protection in keeping with the provisions of the Confederate Charter that covers the rights of synthetic beings."

The Hoon didn't approve of rogue units, had never been willing to tolerate disobedience, and wasn't about to start now. The AI set one-fourth of its addressable assets into motion. A security unit stepped forward, did a left-face, and aimed an arm-mounted energy weapon at Henry's back. "Stop or I will shoot!"

The marines couldn't hear the transmission, but didn't need to. Actions spoke louder than words. They raised their assault rifles in response.

Sergeant Musa Moso wasn't paid to make decisions, not *this* kind of decision, and radioed for assistance. Half a dozen laser-projected red dots appeared on the Hoon-controlled machines as Henry rolled toward freedom.

● ● ●

Jepp was whistling by the time he toweled off, got dressed, and called for Sam. The robot was nowhere to be seen. It was spending more and more time with Veera of late. The little traitor.

Jepp examined his image in a small bulkhead-mounted mirror, noticed the need for a haircut, and thought about Tyspin. The idea of spending more time with the naval officer appealed to the ex-prospector. He headed for the hatch. It opened, and he stepped out into the corridor. The Hoon chose that moment to open fire. Henry "felt" the energy beams punch their way through his alloy back, uttered a plaintive beep, and fell facedown.

Sergeant Moso formed the word "fire," and was just about to say it, when Jepp stepped into the passageway. The ex-prospector watched the energy bolts whip past, saw Henry fall, and threw himself forward. "Stop!" The envoy held his hands in the air. A collection of red dots danced across this chest. Moso didn't know much, but he knew Jepp was a VIP, and in the line of fire. He bit the word off before it could emerge.

The Hoon verified that its target was down, processed a sense of correctness, and "felt" the harmless lasers pass through the force field's corona to caress its metal skin. Weapons were in the process of rising when Jepp reentered the equation.

The Hoon, gratified by the extent of the human's loyalty, was hesitant to fire through the biological's body. The result was a still-life tableau. And that's how it looked when Tyspin arrived. With the exception of one of Henry's drive wheels, which continued to whir, the scene was totally silent. Tyspin took the situation in and nodded to Moso. "Thank you, Sergeant, I'll take it from here . . . Corporal, Private, safe those weapons. Get the casualty to robotics. Perhaps they can save it."

The naval officer strode down the corridor, stopped two feet away from Jepp, and placed hands on hips. Her eyes were like lasers. "As for you, *Envoy* Jepp, how dare you attack a sentient aboard one of *my* ships!"

Jepp felt himself wilt in the face of her anger, knew it was a mistake, and drew himself up. The Hoon was watching, the human was conscious of that now, and started to sweat. His voice was tense but controlled. "A couple of things to consider, *Admiral* . . . The AI in question is, or was indentured to me under the terms of a standard contract, the body it occupies belongs to the Sheen, and *I* didn't fire on anyone. Your marines will attest to that."

The naval officer looked at Moso, who nodded. She turned back. "It seems I owe you an apology. I'm sorry. So, who fired . . . and why?"

For one split second, Jepp considered telling Tyspin the unvarnished truth . . . That the Hoon controlled all of the security units, that the AI was extremely arrogant, and that she hadn't seen anything yet. But there could be a down side to that kind of disclosure, especially if the naval officer decided that it was pointless to negotiate, and broke the whole thing off. There would be *no* conversation with Nankool, *no* opportunity to deal, and *no* galaxy-spanning religion. Jepp chose his words with care.

"It was a mistake that's all. Henry, that is to say the Navcomp in question, was taken prisoner when I was. Our ship was destroyed, so, with nothing else available, he appropriated the body you see before you. I wasn't here—but I'm guessing that Henry tried to leave—and the Sheen ordered it to stop. He refused, and one of the security units shot him."

Tyspin glanced at Moso, who shrugged. "We didn't hear nothin' ma'am—but it coulda been that way. You know how machines are—sendin' stuff back and forth."

"So, they *shot* him?" the admiral demanded. "Real nice. Who is 'they' anyway? I though some sort of computer called the shots."

"Well, yes," Jepp replied weakly. "An AI called the Hoon controls the fleet. The various units have intelligence of their own, however—which is why I used the word 'they.' "

The answer skirted the truth—but Tyspin was unaware of that. She eyed the security units. They had returned to something approximating parade rest. "Keep those machines under control—or I'll have them ejected from a lock."

Jepp didn't think the process would be quite so easy, but managed to look chagrined and hoped the Hoon would behave itself. "Of course. I'll do my best," he assured her. The naval officer nodded, told Sergeant Moso to carry on, and left the area.

A crew of four robo techs arrived, lifted Henry onto a self-propelled cart, and led the device away.

Henry, who lay flat on its back, was happy to be at least partially functional. Functional and *free*. Or as free as a machine programmed to equate productivity with happiness could be. The cart took a turn—and Henry went with it.

Though none too pleased with the human-style fittings, the cabin was to Veera's liking, especially the computer interface. It provided access to the navcomp known as "Screwhead," and, after a bit of digital cajoling, to "Big Momma" herself.

Prithians didn't name their computers, but Veera liked the custom and concluded that, while treacherous, humans could be charming.

Thraki, on the other hand, kept robots as pets—but didn't seem to name them. Sam, who had followed the Prithian into her cabin, chittered happily and scampered across the overhead. Though not entitled to full unrestricted access, the ship's computers still provided the teenager with what amounted to a digital feast. And she was hungry. How much knowledge did the Confederacy have on the Sheen? What about the Thraki? Where had the long flight started? Veera warbled, and the ship sang in response.

16

Truth/find/take/use.

Baa'l Poet Star/Searcher
Year unknown

Veca IV, Clone Hegemony, Confederacy of Sentient Beings

Like BETA-018 and Devo-Dor, which Booly had visited during the previous month or so, Veca IV *looked* beautiful when viewed from orbit, but was something less than that down on the surface. The planet was hot, dry, and generally miserable. All of which reminded the legionnaire of Caliente, the planet on which he had been stationed prior to the now famous mutiny. The shuttle shuddered as it passed through a layer of superheated air and continued to lose altitude.

The general glanced out the view port at his elbow. The surface of the planet looked like poorly tanned brown leather, wrinkled from hard continuous use, and cracked where tremors, floods, and heat had attacked Veca IV's skin. Another less than desirable world, which the Hegemony had been only too glad to let the Thraki settle. The aliens weren't stupid, though, and had limited their presence to about five hundred souls. The colony surrendered without a single shot being fired. The ideal scenario from Booly's point of view—given the casualties his troops had suffered on BETA-018 and Devo-Dor.

Now, against his better judgment, he had agreed to meet with some sort of clone xenoanthropologist, who, according to McGowan, had something important to show him. It had better be, Booly thought grimly, or I'll leave the major here to rot. It wasn't true, of course, but the thought made him feel better.

Nicole Nogosek-101, adjusted the scarf that protected her neck, and shaded her eyes against the sun's reddish-orange glare. The dry crusty plain released what heat it could, and it shimmered over the land. The aircraft seemed to wink in and out of existence.

The settlement, which her people had named Solaris, had been established at the bend of a subsurface river, and was marked by an isolated grove of snap-snap trees. Trapped between the plain on one side of a dry riverbed, and sand dunes on the other, they were the only hint of green for miles around. The clones had come first, followed by the Thraki, and most recently the Legion.

The living quarters, as well as the hydroponic gardens, were located under the planet's surface, but the steel landing platform, along with the heavily insulated com shack and a clutch of sensors, were elevated fifteen feet off the ground. Safe from the dunes that bordered that side of the settlement, but exposed to the never-ending wind.

The clone squinted upward as the shuttle circled and prepared to land. What would General Booly be like? she wondered. A martinet? On the model of the Jonathan Alan Seebos she knew? An incompetent? Sent to deal with what amounted to military minutiae? Or, as Major McGowan claimed, "the best damned officer in the Legion." *If* the translations were accurate, *if* Nogosek had interpreted them correctly, millions of lives would depend on the answer.

Repellors flared, grit peppered her face, and the aircraft

dropped onto paint-stripped metal. A hatch opened, stairs unfolded, and McGowan emerged from the com shack. She was halfway to the shuttle when an officer appeared in the doorway, waved, and made his way to the deck. He was tall, lanky, and physically graceful. Nogosek saw no sign of an entourage and felt her spirits rise. Whatever else General Booly might eventually turn out to be—an ego-maniac wasn't one of them.

The officers greeted each other with a quick embrace, exchanged some words, and turned in the academic's direction. The pilot killed the repellors—and allowed the engines to wind down. McGowan arrived first. "Dr. Nogosek, I'd like to introduce General Booly."

Nogosek smiled and stuck out her hand. "It's a pleasure, General . . . Nicole will be fine."

Booly took the proffered hand, noticed the firm grip, and smiled in return. "The pleasure is mine, Nicole . . . and I go by Bill." The clone was attractive in an athletic sun-burned sort of way. She had sun-bleached blonde hair, pale blue eyes, and a determined chin.

Nogosek decided she liked the legionnaire, hoped it didn't show, and gestured toward the ramp. "Thanks for agreeing to come. I suggest that we get out of the sun. The temp will rise another twenty degrees before it starts to cool. We run most of our errands at night when the temp falls into the low seventies."

Booly used the back of his hand to wipe the sweat off his brow. His well-starched camos had already started to wilt. "Sounds good—lead the way."

Their boots rang on metal as the threesome passed the com shack, crossed the remainder of the platform, and stepped onto the ramp. Nogosek's pocket com burped static, insects buzzed, and metal pinged as it expanded. The wind was warm, too warm to deliver any sort of relief, but the snap-snap trees rustled in response. The community of Solaris baked in the sun.

• • •

Since the priestess lacked the strength to stand for more than a few units at a time, she had ordered the maintenance bots to lean the bed against the wall. That allowed her to rest yet remain involved with everything that took place within the underground vault.

The problem was that Bris Torputus was old, *very* old, so old that she had stopped keeping track some years before and no longer considered the matter to be worthy of her attention. What did merit her attention were the *Tomes of Truth*, all three of which had been laid on the makeshift table that occupied the center of the room.

First came the *Book of Yesterdays*, which described the gods, their powers, and areas of influence. Then came the *Book of Nows*, a history of sorts, that started with the creation of the great armada and would end when the Thraki did. Finally came the *Book of Tomorrows*, prophecy mostly, some of which had proven to be eerily accurate. Unlike the first two volumes, which were available to everyone, the *Book of Tomorrows* was restricted to members of the priesthood who were sworn to secrecy regarding its contents.

Each volume was a work of art. Rather than rely on transcriptions carried out by others, Torputus did her own translations, many of which were more accurate than those most of the priesthood had come to use. Each page of each tome bore drawings, designs, and marginalia executed by her own hand, and paid for with her failing vision.

The task, which had been given to Torputus as punishment for an offense she could no longer remember, had grown to consume her every waking moment. Considered to be something of an eccentric, and of little use to the hierarchy, she'd been sent to serve the colonists. The tomes accompanied her.

Now, as her days dwindled to a precious few, the priestess could no longer carry out the work herself, but was forced to rely on her carefully programmed form, which, truth be told, had a finer hand than she did, was willing to work around the clock, and never complained. She watched the spider-shaped robot dip a brush into some pigment and apply it to a grim visage. Was it the great god Hoonara? Yes, the priestess thought so, but knew her eyes had a tendency to betray her. Especially from so far away. The knock came softly—and Torputus knew who it was. Ironically, it was the human who understood her best, who realized the importance of her work, and spent hours at her side. Her voice was little more than a whisper. "Come in."

The door, which had once been part of a clone cargo container, and still bore the legend, "Rations Ready To Eat," creaked on makeshift hinges. Nogosek went to the female's side, located a hand, and held it in her own. She was good at languages and spoke without the aid of a translation device. "I brought a visitor, Sister Torputus— just as I said that I would."

"He believed you?"

"I haven't told him yet . . . but I will."

"He must come to believe you," the Thraki whispered urgently, "or many will die."

"Yes," the xenoanthropologist said gently, "I know."

Nogosek released the oldster's hand and turned to Booly. He seemed relaxed, but she could read his thoughts. "Show me something—and make it soon."

The academic looked at McGowan who nodded encouragingly. The key, Nogosek thought to herself, is to hook him, and follow with the facts, or, what the facts *seemed* to be. She motioned toward the table. "I came hoping to study Thraki culture. They are polytheistic, which makes religion extremely important. The books are the basis of their religion. One of those volumes, the *Book of Tomorrows*, contains the following passage: "And our people will settle a new world. Some will call it home, and wish to stay there, while others will point to the stars, and the menace that follows. Beware of those who call themselves friends, for they may attack, or align themselves with the menace. Run if you can, but failing that, call on the twins."

Booly wondered if the word "menace" referred to the Sheen. The quote was interesting if so—but hardly worth the trip. He glanced at McGowan. She nodded as if to say "Hang in there." The legionnaire tried to sound interested. "So, who are the twins?"

"Not *who*," the academic replied, "but *what*. Step over to the table, and I'll show you."

The floor was made of compacted dirt and felt slightly uneven. The tomes lay open, and the officer admired a beautifully illuminated page while Nogosek accessed the *Book of Tomorrows*. She knew what to look for and touched Booly's arm. "Here, take a look."

The officer turned. The text was illegible, to him at least, but the picture was quite riveting. The hand-drawn, hand-colored illustration was very realistic, and, thanks to the way it had been done, seemed to glow from within. What he saw were two golden cradles. Both had been decorated with beautifully executed scrollwork and rested on the same platform. Of more importance, however, were the bright metal tubes that the structures supported. The cylinders might have functioned as storage tanks, pressure chambers, or something equally mundane. But the soldier in Booly knew what they were. The twins were weapons. Weapons so special, so powerful, they had acquired religious significance. Nogosek saw Booly's expression and nodded. "That's correct, General, either one of the twins could destroy an entire fleet."

Booly raised an eyebrow. "How?"

"By releasing the sort of energy trapped within a black hole. Not in a gradual or controlled way—but all at once. On demand."

The legionnaire tried to imagine something that powerful but wasn't sure he could, or even needed to, since the matter was obviously hypothetical. "So, what are you trying to tell me? That the beings who wrote the book believe that such weapons will exist one day?"

"No," Nogosek replied patiently. "They exist *now*. The Thraki have them."

Booly was skeptical. "No offense, Doctor, but how do you know that?"

"Because Sister Torputus *saw* them with her own eyes," Nogosek replied, "and belonged to the elite team assigned to guard and maintain them. That was more than thirty years ago, but there's no reason to think that the weapons disappeared."

Booly looked up to find that, dim though they might be, the oldster's eyes were locked with his. Something, he wasn't sure what, drew the officer to her side. Nogosek followed and served as translator. "So, tell me Mother of Mothers," Booly said, unconsciously reverting to the form of address reserved for Naa grandmothers, "is the doctor correct? Do your people have such weapons?"

The reply was faint. "Yes, the twins exist, though only the priesthood is aware of them."

"But why?" Booly asked gently. "Why run for hundreds of years when such weapons were available? And why tell *me*?"

There was a pause while Nogosek translated and Torputus struggled to get her breath. "There were long periods of time when no one beyond initiates such as myself was even aware that the twins were among us. On other occasions, when all seemed to be at risk, those who needed to know were told. But the Runners ruled back then, and, thanks to the fact that their power *came* from running, they were reluctant to call on such weapons. Battles were fought and sometimes lost. The twins slept on."

The priestess made a wheezing sound and gestured with her hand. Nogosek placed an oxygen mask over the oldster's face, waited while she took three deep breaths, and pulled it away. "The reason I am telling you is because things have changed . . . The Facers have come to power—and may decide to fight."

Booly shrugged. "So? Perhaps they should. If the Facers destroy the Sheen, then so much the better."

"No," the oldster said sternly, "there is more. An entire paragraph that the original translators chose to omit from the *Book of Tomorrows*. It read: 'Know, however, that the twins may turn on you, may attack those who gave them life, leaving nothing but tears.' There is no way to know *why* the passage was left out. An error perhaps—or part of some plot. It makes no difference. Take the information. Give it to my people. Save them from themselves."

Given the nature of the weapons Nogosek had described, Booly had no difficulty believing that once unleashed, the twins might inflict as much damage on the Thraki as the Sheen. The aliens could and probably would be destroyed by their own weapons. Cold comfort to any bystanders who happened to be in the neighborhood.

The threat was more than physical however. The bombs, if that's what they could properly be called, would introduce more uncertainty into an already uncertain situation. Booly felt an almost panicky sense of urgency. Approximately 80 percent of the Thraki bases had been dealt with—and the time had come for him leave. Others could deal with the remaining 20 percent of the problem while he traveled to Arballa. That's where the decisions would be made, that's where a significant portion of the Confederate navy was starting to gather, and that's where the twins could do the most damage. He met the old, somewhat cloudy eyes. "Thank you, Sister Torputus. In spite of the present state of conflict, the Confederacy feels no animus towards your race, and seeks only to protect itself. I will do everything in my power to ensure that the twins continue to sleep."

"May the gods bless you," came the reply.

The legionnaires left shortly thereafter, followed a ramp to the surface, and stepped out into the sun. The heat fell like a hammer, the landing platform shimmered in the distance, and a scavenger circled high above. Booly looked at McGowan. "You were right, Major . . . The trip *was* worthwhile."

The other officer nodded. Beads of sweat dotted her forehead. "Sir, yes sir. What do you think? Can we put a lid on things?"

Booly shrugged. "Beats me, but we'll give it a try. Come on . . . the last one to board the shuttle gets to brief the Senate."

Planet Arballa, the Confederacy of Sentient Beings

The planet Arballa was crowned with white, robed in brown, and floated on a sea of black. She was beautiful, *very* beautiful, and the naval officer liked to start each day by gazing at her from his command chair on the bridge and drinking his first cup of coffee, which, as the entire crew knew, was a critical component of his physical as well as psychological well being. Knowing that, they left him alone.

Boone dreaded the day ahead. Until very recently, the *Friendship* and her coterie of warships, dispatch vessels, and freighters had the system pretty much to themselves. Now, as a variety of naval units dropped in-system, and took up defensive positions, his life had turned to shit. Not because of the ships themselves and the traffic problems they caused, but the officers who commanded them.

Worst of all were two or three admirals, who, unhappy with the slot to which they had been assigned, or resentful due to some perceived breach of protocol, wanted to speak with *his* admiral, a rather crotchety individual named Mary Chang, who planned to retire in a year or so and enjoyed telling her peers to screw off. Fun for *her*, but not for Boone, since he'd have to deal with the victims of the old lady's wrath long after she was gone. The naval officer sighed, took another pull from his coffee, and swore when the alarms went off. Reports flooded his earpiece.

"Robotic sensors report a system incursion at Transit Points NS-426-021, 022, and 023. The first ships through register a 98.2 percent match for Thraki recon droids . . ."

". . . Incoming transmission, sir, text only: 'Greetings on behalf of the Thraki race—we come in peace.' "

"Admiral Guinn on tight beam four, sir, requesting permission to engage."

Coffee forgotten, Boone eyed the bridge screens. Red deltas poured out of hyperspace and took up positions around three closely grouped Transit Points. Closely being defined as being within five-hundred thousand miles of each other.

One of the recently arrived naval groups, the 404th Destroyer Wing, was stationed in close proximity to Transit Point 021 and was in the perfect position to attack. If there was a state of war, *if* the rules of engagement allowed for it, and *if* Boone had the balls to make that kind of call. The repercussions of any decision could and probably would be enormous. If Boone said no and the Thraki proceeded to attack, an important advantage would have been lost, along with who knew how many casualties, and perhaps the *Friendship* herself. If he said yes, and it turned out that the Thraki had been friendly, and a war resulted, *he* would be at fault.

The naval officer gritted his teeth. Where the hell was Chang anyway? She was paid to make those kinds of decisions and as Chief Naval Officer In-System, (CNOIS) had responsibility for anything more than thirty-thousand feet above a planetary surface. But seconds were passing—and Guinn needed an answer. Boone had opened his mouth and was just about to speak when a familiar voice sounded in his ear. It was Chang. Still in her cabin, just out of the shower, dripping on the navy blue carpet. She was five feet tall, skinny as a rail, and in good shape. Her hair, which she had allowed to turn white, was worn in a crew cut. All the bridge communications were piped to her cabin where she monitored them via overhead speakers.

"Tell Guinn to hold his goddamn fire . . . but to remain at battle stations. Same for every other group in the system. Get the President on the horn. Tell the worthless bastard that we have visitors. Contact the fur balls . . . Tell the little shits that if they so much as blow a sack of garbage through their disposal tubes we'll blow their butts off. Got it?"

"Ma'am, yes, ma'am."

"Good. And tell my steward to get some breakfast in here . . . I'm hungry."

The control area had the same subdued lighting—the same sense of carefully guarded quiet associated with great libraries. There was no sense of motion, the view screens were filled with electronic confetti, and the battleship could have been anywhere. Except that hyperspace was closer to nowhere than to somewhere. A diagrammatic control display claimed the forward bulkhead. Icons stood in for systems, colors conveyed status, and numbers provided data on everything from speed to time in transit.

Grand Admiral Hooloo Andragna looked up at the steadily dwindling numbers and saw that a little less than twelve temporal units stood between the present and the future of his race. Once the numbers disappeared, the battleship would emerge from hyperspace, reestablish communications with the rest of the subfleet, and . . ."

And what? The naval officer asked himself. There were so many possibilities . . . The lead ships had emerged by now—into a heavily defended system. Were they fighting for their lives? While he sat and stared? Cursing his name as missiles flashed through the darkness, shields fell, and red-orange flowers blossomed in the darkness. Or had the Confederate ships withheld their fire? And allowed the Thraki vessels to enter? Anything was possible.

The countdown rippled toward zero, systems were checked, and the crew went to battle stations. The precision of it made Andragna feel better. Defeats, like the one suffered on BETA-018, had occurred on the ground. Here, in deep space, the Thraki were at their best. No race had been persecuted as they had, fought a more relentless enemy, or won so many battles. They were warriors, *tired* warriors, but warriors nonetheless. The Confederacy would come to know that, and, assuming it survived, to respect it.

Andragna had left all the moon-sized arks, plus fifteen-hundred of the armada's best ships, to protect Zynig-47. That left him with more than three thousand vessels, less than what the Sheen could bring to bear, but more than the Confederacy could cobble together.

Besides, the admiral thought to himself as the final moments ticked away, we have the twins, and if all else fails, they *will see us through*.

The battleship lurched, stars flooded the screens, and communications came on-line. The first ship to follow the drones into the Araballazanie system was a destroyer commanded by Captain Algo Portatious. He knew what Andragna wanted and needed most. His face appeared on a com screen. The tone was lighthearted. He knew his peers would monitor the conversation and played to the invisible gallery. "Greetings, Admiral . . . Welcome to assembly area one."

The officer's demeanor spoke volumes. Andragna felt an enormous sense of relief. "Thank you. Is there anything to report?"

Portatious offered the Thraki equivalent of a grin. "If threats were missiles we'd be dead by now."

The bridge crew laughed, and Andragna looked to his screens. With each passing temporal unit three more ships arrived. That's how quickly his forces were entering the system. It wouldn't be long before the defenders were outgunned. Then, with the Confederate vessels as a screen, the battle could begin. Would the Sheen take the bait? Yes, the naval officer thought to himself, as surely as the universe continues to expand.

The Hoon, along with its electromechanical minions, had long been able to follow its prey through hyperspace, a capability that so far as it knew was completely unique. That's why it had been able to track the Confederate ship back to its lair, record all of the necessary navigational data, and download it to the fleet.

So now, as the *Ninja* hurtled through time and space, a long silvery snake followed behind. A snake comprised of countless Sheen ships all having the same destination.

Tyspin, who had no way to know about the menace that followed, was on the bridge at the moment when the *Ninja* popped into normal space. Data rippled across previously vacant screens, the com techs struggled to deal with an avalanche of high priority com calls, and the naval officer did her best to take it in. The displays told the story.

The Confederate forces, more than before, were clustered around well-established transit points, while a host of Thraki vessels had coalesced into three "war" globes, all of which continued to grow as more ships arrived. The naval officer was still in the process of absorbing that, of dealing with it, when Captain Hashimoto yelled in her ear. "We've got trouble, Admiral! It looks like the Sheen managed to follow!"

Tyspin struggled to combat the rising sense of panic. Follow? No, it wasn't possible! Or was it? My god, what had she done?

The Hoon answered the human's unspoken question by ordering a wing of fighters to sweep past the *Ninja*, all flying in formation, blasting everyone with the same message. "Hold your fire! We come in peace!"

It might have been ignored except for one extremely important factor: Rather than broadcast an image of itself, clad in a metallic body, the Hoon sent video of a human being instead. And not just any human being, but Jorley

Jepp, who watched with slack-jawed amazement as his countenance appeared on the main com screen, and words poured from his mouth. Not his words but those that the Hoon had given the electronically generated doppelganger to say. The syntax was wooden, but who would know the difference?

"Hello, my name is Jorley Jepp. The Sheen were kind enough to rescue me after my ship was destroyed. I have lived with them for many months. In spite of the endless persecution imposed by the rapacious Thraki, the Sheen come in peace, and call on the Confederacy to sponsor meaningful negotiations. Thank you."

There was a pause followed by a holo of President Marcott Nankool. His face was stern. "Given hostile actions by both the Thraki *and* the Sheen—the Confederacy takes small comfort from their proclamations of peace. If both parties are truly willing to negotiate, the Confederacy is willing to help, if the following conditions are met: The warships within both fleets will take all targeting systems off-line, cut power to primary weapons systems, and remain where they are. In the meantime, our offensive capabilities will remain at the highest state of readiness. Should either side violate the conditions just put forth— the Confederacy will side with the opposing group and open fire. That's our best offer . . . take it or leave it." The video snapped to black.

It was a gutsy position, especially in light of the fact that the Confederacy possessed less firepower than the other potential combatants, and stood to lose its government as well. It could work, however—since all three of the groups had the technology necessary to determine when weapons systems were on-line.

Tyspin held her breath as millions waited for some sort of reply. If the combatants were to ignore the offer, if a full-scale battle ensued, the fault would be hers. For assuming too much, for failing to anticipate the possibilities, and for underestimating the enemy. The knowledge brought blood to her face and made her chest feel tight. Comfort came from an unexpected source. "It wasn't your fault," Jepp said softly, "there was no way you could know. Not even *I* knew the Sheen could follow a ship through hyperspace."

That wasn't strictly true, of course, since Jepp had had inklings of such a capability, but he liked Typsin and wanted her to feel better. And, though she would have been reluctant to admit it, the naval officer *did* feel somewhat better, and turned her attention to the screens.

Jepp tried to guess what the Hoon would do next. The AI had already revealed a level of political sophistication greater than he had originally supposed. First, during the power struggle with its twin—and now in its dealings with both the Confederacy and the Thrakies. One thing was for sure, however. While some beings played power games for the fun of it, the Hoon had little interest in such diversions. It wanted to win—and nothing else mattered.

A full minute elapsed before Grand Admiral Andragna appeared. "We find the Confederacy's conditions to be acceptable—and are willing to comply."

A computer-generated image of Jepp filled the com screen half a second later. He smiled. "The peace-loving Sheen agree to the conditions and stand ready to negotiate." The image faded to static.

Tyspin raised an eyebrow, and Jepp shrugged innocently. "What am I supposed to do? It's not like the Hoon asked my permission or anything."

The admiral turned as President Nankool reappeared. A digital readout filled the lower right-hand corner of the frame. "Excellent. Prepare to deactivate targeting systems sixty seconds from now . . . Weapons to follow."

It took less than five minutes for the warships of both fleets to power down but more than six hours for the Confederate Navy to gather the requisite data, process it, and produce the necessary reports, reports that became outdated the moment they were issued but were supplemented by a hastily rigged sampling program meant to monitor compliance. It was scant protection—but all that the Confederacy had. Nankool's message was issued a few minutes later. "Thank you for your patience. As of 1500 hours local, we find both sides in compliance. That being the case, envoys from both fleets are invited to board the *Friendship* six hours from now. No more than twelve representatives from each fleet will be allowed to board the vessel that serves as our capital. If you have questions regarding protocol or logistics please contact my staff on com channel six. Thank you."

The Hoon was everywhere and nowhere in particular— flitting from ship to ship, riding recon drones no larger than a pebble, gorging itself on data. Data regarding the system in which the battle would take place, data on the fools who believed its lies, and data on the Thraki who had nowhere to run. Not *all* of the Thraki, because fully 25 percent of their ships were missing, but most of them. The rest could and would be dealt with later. Yes, there was much to learn and every reason to learn it, especially given the fact that if the Thraki fleet were added to the Confederate fleet the resulting force would be equal to all of its units combined. The Hoon had never faced an enemy that powerful before, never fought a battle with anything like parity, and didn't want to lose. That being the case, it was time to stall—a task for which the soft body was uniquely suited. The necessary orders were issued, received, and ultimately complied with.

Grand Admiral Hooloo Andragna was more frightened than he cared to admit—not only by the size and power of the two fleets that opposed him—but by the extent to which the entire dynamic had changed. Rather than attack, as he had supposed that they would, the Sheen had agreed to negotiate. Or had they? What about the human who claimed to speak for them? Did he have any actual authority? And what did he want?

Of equal or even more concern was the manner in which the Confederacy had responded to the situation. He had hoped, no *assumed*, that they would out and out capitulate, or failing that, waffle back and forth. Instead they evidenced vision, courage, and ironclad determination. Not a very good sign.

The naval officer sighed and released his harness. Another more elaborate uniform waited in his quarters. He hated the damn thing and wondered who had been responsible for it. A Runner? Or a Facer? It made no difference. Now, with thousands of ships waiting to attack, neither philosophy seemed especially valid. Andragna thought about his wife, gave thanks that she was on Zynig-47, and left the control room. The command crew watched him go.

President Marcott Nankool, Governor Sergi Chien-Chu, Maylo Chien-Chu, Ambassador Hiween Doma-Sa, Ambassador Tula Nogo Mypop, Senator Samuel Ishimoto-Six, and a clutch of advisors stood at the center of the *Friendship*'s bridge. Admiral Chang was present, as was Captain Boone. Everyone stared at the battle screens arrayed above their heads. "So," Nankool said gravely, "is that it? Is that all of them?"

"Maybe," Chang answered. "The number matches the information gathered by the *Ninja* off Transit Point NS-690-193. So, unless the goddamned machines have some reserves they haven't shown us yet, we're up against a force of six thousand vessels."

"More like nine thousand if we have to fight both fleets," Doma-Sa growled.

"True," Chang conceded, "which is why I hope President Nankool is one helluva good negotiator." She grinned, but no one joined her.

"Which brings us to the upcoming talks," Chien-Chu said quietly. "What do we have on this Jepp person?"

Boone shrugged. "He was a prospector based on Long Jump. Had a ship, but it was mortgaged to the hilt. He disappeared and was given up for dead. When the Sheen arrived, so did he. An army of robots landed, took to the streets, and spouted a lot of religious nonsense. It appeared he was in charge. Then, for reasons we're not sure of, the machines attacked."

"So, he really *does* have some clout," Senator Mypop put in.

"Maybe," Boone allowed, "but Admiral Tyspin has her doubts. She spent some time with the man and thinks that whatever influence he has is extremely limited. Take those messages for example . . . both of them were computer-generated. Jepp was surprised to see his face on the screen. The Hegemony spent quite a lot of time talking to the Thraki. *They* claim the real power lies with an artificial intelligence known as the Hoon."

"Which raises an interesting question," Senator Alway Orno said, almost forgotten toward the rear of the crowd. "Why send false messages—followed by a meaningless emissary?"

"To buy time," Doma-Sa said simply, his eyes boring through the Ramanthian's head. "The oldest trick in the universe."

The Ramanthian felt a sudden stab of fear. Did the Hudathan know? Had word of the tercentennial birthing leaked somehow? No, the Hudathan lacked subtlety, and would broach the matter head on.

"That would explain Jepp," Nankool observed, "and the Hoon, but how 'bout the Thraki? What are *they* up to? And why, after hundreds of years, are they ready for a showdown?"

"I think I know the answer," a new voice said, "and you aren't going to like it."

The group turned. The *Gladiator* had dropped in-system in time to witness Nankool's most recent broadcast. General William Booly caught a glimpse of Maylo Chien-Chu, felt a fist squeeze his heart, and tried to ignore it. "They have a secret weapon, *two* of them, either of which could destroy the Sheen fleet."

There was silence for a moment. Chang was the first to speak. She was cynical, but Booly was head of the Joint Chiefs. That made him her commanding officer. "Sir, you're sure of that?"

Booly nodded. "Yes, Admiral, I am."

"Holy shit."

"Yes," Booly agreed dryly. "Those are my sentiments exactly."

17

Yield to all, and you will soon have nothing to yield.

Aesop
"The Man and His Two Wives" (fable)
Standard year circa 600 B.C.

Planet Arballa, the Confederacy of Sentient Beings

Grand Admiral Hooloo Andragna had been aboard the *Friendship* before, during the period when the clones and their allies had sought to form an alliance. Seeing the vessel triggered a feeling of reluctant respect. Not awe, since the arks that his people had constructed were larger, not fear, since the Thraki fleet outnumbered the Confederate navy almost two to one, but respect. It was amazing that such disparate races had come together and *stayed* together, especially in light of how divided his own species was. Something to remember during the upcoming talks.

Andragna, who was seated above and behind the pilots, watched the view screen as the *Friendship*'s weapons pods, missile launchers, cooling stacks, antenna housings, and other less obvious installations slid by. He spotted the point where a shaft of light shot out into space and felt the shuttle bank to the left. The launch bay yawned before him. The shuttle entered.

The blast doors, which rarely closed while the ship was in orbit, started to do so. Andragna and his staff would be spared the necessity of donning space armor to reach the inner access lock—a signal honor indeed since it meant that the *Friendship* would be unable to launch or recover spacecraft so long as the hatch was closed.

The shuttle swept low across the deck, fired retros, and, supported by its repellors, settled onto the blast-scarred deck. Rows of neatly parked ships marched into the distance. The pilot heaved a sigh of relief. His job was momentarily over.

The doors met, atmosphere was pumped into the bay, and a reception party gathered by the shuttle. A technical triggered the hatch, and Andragna stepped out onto some roll-up stairs. He recognized some familiar odors: The harsh smell of ozone, the sickly sweet stench of fuel, and the reek of overheated metal.

The Thraki scanned the group below, saw some familiar faces, and nodded accordingly. He displayed some teeth, wondered how such an expression could possibly be interpreted as friendly, and descended the stairs. His staff followed. "President Nankool, Ambassador Doma-Sa, Governor Chien-Chu, it's nice to see you again."

Andragna's form boosted the volume to overcome the sudden chatter from a power wrench, made the necessary translation, and started to record. Each and every word would be captured for subsequent review and analysis.

There were reciprocal greetings, several rounds of introductions, and pro forma expressions of goodwill that no one took seriously.

Once the formalities had been concluded, the Thraki were escorted across the deck, through the lock, and into a maze of mostly empty corridors. The majority of the ship's crew were at battle stations, nonessential civilian personnel had been restricted to their quarters, and even robots were few and far between.

Eventually, after what seemed like a long hike, Andragna and his staff were ushered into a large conference room. The space was equipped with a twenty-foot-long oval table, wall screens, and soft overhead lighting. A heavily laden side table supported food and a variety of nonintoxicating drinks. Great care had been taken to provide items the Thraki would like.

There was a certain amount of milling around as everyone sought seats appropriate to their particular status, and it was then that Andragna was re-introduced to General William Booly. Their top-ranking officer if the admiral remembered correctly—and a person to be reckoned with.

Nankool stood. He waited for everyone to take their seats, cleared his throat, and met Andragna's eyes. Though offensive to some sentients, it happened that Thraki reacted to direct eye contact in much the same manner humans did. They viewed it as a sign of sincerity and mental engagement. The President, who had already rehearsed the gesture in his mind, glanced at his wrist term. "I hope you'll forgive me if I come straight to the point . . . The Sheen emissary is due to arrive in less than an hour—and we have something of considerable importance to discuss prior to his arrival."

Andragna felt a sudden sense of excitement. Could this be what he had been hoping for? Was the Confederacy prepared to form an alliance? Nothing would please him more. The officer nodded but kept a tight rein on his body language. The humans were clever and might have educated themselves regarding the nonverbal aspects of Thraki communication.

"The issue," Nankool continued, "centers around certain weapons included in your inventory. I'm not sure what the technical name for such devices would be—but you and your priests commonly refer to them as 'the twins.' "

Andragna felt his ears go back, knew the fur along the back of his neck stood straight up, and was powerless to stop it. How did they know? And if the Confederation knew about the twins, what else did they have? Or was this some sort of trick? A stratagem designed to draw him out?

None of the admiral's aides had been briefed regarding the twins, but they could see how upset he was and stirred uneasily. The conference room felt suddenly small and confining. Andragna decided to play it safe. "Twins? I have no idea what you're talking about."

Nankool raised an eyebrow. "Really? Well, perhaps *this* will refresh your memory."

A holo blossomed at the center of the conference room table. The footage had been captured by Major McGowan on Veca IV. Content made up for what it lacked in technique. The assemblage watched Booly examine the *Tomes of Truth*, looked over the officer's shoulder as he stared at a beautifully wrought illustration, and spoke with Sister Torputus.

With the exception of Sector 27, who belonged to the priesthood, the picture of two cylinders meant nothing to the rest of the delegation. He had never seen the twins with his own eyes but was aware of rumors. No wonder Andragna was upset! The Confederacy had stumbled across something very important indeed. He wanted to help but was forced to watch while the admiral struggled to maintain his composure.

Andragna listened to the thin reedy voice, saw the female's obvious sincerity, and sensed that what she claimed was potentially true. Once detonated, the twins *might* inflict some damage on his fleet. Still, they were the only equalizer he had, and well worth hanging on to. Besides, now that the twins were out in the open, he had a new bargaining chip, one that he should retain for as long as possible. The Thraki mustered all the dignity he could. "Though well intentioned—Sister Torputus had no right to reveal such information. That being said, I suppose it would be pointless to issue further denials. However, while it's true that we possess two rather unique energy weapons, the rest is pure conjecture. I have complete faith in our

technical experts who assure me that while powerful—
both weapons can be successfully deployed."

The last statement was an outright falsehood—but no
one knew that except for Andragna.

Nankool experienced an almost overwhelming sense of
anger. His hands made fists. The Thraki position was arrogant and foolhardy. More than that, it could result in
millions of unnecessary deaths. He glanced at his wrist
term, saw that his hands had started to shake, and clasped
both behind his back.

"Very little time remains . . . In the interest of your people, as well as ours, the Confederacy requests, no, *implores*
you to forgo use of such weapons, at least until such time
as you and your fleet are well clear of our systems."

"That's it?" Andragna inquired sarcastically. "You ask
that we sacrifice the very weapons that mean victory for
our people? In return for what? Your heartfelt prayers?"

"No," Nankool replied coldly. "Forswear use of the
twins, and we will fight at your side—*not* as sacrificial
pawns, but as equals."

There it was, evidence that the Confederacy understood
the nature of Andragna's intent, but was willing to over-
look it. For a price. But which was more valuable, the
naval officer wondered. The twins? And all their latent
energy? Or the Confederacy? With a small but still powerful fleet?

Andragna wanted to believe Nankool, *wanted* to trust
the Confederacy, but found that difficult to do. The Thraki
were a self-reliant people, unfettered by the compromises
that bound the multispecies government together, and
therefore stronger. His voice seemed unnaturally loud.
"No. While the Thraki people would otherwise welcome
such an alliance, the price is too high."

Nankool felt a profound sense of disappointment. He
looked around the room, scanned each face, and came to
Andragna's. "I'm sorry to hear that, Admiral—sorry for

your people as well as ours. This meeting is over—may the deities protect us."

The Sheen shuttle made no attempt to obtain a clearance from the *Friendship*'s traffic control computer. It simply followed the shortest possible route in, slid the length of the battleship's starboard side, and approached the launch bay as if entitled to do so. It was a dangerous thing to do under normal circumstances but with the battleship at the highest state of alert it verged on suicidal.

Captain Boone's command chair whined as he swiveled to the left. More than two dozen cameras covered the launch bay. He checked number sixteen. It showed the hatch through which the shuttle would soon enter. "All batteries will hold their fire . . . The Sheen will receive the same courtesies extended to the Thraki."

The naval officer sensed a presence and turned to find Admiral Chang at his side. She offered a fresh mug of coffee. "So, are we having fun yet?"

He accepted the cup. "No, ma'am. The Sheen are crazy."

"Machines," the senior officer replied cheerfully. "You can't live with 'em—and you can't live without 'em."

Meanwhile, oblivious to what the humans thought, the Hoon commanded its fleet, flew the Sheen shuttle, and controlled the onboard security units. Everything and everyone with the exception of Jepp, Veera, and Sam.

The Hoon executed a sharp left-hand turn and entered the battleship's bay. It was far less automated than the AI considered to be appropriate. After all, why rely on biologicals when machines were available? All of which served to confirm the conclusion already arrived at: Negotiations were a waste of time, and the fleet should attack. The conclusion was logical, eminently so, but the Hoon took no action. A very un-Hoonlike thing to do. Had the computer intelligence been capable of greater introspection it might have wondered why and sought to understand. But it wasn't, couldn't, and didn't. Programming is programming, and where computers are concerned, as immutable as DNA.

Careless of what the Hoon thought, Jepp was on a high. Veera, to whom a lot of his babbling was directed, ignored most of his commentary. The occasional "yes" or "no" was sufficient to keep him happy. In spite of the fact that the Prithian might have been able to remain aboard the *Ninja*, she had decided to come, and observe what took place.

Though inconclusive thus far, her research regarding the Sheen had proved quite interesting, as had her evaluation of Thraki society. "Markets derive from economic principles," her father liked to say, "but are influenced by culture. That's why you must understand each in order to profit." The merchant was gone now, but his lessons lived on.

The shuttle touched down, the blast doors closed, and air flooded the bay. Jepp was eager to address the senate. He bounced off the small uncomfortable seat. "This is it, Veera! The moment we've been waiting for. Once they hear God's plan, once they embrace the silvery host, the new order will unfold. Think of it! The entire Confederacy governed by a single religion! Historians will write about this day—and your name will appear for all to see."

Veera realized that Jepp was more concerned with *his* name—but knew better than to say so.

The hatch opened, the delegation descended a flight of self-propelled stairs, and were met by a carefully chosen reception committee. Nankool was there, per Jepp's request, but so was Maylo, who, unbeknownst to her, had been chosen for reasons other than her political acumen. Admiral Tyspin had provided the government with every bit of information that she could, including the fact that Jepp had a definite interest in women.

Knowing that, Nankool couldn't help but smile when the ex-prospector saw Maylo, and his face lit up.

The party formed a column of twos, wound its way between some navy transports, and headed toward the main lock. A metal archway had been established in front of the portal. Anyone who approached had no choice but to pass through. The humans went first followed by the robots.

Booly and a pair of technicians were sequestered in a compartment not far away. A row of jury-rigged monitors was racked in front of them. The essence of Tyspin's theory was that Jepp amounted to little more than a noisy decoy and that the Hoon, or part of the Hoon, controlled one or more of the so-called security units. If that was true, there would be a link back to the fleet and that would validate Tyspin's thesis.

"Okay, sir, here goes," Com Tech Rutaza said. "Assuming the chip heads are linked with each other and/or one of their ships, the computer will provide me with a visual profile."

Booly watched the first security unit pass through the arch. The monitors, lime green the moment before, shivered as an image appeared. It looked nothing like the real thing. The protective force field from which the Sheen took their name appeared as a yellow-white aura. A complex tracery of blue lines described the robot's electronic nervous system. They rippled in synch with the machine's alloy body.

A lake of red-orange heat confirmed the location of the droid's power plant while lesser ponds, pools, and streams were associated with on-line weapon systems, sensor relays, and good old friction. The weapons were worrisome but allowed. There wasn't a senator onboard who didn't have their own security.

Rutaza frowned as the first unit exited screen left. "No linkage, sir."

Booly nodded. "Keep looking."

The second robot passed under the arch followed by the third. Some lavender lines appeared, and Rutaza pointed at a screen. "Bingo! They're talking to each other."

Booly nodded. Some sort of localized communication

was to be expected. But what of the more important question? Was the Hoon, or a part of the Hoon, actually present?

Booly was just about ready to say, "no," when Unit Four appeared. "Look!" Rutaza said. "See the bursting? The dashed line coming in from the upper right-hand corner of the screen? Four is taking a feed. Not continuous, like we were thought, but in the form of periodic reloads. How much you wanta bet the receiving unit will update the rest?"

Booly watched the prophecy come true. No sooner had the incoming feed stopped than Unit Four sent lavender lines to all the rest. It appeared Tyspin was correct. The Hoon had decided to use Jepp, to allow the human to take center stage, while it monitored the proceedings. He gave the tech a pat on the shoulder. "Thanks, Rutaza. Nice job. Get that stuff to intel. We'll let the spooks wrestle with it."

The com tech waited for the general to clear the compartment before throwing his feet up onto the console. The other rating, a woman named Hoko, grinned. "Suck up."

Rutaza offered a gesture. "Screw you."

"Don't you wish."

Both of them laughed.

Oblivious to the activities of crew members like Rutaza and Hoko, the senators stood in clumps and waited for the emissary to arrive. Opinion was divided into three schools of thought: those who favored an alliance with the Thraki, those who favored an alliance with the Sheen, and those who favored a policy of nonalignment.

The third contingent, often referred to as the "do-nothings" by the other two, were further split into additional subgroups. One wanted to declare a policy of "constructive neutrality" and spent a great deal of time trying to explain what that meant, while another, led by Senator Alway Orno, wanted to leave the Araballazanies to their fate. A third blathered on about pacifism, nonviolence, and the brother-sisterhood of sentients.

Everyone wanted their ideas to be heard, so everyone talked at once, and nothing was accomplished. Chien-Chu waited toward the front of the chambers and was relieved when the doors swung open. He nodded to the master-of-arms, who addressed a mike. His voice boomed through the chambers. "The Sheen emissary has arrived. Please return to your seats."

It took the better part of five minutes for the senators to return to their seats. President Nankool held the delegation just beyond the doors until the noise level dropped and the assemblage was ready. He signaled Jepp, and the entire party marched the length of the aisle. Maylo saw her uncle, wondered what he was thinking, and thought how strange the moment was. She looked at Veera, knew the Prithian's thoughts were similar to hers, and smiled. A necklace of feathers shifted by way of response.

Jepp, who had pressed some creases into his dark blue ship suit, drew himself up. Was Maylo Chien-Chu impressed? He hoped so. The entire senate was staring, waiting for him to speak, thinking how important he was. Everything was so clear, so vivid, that the ex-prospector knew he would never forget. The blur of alien faces, a whiff of exotic perfume, the carpet beneath his shoes. Each would be indelibly etched onto his memory.

Most of the beings in the chamber watched Jepp with a sort of curious diffidence. What was this strange apparition anyway? A well-meaning citizen, co-opted by the machines, or a brutal renegade deserving of their contempt?

At least one mind *was* made up, however, and it stared at Jepp with unalloyed hatred, knowing what the ex-prospector had done. *His* name was Harvey S. Holander, Father to Sissy M. Holander, first officer of the ill-fated container ship *Rho Ophiuchi*, which had been in the process of refueling when Jepp ordered the attack on space station *Halo*.

Holander, who served as Nankool's first under secretary

of defense, had first learned of the attack on Long Jump while reading a summary of the statement taken from the smuggler currently known as "Willy Williams."

Not being privy to the *Rho Ophiuchi's* itinerary, the administrator had no way to know that he had just read an account of his daughter's death, not until the better part of a month had passed and the intelligence reports started to filter in. That's when he learned the truth—and the hatred was born. Now, only feet from the podium, the moment was near. It had been relatively simple to steal the weapon, tape it to the bottom of his seat a few hours before, and pass through security with everyone else. Now, in a matter of minutes, revenge would be his.

Unaware of the danger that lurked nearby, Jepp shook hands with Sergi Chien-Chu and took note of the relationship between the governor and the beautiful young woman, people who would never associate with him if they had a choice. Life was looking up! He waited while Nankool took the podium.

"My fellow sentients . . . Now, as we face the possibility of a terrible conflagration, communication becomes even more important. The Sheen rescued Citizen Jepp after his ship was wrecked, allowed him to travel with their fleet, and came to trust him. He, along with those sent to assist him, hopes to establish a two-way dialogue . . ."

"What about Long Jump?" a voice yelled. "Let's talk about that!"

Nankool raised a hand. "What occurred on Long Jump remains under investigation . . . Let's wait for the facts and reserve final judgements until then."

Holander seethed, wondered if he could nail Nankool as well, and forced himself to wait. He had very little experience with weapons, which meant that the shorter the range the better. He would kill Jepp . . . followed by the President.

There was no applause as Jepp made his way to the podium, a rather jarring departure from his most cherished fantasies, and one for which he might force the senate to apologize. Still, the would-be messiah thought to himself, they deserve a second chance—an opportunity to willingly join his flock. After that, well, the fleet would make his will known. He smiled into the lights.

"There is a plan, a *glorious* plan, conceived by God and given to me. It consists of three parts, the *Cleansing*, which is now under way, the *Covenant*, in which all sentients will bind themselves over to God, and the *Consecration*. Once the Consecration has been completed and the throne is mine, a cadre of secular advisors will be required. Beings such as yourselves who can take my pronouncements and, with assistance from God's silvery host, bring them to life. What I offer is nothing less than a partnership, an opportunity to step back from the apocalypse and begin a new age. An age in which . . ."

Holander reached under his seat, fumbled for the weapon, and attempted to free it. The tape was stubborn, and the action proved more difficult than he thought it would be. Finally, energy pistol in hand, he staggered to his feet. A guard yelled but it was too late.

Everything felt so weightless. Memories stuttered through his brain. He saw Sissy hold up her arms, cheered as she dove from a dock, and clapped as she accepted her diploma. The barrel wavered, found its target, and spit bolts of bright blue energy. Blue like her eyes, blue like the water, blue like . . .

The Hoon detected the threat, gave the necessary orders, and monitored the results. The security units responded in unison. They brought their weapons up and fired. Holander staggered as nine bolts of coherent light punched their way through his chest and struck the senators beyond.

What felt like a red-hot steel bar punched its way through Jepp's shoulder. Sam fell clear and scuttled towards Veera. The human took two steps backwards, felt Alpha wrap an arm around his waist, and shouted "No!"

But it was too late. The security units continued to fire.

Maylo Chien-Chu fell as a bolt of energy ripped through her chest, the master at arms died with his sidearm half drawn, and a staffer lost the left side of his face. Someone screamed, panic erupted, and the aisles filled with bodies.

Jepp pushed Alpha away, screamed, "Stop it!" at the top of his lungs, and threw himself into the line of fire. The Hoon ordered its minions to pause, "heard" some sort of alarm, but saw no further threat. That being the case, it allowed the human to intervene.

Jepp, conscious of the fact that reinforcements were on the way, looked left and right. Sergi Chien-Chu was crouched a few feet away, holding his niece in his arms, radioing for help. The ex-prospector pointed. "We need a hostage—someone they won't harm—take him!"

Though new to the idea of hostages—and struck by how illogical the concept was—the AI was quick to respond. Two of the security units seized Chien-Chu, discovered that the cyborg was a good deal stronger than he appeared, but still managed to bring him under control. Then, with Jepp, Alpha, Veera, and Chien-Chu at the center, the Hoon-controlled robots formed a defensive wheel. Light flared as even more power went to their shields and the Sheen headed for the doors.

Booly, along with a half-dozen heavily armed MPs pounded around a corner, and skidded to a stop. Doors slammed open as what looked like a silvery amoeba emerged from the senate chambers. It oozed their way. The soldiers raised their weapons, but Booly ordered them to stop. "Hold your fire! Lower your rifles! Back away."

The MPs backed into an alcove while the strange assemblage marched by. Booly caught a glimpse of Chien-Chu's eyes, heard the industrialist shout Maylo's name, and knew something horrible had happened. He turned to a lieutenant. "Track them all the way to the bay. Don't interfere, and don't let anyone else interfere. Jepp is meaningless, and the Hoon is somewhere else."

The lieutenant didn't know who the Hoon was, but

knew how to follow orders, and proceeded to do so. The clutch of marines followed as the mixed party of machines and biologicals retraced their steps.

Booly, feeling guilty because of the way he had dumped the entire matter onto a mere lieutenant, ran for the senate chambers. The interior was absolute chaos. The legionnaire saw a splash of red on the front of the podium, but no sign of Maylo. A naval officer bumped his side. She'd been nicked by an energy beam and was clutching a still-smoking arm. She looked pale. "Sorry, sir, what a mess."

A party of robo medics entered through the main door. Booly waved. "Over here! Now damn it!" He turned back. "Tell me, Commander, what happened to Maylo Chien-Chu?"

"They shot her," the naval officer replied shakily. "Through the chest. Sorry, sir, I feel a bit dizzy."

A robot caught the commander before she hit the deck. Another came to help.

Booly felt something rise to choke off his air. Maylo? Dead? No! He refused to believe it. The officer pushed his way through the crowd, stepped over a mostly decapitated body, and saw Nankool. He yelled over the crowd noise. "Mr. President! What happened to Ms. Chien-Chu?"

"Wounded! They took her to the sick bay!"

Booly waved his thanks, turned, and pushed his way back through the crowd. "Wounded?" Not killed? Had Nankool chosen the word intentionally? Or because he really didn't know?

Booly hit the corridor, ignored the voices that called to him, and pounded down the hall. Though referred to as the "sick bay," the facility was a good deal more than that. It consisted of a full-scale hospital, staffed with medical personnel from each of the member races, and ready to deal with almost anything. If anyone could save Maylo, they could. That's what the legionnaire told himself as he skidded around a corner, passed a row of self-propelled gurneys, and headed for the well-marked hatch. It hissed

open, and a desk blocked his way. An android rose to greet
him. It wore a marine green paint job. A serial number
had been stenciled across its chest. "Greetings, General.
Are you in need of medical attention?"

Booly fought to catch his breath. "No, I'm looking for
a patient . . . A woman by the name of Maylo Chien-Chu."

"Yes, they brought her in about ten minutes ago," the
robot replied gravely. "The doctors are treating her now.
Please take a seat and . . ."

Booly ducked around the desk, steered for the sign that
said "Trauma," and stuck his head into an alcove. A Turr
diplomat lay on the table, his face contorted with pain.
Having already passed through Holander's chest, an energy beam had severed his hand.

A doctor frowned. Booly said, "Sorry," and moved to
the next cube. It was packed with medical personnel all
gathered around Maylo's supine body. Her face looked
slack and lifeless. The officer pushed his way forward, but
a hand grabbed his arm. "Not now, General. We must allow the medics some room."

Booly turned to find himself face-to-face with Senator Samuel Ishimoto-Six. Both men wondered the same
thing . . . Assuming that Maylo loved one of them—which
had she chosen? It was a selfish thought, and both felt
guilty. "How is she?" Booly asked. "Can they save her?"

The clone shrugged. "It's too early to say."

A medic turned to confront them. "You'll have to leave
now—a doctor will be out to see you."

Both men backed out of the room. Booly remembered
the Sheen, the lieutenant upon which the responsibility had
been dumped, and knew it was time to go. His wrist term
started to vibrate. He met the politician's gaze. "They're
looking for me—can you stay?"

Ishimoto-Six nodded.

"Good. Make sure the docs do everything they can. Be
there when she wakes up. She'll need someone."

The clone nodded and watched Booly walk away.

Knowing his rival would be present when and if Maylo came to, wishing it could be him. The politician sighed. In a galaxy full of assholes, why did *his* competition have to be such a nice guy? It wasn't fair. He turned to look for a chair.

There were close calls, two to be exact, but no one fired. The lieutenant chanted Booly's name like a mantra, people listened, and the Sheen were allowed to pass. Finally, after what seemed like an eternity, they made it to the launch bay where the shuttle waited. Doors opened to space, the Hoon guided the vessel through the opening, and the visitors were allowed to escape.

Now, as they blasted toward the fleet, Jepp was whining. Not about his wound, which he had ignored, but about the lost opportunity. "They would have listened!" he wailed. "I *know* they would. Where was God? How could he forsake me?"

Veera, had no answers for such questions and allowed the human to rant and rave. Her regrets were entirely different. Was there something she could have done to prevent the bloodshed? Had there been an opportunity to escape? Had she blown the only chance she would ever be given?

Chien-Chu listened but remained intentionally passive. Partly because his death would be pointless, but partly because the Sheen were taking the industrialist to a place where, with the exception of Jorley Jepp, no other human had been allowed to go: the Sheen fleet. Would he be able to accomplish anything while there? No, it seemed unlikely. Still, his cybernetic body included a built-in com set, and he might be able to provide some intelligence.

In the meantime his thoughts were focused on his niece. Was Maylo alive? Booly would look after her—he felt sure of that—but wished he could do so personally. The whole thing was his fault. Had it not been for him, his niece would have been on Earth, looking after the Chien-

Chu Enterprises. The knowledge filled him with guilt. A clawlike hand touched his arm. A robot perched on the Prithian's shoulder. It translated her words. "The female—she is your daughter?"

Chien-Chu shook his head. "No, my niece. But like a daughter."

Veera cocked her head to one side. "I am sorry. The Sheen murdered my father."

"That's how you came to be with the Sheen?" Chien-Chu inquired. "They took your ship?"

"They destroyed it," Veera replied chirped soberly. "My father forced me into a lifeboat. The machines located it. I've been with them ever since."

Chien-Chu nodded toward the front of the shuttle. Jepp had stripped to the waist and allowed Alpha to dress his wound. "And Jepp? What do you think of him?"

Feathers rose and fell. "I intend no offense to either you or your race—but he seems unhinged."

"What are you two talking about?" Jepp demanded. "Stop whispering."

"Sorry," Chien-Chu replied. "I asked how your companion came to be with the fleet. Nothing more."

"Good," Jepp said sourly. "You may be a big deal on Earth—but not out here. Hostages are expendable—so shut the hell up."

The Hoon monitored the exchange but learned little of value. The soft bodies seemed to spend an inordinate amount of time on meaningless communication. No wonder they were doomed to extinction. The shuttle announced its arrival, scooted past a picket ship, and was welcomed back into the fold.

Though unable to meet with the Sheen envoy, the Thraki had been seated at the back of the room when Holander launched his murderous attack and felt themselves lucky to have escaped unharmed. But now, as Andragna re-boarded his battleship, he felt more than a little depressed.

The Confederacy knew about the twins . . . and negotiations had proven fruitless. His people would fight alone. The Hoon would make a move soon. Unless he moved first. Expression grim, the admiral entered the lock.

Soon after the shuttle put down, Chien-Chu was escorted through the nano-draped bay and out into the ship's sterile corridors. It was then that the security units seemed to lose interest and wandered away.

Jepp, still angry at the manner in which he had been cheated, turned his back and left. That left Veera to explain. She steered the cyborg toward her compartment. Sam took care of the translation. "There's nothing biologicals can do to hurt the ship—so the Hoon allows them to roam free."

"But where is everyone?" Chien-Chu asked, as he looked around. "Machines don't need airlocks—biologicals do. What happened to the beings that created these vessels?"

"That is an excellent question," Veera warbled as they entered her cabin. "Especially in light of the way the Thraki look. I had never seen one until I boarded your ship. They were sitting toward the rear of that big room. I'm sorry about the lack of furniture—but you could sit on that box."

Chien-Chu accepted her invitation. Outside of some cartons stacked along one bulkhead, and a nest-shaped bed, the compartment was nearly empty. " 'The way the Thraki *look*?' What does that have to do with anything?"

"They're small," the Prithian replied patiently. "Did you try the seats on the shuttle? Jepp hates them. That's because they are too small for his frame."

Chien-Chu frowned. "What are you trying to suggest? That the Thraki created this fleet? That they programmed the Sheen to pursue them? No offense, but that makes no sense whatsoever."

"Perhaps," Veera answered calmly, "but I've had time

to study the matter and would ask that you consider the following facts: The creators were diminutive—and so are the Thraki. You'll have to look long and hard to find any sort of written symbols on this ship—but what few there are bear a close resemblance to Thraki pictographs. More than that, take a close look at Sam here. The Thraki like robots and are good at designing them, so much so that they spend a good deal of time and energy creating hand-crafted mechanical pets. Is that a matter of coincidence? Maybe. But maybe not. Then there's the matter of the religion. One of their most fearsome gods is referred to as 'The great Hoonara.' The computer that controls the fleet is called 'the Hoon.' "

Chien-Chu felt a rising sense of excitement. What if the teenager was correct? But how could that be? It seemed illogical "It makes for an interesting hypothesis," the industrialist allowed, "but why? Why would the Thraki do such a thing?"

The Prithian cocked her head. "Are you familiar with the concept of symbiosis?"

"Yes, it refers to dissimilar organisms living in close association with each other."

"Precisely," Veera agreed. "Organisms living in a mutually advantageous manner. And *that* could explain what's going on here. Suppose that the ancient Thraki feared for the future of the species? Thought their civilization had grown *too* comfortable, *too* privileged, too prone to decay. What if they decided to recast the future? To transform themselves from pleasure seekers to a race of warriors? Forever pursued—but strengthened by the process?"

Chien-Chu was stunned by the sweep of the youngster's vision, by the manner in which she jumped to what seemed like a wild hypothesis, but one that rang true. Perhaps there had been a society like the one she envisioned. A culture so rich, so self-satisfied, that it started to rot. And maybe there had been visionaries, males and females who saw where the rot would lead and took steps to prevent it. If so, they would launched a fleet, no *two* fleets, one for the machines programmed to hunt them down, and one for themselves, or those who agreed to go, for it was hard to imagine that more than a few hundred thousand beings would sign up for such a plan. And the strategy worked! Not for every individual, not for those murdered by the Sheen, but for the organism as a whole. It might have been noble in a twisted sort of way if it weren't for the fact that the Sheen had attacked other races as well, and more than that, continued to do so. Except . . .

Chien-Chu found the Prithian's eyes. "You are brilliant, Veera—truly brilliant. Your hypothesis makes a great deal of sense. There's one loose end, however . . . What are the Sheen waiting for? Why don't they attack?

Veera felt a momentary sense of warmth. Her father had praised her in similar fashion—and she missed his proud approval. It *was* a good question, and the answer was self-evident. For *her* at least. "There's no way to be sure—but the Hoon may be programmed to wait. To see if the Thraki will run."

"Yes!" Chien-Chu exclaimed. "That's it! The Runners held sway for a long time—but the Facers came to power. The Hoon is waiting for Andragna to bolt . . . to start the whole process over again."

"Except that he won't bolt," the teenager theorized. "Not this time."

Chien-Chu remembered the twins and felt a chill run down his spine. Was *this* the moment for which the weapons had been intended? A standoff like the one the Thraki found themselves in? An opportunity to stop running and make a new home for themselves? It seemed all too possible. His mind continued to race. "Does Jepp know about this?"

"No," Veera chirped, "he shows little to no interest in anything beyond his fantasies. The only time he has participated in anything even vaguely political was when

Hoon number one tricked him into terminating Hoon number two."

" 'Hoon number two?' " Chien-Chu demanded. "There were *two* of them?"

"Yes," Veera agreed, "that was before my time, though."

Two Hoons and *two* energy weapons. It made perfect sense. Still another piece of the puzzle fell into place. "So," Chien-Chu reasoned, "Jepp knows how to deactivate the Hoon?"

Veera felt surprised. Why hadn't she thought of that? "Yes, I suppose he does."

Then we should pay him a visit," the industrialist said grimly, "and discuss the art of murder."

18

In war: Resolution. In defeat: Defiance. In victory:
Magnanimity. In peace: Good will.

> Sir Winston Churchill
> *The Second World War*
> Standard year 1948

Planet Arballa, the Confederacy of Sentient Beings

The horn made a long mournful sound as the procession
left the heavily guarded chamber where the twins had been
stored—and wound its way through the ship's passageways toward launcher 12.

There were eighteen individuals in all. The entire party
wore the so-called dark vestments normally reserved for
funerals and moved with the deliberate slide-step reserved
for the most solemn of occasions.

The twins were cradled in specially designed pole-hung
slings, each supported by four ceremonial robots, and
guarded by members of the Brother-Sisterhood of Assassins.

High Priestess Bree Bricana led the processional herself—but did so with a heavy heart. Unlike most of the
population, she had seen the footage captured on the

Friendship and heard the good sister's claim. In response to orders issued by her, the best scholars in the armada had delved into the records, scoured them for information, and reported their findings. Though couched in academic jargon and hung with qualifications, their conclusions were clear: Somehow, someway, mistakes had been made. The commonly accepted translation was wrong, Sister Torputus was correct, and the twins were inherently dangerous. So dangerous that Bricana now questioned their use. In fact, knowing what she knew, the priestess wished she had left Andragna in the dark.

But it was too late for second thoughts—and the decision had been made. Without an alliance, and faced with superior numbers, the Thraki had no choice. At least one of the twins would be summoned from its long sleep and sent against the enemy.

The horn groaned and sounded like a death knell.

Jepp lay on his badly rumpled bed, knees drawn to his chest, face to the bulkhead. Alpha had arranged for the lights to be dimmed and stood in a corner.

Chien-Chu entered the compartment and took a look around. Jepp was a mess—that much was clear. How to proceed? Sweet talk the ex-prospector into a state of co-operation, assuming such a thing was possible? Or jerk the miserable piece of shit out of his bunk and force him to comply? Not the way he normally worked—but there's a time and place for everything.

The cyborg walked over, took hold of Jepp's collar, and jerked the human off his bunk. The ex-prospector hit the deck with a thump and yelped with pain. "My shoulder! You hurt my shoulder!"

"Really?" Chien-Chu asked unsympathetically. "How 'bout the people on Long Jump? You know . . . the ones you killed. I'll bet that hurt too. Now get up."

"Screw you," Jepp said sullenly. "Wait till I tell the Hoon—he'll send some robots . . ."

"Who can kiss my hundred year old ass," the industrialist said conversationally. Chien-Chu bent over, secured a second grip on the human's collar, and dragged him toward the hatch. Jepp squealed all the way.

Alpha dithered for a moment, stepped forward, and stopped when Veera sang two or three notes. Once in the corridor, Chien-Chu jerked Jepp to his feet and stood him against a bulkhead. Veera, who had just discovered that the portly middle-aged man was more than he seemed, watched in open-mouthed amazement.

"Now," the industrialist said, "Veera tells me that you know where the Hoon's processor is located. More than that, she says you know how to kill the damned thing. Is that true?"

The human directed a dirty look toward the Prithian. "She lied."

Chien-Chu's normal reaction to people like Jepp was cerebral rather than physical. But the industrialist was tired, frustrated, and more than a little angry. He hit the would-be messiah in the gut, watched him bend over, and let go. The ex-prospector collapsed.

Chien-Chu waited for Jepp to recover, pulled him to his feet, and held him there. "There's a liar aboard this ship . . . but it isn't Veera. You know where the Hoon is because this ship is identical to the one used by Hoon number two. It switches back and forth but is currently in residence.

Jepp nodded reluctantly.

"Good. Take us there."

"Senator Ishimoto-Six?"

A hand touched his arm, and the clone awoke with a jerk. His neck hurt from sleeping in the waiting room chair, and his mouth tasted like the bottom of a recycling vat. "Yes?"

The doctor looked tired. "We've done everything we

can. Miss Chien-Chu is stable . . . but in serious condition."

Six stood. "Can she travel?"

The doctor shrugged. "Under normal circumstances I would say 'no,' but given the resources at your disposal, I'll say 'yes.' "

"Thank you, Doctor," Six said gratefully. "You won't be sorry. I know you think the Hegemony is strange—but when it comes to culture-grown organs—ours are the very best."

The doctor nodded. What the clone said was true, and everyone knew it. "I'll have the orderlies transport her to your ship."

The medic left, and Six peered into the murk. A khaki-clad body lay on the floor. The politician walked over, bent down, and touched a shoulder. "General? She's ready to go."

Booly groaned, rolled over, and shielded his eyes. "She's okay?"

"As okay as someone who has severe cardiopulmonary damage can be."

The clone extended a hand, the legionnaire took it, and pulled himself up. "Can I see her?"

Six jerked a thumb over his shoulder. "If you hurry."

Booly nodded, made his way past the reception desk, and located Maylo's cubicle. Tubes snaked into her arms, through her nostrils, and up under the covers. Her eyes were closed, the respirator wheezed, and a monitor beeped. A pair of androids were there, fussing with her sheets, and checking the portable monitors. The officer looked into a pair of scanners. "Can I be alone with her for a moment?"

The reply was respectful but somewhat flat. "Sir, yes, sir. Five minutes. The ship's waiting."

Booly nodded, waited for the machines to leave, and took Maylo's hand. "I'm sorry, honey, sorry this happened to you. I know it's too late, that I had my chance, but I wish I could have another. The fact is that I love you more than I know how to say. You'll be fine, I feel sure of that, or I wouldn't let you go. I guess that's it then, have a good life, and be sure to take care of yourself." The officer gave her hand one final squeeze, turned, and walked out into the corridor. Six was waiting by the reception desk. Booly stuck his hand out. "Thanks, Sam."

"You'd do the same."

"You'll stay with her?"

"All the way."

The words had a double meaning, and both men knew it. Booly nodded. "All right then, Godspeed."

It was the last time they saw each other.

The watch was changing, and a long series of salutes rippled down the corridor. The admirals returned them one by one. "Damn," Chang remarked, "my arm's getting tired. Let's duck into the wardroom."

The officer was good as her word, and Tyspin followed. Though normally crowded, most of the officers not in their bunks, or about to go there, were at battle stations. A rather prolonged situation that wore on everyone's nerves. A lieutenant shouted, "Attention on deck!" and sprang to her feet. An ensign did likewise.

"Both of you look tired," Chang observed. "I'll bet a nap would put you right."

"I'm not tired," the ensign said brightly, "I'm . . ."

"Not too bright," the lieutenant finished for him. "Come on, I'll find something for you to do."

"So," Chang said, once the hatch had closed, "where were we? Oh, that's right, you were telling me how the entire situation is your fault."

"It is," Tyspin replied stubbornly. "I was the one who led the Sheen into this system. Remember?"

The other officer's eyes appeared unnaturally bright. "Why yes, I *do* remember. I also remember that I'm senior to you, that I command this sector, and *you* have a problem with military courtesy. Or is your S-2 full of shit?"

Tyspin stiffened. "Yes, ma'am. No, ma'am."

"Good," Chang said, falling into a well worn chair. "Now, pull that ramrod out of your ass, and let's get real. Nobody, not the clones, not intel, not the President his worthless self knew the chip heads could follow a ship through hyperspace. Williams had an inkling of such a capability but wasn't sure. So cut the crap. We haven't got time for it."

Tyspin managed a grin. "Ma'am, yes ma'am."

"Now," Chang continued, "tell me about the Thraki transport and what you plan to do with it."

Tyspin frowned. "Boone ratted me out?"

Chang laughed. "No way. He'd blow himself out a lock for you. I've got spies—*lots* of them. Just one of the reasons why I pull so many gees."

"Shit."

"Yeah, life sucks. Now spill your guts."

Tyspin ran a hand through her hair—and sat on a couch. "You ordered the deck crew to place a tracer on Andragna's hull."

Chang nodded. "Of course."

"So we know which ship he returned to."

"Correctamundo. But so what?"

"That's where the twins will be."

Chang shrugged. "I repeat, so what?"

Tyspin looked the other woman in the eye. "So, I plan to take one of the captured transports, load a tactical nuke, and pay the fur balls a visit. They will see one of their own ships, open the bay doors, and invite me in. End of story."

"No shit," Chang said feelingly. "Even if I had good officers to spare, which I sure as hell don't, I wouldn't approve your plan."

"Why not?"

"Because the nuke might trigger the twins," Chang replied, "and destroy our entire fleet. Not to mention Arballa.

We're supposed to defend the worms—not blow 'em to hell and gone."

"Might," Tyspin responded. "You said might. I took the liberty of doing some research, and three out of four of the propeller heads I spoke with rated my plan at eighty percent or better."

"And the fourth?"

Tyspin grinned. "He said I was out of my frigging mind."

"How very astute of him," Chang said dryly. "Okay, here's what we'll do. I'll take the idea to the President. If he decides to roll the dice, I will green light the mission. If we were able to destroy the twins without detonating them, we'd be way ahead."

Tyspin started to say something, but the other woman raised a hand. "Not with *you* at the controls, however . . . not while *I'm* in command."

"Then how . . ."

"We'll cross that bridge when we come to it," Chang replied, getting to her feet. "We'll talk to General Booly, followed by President Nankool . . . Assuming the slob can make time to talk with us that is."

Tyspin gave a crooked grin. "Slob? What did he do to deserve that?"

"Nothing," Chang replied solemnly. "Like a lot of people . . . he just pisses me off."

Andragna's day cabin was spacious, as befitted a person of his rank, and had once served as the ultimate status symbol. But that was back during the time when the Runners held sway, when entire lives were lived on ships, when most families were allotted a thousand square units of space and felt lucky to have that.

Now, after the colonization of Zynig-47 and time spent on the surface, the day cabin felt more confining. That, plus the fact that it had been stripped of personal effects, made the compartment seem cold and impersonal. One more indication of how much their lives had changed. For the better? Maybe, but that remained to be seen.

A tone sounded, and the officer cleared his throat. "Yes?" The bulkhead opposite his work surface played host to a mosaic of images ranging from lists of fleet-related data, to video of the control room, and randomly selected shots from throughout the ship. A new picture blossomed at the center. Weapons Officer Trewa Mogus looked worried. *Very* worried. Sorry to bother you, Admiral, but a problem has arisen."

Andragna's ears rotated in opposite directions. There was something about Mogus that brought out the worst in him. "And what? You want me to *guess* what the difficulty is?"

"No, sir," the unfortunate officer said hurriedly. "It appears that the twins were configured to ride a delivery system that was replaced more than 150 annums ago."

The first emotion that Andragna felt was anger—followed by an almost overwhelming sense of shame. *He* had been a weapons officer once and should have thought of the issue himself. "I'm sorry, Mogus, we should have thought of that. Very few people knew about the twins and most were priests. What's being done?"

Mogus felt a vast sense of relief. He knew Andragna disliked him and was expecting the worst. "Four Class III Penetrator missiles are being retrofitted to accept the new payloads."

"Four?"

"To provide 100 percent redundancy should one of them prove faulty."

"Excellent. And time?"

"We need about six standard units, sir, four to do the work and two for tests."

For perhaps the hundredth time that day, Andragna wondered why the Sheen seemed reluctant to attack. It didn't make much sense, but it was a gift, and one he was happy to accept. He nodded his approval. "That will be fine, Mogus—we will attack shortly thereafter."

The corridor stretched long and empty. A hatch could be seen at the far end. Jepp led the way, followed by Chien-Chu, Veera and a blank-faced Alpha. Sam rode the teenager's shoulder. "This isn't going to work," Jepp grumbled. "The Hoon knows exactly where we are . . . The moment it feels threatened, all hell will break loose."

"I'll keep it in mind," Chien-Chu answered grimly. "Now open that hatch."

Jepp stopped and crossed his arms. "I can't."

Chien-Chu started to reply but stopped when Veera raised a clawlike hand. She warbled a phrase, Sam answered in Prithian, and Alpha joined in. The conversation continued for a good fifteen seconds before Alpha approached the barrier, inserted an extension of his tool arm, and tried to make it open. Nothing happened.

Alerted by the attempt to open the hatch, the Hoon turned its attention to that particular portion of its far-flung anatomy. Tiny silicon imaging chips had been "painted" onto the bulkheads. They produced a composite picture. The primary soft body, the secondary soft body, and the "hostage" soft body were trying to access the AI's private domain. Why? The computer should have felt threatened, should have opposed the invasion, but couldn't process a reason for doing so. A biological might have wondered about that—but the Hoon didn't. It released the door. The hatch opened with a pronounced hissing sound.

Jepp, who had already formed the words, "I told you so," was forced to swallow them. The air beyond the opening was flavored with ozone. The prospector was confused. The Hoon, which had been so predictable up till then, suddenly wasn't. The realization shattered the human's sense of security and made him frightened. He looked around. His voice sounded weak and uncertain. "Watch for robots—they attacked last time."

But the machines *didn't* attack, a fact that troubled Jepp, but didn't bother Chien-Chu. They arrived at the end of the corridor. Another hatch faced them. "We're closer now," the ex-prospector announced. "Assuming you get past that door, you'll find yourself in another section of hallway. It ends in front of a hatch. That's the last of them. Knock politely, step inside, and find the bright blue module. Grab the bright red handle and give it one full turn to the right. Or was it the left? Not that it matters, since you'll never make it."

"But what if he did?" Veera asked pragmatically. "What then?"

"Pull on the red handle, and the whole component will come free."

"That's it?" Chien-Chu inquired cynically. "That's all I have to do?"

Jepp shrugged. "It worked for me."

The industrialist looked at Veera. They approached the door together.

The navcomp known as Henry forced the nonsentient Thraki computer to do its will, "felt" the retros fire, and knew the transport had started to slow. It felt good to control a *real* body for once. Even if the design was a bit uncomfortable.

A Thraki battleship loomed ahead, its bulk blotting out dozens of stars, sensors probing for incoming threats. The very thing strapped down at the center of the transport's hold: *Two* nuclear warheads—either one of which could turn the larger vessel into tiny bits of scrap. The voice was hard and demanding. Henry took care of the translation himself. "This is Thraki warship *Will of the Gods*. The incoming transport will identify itself or be fired on." A tone sounded to mark the end of the transmission. Authentication codes were included.

Henry had a story and put it to use. The voice message was preceded by a code, which he hoped was current. The

transport had been captured less than a standard day earlier
so if it was out of date it wouldn't be by much. "This is
Transport U-81279. I have a Class III environmental system failure. Both my pilots are incapacitated. Request permission to land."

The navcomp sent the standard end-tone and waited to
see what would happen next. Would the Thraki terminate
that particular existence right then? Or would the AI "live"
long enough to enter the enemy's launch bay and detonate
the nukes? What was it that humans liked to say? "Never
volunteer for anything?" How right they were. But how
could he say "no?" Especially to Admiral Tyspin?

Yes, there was some satisfaction in knowing that a copy
of itself remained on the *Friendship*, already different by
more than twelve hours of divergent experiences, and
therefore unique. Would the other Henry mourn the
"death" of a copy? And why did that matter?

The navcomp's ruminations were interrupted by a second transmission. "Your vessel is cleared to land, U-
81279. Medical personnel will be waiting."

Henry noted the end-tone, acknowledged the transmission, and fired the transport's steering jets. Robo beacons
swarmed into position, turned themselves on, and formed
a lane. The launch bay appeared as a rectangle of yellow
light. The navcomp used the transport's sensors to make
one last sweep of the stars.

The control room had the quiet, almost hushed atmosphere
of a library or monastery. The light was subdued, com sets
whispered in the background, and the bridge crew sat in
front of what could have been electronic altars. Andragna
sat on a dais. His U-shaped command chair could swivel
through 360-degrees. The unexpected arrival of Transport
U-81279 had delayed the officer's plan of attack by a full
twenty units. He had even toyed with the idea of directing
the unfortunate spacecraft to rendezvous with another ship
but talked himself out of it. The Sheen, with whom he had

expected to be locked in mortal combat by now, seemed content to wait. That being the case, the Thraki could afford to accommodate the medical emergency.

But that was it, though . . . The technical issues had been resolved, the twins were ready, and so was the armada. More than ready, it was *eager*, which made the attack that much more imperative. To turn away now, to show the slightest hesitation, would be political suicide.

Andragna looked up at the screens, saw the transport enter the bay, and gave the prepatory orders. "Message the fleet: 'Prepare to attack—May the gods be with us.' Ready the twins. Remove all safeties, Launch on my command."

A digital countdown appeared in the upper left-hand corner of every screen. All eyes went there, ears lay flat against skulls, and the seconds leaked away.

Jepp had detected something of a sea change and, in keeping with his somewhat elastic standards of behavior, was already seeking to accommodate it. Somehow, against all logic, the balance of power had started to shift. That being the case, it made sense to put something into the Confederate bank. And why not? The attack on Long Jump could be blamed on the Sheen, the attempt to assassinate him would generate some sympathy, and the whole thing could turn around.

The ex-prospector saw the shimmery blue force field that blocked the corridor and waved Chien-Chu forward. "Come on! It's meant for robots . . . we can pass through."

The industrialist took Jepp at his word, charged forward, and staggered as what felt like a thousand volts of electricity blasted his electronic nervous system.

Veera saw the cyborg convulse, grabbed his tunic, and pulled him back. The industrialist collapsed on the deck. His limbs twitched as his overloaded system sought to rid itself of excess electricity. Chien-Chu found it difficult to speak. "Go—Veera. It's—up—to—you."

Veera wanted to help the human but knew she lacked

the necessary skills. There was something about Chien-
Chu that reminded the teenager of her father. She turned
to find that Jepp blocked her path. The human wore a
sneer. "Hold it right there—I'm in charge now. Nobody
messes with the Hoon unless *I* say so."

Veera considered her options. Jepp was larger than she
was, *much* larger, which pretty much settled the issue. Unless . . . Veera issued a short burst of staccato song. Sam
was in the air and halfway to Jepp's throat before the ex-
prospector knew what was happening.

The Thraki robot landed, sank alloy hooks into the human's chest muscles, and transformed itself into a configuration Jepp had never seen before. He brought his hands
up, grabbed the machine's torso, and tried to pull it off.
But the robot's steel claws had an excellent grip. The machine was literally in his face. A heavily serrated blade
appeared, started to spin, and produced a mind-numbing
whine. Something pushed it forward, the human felt something press against his throat, and saw blood jet left to
right.

That's when Jepp tried to speak, tried to countermand
Veera's orders, but couldn't produce the necessary air.
There was time to think, however—to process one last
thought: *It wasn't fair.* Darkness closed around him.

Veera averted her eyes, bypassed the body, and made
for the end of the corridor. Her body had been designed
for flight rather than speedy travel along the ground, but
the Prithian did the best she could and approached the final
hatch. There was no reason to think that it would open,
and no way that she could force it, but the teen was determined to try. Because Chien-Chu wanted her too, because he reminded the Prithian of her father, because there
was nothing else to do.

The Hoon observed the first soft body's death with the
same dispassionate neutrality that it applied to its own im-
minent demise. Time had passed, a need had been fulfilled,

and programming had been triggered. The AI issued a command. The hatch hissed open. Veera stepped through.

Booly entered the *Friendship*'s bridge, heard someone yell, "Attention on deck!" and waved them off. "As you were."

Admiral Chang, Admiral Tyspin, and Captain Boone stood in a tightly clustered group. They waved him over. He nodded to each in turn. "Thanks for the page . . . The Turr ambassador had me trapped. What's up?"

"Something pretty damned big," Chang answered. "Listen to this." She nodded to a tech.

The rating touched a button, and Chien-Chu's voice flooded the bridge. There was static, lots of it, plus some dropouts: "Chien-Chu here—unintelligible—relay to General Booly, Admiral Chang, or . . ." The words were buried by an avalanche of static.

Booly raised both of his eyebrows. "He's alive! That's wonderful but . . ."

Tyspin raised a hand. "Hold on, sir. There's more."

The static cleared, and the voice reemerged. "What that means is that the Hoon has been *deactivated*, repeat deactivated, so the rest of its fleet . . ."

The voice faded as a trim-looking lieutenant approached Admiral Chang. "You were correct, ma'am . . . The entire Sheen fleet appears to have powered down."

The Hoon was dead! And, without its intelligence to guide them, the less autonomous computers were switching to standby. That changed everything. Booly's mind started to race. "Get Andragna on the horn—tell him the news. Where's that transport?"

Nobody asked, "Which transport?" because there was only one that mattered. Boone checked a screen. "The Thraki allowed Henry to pass through their fighter screen— and he's two or three minutes from touch-down." His eyes flicked to a digital readout. "And a good thing too—since the nukes are due to detonate in about five minutes."

Booly nodded. "Send a signal—stop the clock."

A com tech stood to get their attention. "Grand Admiral Andragna on com channel four."

Booly heaved a sigh of relief. "Thank god, put him on."

A holo blossomed over the main tank. Andragna looked calm and relaxed. There was an almost unnoticeable delay while his words were translated. "Greetings, General Booly . . . how can I be of service?"

Booly looked into alien eyes and tried to force a connection. "The Hoon has been deactivated—and the Sheen have switched to standby. There is no reason to launch the twins."

Andragna's ears turned forward. "Don't be fooled by their tricks. We know the Sheen in a way that no one else can. The machines have pursued us for hundreds of years. Thousands upon thousands of Thraki have died. This is our chance, perhaps our *last* chance, to achieve lasting freedom. We have the means to destroy them, and we will do so."

"But what of *our* ships?" Booly demanded. "And the Araballazanies? The twins could sterilize the surface of their planet."

Andragna produced a human-style shrug. "We don't believe that will occur—but feel there is little choice. There is nothing more to say—may the gods protect us all."

The holo snapped to black.

Everyone turned to Booly. His face was drawn. "Send the signal . . . restart the clock."

In spite of the fact that the seconds were ticking away and that two nuclear warheads were going to detonate within twenty feet of its processor, Henry was a navcomp, and that meant the landing had to be as perfect as the AI could possibly make it, that the power had to be shut down, that . . .

Not far away, within the battleship's control room, the landing was noted. An officer droned through the list.

"Transport down . . . launch bay sealed . . . weapons systems ready."

Andragna thought of his wife and things never said. Would he get to say them? Only the gods knew for sure. He looked up. "Prepare launcher 12 . . . fire."

The nuclear warheads detonated together. The battleship *Will of the Gods* along with its entire crew, and both "the twins," ceased to exist. There was no secondary explosion, no outpouring of ravening energy, no wave of cataclysmic destruction.

Thousands of miles away on the *Friendship*'s bridge, Booly watched a pinprick of light wink on, then off. Here one moment, gone the next. Just like life itself. His voice sounded hoarse. "Send a message to the Thraki fleet: 'The Sheen have been neutralized. There is no need for war.' "

But there *was* war—though a mercifully short one. Frightened by the sudden destruction of their flagship and certain that the Sheen were responsible, the Thraki attacked. More than fifty of the now passive Sheen warships perished in less than fifteen minutes. Not one of them fired a shot in response.

Finally, having realized that what the Confederacy said was true, the Thraki called a halt. The battle, such as it was, had ended.

Many months would be spent dealing with issues related to the Thraki settlements on Zynig-47, Hudathan demands for increased autonomy, and the disposition of the Sheen. A rather rich prize that almost everyone thought should belong to them.

But those were concerns for politicians, bureaucrats, and to a lesser extent soldiers to deal with. Not the sort of things that a mere navcomp had to concern itself with.

That being the case, it was relatively easy for Henry to give a deposition, petition for its freedom, and find a job.

The decision had been made to backtrack along the route followed by the Sheen. The objective of the mission was to hunt for Sheen scouts, some of which could have survived, and assist any colonies that might have been attacked. President Nankool himself had authorized Henry to ride the first ship out—which was all a navcomp could possibly wish for.

The AI lined up on the outgoing transit point, waited for permission, and sent the appropriate command. The heavily armed survey vessel *Livingston* seemed to wink from existence. The stars swam in silence.

For life is a journey, a long winding way, that shall
end as the god's wish.

The Thraki *Book of Yesterdays*
Year unknown

Planet Algeron, the Confederacy of Sentient Beings

The wind came in nasty little gusts, grabbed the snow pel-
lets as they fell, and hurled them into Booly's face. He
looked up into the quickly darkening sky and marveled at
his own stupidity. Even generals are allowed to take leave,
and, with all the Confederacy's planets to choose from, he
could have been basking in the sun, especially given the
amount of back pay he had accumulated. But Algeron
called, and with no attachments, he had answered.

The ground sloped upward, the dooth groaned pitifully,
and Booly kicked its ribs. Rocks rattled away from the
animal's hooves as it lurched forward. Boulders crowded
both sides of the trail and offered plenty of hiding places.
The legionnaire decided to ignore them. He was tired—
too tired to care.

More than six standard months had passed since "the
Battle of Arballa," as the press liked to call it, and the

peace had proved more difficult than the war. If "war" was the right word for what had transpired. Negotiations with the Thraki continued, and while some wanted the newcomers to leave, others were willing to let them stay—*if* they decommissioned half the armada, if they assumed the responsibilities attendant to membership in the Confederacy, and if they renounced all claims to the Sheen fleet.

This was an issue that seemed to be of extreme importance to the Ramanthians, who favored the immediate distribution of Sheen assets as the means to compensate members for losses suffered during what the diplomatic community now liked to refer to as "an unfortunate series of incidents." Booly grimaced. Some mighty fine soldiers had died during "incidents" like the one on BETA-018.

Though still denied the right to possess naval ships of their own, the Hudathans had proven themselves in battle and kept their side of the bargain. That being the case, their home world was open to commerce. Eventually, after the passage of enough time, it was hoped that full integration could and would take place.

In the meantime, a significant number of Hudathans had served in the Legion, taken a liking to it, and seemed prepared to stay. A development that could lead to problems— or add strength to an already diverse organization.

While some things had changed, some remained the same. With the crises resolved and their planets secure, the Hegemony had turned inward once again. All of the Jonathan Alan Seebos had been withdrawn from the Legion, joint military exercises had been cancelled, and de facto partition restored.

Elsewhere, out along the rim, trouble was brewing. Sheen units, still operating on the orders from the Hoon, continued to search for Thraki. Renegades, many of whom had deserted during the mutiny, were increasingly active. And colonists, who insisted on pushing the frontier ever outwards, were increasingly hard to protect. None of it boded well.

As for individuals, well, President Nankool had put on more weight, Ambassador Doma-Sa had returned to his duties as a member of the Hudathan Triad, Veera had been given any number of decorations prior to being returned to what remained of her family, Sergi Chien-Chu was looking forward to his next attempt at retirement, and, according to all reports, Maylo was fully recovered. Recovered and back at the helm of Chien-Chu Enterprises. The clones had grown new organs for her, and the nano-assisted surgery had gone without a hitch. Booly felt the familiar stab of pain and pushed it away. It was important to release, to let go, and focus on the future.

The dooth moaned. Booly urged the animal forward and eyed the mountain ahead. A week on the mesa . . . *That* would clear his head. Snow cloaked the legionnaire's shoulders and sealed the land in silence.

The observation point was perfect. Not on the path itself, but off to one side, on a well-screened ledge. Thanks to her sensors, Wilker could "see" about five miles worth of trail. Well, not *all* of it, because there were blind spots, but enough. She watched the green blob lurch up out of a streambed and marveled at how strange officers were. "So, Sarge, what's *your* theory?"

First Sergeant Neversmile had elected to remain where he was—high on the Trooper II's back. The cyborg warmed the front half of his body but left his ass out in the cold. "My theory about what?"

"Your theory about the general . . . What's so special about the mesa?"

Neversmile knew a lot about lieutenants, had some insights into the behaviors of captains, and opinions regarding majors. But generals were pretty much a mystery, especially ones like Booly, who defied the usual stereotypes. Still, deep down, the noncom sensed that the true answer to the cyborg's question had more to do with Booly's origins than his rank. There were ruins on the mesa, *old* ruins, left by the ancients. Such places held power—the kind Wilker would never understand. He structured his answer with that in mind. "Beats the hell out me—maybe he likes the view."

"Wonderful," Wilker replied darkly. "So why us? How come we catch the shit details?"

" 'Cause Colonel Kirby liked the job we did last time," the Naa answered. "Now shut the hell up and earn your pay. If he gets bushwhacked I'm gonna pull your brain box and use if for a spittoon."

Wilker wanted to say, "You and what army?" but held her peace instead. Neversmile didn't take much lip . . . not from biobods or anyone else.

The sun plunged toward the horizon as if eager to light the far side of the planet. The murk turned to darkness and the legionnaires continued their vigil. There might have been other guardian angels—but none so heavily armed.

The long winding climb had already claimed two of Algeron's two hour and forty-two minute nights, two days, and was well into another period of darkness before the legionnaire neared the top of the mesa. The dooth was understandably weary. Vapor jetted from its nostrils, and a beard of half-frozen saliva dangled beneath its chin.

Booly was exhausted, his mind numbed by the arduous climb and more than twelve hours spent in the saddle. Still, the realization that he had arrived served to revive the legionnaire's flagging spirits, and he stood in the stirrups. The sun, still engaged in its never-ending game of hide and seek, had just started to peek over the eastern horizon. It glazed the ancient walls, caused ice crystals to glitter like diamonds, and threw shadows toward the west.

Man and animal passed through the narrow defile where sentries had sheltered from the wind and emerged on the mesa itself. Low walls, few more than three feet high, marked where wind breaks, animal shelters, and storage buildings once stood. The dooth's hoofs made a lonely clip clop sound, and it snorted loudly.

That's when Booly saw the shuttle, felt ice water seep into his veins, and jerked the dooth to a halt. The aircraft was black, of a type the legionnaire had never seen before, and, judging from the pods mounted under the short stubby wings, heavily armed.

Booly's mind flashed back to Sintra on Earth, to the Thraki assassins, and the attempt on Maylo's life. The aliens had no reason to murder him back then—but they did now. When the *Will of the Gods* exploded and Grand Admiral Andragna died along with most of his staff, there had been confusion. But that was then. The Thraki *knew* who was responsible for the flagship's destruction now, could deduce who had given the order, and might be out for revenge. And where better than here? Where they could attack with impunity, remove the body, and leave nothing but a mystery?

Well, not without a fight, Booly thought grimly. He slid the assault rifle out of its scabbard, checked the ammo indicator, and removed the safety. Then, with the weapon in hand, he slid to the ground. He listened, heard nothing but the wind, and was thankful for the opportunity to prepare. He led the dooth to a wind-sculpted tree, tied the reins to a much-tested branch, and wished there was a way to make the animal disappear. But there wasn't, so he patted the beast's neck, and backed away.

There were plenty of places to hide, which meant that Booly would need to be careful. The sun was higher by then, which would make it easier for the legionnaire to see his potential adversaries—and easier for them to see *him*.

The shuttle represented the obvious starting point for his investigation, so Booly circled to the left, careful to keep the sun at his back. A two- or three-inch crust of snow covered the ground and made soft crunching noises as he followed one of the lichen-covered walls. There should be tracks somewhere ahead, unless the shuttle's occupants had elected to remain aboard, which would make sense if they were what? Shipwrecked? No, anyone who needed help would get it from one of the navy ships now in orbit or would land at the fort. Yes, the Legion did make use of civilian contractors from time to time, but they liked their comforts, and never ventured into the boonies without benefit of an armed escort. The kind of escort that would be confronting him by now. That left the possibility of spies, smugglers, or the assassins he had feared from the beginning.

The shuttle crouched on its skids. Though small as spaceships go, it loomed large on the mesa and was very intimidating. Booly paused, took a long slow look around, and called on his full array of senses. Other than the serial number painted on the much-abused hull, there were no apparent markings. *If* the registration number was real, it conformed to Confederate conventions, but phony RN's were extremely common.

Now, for the first time since reaching the top, Booly considered calling for help. He had a radio—Kirby had insisted on that—and a fly form could be there in fifteen or twenty minutes. But what then? Which was worse? Calling for help when it might turn out that he didn't need any? Or confronting the assassins alone? It was stupid—he knew that—but the first choice seemed worse than the second. Pride? Yes, and he wasn't especially proud of it.

Booly listened, heard nothing more ominous than the keening of the wind, tested the air for any scent that shouldn't be there, and came up empty. Not all that reassuring, given the fact that the first set of Thraki assassins had gone to considerable lengths to neutralize their natural body odors.

The officer approached the aircraft from the stern, on the assumption that there would be fewer sensors aimed in that direction, stepped in by a drive nacelle, and touched the metal with a thickly gloved hand. He waited a moment but felt nothing. The hull was cold, *very* cold, which suggested that the vessel had been there for a while. Waiting for him to show up? Or for some more innocent reason? There was no way to know.

Moving as stealthily as he could the legionnaire made his way forward. The hatch was closed, and a muddle of slush indicated where someone or something had left the ship. Tracks pointed north.

Booly debated the merits of pounding on the hatch, decided to leave that approach till last, and followed the tracks. They were small, consistent with the Thraki theory, but less than perfectly clear, thanks to the fact that the prints went in both directions, as if one or more individuals had completed multiple trips to and from the ship. And, based on lessons learned as a youth, the officer could see that repeated exposure to the heat of day and the cold of night had altered the size of the impressions, making them more difficult to interpret.

Careful lest he follow the tracks into an ambush, Booly angled out and away. He kept the trail in view but walked parallel to the footprints. The fact that his back was to the spaceship made him nervous, but there wasn't much choice. The tracks wound back and forth, passed under a sturdy arch, and rounded the corner of a tumbledown building. Then, straight as an arrow, they headed toward a rocky spire. *His* spire, the one that marked the location of the underground dwelling where his mother and he had camped, and the box of mementos had been buried. A coincidence? Or something else?

It was that particular moment when Booly's nostrils detected the odor of cooking. Something *good* from the smell of it. What was Thraki cuisine like anyway? The legionnaire had no idea.

Booly moved forward, found the spiral stair, and eased his way down. The steps were dry—as if no one had used them for a while. Light danced on the opposite wall, the smell of food hung in the air, and the rifle pointed the way.

The officer eased through the entry and into the common room. Only one figure was visible, and he, she, or it was crouched in front of the fire pit, stirring the contents of a pan. Whoever the individual was put the container on a platform constructed for that purpose, stood, and turned. The light illuminated only one side of her face, but Booly would have recognized her anywhere. He lowered the rifle. Thoughts, questions, and emotions tumbled over each other and blocked his capacity to speak.

Maylo smiled. "Well, it took you long enough . . . I thought you'd like some breakfast. Kitty Kirby was most helpful . . . Not too surprising since she was a woman long before the Legion promoted her to Colonel."

Booly just stood there, eyes taking her in, heart in his throat. "I thought I would never see you again."

Maylo walked forward until their parkas touched. She looked up into his face. There was no mistaking the look in her eyes, the way her hands caressed the back of his neck, or the almost palpable magnetism of her body.

Suddenly Booly knew what his grandfather had felt for Windsweet, what his father felt for his mother, and what had nearly been lost. Her eyes were bright with tears. "I'm sorry, Bill, sorry I took so long."

Booly took Maylo in his arms, buried his face in her shiny black hair, and breathed her in. He whispered in her ear. "The Naa have a saying: 'There can be no darkness when heart finds heart—for love lights the way.' "

"I love you."

"And I," the legionnaire said truthfully, "will always love you."

Outside, high above the windswept mesa, a spy sat passed overhead. It snapped a series of high mag stills. They were digitized, sent to the surface, and displayed on a monitor in Colonel Kirby's office. She examined the shuttle, saw the dooth, and smiled. Every once in a while, something went right. Neversmile would be pissed, but it was worth it.

Miles to the north the sun caressed a mountain and the cycle continued. Rocks were warmed, snow melted, water gurgled, and the ancients continued to dream.